N.C

D1614469

Rogue's March

ALEXANDER CORDELL

Rogue's March

HODDER AND STOUGHTON
LONDON SYDNEY AUCKLAND TORONTO

British Library Cataloguing in Publication Data
Cordell, Alexander
    Rogue's March
    I. Title
    829'.9'1F

ISBN 0 340 25351 7

Hodder and Stoughton Editorial Office: 47 Bedford Square, London WC1B 3DP.

For Ian Stuart and his fellow
educationalists, the
librarians

Those whom the gods destroy, they first make mad.

Euripides (attributed)

My thanks are due to many who have helped me in research for this novel, especially to the following:

Mr. G. A. Dart, the County Librarian of South Glamorgan; Mr. Brian Luxton, the Barry historian; Mr. Harry Brooke, a seaman of old Tiger Bay, Cardiff; Mr. Jack Donovan and Mr. Jim Robinson; also to Mr. Roger H. Smith LL.B., for legal advice, and the Swansea coastguards for nautical assistance.

To Mr. Ian Stuart, to whom this book is dedicated, my grateful thanks for happy evenings of constructive criticism, and wine.

Book One

Book One

1

1940

William Seddon, of Seddon and Partners, Solicitors, was unaware that summer morning as he left his office that he had less than an hour to live.

He crossed the Strand at the pedestrian crossing. With his brief-case under his arm he entered the Savoy Hotel.

Pilot Officer John McAndrew, slim, fair, was awaiting him in a cocktail bar.

The airman's back was to Seddon. He was sitting on a high stool in the hunched despair of isolation.

Wandering the counter before him, seemingly unaware of the young man's existence, a barman polished a glass with an equally desultory air.

"Pilot Officer McAndrew?" The solicitor offered his hand.

"That's right. How did you know me?"

Seddon put his brief-case on the bar. "Actually, old chap, I've seen a photograph."

"My God," muttered McAndrew. "Really? You little chaps do get around, don't you?"

Seddon nodded. "In the interests of our clients, although they're rarely as rude as you were on the phone, Mr. McAndrew. Another drink?"

The young man pushed his glass towards the barman. Seddon said, glancing around, "The rendezvous I find impressive, but I'd rather we'd met in my office. It's only across the Strand, you know."

"I'd rather we met here."

"Any reason? A hotel's not always the best place in the world in which to conduct business."

"Business with pleasure, Seddon. I'm meeting a girl. Also,

this place is central. Furthermore, it stays open despite any particular hell coming loose at the time. Or would it have been poetic expediency to have met in the National Gallery?"

"What makes you say that?" Seddon's expression didn't change. He paid for the drinks and lifted his glass.

"That's what you've come about, I take it? It's usually the subject of conversation the moment I meet a reporter or solicitor . . ." McAndrew gulped at his whisky.

"As a matter of fact that's not the subject at all."

"Then for Christ's sake come to it. You fluffed about enough on the phone, and we've been here too long already."

The man's impatience was understandable, thought Seddon, with James Alexander McAndrew for a father.

He drank slowly, watching his shadowed eyes and drawn cheeks; he was possessed, thought the older man, of the sickness and the pallor of war.

There was a criminology about this particular war that went beyond the bounds of mere slaughter, Seddon considered. It was a decimation of innocence, of the impossibly young who possessed all the impossible dreams. They sat out their lives in personal dungeons of despair, either in the seats of fighter aeroplanes or on plastic-covered high stools, affronted by the gaudy tinsel of battles or cockpit instruments . . . usually amid the high-pitched mundanities of girls a quarter of their intelligence, the easy lays. Their expectation of life, now that the Battle of Britain had begun in earnest, was in the region of twenty flying hours. It was a crime from which they would never recover.

Naturally they were touchy, thought Seddon, and often to the point of rudeness. Their front was a façade of vast understatement, a hostile verbiage that paid the bills of death.

McAndrew added, more amenably, draining his glass, "I suggested this place because I might have a date here, as I say. So come clean, Seddon. I take it that you've had yet another application from some obscure faculty of art?"

"No. But I'll come straight to the point as you suggest. Does the name Antonio Salieri mean anything to you?"

"Nothing."

12

"Or Mama Meg?"

"Christ, what is this?"

"Only that under the terms of that lady's will you've been left a considerable amount of money."

"So you said on the phone. But surely it's a joke. Who is she, anyway?"

Seddon answered brusquely, "It is not a joke. It's a legal fact. Would I have brought you all the way from Biggin Hill for nothing at a time like this?"

The other said, smiling, "Right, I'll buy it. How much has the old clown left me?"

"Eighty thousand, all told, I'd say."

"She's nuts."

"Mama Meg? Perhaps."

"Therefore the will might be contested."

"Probably not."

There was a faint air of pomposity about Seddon which McAndrew resented. The puzzle would be unravelled, apparently, but at Seddon's legal pace and within the accepted jargon.

The solicitor added, "No, not necessarily, and any such claim would fail, I think. The lady who left you this money has undoubtedly had some sort of contact with your family in the past. True, she died in a mental home. But she was housekeeper, she says, to a man called Uncle Dumb, who, in her will, she refers to as God. Immortal or not, it appears that he left her not only the residue of his fortune, but also a place called Atopia House."

"Go on." McAndrew lit a cigarette.

"Meanwhile, the will . . ." Seddon lifted his brief-case. "And I have it in here, appears legally sound, as I say. Psychological aberrations of this kind rarely affect the legality of bequests, providing, of course, that the beneficiaries can be properly identified . . . as I have identified you." He frowned at the other and began to unlock the brief-case.

"Not in here."

"Over in my office, then? That's what I originally suggested."

The younger man asked, "What's Mama Meg's real name, do you know? And where's this Atopia House?"

"In East Yorkshire. As for the lady, she lived for years in the old place . . ." Seddon smiled suavely. "In case you don't know, incidentally, Atopia is a Greek derivative of eccentricity. Other people were there, it seems, and she names some, including, she says, your father, James Alexander McAndrew." Seddon raised his eyes. "Are you *quite* sure you've never heard the name Salieri used in your home? By your mother, perhaps?"

"No. I keep telling you."

"Or Constanze, Conrad, Mr. Toppam, Banker – unusual names like that?"

McAndrew said, "Look, this is getting us nowhere." He slipped down off his stool. "Write to me, for God's sake, I've got better things to do."

"They're important names. The old girl mentions them more than once," continued Seddon, unperturbed. "And she specifically identifies you as the son of James Alexander McAndrew, alias Antonio Salieri."

"She was mad. You said as much yourself."

"Maybe, but yours is a very strange reaction to someone who's left you nearly eighty thousand pounds. What are you hiding?"

McAndrew replied with hostility, "Nothing. And it so happens that I'm not particularly short of that kind of money."

"I'm aware of that also."

People were drifting into the lounge now. Jostling at the bar, they called their orders, and their confusion invaded McAndrew's thoughts. Seddon guessed them.

The lad was thinking that tomorrow he might be dead; that there was no good reason to rake up the past. The motto of the McAndrews clan (properly spelled MacAndrew) was *Nemo me impune lacessit* – 'No one threatens me with impunity' (rightly or wrongly claimed) and the lad, thought Seddon, was living up to it. Among its heroes and historical holies the clan had harboured alcoholics, sheep-stealers, murderers and power maniacs; he could be forgiven for not adding to the list . . .

Seddon said now, staring into his glass, "There simply must be some significance in the appendage '. . . the son of Antonio Salieri.' The woman couldn't have just picked it out of the air, mad though she may have been . . ." He added, "Young man, one way to stop a muck-rake is to nip all the facts in the bud. Ignore them, and they breed. Clearly your father's involved, isn't he. . . ?"

John frowned. "I've got a marvellous mother, Seddon, and I'm not having her brought into this."

"All right, but look, son – establish your identity – that's all I'm asking. The files will stay open all the time you don't. Listen to me." Seddon spoke with sincerity. "Solicitors are not always versed in the purism of art. But if my firm doesn't handle this will, somebody else is going to, and probably after a lot of embarrassing publicity to one of the most important families in Scotland. You know, do you, that Salieri was supposed to have confessed to poisoning Mozart, and made attempts to seduce his wife, Constanze?"

"Christ, man, where are you going now? You're back in the eighteenth bloody century!"

Seddon lifted the brief-case. "It's all in here. Even your date of birth is in the will."

There was a silence of noise and discord. People were coming up to the bar.

"How . . . how did you get my address?"

Seddon shrugged and sipped his whisky. The younger man said:

"You've been to Duke Street, haven't you. . . ?"

"Yes. And that's mentioned in the will as well."

"And talked to my housekeeper."

"Actually, your housekeeper was away. One of the servants gave me your Biggin Hill address. Your mother, the Princess, is out of the country."

"Keep away from my mother or I'll bloody kill you!"

"You really are the most pugnacious beneficiary it has been my sadness to meet," said Seddon, drolly. "What do I do with this eighty thousand?"

15

"Tell her to stuff it." McAndrew left him, pushing through the growing press of people.

The solicitor followed him to the door.

Here a young girl was standing.

Her name was Hilary and she was wearing the uniform of the W.A.A.F.

She was chattering vivaciously to an escort, a somewhat languid young man with a stoop, meanwhile flashing glances in McAndrew's direction.

"Is tonight on, then?" McAndrew asked her.

She averted her face, whispering as Seddon went past, "Well yes, Johnny, but I've got to get rid of Stephen. I can't just . . ."

"Yes you can. If you don't, I will. See you here tonight at seven-thirty for dinner."

"And what about this, then?" interjected Seddon, tapping his brief-case.

McAndrew swung to him.

"Do I have to keep telling you? Do what you like with it, will and testament. This time tomorrow we may all be dead."

"That," said Seddon, "is a distinct possibility," and he walked through the foyer entrance.

The commissionaire said as the air-raid siren wailed, "Why not wait a bit, sir? You'd be safer under cover 'till we know what's happening . . ."

"That's all right, old man," said Seddon. "My office is only across the way."

The bomb dropped, said the commissionaire later, just as the poor gentleman reached the Strand. "Honest to God, sir, it seemed to fall right on top of him. I remember him, you see, because he was carrying this brief-case." He touched it with his foot.

Book Two

2

1896

Outside the gate of the Hendon Annual Camp, Head-
quarters of the 53rd Medium Brigade R.A., forty-four years
before the preceding event, a small group of people had
gathered with ghoulish expectation; akin to the curiosity,
James Alexander McAndrew said later, of those awaiting an
official execution.

Gunner McAndrew was about to be drummed out of the
Royal Artillery.

Beyond the walls of the barracks, the evening sun swept
distant London spires; cavalcades of light lit the barrack
square with each fresh rush of the sun.

All that day it had rained.

Imprisoned in the guard room, McAndrew had heard it
beating on the corrugated iron roof like castanets. Now, lying
on the floor of the cell with his feet cocked up on a chair, he
heard his brigade resounding with dusk activity.

In his stolen cloak of a hussar around his shoulders, a
broad-rimmed hat upon his head and a cheroot in his mouth,
he listened to stamping feet and barked commands with
bored equanimity, glancing up as the cell door opened. The
guard bombardier said:

"You'll bloody get it when they see you in that rig-out,
McAndrew."

"Also you, my Sassenach friend," said McAndrew.

"Breaking out of barracks is one thing," said the bombardier, "breaking into a regimental museum is another, ye
know. It's a punishable offence. And the sergeant-major's in
hospital, too, poor sod."

"You shouldn'a let me go," replied McAndrew. "Ye left the door open and it were a terrible temptation. And the sergeant-major put his chin up."

"You big Scottish whore," said the bombardier. "I'll be busted for this, you know."

"Count yourself lucky. They'll hang me, the bastards."

"No more'n you bloody deserve," said the bombardier. "B.C. for Bad Character. Thirty year ago you'd have been branded, you realise?"

"They can do it now, providing it ain't on me arse."

"God help us. The army's better off without you."

"The feeling's mutual," replied McAndrew. "Now shift yersel', for I'm getting me feet up."

"By the left, who do ye think you are? Lieutenant bloody Fireworker?"

"Now you're talking, for he were a man," said McAndrew, "not a narrow-gutted apology for one like you. Bugger off, or I'll kick your arse from here to Madras."

The guard bombardier said, "If we was on active service, I'd 'ave you, McAndrew. I'd bring the guard in 'ere and we'd work you over."

"Violence, is it?" said McAndrew, starting forward. "Away, ye scoot, or I'll be out there and do the bloody lot of ye in peace time." Lifting a hip-flask he drained it and tossed it to the bombardier. "Take this or they'll 'ave that on your two-five-two as well." He began to sing then, a bass roar of a song, beating time with it by stamping on the floor.

> "Fifty lashes they give me for selling me coat.
> Fifty for selling me blanket.
> If ever I list for a sojer again,
> May the Devil promote me to sergeant."

"Gawd, hark at that," said the bombardier to the guard. "Drunken bugger. Get us all hung, he will, breakin' outa' barracks. Desertion, drunk and disorderly, striking a superior officer. I tell ye, in all my time, I never met a man like him."

20

"Long service, bad stations, good beer and wicked women, Bomber," said a soldier. "That's my trouble, too."

"And no lip from you, either. Get on wi' ye brassing."

"Mind you, he didn't half land the sergeant-major one. I never did see a chap done better."

McAndrew was now singing a song of incredible vulgarity.

"Gawd help us," said the bombardier. "Just 'ark at him! How long is it till morning?"

"Twelve hours and the orderly officer." The soldier lay back on his palliasse with his hands folded under his head. McAndrew roared:

> "He were known as Sergeant Who
> And a yellow bastard, too.
> He were hotter than a regimental Hell
> And because of foolish pranks
> He were drummed out of the ranks
> And the colonel's daughter bedded him as well.
> As he crossed the barrack square
> Ten defaulters stripped him bare . . ."

"Cor, bloody hell," said the soldier. "He can't sing that to the orderly officer."

"Can't he? You listen," replied the bombardier.

In the morning the sun rose with a new and violent splendour.

McAndrew awoke; sober, he sniffed at the air coming through the cell window, bringing to his nostrils the chaotic perfumes of crushed flowers. Smiling, eyes closed, he tried to identify them. Beyond the brick and concrete jungle that was London the woods would be in full bloom now, he thought; primrose and the early orchid, wood-sorrel and cuckoo-pint; in his mind's eye he saw them, and rose on an elbow, staring about him. Staggering up, McAndrew battered on the cell door with a huge fist. "Open up!"

"What for?"

"I need a leak. A prisoner's entitled to a slash, ye know."
"Tie a knot in it," said the bombardier.

Later, when the sun was high, McAndrew gripped the bars of the cell and looked out over the square.

Here was a dress rehearsal of the drumming out ceremony. Soldiers with fixed bayonets were lined up in a double rank that stretched from the saluting base to the gate.

"What's happening out there, Bomber?" shouted McAndrew.

"They're goin' to do you, mate, that's what's happening."

"Is this the rehearsal?"

"It's the real thing, boyo. Half an hour hence you'll be off my hands and down on your arse."

"The brutal buggers. Whose this comin', then?"

"It's the provost-sergeant. Now straighten up, McAndrew; we all got to serve in this sodding army till ye gets your ticket. Come on now, I'm the fella who gets the boot, remember?"

"Ach, you're right, son, I'll do me best," said McAndrew. He was standing to attention as the cell door swung open.

"God help us. What's he doing dressed like that?" gasped the provost-sergeant. Bucolic, breathing heavily from his square exertions, he was pointing at McAndrew's hussar tunic with its layers of gold braid and buttons.

"Last night he got into the regimental museum, Sarge. Thought you was told," said the bombardier, trembling to attention.

"You thought I was told?" The sergeant slowly swung to him. "But I was not told, see? You thought wrong, didn't you, bombardier!" The sergeant's voice rose. "The brigade's waiting. The colonel's waiting! Do I have to take the prisoner out like that? Number 5357, Gunner McAndrew of the 53rd Medium. Is that you?"

"Yes, sir!"

"Breaking into a regimental museum, eh? That's another charge you'll 'ave to reckon with. Fall in behind the escort, man. Move. *Move!*" The provost-sergeant whispered to the bombardier, "My God, young fella, I'm goin' to see to you." He strode out, his black-bulled ammunition boots thumping after McAndrew and his escort guard. "Left, right, left, right, left. Quicken it up, move, *move!*"

A pigeon, watching from a high vantage point on the barrack clock tower, saw the provost-sergeant driving McAndrew before him with a guard either side, to the square saluting base. Here the commanding officer stood with his aide.

"Oh my God, what have we here?" asked the colonel.

"Gunner McAndrew, sir. For drumming out, sir," said the captain.

"But dressed up as a ruddy hussar?"

The aide's expression fell. "I'll . . . I'll make enquiries, sir."

"I should do that, if I were you," said the colonel.

"It appears, sir," said the captain, his ear inclined to the provost-sergeant, "that the regimental museum has been broken into . . ."

"So it seems," replied the colonel. "The prisoner is copying Lieutenant-Fireworker West of the Madras Artillery. Monday the 23rd of August, 1769. His knowledge of military history appears appropriate, to say the least. The intention, you may now be aware, is to extract urine from the military establishment. Halter him and march him through the ranks. Details of his crime to be read at every thirty paces. Remove the cockade hat from his head and knock that bloody cheroot out of his mouth." The colonel's monocle dropped from his eye.

"Yes, sir." said the aide.

"And report to me afterwards in my office."

"Yes, sir."

"God Almighty," added the colonel. "He's got enough gold braid across the front of him to blunt the regimental scissors." His toothbrush moustache bristled. "God preserve me from the antics of educated bloody soldiery."

*

23

Silence, now broken only by bawled commands and the stamping of boots.

McAndrew stood below the saluting base, looking down the double rank of soldiers. With a rope halter around his neck he was unaware of others, for he was watching a bird; a linnet, was it? No, just a sparrow; perched on the ridge of the married pads quarters.

"Prisoner ready for drumming out, sir," yelled the provost-sergeant in a shrill falsetto.

With pale faces the soldiers of the 53rd stared doggedly to their front.

"Carry on, please, Sergeant," said the aide.

His presence in this place was of indifference to McAndrew.

Soon, he was thinking, now that it was April, summer would come flying in to the Yorkshire dales; the mountains of Wales, to which he would inevitably go, would be lying on their backs, winking at the sun.

And the blossom-lined avenues of the Parisian boulevards, gay with the coloured dresses of women in summer, also beckoned him with humanity's warmth.

His friends would be in their appointed places – Rosa Florence (a tinker girl of untold generosity . . .) would be with the caravans along the Usk near Abergavenny: Miss Pan and Conrad, equally deranged, would be wandering the grounds of Atopia House up in Yorkshire – always his second home when in search for freedom. And . . . (he remembered this with a sudden surge of trepidation . . .) the mural he was painting on the wall of Uncle Dumb's banqueting hall up there was still unfinished . . . an outraged Uncle Dumb was extremely hard to handle.

But better still, thought McAndrew, Henri, his beloved Toulouse-Lautrec – artist and friend – would be waiting for him in the Moulin Rouge – if only he could rid himself of this man's soddin' army.

Why he'd joined the outfit in the first place was now beyond him, thought McAndrew.

*

A lark was singing above the barrack square and he turned up his face to the sun.

A lark such as this, thought he, would be singing above the turrets of Atopia House, above the gay Parisian boulevards, above the caravan of Rosa Florence – his immediate thought. It was nearly a week since he'd had a woman, and the situation was becoming intolerable. And, on his way to her – before jumping a ship down in Wales for Montmartre again, he would drown his teeth in some ale – quarts at the Bell, at the Black Boar and whisky at the Bear, Crickhowell, where he had a soft spot for the landlady's daughter.

Yet, despite his attempts to philosophise the situation there grew within McAndrew a strange sadness at leaving the army.

In the barrack rooms, he thought (sod the Officers' Mess) lay unequalled comradeship. The spit and polish button-sticks, bull-blooded boots and boning of toe-caps, though an anathema to him, snatched him up into the universal, blind acceptance of military discipline.

The bawdy ballads, many Kiplingesque, of the barrack rooms; the Crown and Anchor boards, Pitch and Toss, with Urq the Firk and Bloop (Bill Hooper), Evil Eye Evans of Penrith and Ponce Heldanby (a pugilist) playing hell down the Blood Tub boozer on a Saturday night – all fashioned nostalgia into something akin to love . . .

There was Gunner Jenkinsop (the kidney-wiper) for instance, in the next bed-space – his charm lay in large privates and an idiocy of innocence – Jenkinsop, whom the M.O. greeted with down-cast eyes (the inspecting doctors never looked up on short-arm inspections) and a muttered 'Good morning, Jenkinsop'.

There was Ianto Rumblebum, of Swansea, who performed most beautifully on the piccolo . . . Baccy Buntin, who, now paying six affiliation orders, reckoned that all his lovers were expecting before he met them, and Randy Raper, who was changing his name by deed poll, having ambitions for the

Church . . . also Alfie Gillie, the Edinburgh Scot who claimed he'd slept with Queen Victoria.

Thought McAndrew, I could go on and on and on . . . God, he was goin' to miss 'em . . .

The lark began joyously to sing again, but its song was cut short by the ceremonial crashing of drums and fifes.

A command rang out. The double rank of waiting soldiers turned inward; a unison crashing of boots that brought McAndrew back to the present. The provost-sergeant clattered up, his chest pigeoned with medals, his boots, polished with ox-blood, their blaikies loose and metallically crashing on to the tarmac. He shrieked: "Escort to the rear. Prisoner and escort, quick march!"

The drums and fifes of the 53rd struck up 'The Rogue's March'.

Led by the provost-sergeant, McAndrew, still haltered, was marched down the avenue of rigid soldiers.

"*Halt!*"

With a paper in his hand, the provost-sergeant turned about and fiercely cried: "Number 5357 Gunner James Alexander McAndrew. Accused and convicted on the 10th of March 1890 of two months and eleven days desertion. Drunk and disorderly on two occasions between July and September 1892. Sentenced to a total of a hundred and twenty lashes."

There was a silence. Then the lark began to sing again.

McAndrew was remembering that first desertion.

There was a wildness in the Brecon Beacons that called to him in springtime.

There, in summer, the brooks sparkled like Moselle wine, and all was bee-hum.

Once he had met a shepherdess alone on the hills. Her arms, bare to the elbows, were honey-coloured; the dress she wore had been inflated by nature to exactly the right proportions. Making love to her, he remembered, was like worshipping a nun in a flower shop.

"Take that smile off your face, McAndrew."

The sergeant stamped about, shouting: "Another thirty paces. Quick march!"

And the drums and fifes struck up again. With his rope halter dangling, McAndrew went, thumped from behind.

"*Halt!*"

The provost-sergeant bawled, his face beet-red and sweating ale:

"Arrested in France. Sentenced for desertion to sixteen hours field punishment and fifty lashes. Sentenced to a further hundred lashes for six months' desertion – arrested in Paris in September of last year . . ."

Approaching McAndrew the sergeant halted, seized the plaited gold braid of the stolen hussar's tunic and began to tear it off, throwing it over his shoulder.

Ach! – but it was worth it, thought McAndrew. Those months of freedom with the great Henri Toulouse-Lautrec in Montmartre, were the best months of his life.

The sun blazed down on to the barrack square, the lark sang; there was now no other sound but the wheezes and gasps of the provost-sergeant, as he tore at McAndrew's cross-braid and epaulettes, but McAndrew was not really there.

He was strolling, in his mind, down Rue de Steinkerque with Henri, and exhibiting his canvases in the square off Rue Norvins.

The giant Scot McAndrew, the dwarfish Frenchman Toulouse-Lautrec, the darling of the Moulin Rouge, walking together in the sun . . .

"*Mon ami,*" Henri had said, "you will never make an artist if you insist on being *taught!*"

The tiny man opened his hands. "You have great ability – all right, but do not tamper with it. Did Leonardo de Vinci take private instruction? Balls! He did not!"

"It's all right for you, because you've achieved it," protested McAndrew. "D'ye know I haven't earned ten francs in a fortnight? But you. . . !"

"Yes, I earn now, my friend, but only after a struggle! All art struggles! To starve is the destiny of artists. All right, all right!" continued Henri. "Go to school – go to the Ecole des Beaux-Arts – even go to Cormon's school, as I did once – and you might become a Bonnat. I will even pay for such an education! Think of it, Big One! A painter of Kings and millionaires – is there an easier way to earn one's money? Except upon one's back? At least a good whore gives something in return. Now then, if you were a Princeteau . . ."

"If I were a Princeteau or a John Lewis Brown, I'd not be askin' your help, ye bloody little fool," said McAndrew.

"It is you who is the fool!" replied Henri, and stopped amid the rushing bustle of Steinkerque and prodded McAndrew in the stomach. "You, my stupid friend, are the centipede who stopped beneath a tree, and said to the tortoise, 'Just think of it, my slow and clumsy tortoise – you possess four legs yet you can scarcely walk. I possess a hundred. What precision from God! Consider, my lumbering comrade, the nerve construction required to govern my movements! The million messages that flash to my brain, every time I take a step.'"

Henri stared up at McAndrew from his bulbous face, raised his top hat to a passing flower-seller, thumbed his prod-nose at a passing gentry carriage, and added:

"'Consider me well, my friend,' said the centipede, 'for I am the most excellent of God's handiwork. Allow me to explain the marvellous intricacy of my engineering . . .'"

Henri grinned up at McAndrew. "And, after explaining this, the centipede raised his hat and prepared to leave, then found he was paralysed by uncertainty."

The day was hot with bustle and sun; Paris was in her flowering mood of summer. The windows of pretty Rue de Steinkerque, the brothel quarter haunted by Toulouse-Lautrec, lent their flower-box perfumes to the Apache stinks of Montmartre.

Henri added, "Soon the gendarmes will catch you in any case, so why worry about your art? They will catch you and

28

send you back to the English army, which is the place, *mon ami*, for artists who desire to be instructed. What more can I say?"

McAndrew wiped his sweating face. "Mark, Mary and Joseph, mun! It's bloody good for you isn't it!"

"All right, all right! Do not swear at me!" The tiny man patted and cajoled McAndrew. "Or soon I will be in tears.

"Listen to me – draw, draw, *draw*! Paint, paint, *paint* – and it will come, you hear me? Open your heart, your soul, open your eyes – abandon technique, forget stylised line – stop *thinking* about it, Big One! Do not consider it, do not tamper with it! The gift is yours, it comes from the womb – let the womb do the drawing – bright, *bright* colours, yellow for womb blood, pink for trees! – were not van Gogh's cypresses purple? Listen to me, Big One! The moment the artist stops to think, his art is lost! Like the centipede. Next time I draw a woman's breast I am putting no nipple on it. *Voila!*"

"You're mad!" said McAndrew, and Henri Toulouse-Lautrec emptied small hands at him, smiling up, his pince-nez perched on the end of his nose.

"Monsieur, you flatter me with your caprices, so continue with your stupid conventions and fail to be an artist."

"But the font of life . . . without a nipple? It would not be possible. . . !"

"I refuse to accept this nipple," said Henri. "A billion people call it the font of life; I shall not. A nipple the font of life?"

"Ach, I'll never get the hang o' this," said McAndrew.

"In future, also, all my pigs will carry umbrellas and wear black boots."

"I still say you're mad!"

Henri bowed to him.

"*Halt!*" screamed the provost-sergeant, returning Mc-Andrew to reality.

The drums and fifes were silent on the barrack square. The sun burned down, and the sergeant chopped and tore at what was left of McAndrew's hussar uniform, and, as he did this, whispered: "You bastard, McAndrew, we're glad to be rid of you, you and your bloody drawings."

"Ach, you're bein' awful unkind to me," said McAndrew.

"*Right!* Quick march!"

The band struck up again, and again McAndrew marched down the ranks of soldiers towards the barrack gate. A little drummer-boy, his face pale with fright, was standing by the barrack gate to which McAndrew was marching. Poor little sod, he thought.

"*Halt!*" The sergeant shrieked, reading from his charge sheet:

"Desertion again in January this year. Arrested in Yorkshire. Selling his kit and blanket. Drawing on walls – defacing government property; breaking into a regimental museum, stealing a hussar uniform and striking a superior officer.

"Sentenced to be discharged from the army with ignominy."

The band blared again.

With his hussar's tunic hanging in ribbons went McAndrew, until he reached the barrack gate.

There he was momentarily held until a well placed boot by the drummer-boy sent him sprawling into the gutter.

"And don't show hide or hair o' yourself round 'ere no more!" yelled the sergeant. "Not never again – no more!"

The gates slammed shut.

After a moment or two McAndrew raised his head.

A white bull-terrier was sitting within a yard of him; dishevelled, bitten, covered with mud, it regarded McAndrew with a quizzical stare.

From a little knot of watching people, an old man called:

"You want to keep clear o' that one, mister – he's bad company. Wanted for murder in three countries, I heard say. You got trouble enough."

McAndrew rose, brushing himself down. The dog stared up at him.

30

"Away, ye daft thing." McAndrew swept the dog away with his foot.

"He boozes, too," said the old man. "They just flung him out o' the Coach and Horses."

"Is that a fact." said McAndrew of the dog. "Ye sup ale, too, is it? D'ye fancy a pint just now, son?"

The bull-terrier licked its lips.

"Away, then," said McAndrew, "and we'll see what we can do for ye. When did you eat last, for instance?"

The bull-terrier wagged its tail.

"Almost human, ain't he?" exclaimed the man, delighted.

"Don't insult the bloody dog," said McAndrew.

As he walked clear of the town, and with the dog swaying at his heels, McAndrew glared at the sky, and said: "Ye made a right cock o' that now, didn't ye? Didn't I tell ye I wanted to stay in the Gunners a bit longer? No money! In future we'll have this on a purely business basis."

He looked over his shoulder at the dog lagging behind. "As for you, you're drunk, ye boozy ponce. Come on!"

31

3

There was a tinker girl McAndrew knew.

Her name was Rosa and she came with the caravans every springtime to a field in Govilon on the canal, for the annual Gilwern Fair. McAndrew had the Fair in mind for pugilists attended it, the thick-eared community of the Welsh valleys, and he had an eye on a sovereign or two bare-knuckle.

For the past six days he had marched from Hendon to Wales.

He had marched at a military pace, a hundred and twenty strides to the minute and ten minutes rest in every hour. He went with his head back, his chest out and his arms swinging, and he sang as he marched, the bawdy songs of the barrack rooms where he had spent his youth. He shouted greetings to birds, he discussed the weather with watching cows. The sun was in his stomach, he used to say, and his belly was in his boots. At night he slept in barns and under hedges, making his camp fires by the roadside, sweeping and rough digging for pin-money, begging when there was none.

The dog, always behind him, trotted with the desultory mood of one who has no option. He ate when McAndrew ate and slept when he slept, within the warmth of his coat with his muzzle against his master's face.

McAndrew was still thinking of Rosa Florence when he came to the Bell, near Crickhowell, six days later. Light and smoke struck him as he pushed open the door of the public house with the dog in his arms.

Here, in the four-ale, were drinking the old poachers of the Usk, men who could ease a salmon out of the river without a ripple. The bailiff of the nearby Sandeman estate was here, swallowing port alone in a corner. Here bewhiskered labourers rubbed shoulders with gentry, who largely used the private bar called Gentlemen's Relish. In another corner a melodeon was playing accompaniment to a fiddler who was sawing out a merry Irish tune, and a bent old navvy from the Crumlin viaduct was clog-dancing in the middle of the floor, slopping his ale.

McAndrew quietly closed the four-ale door, turned, and entered the door for gentlemen.

Here a solitary customer was sitting on a high stool at the bar; a tiny misshapen crow of a man dressed in black from head to foot, and with a flat straw hat perched on the back of his head.

Jean Pierre, known in the south as the French Dwarf, raised heavily-lidded eyes to the mirror over the bar as McAndrew came in.

"'Evening."

The little man did not reply.

For a sailor he was a long way inland, come to visit his sister who had married a Welsh blacksmith. The dwarf's ship, the *Marie Prey*, was loading coal at Barry docks; within a day she was due out for Brittany. Meanwhile, Jean Pierre was watching the plump, white arms of the landlord's daughter who was serving in the four-ale; he could see her reflection through the adjoining hatch.

Through the crooked, clandestine years Jean Pierre had known few women. But, if the *Marie Prey* put into Brest this spring, he reflected as McAndrew joined him at the bar, there would be such a girl awaiting him; she, Mignon Marat, ignored his ugliness, finding in his love a symmetry and grace. True, once she had rejected him for a penniless poet who showed her neither respect nor concern, so Jean Pierre had tracked and killed the poet, and Mignon, his wayward lover, pined for but a few weeks.

33

"'Evening, mister," said McAndrew again.

The dwarf lowered his glass of absinthe. His small eyes, one crossed, moved in the vestal whiteness of his thickened features. The landlord appeared before them both, a lanky, skeletal man whose eyes stared from the bony quiet of his face.

"What can I do for you?"

"You can settle an argument, me sweet man," replied McAndrew.

The eyes of the dwarf flickered with interest. McAndrew said, "In the four-ale next door there's a fella who claims there's two gills to a pint."

"Two to the half-pint, Mister. Eight to the quart, thirty-two to the gallon."

"You're sure?"

"Sixteen year I've been in this trade, and some of them north of the border, where you come from. Tell him that from me."

"Hold it here while I settle the fella's hash." With the dog held against him McAndrew went through the porch to the bar next door.

"Will ye drink with me, son?" he asked the Irish fiddler.

"With the devil, if he pays." The man fiddled on; the navvy dancer, with his mug held high, went in a circle while the customers clapped the time.

"Two pints, please," said McAndrew to the landlord's daughter, and her chin went up and she looked him over. She thought she'd never seen a man as handsome, with his bright hair and face tanned by the sun.

"Ach, you're a beautiful creature" said McAndrew, leaning. "I've never seen such a lovely girl in a day's march, then some. By the way, the drinks are on the landlord," and the girl shouted over her shoulder:

"Is this all right, Pa? Two?" And McAndrew thrust his head through the hatch, crying:

"Two, landlord – that right? The foreigner in here still won't believe it."

The landlord, talking to Jean Pierre, nodded a smile.

34

"You'm lucky," said the girl. "I've never known him give a pint away, let alone quarts."

"And you're a darling thing, me pretty little Welsh. This is the best pub between here and Princes Street."

"Is one o' them for me?" asked the Irish fiddler, seeing two glasses.

"Hop it, ye big Irish yob, before I bloody kill ye," said McAndrew, and he drained one of the mugs and put the other on the floor for the dog.

Jean Pierre, his glass against his lips, watched through the hatch.

Later, out on the Abergavenny road when the moon was high, McAndrew strode out down the lane on a short cut to Gilwern and the Spring Fair, for there was money to be earned knocking out the pugilists.

On the way to Gilwern fields, he entered an allotment, plucked a little beetroot out of the ground and put it into his pocket. For one who would cartoon for a living, it was fruit of some importance . . .

The Bridgend Inn, when he reached it with Caesar, was jam-packed to the doors with railway tradesmen. McAndrew had almost to fight his way to a corner, such was the confusion of tables and bodies, and he lifted a quart pewter from under a navvy's nose as he went, blew off the froth and drank deep.

These were the railwaymen of Crawshay Bailey's greedy empire of iron, but whose genius had built the famous railway (of University doggerel) from Brynmawr to Monmouth, and all the trades were there in the Bridgend Inn that night, and mostly Irish (McAndrew knew this) gaugers, wheeltappers, ballasters and platelayers – men who, 'end-on', could lay a mile of the standard four-foot a day.

Now, their ten hours labouring finished, they jostled around the bar-counter where the fat landlord and his spinster, floss-headed daughter poured the quarts.

In a corner, McAndrew took the beetroot out of his pocket

and crushed it in one big hand, letting the scarlet juice run through his fingers into the half-filled pot: ale and beet he stirred with a finger to the colour of blood, and an Irish voice suddenly cried:

"*Arrah!* Where's me bloody ale then?"

The men turned in surly banter. "Ye've drunk it, mun!"

"I have not! It was under me blutty nose scarce a moment back!"

"Did the bulldog sup it? I saw one come in just now!"

"Aw, no!" said McAndrew, coming up with the pewter. "Did some fella steal your ale! Ach, for God's sake, that's a dreadful thing to do," and he crossed himself.

"What you got there, then, stranger?" This from a Connemara gnome less than five feet high, and in him stared the hungers of Cromwell.

"Port and lemon, my son," replied McAndrew.

"Holy Mother," said the gnome. "The ponces are with us – port and lemon, for God's sake!"

"Me ale was here not a second back, I tell ye!" cried the first man, aggrieved. "On me mither's grave, I'd scarce got it to me teeth, so I hadn't, and up comes some whore's aunt and bloody lifts it."

"Ach, there's little honour in the world these days," said McAndrew. "Sure to God, I'd be buyin' ye another, if I possessed the makings."

"Who the hell are you, then?"

"I'm the priest o' Crow Head, off Bantry, and I'll bother ye to moderate ye language, my son."

"Holy Mother – a priest, is it!" The man removed his hat.

"In that rig-out, beggin' ye pardon, Holy Father?" whispered another.

"Aye, well, me parish is small," said McAndrew, in a fine Irish brogue, "so I'm on the road, d'ye see. I'm a seller o' coloured Bibles for the poor – and didn't the good Lord Himself have nothin' more'n a rag to cover His decency. . . ?"

The conversation was dying.

"That He did not, Father. Ach, that's for sure!"

36

"There's only me and me wee dog in the world, ye see," said McAndrew. "So to quench the dust o' the road, we just slipped in for a port and lemon, ye understand, and a bowl of water for the poor beast, I'd be obliged to ye."

Caesar sniffed at the water the landlord's daughter hurriedly brought, and turned away, disgusted.

The conversation had started up again. More men were thronging in, hammering the bar for ale, and a man shrieked, falsetto:

"Will ye moderate ye language ye damned big apes, for we're blessed wi' the presence of a man o' the cloth!" He crossed himself. "Are ye travellin' hard then, Father?"

"I'm spreadin' the Word, me son," said McAndrew.

Out of the corner of his eye he saw Caesar, paws on a table, lapping up a platelayer's ale, and inwardly cursed him. "In a manner o' speaking, I've come to bless the pub, so I have," and he cleared a space facing the bar, and with the quart pot in his left hand began to draw on the wall.

"Holy God," whispered a navvy, "just look!"

The face of a young girl was taking shape on the wall.

Under McAndrew's dripping fingers, she grew in scarlet on the white-wash.

He painted with his fingers, inscribing quick arcs, dipping into the pot; sometimes using the back of his hand, sometimes the front, each finger moving independently, to quicken the effect, and the beefy landlord cried:

"Be Jesus! What's he up to? He's defacin' the bloody premises!" and he opened the flap of the bar, struggling through the crowded room, but his daughter shouted:

"Oh, Feyther, leave him, for God's sake – look! *Look!*"

The noise of the public bar quietened to a whisper, then hushed into silence.

There was no sound now but the brushing of McAndrew's fingers.

And there was growing upon the whitewashed wall a woman of full size and great beauty.

Her face, in scarlet, was oval, and of dignity: her red lips were parted in a smile. Her eyes, large and slanted in her high-boned, clearly Jewish face, held the luminous quality of absolute peace: serenity lay in every contour of her expression.

And, even as all there watched, their drinks lowered, so the portrait grew in shape before them. The profound vision, appearing so magically in their midst, stilled their tongues.

The fat landlord, now behind McAndrew as he worked, was staring with incredulity.

For there came from the face on the wall something greater than mere beauty: it touched their Celtic blood with poetry: a sudden purity that banished the blasphemy of their existence.

A man said in the silence, his voice a whisper: "Dear God, it's me darlin' departed . . . me sweet Kathleen . . ."

McAndrew worked on swiftly, his hand now inscribing scarlet robes. The woman's arms were bare and lying across her breast, as if in prayer. Now McAndrew stooped, the better to capture her form, drawing with quick curves, the slim waist and hips, the folds of her gown right down to her feet.

Full height now, she held herself erect, smiling into the room, and the men gasped.

McAndrew was now upon his knees, working at her feet.

"God Almighty," said a man. "She *lives!*"

With the pewter-pot on the table now, McAndrew painted with both hands, and life came to the face he smoothed and touched; the dark-shadowed eyes, the hollows of her cheeks, and her hair, bright scarlet, fell in swathes over her shoulders.

"Who is it?" asked a man, but they knew who it was, and McAndrew said, as he worked:

"I kissed the ring o' the Bishop of Derry, and I took the cloth in that town. But He called me to a trade, and I walked the roads of County Connaught. *Aye. . . !*" and he worked on deftly, "I travelled the roads in search of good works, and one day met a woman in the mountains, and she says to me, she says: 'To you, my son, I will grant a gift. That ye take me from this place and fashion me before the heathen, for drink is the Devil Incarnate and a curse to decent women. It degenerates the man, it bruises the faces of his children. So put me on the walls of the publicans and sinners . . .'" and the landlord cried:

"Spare us, Father! Would ye have me life-blood? Ye'll be takin' me living, so you will."

"God bless the Pope," whispered a man, "I'll never touch another drop . . ."

McAndrew was drawing a baby in the woman's arms; this done, he reached up and inscribed around her head a scarlet halo.

"Heaven be praised!" said a Dublin voice, "It's the Mother and Child," and he knelt.

There was no sound now but breathing and the uneasy shuffling of boots in saw-dust. And then the landlord's daughter cried, harshly: "Will ye kneel, you lot? Ye numb-skull cursed heathen? D'ye realise we're in the presence of the Deity?"

One by one, they knelt, and those who did not wish to kneel, put down their drinks, and left.

While the prayers were being said, and after he had collected three and sixpence, McAndrew went quietly around the tables finishing their beer.

Caesar was flat on his back outside in the yard, paws up, sleeping it off, when McAndrew reached him. He said: "In future, ye stupid nut, will ye lay off the ale till I give ye the word? Five minutes back in there ye nearly put a bloody end to us."

Always in April the tinker caravans would come to the Govilon field and sit in a circle around a bonfire. Unsteady on his feet, McAndrew could hear the laughing of children and the squalling of the babies who came nineteen to the dozen.

He envied these dark-skinned people their communal

freedom. Nothing pleased him more than to see their hooped caravans wending in a line across the dull forbidding country and hear the clip-clopping of their little New Forest ponies.

They claimed an aristocratic origin, these tinker folk, the remnants of a dispossessed nobility; their smooth classical features giving the lie to a riff-raff of the road.

And Rosa, now aged twenty, was the epitome of her race, with her delicate face and fine, black hair.

Now, as he strode along, McAndrew hoped she would be as generous as she had been twice before – and would be, he acknowledged, were she not pledged. Were she pledged then his visit would be a waste of time, for there was none more virtuous than a tinker maid with a tinker lover in the offing.

McAndrew wanted a woman. His affection for women moved within him like an elegant ceremony. Rosa Florence, he thought, could please him most of all.

The full moon was blazing down on the narrow road; the fields either side of the Usk River gleamed white, each grass blade tipped with a diamond of light. Aware that the dog was no longer following him, he stopped and turned. The animal was staggering, its legs buckling.

"Aye, it's a good sup of the hops ye get in Wales, and I agree with ye," said McAndrew. Bending, he picked up the dog. "After a month or two wi' me, son, you'll learn how to carry your ale.

"What shall we call you, eh? Would Caesar suit you, little fella?"

The dog's eyes were shining in the light of the moon.

Man and dog heard the Spring Fair long before they came to Gilwern; the singing of the hurdy-gurdies, and saw the red flashes in the sky. Also, the ironworks was pouring up at Blaenafon, for the clouds were pulsating and glowing with light.

Breasting a rise, McAndrew smelled the tinkers' caravans long before he saw them; the smouldering wood ash, the perfumes of the big cooking-pots that hung on tripods over

40

the flames. The fattest leverets and rabbits found their way into a tinker's larder.

Six caravans McAndrew saw, with the bonfire burning in the middle of the clearing and the sparks flying up, lighting crimson the faces of the tinkers squatting around. But the only tinker he had eyes for was Rosa.

How to tell of her, he thought, with only words to use?

She was sucking the thigh bone of a leveret, her head held back and her black hair ruffling in the wind. The flames of the fire painted red her high-boned face.

With the dog held against him he stood in the shadows, watching.

She was wearing a white blouse pulled in at the waist and beneath that a skirt; the skirt was stretched wide at the hem because she was squatting; her legs were raked to the fire, her knees cocked up.

But it was her eyes.

Often he wondered where she had gained such beauty, for her mother was a dump of a woman and her father, now dead, had the face of an ingratiating poodle.

There was a woman down at Barry; he had seen her last summer on the steamers with her father. She was small, well defined, and had the features of a delicately painted Chinese vase. She had been doing her books and arguing with an agent like a man, so he presumed that she was educated. One could take such a woman and pass on, he thought, leaving behind but the memory of relief. But not so with Rosa. Her instincts were those of an animal, fierce and uncontrolled; yet she possessed a sensitivity he had discovered in no other, a victim unprepared for the hurt.

Unease touched McAndrew into movement. Only a soiled specimen of life, he thought, would return. Rosa had given to him before, but now, no doubt, she was pledged.

Public opinion was wrong about the tinkers. Theirs was a high moral code. You could earn favours of a tinker girl with kindness but never money, he knew. Once they were pledged to marriage, there wasn't enough gold to buy them.

*

Pinta, too old to die, was playing on his melodeon, his bearded face sunk low on his chest. Mr. Florence, the step-father of Rosa, was whittling pegs, and Evan Kinto, his cousin, was polishing a harness.

None of the men looked up as McAndrew approached; all had the ability to know a male presence without the use of eyes. The ponies and donkeys stood statuesque in the moonlight. Rosa leaped up.

"Jim McAndrew! *Jim!*"

"Siddle you down," said her mother and her hand fastened on Rosa's wrist. "You'm pledged, remember?"

Other tinkers, men and women at the fire, went on eating as McAndrew and the dog approached. Mrs. Florence said, raising her walnut face out of her rags, "They got you in November, Scotsman, now its April. Are ye out for good?"

"Aye, Missus, and back on the road," came the reply, but his eyes were on Rosa.

McAndrew squatted beside her and the terrier sat distantly.

"Come and eat," said Rosa, and her mother took a bowl and filled it with broth from the cauldron, saying:

"What you want with us, man? You anna tinker and you anna Romany. Reckon you come this way only when you got the moon in your pocket?" She offered the bowl.

"That's right, Missus." In both hands McAndrew grasped the ribs of a ewe, sucking voraciously, tearing away the bones and throwing them to the dog. "All the chalked signs led me here," he said. "The Tramps' Circuit knows the Gilwern Fair for sure."

"And you know that Rosa's pledged? Did they chalk that up, too."

He stopped eating and looked at Rosa. The girl said in halting explanation. "I got Tam Shenks, Jim. You remember the shoeing lad?"

"God alive, couldn't you have done better than that?"

"Tam Shenks is tinkering, remember," said Mrs. Florence. "More'n you are, I say, you'm just rovering."

42

McAndrew shrugged. "He'll still be shoeing when he's bloody ninety."

"Maybe, but I hopes you anna staying," said the woman bitterly. She tore the flesh from a bone and tossed the bone on to the fire and the fat flared, lighting her face.

She was young, with the face of age. Her first husband was dead, but when he was alive his hands bled with beating the donkeys, and she had learned in her girlhood to bite the cloth to save herself screaming when he was beating her. Most horse fair days it were worst, she used to say, when he came back on the ale and the horses gone to some far country. A man got to beat something, lest he anna human, the old ones said.

"You don't have to worry," said McAndrew, "I'm only passing through."

"That's all right, then, for Rosa's pledged, and she's only a kid to you. Don't you come here with a little shovel of ashes for her babbies, for that's Tam Shenks's ground, and all her tackles are his." She raised bagged eyes. "Leastwise, were her pa here he'd be givin' you hard knocks for even callin', ye understand that?"

"Ach, still your tongue, I can take care of meself," said Rosa.

"Right, but comb the meat out of him and I'll tell your fancy chap, and he'll beat the bones of ye black and blue – before wedding, never mind after."

Rosa said, pouting at the moon, "Anyway, I don't care so much about Tam Shenks now, I don't."

McAndrew, munching, gave her a grin. He nudged the old woman. "It's not your Rosa I'm after, Mamie girl, its a size of your dead chap's breeches and a decent coat to cover me."

"The army don't do you much good with that." Rosa looked him over.

Her mother said, "Tell you what. If I rig ye, and no charge, do you promise to leave us in peace?"

"I swear on the life of me mither."

"Where are ye bound?"

"South Wales – to Barry and the ships."

"And never come back?"

"Jesus, woman, do I have to cut my throat for ye?" He snapped his fingers and the dog leaped into his arms, and he rose, looking down at them; the brightest eyes of all there were the eyes of Rosa.

"I couldn't wait for you, Jim," said she. "Honest, I tried."

"Five months? God, you didn't waste much time."

He wandered away into the shadows and Rosa joined him, saying, "It was me mam, really speaking. But he's an enchantin' chap is Tam Shenks, mind. Once he's got his teeth under your jumper he holds real tight."

"He'll sow you babies, you realise that."

"Aye, I do. But that's what I'm made for, says me mither, to make babbies in the van on the nights of full moon."

"You'd not make babies with me," said McAndrew.

"Mebbe, but ye're rough with a girl," said Rosa, no higher than his shoulder. "You're a boozing chap, you'm no good at tinkering. You canna spring a gin or cover bad spots on a horse's teeth. I'd likely starve to death wi' you."

Her stepfather called from the bonfire, "If ye go to the Fair, come back early, remember. I'm not scratching me ears with midnight goings on, McAndrew."

"Sleep easy, old man."

"So you're going?" asked Rosa.

"If your mam rigs me out, I'm away. A man's a fool to stay when he's not wanted. Where do you sleep these days?"

"With Brookie, me brother, but when Tam and me are married, we'll give him a penny and turn him out."

"I'll give him sixpence tonight."

"Don't you dare, ye wicked zoul!"

"Och, I will. Rosa Florence is worth any man's bob, never mind sixpence."

"Me mam has ears to hear dead grass growing. She knows the difference between lovering breathing and the scratching o' goats."

Unseen by the others, McAndrew held her.

He thought she was astonishingly young. And Rosa turned down her face from his mouth as if hatred of herself was moving within her. He said, "Just once more, for old time's sake? I've never loved any girl but you, Rosa Florence."

Last spring, in a wheatfield not yet born, he had made love to her in the rain. And the rain had tufted her hair, making her look like some small creature in alarm; there was about her a nymph-like beauty. Later, he was surprised that she had never made love before; her movements being filled with anxious desire, lying there beneath him while the rain dripped tearfully.

"There now, Jim McAndrew, you've gone and done for me," she had said.

Later, her youthful ardour had tired him. Even the moon, he thought, seemed to be standing on its head; then he knew that her very immaturity had bored him. Making love to a child only reminded him of women.

"I'll come back," said McAndrew now.

"Please don't!"

"I'll go to the Fair and pick meself up a sovereign or two at the boxing booth, then I'll come back."

"I'll call for me mam, mind."

"I doubt it."

"You'm rough with a girl, Jim. Tam Shenks is easy. Last time me arms and legs were as black as a hawthorne bush . . ."

"I'll give your Brookie sixpence," said McAndrew.

4

The morning was bright, with perfumes of spring in the April air, as McAndrew set off from Rosa's caravan next day. With the bull-terrier trotting behind him he went, and there was a fine swinging gait in him as Rosa watched him go.

Her mood was a context of rage and joy, as, with her hand on the curtain of the caravan window, she watched McAndrew: the usual, absurd, cockerel-like male, she thought in tinker-tongue – full of arrogance, bound on drink and fornication.

Hands in pockets, McAndrew marched. Once clear of the tinkers' camp, he began to whistle, his face cocked up to the early sun, his boots thumping a rhythm on the metalled road that led to Abergavenny. Rosa watched him until he was lost in distance, then gripped her hand and bowed her head.

His lovemaking had enveloped her: it had possessed the delicacy of a male tiger, giving nothing, taking all. Rosa wondered what she was going to tell Tam Shenks. Time might tell, she thought bitterly.

The door of the van opened and Brookie, her brother, entered. His grimy face was alive with smiles; his face, with teeth missing in front, leered up at her.

"He give me threepence."

"Don't you say anything," warned Rosa, and she reached out and gripped his arms. "You tell anyone he gave you money and I'll damn fry you."

"What did you get?" asked Brookie.

She did not reply at once, but looked through the window

46

to the whiteness of the fields. The tops of the poplars on the westward road were ringed with sunlight. Faintly, in quick buffets of the wind, she could hear McAndrew whistling.

"I got trouble," said Rosa.

In the clothes of Rosa's dead father, McAndrew felt confident and renewed; a fine pair of corduroy breeches and woollen stockings under; his boots were his own, army issue and of Number One quality. The thick worsted jacket he wore now had seen better days, but upon his head was a bowler hat set at a jaunty angle.

True, he had not yet breakfasted, but there were ports of call well sign-posted by the élite of the Tramps' Circuit, the directions being arrowed on trees or indicated by tufts of grass planted in hedgerows for the soft touches; hard cases were designated by chalked circles around small stones. During his many desertions of his eight years army service McAndrew had learned the signs and etiquette of the Circuit; when not to poach upon another traveller's preserves; conversely, to avail himself of all opportunity when the way was free.

He went gaily, smiling up at the sun, often laughing aloud: stopping at times in his military march to cup his hands to his mouth and mimic the birds. This brought about him a chorus of replies. The cuckoo he imitated, the sparrow and the wren; now stopping to repeat the hoarse 'Caw-cawing' of rooks and crows.

Vaulting a gate, he walked through Abergavenny, along a bank of the Usk. There, dozing in the afternoon sun, he watched misty haloes forming around the summits of the Sugarloaf and Blorenge mountains.

Beneath his head, when he slept in bee-hum, he heard the salmon splashing in the higher reaches; and faintly, too, the drop-hammers of the Top irontowns thudding in the grass.

From the Usk he poached two trout, tickling them with his fingers, and cooked them over the red embers of a wood fire, eating them in the dusk and drinking from the pools. The

47

bones of the fish he left on the grass for other wayfarers to find, and learn of the bounty of the river.

In this manner McAndrew lived his life, chained by fate, unchaining himself.

When stationed up north, for instance, he had travelled the length and breadth of the Ridings, knowing where he would find generosity or where he would be set upon by dogs. In the dales, from Swaledale, through Wensleydale to Wharfedale he had followed the route of the river from its source on the Roof of England.

Here, in the grey hills that had given up their lead to the Romans, he had sought shelter in the old workings and begged food from wandering tribes of gipsies. He had shared an earth bed with a yowling cave-dweller and served at the table of the Duke of Devonshire in Chatsworth; an elaborately uniformed flunkey by night, a coach postilion by day.

After a few weeks of desertion, the police would track him and hand him over to the army, after which would come field punishment or public flogging. Then would follow a disciplined life of soldierly refinement, when he would gain the respect of officers and men.

None was smarter on parade than James Alexander McAndrew, at such times; none more fitted to wear the Queen's uniform.

But then the freedoms of the wild places would call him; some new scent in the wind, and his comrades would awake to find him gone. His bed would be made up, the bed-space swept clean. His equipment, with its brasses freshly polished, would be meticulously hung on its wall pegs; his rifle cleaned, oiled and pulled through, the breech bound with cloth to preserve it against rust.

While serving with the 53rd (London) Medium Brigade, Royal Artillery, McAndrew was captured as far north as Hubberholm, and returned to Hendon under heavy escort.

The written evidence of one, Gunner R. Jenkinsop, during the ensuing court-martial (who was unfortunate enough to share the next bed-space to McAndrew) is of interest.

*

'He were an immense bloke. There was a chap in the brigade who was six foot four, and McAndrew topped him. When sober he could be a gentleman. Once, in drink, he told me he were a Scottish laird, and I believed him. He showed me a white scar through his hand and said it was caused by a bullet while serving on the Afghan Frontier, but now I hear he'd never been near the Khyber Pass – never ever been overseas, to my knowledge.

'He were a terrible man for fighting. I saw him knock a Negro pugilist flat and win a golden guinea in a boxing booth in Premierland and the military police always had a terrible time in catching him, coming back with cut eyes and that, and though they took him rough, they never broke him. He were an artist, too, though few know this. Major McMillan knows it, for I were there when he got the proof of it.

'I were dozing off one night in the room when McAndrew comes in drunk. He 'ad been fighting again and I saw blood on his greyback when he stripped off his tunic. Then he rolls up his right sleeve and goes to the combustion stove in the middle of the room; it being summer, the thing weren't lit. So McAndrew takes off the top and puts his hand in up to the arm-pit and his hand is covered with soot.

'I watched, one eye open; all the other chaps was snoring. Then he went to the wall of the hut and begins to draw upon it. First he draws the head and shoulders of a naked Roman soldier with his arms out, his hands gripping the reins of two horses who was pulling a plough. True, sir, I ain't never seen anything more beautiful.

'Down to the waist he draws this Roman soldier, with his buckler on, and his sword scabbard, but no sword in it. And, as I watched, so it all come into shape; the Roman soldier drivin' a twin of horses pulling a plough with 'is broken sword across his back. You could see the rears of the 'orses, their plumed heads and harness; it just grew before my eyes, sir; the plough going in and the earth turning up, and the fields right away to the distance. And McAndrew kept coming back and dipping his hand into the soot, dabbing here and there on the wall, making the muscles in the back of the

49

Roman soldier, and his great head with its helmet and wavin' feathers. I tell you, sir, it were marvellous.'

'And then?' asked the defending officer.

'Then when Major McMillan comes in the morning he puts McAndrew on a charge for defacing government property.'

'Very rightly,' said the president.

The court went silent. The defending officer asked, 'Anything more, Gunner Jenkinsop?'

'Only one thing, sir. I been a farmer, see, before I come for a soldier. There were a mistake in the drawing. The plough was throwin' the wrong way.'

'Scarcely relevant, all of this,' said the prosecuting officer.

The president said, 'Yes, but allow the evidence of Gunner Jenkinsop to stand. It may be useful to the medical authorities later, when assessing the prisoner's ability to plead.'

'It . . . it were a wonderful drawing, mind,' said Gunner Jenkinsop.

'You're casting pearls before swine, man. Don't waste your time on 'em, ye damned idiot,' said McAndrew.

'*Silence!*' roared the provost-sergeant.

'And then, Jenkinsop?' asked the court president sighing.

'Then . . . then he just puts his coat back on and walks out, don't he?'

'You mean, he left barracks.'

'Aye, sir. And the next time I sees him, sir, was under guard four months later.'

'Thank you. Next witness, please.'

There was a clattering commotion in the court. A new witness came in.

'Number 42162, Bombardier Henry Manders, is that you?' asked the prosecuting officer.

The bombardier stood rigidly to attention. 'Yes, sir.'

'At the time of the arrest of the accused, Gunner James Alexander McAndrew, you were bombardier of the guard at Barnsbury Park, is that correct?'

'Yes, sir.'

'What time was the prisoner brought into barracks under escort?'

The court was hushed. McAndrew appeared a man removed, staring through a window of the room to distant fields.

'Just after midnight, sir. I entered the time in the Guard book.'

'What state was the prisoner in?'

'Drunk and disorderly, sir. He weren't marked, but two members of the escort were sort of battered about . . .' the bombardier faltered.

'Battered about? Explain their injuries.'

'Well, Sergeant Holder had his eye filled up and the two privates got blood on their tunics.'

'What action did you take?'

The bombardier stiffened. 'I called out the guard, sir, and incarcerated the prisoner in one of the cells, didn't I?'

'What happened then?'

'At one o'clock in the morning the R.S.M. comes round.'

'The regimental sergeant-major came round at one o'clock, to inspect the guard. He was standing in for Captain Falkener, I understand,' explained the prosecuting officer. The president wrote carefully in his notes.

'Then what happened, bombardier?'

'The sergeant-major asked to see the prisoner, didn't he?'

The president looked up wearily. 'Bombardier Manders, the prosecuting officer is asking you. Please do not insist on asking us. Proceed.'

'And did he inspect the prisoner?'

The bombardier's eyes flickered with an inner emotion. 'Oh yes, sir. I called the guard as an escort and opened the cell door and let the sergeant-major in.'

'Was the prisoner violent at this stage?'

'Quiet as a mouse, sir, sleeping . . .'

'And then?'

'Then the sergeant-major ordered McAndrew on to his feet and he got up and stood to attention.'

'Go on.'

'Then the sergeant-major said . . .' The bombardier looked about him, pain growing on his taut features.

'In your own words, please, Bombardier Manders. You are not being arraigned here, no punishment will fall upon you for your evidence. It is only necessary that you tell the truth – in your own words – just tell the truth.'

The bombardier drew himself up, staring doggedly to his front. 'The . . . the sergeant-major said, "Ohoho! Here we are again, are we? Gunner James Alexander bloody McAndrew, eh? What you in here for this time, my little lovely. . . ?"'

The bombardier gazed across the room at the sergeant-major, who sat as one bucolic.

'Did the prisoner reply?'

'Yes, sir. He said, "I'm in here for desertion, resisting arrest and striking a sergeant," that's what he said, sir. Then the sergeant-major said, "Well well, well! Is that a bloody fact? Desertion, resisting arrest and striking a sergeant, eh?" and he poked McAndrew in the stomach with his stick. "A regular little who-ha, ain't we, McAndrew? Going from bad to worse, ain't we? Well, here's your chance to improve yourself." And he closed his eyes, sir, and stuck his chin out, sir, and said, "Before you, my son, stands your own regimental sergeant-major – a real live regimental sergeant-major, McAndrew. *Strike me!*"'

The president looked pained. 'Proceed, Bombardier Manders. Do not spare us.'

'The prisoner took one pace forward and . . .' the bombardier hesitated.

'In your own words, remember. Just give the evidence, man – the exact words, if you like, that you used to the orderly sergeant at the original regimental enquiry, bombardier.'

'The exact words, sir?'

'The exact words, bombardier, if that makes it easier.'

'McAndrew took one pace forward and hit him arse over tit, didn't he?'

'Oh my God,' muttered the president. 'Do we really have

52

to admit such expressions in an official court?' and the defending officer said:

'It is necessary, sir, to get at the exact order of command, provocation and ensuing action on the part of the prisoner. Continue, Bombardier Manders.'

'We thought he were dead, sir – the R.S.M., I mean. We was twenty minutes bringin' him round . . .'

'And what was the prisoner doing during this period?'

'Back asleep, sir. He laid on 'is bed and got his head down.'

'The bastard gave me an order and I complied wi' it,' growled McAndrew. 'What else d'ye want?'

'*Silence!*'

The prosecuting officer was rubbing his chin, instantly immersed in his notes. Raising an unemotional face, he said:

'Yours has been a very painful duty, bombardier. What happened then?'

'We got the R.S.M. to the hospital, sir.'

'And because of the injuries he was there for three days.' The president added:

'You distinctly heard the R.S.M.'s order to the prisoner, bombardier? The defending officer, in his plea for mitigation, has made much of this – that the prisoner, Gunner McAndrew, received from the regimental sergeant-major a clear and precise order that was intelligible and understandable. Did you yourself understand it?'

'Oh yes, sir,' said the bombardier joyously.

'To do what, bombardier? Please be precise.'

'To . . . to give 'im one.'

'It was an order to the prisoner, from the R.S.M. to strike him, the R.S.M.?'

'Yes, sir. I'd 'ave done the same meself.' He beamed around the court. 'I'd have had to, wouldn't I?'

The president nodded and said peremptorily. 'Court writer, please erase the accusation in respect of the prisoner striking the R.S.M. from the record. It is now inadmissible.'

'About bloody time,' said McAndrew.

*

Jean Pierre, the French dwarf, was sitting on a high stool at the bar of the Barry Chain Locker, the biggest public bar in Wales, when McAndrew entered with the terrier under his arm.

Since he was facing the street, the dwarf had a clear view of the entrance. Despite his poor eye-sight he recognised McAndrew immediately: the innate power of the big man seemed to reach out to him over the crowded floor.

"Sorry, boy, no dogs in here," said the barmaid, one of six who were filling the glasses and mugs as fast as the clients could sink them.

Because of his deformity, Jean Pierre found himself, through challenge, attracted to strength and virility.

When young, he would sit on the little stone quays of the Brittany villages and watch the coalers at work; poetry lay, for him, in the muscular sweating of the navvies; the bulging arms that served the winches. Strength depicted for the dwarf the sensual masculinity which he coveted. It went further. It represented an element to be conquered and destroyed.

His small, squinted eyes drifted over McAndrew as he pushed aside the entrance door and entered with grandiose style; an affront, almost, to any man in the room who might take a chance.

Momentarily, he waited, looking about him. He saw the labourers of Number Two Dock; the stunted faces he saw, the crude strength that submerged the beards and quart pewters. The navvies glared back, momentarily stilled and quiet, accepting his arrogance.

The thunder of the bar began anew as McAndrew unexpectedly turned and went out again.

The dwarf smiled knowingly; lifting his glass he drank his wine with fastidious grace, watching McAndrew in the adjoining bar through the glass of the serving-hatch.

The landlord, he could see, was now talking earnestly to McAndrew; the dwarf licked his thick lips and smiled wider.

McAndrew entered the public bar again and this time

pushed his way through the navvies to the counter.

"Two pints," said he.

The barmaid raised her eyes in silent appraisal. McAndrew winked at her, then smiled happily around the mud-stained faces of the navvies.

"Good pub, this. Best pub between Wales and Princes Street. Is there money round here?"

"On Number Two Dock, but Mister, you got to work."

The barmaid was pouring the ale now; McAndrew's eyes moved over her.

Her Nordic beauty attracted him; the gas lamps flung flickering shadows deep into her eyes, making bright her fair hair. He wanted to hear her speak again; her tongue held a lilting Welsh charm; fair down was upon her cheeks, her forearms shone. She poured the two pints and slid them towards him over the counter.

"Twopence."

McAndrew lifted one and blew off the froth. "On the landlord, Missus," he said, and drank.

"On the house? He didn't say." The girl glanced over her shoulder at the serving-hatch. The landlord's bald head gleamed on the glass. Leaning across the counter, McAndrew tapped the glass of the hatch. The landlord slid it aside.

"Two, you said – that right, landlord?" McAndrew jerked his thumb at the dwarf. "He don't know a gill from a litre, this one."

The landlord laughed, nodding.

"Cheers," said McAndrew, drained one pint and lifted the other.

"You're the only one I've met who orders two at a time," observed the barmaid.

"Watch me when I get going," said McAndrew. He put his arm around Jean Pierre's shoulders. "How're ye doin', son?"

The dwarf's face was expressionless.

In McAndrew's embrace he lifted his wine glass, drinking steadily. Under the pressure of the arm the dwarf felt

55

narcotised, palsied by the affront. The warmth of McAndrew bit deep into him; a sensation of disgust that he fought to contain. '

"Don't they talk English in here, then?" asked McAndrew.

"Let him be, mister or you're in trouble," said the barmaid.

Jean Pierre was experiencing a physical insensibility; a revulsion that rendered him momentarily inert.

Once, when a child, another man had so held him, rendering in him a paralysis of fear and pain. The act had induced into his childhood nightmares of dreams.

Now the shouted insults of the circus crowds he heard again; the chattering jumble of the navvies; it pierced Jean Pierre's present with his disreputable past, before his escape from the circus to the sea: a sea that had washed him clean of a personal vivisection.

McAndrew removed his arm. The dwarf closed his eyes and bowed his head with relief.

"You all right, Jean Pierre?" asked the barmaid.

"Oh, he's fine, anna ye, Frenchie?" McAndrew elbowed him.

He could see the dwarf's reflection in the amber slant of the ale; the narrowed eyes, the humped cheeks, flattened nose; the thick lips drawn back. McAndrew drank and the vision disappeared. Gasping, he wiped his mouth with the back of his hand.

"You'd get taken on at Two Dock, more than likely," said the barmaid. "No brains and all brawn is what they're after."

"What you say?"

She leaned towards him, shouting through the noise, "I said you'd likely get a job on Two Dock."

"Where's that?" McAndrew could see two of her. He was finishing the second pint and he'd played this trick before that day, once at the Hen and Chickens in Abergavenny and once at the Bear in Crickhowell. The ale doing much to dispel the nagging ache for food.

"Out of the door, turn right," said the barmaid. "Any-one'll tell you."

Banging the glass down on to the counter McAndrew turned to go. "Thanks, and good day to ye."

Jean Pierre Paul put his foot out and McAndrew fell headlong.

"Two pints he drink, and do not pay," said Jean Pierre, the dwarf.

The bar clattered into silence. The small man calmly lifted his glass to his lips. McAndrew lay on his face, momentarily unmoving. Then he slowly turned, staring up.

"You little bugger," he said.

Jean Pierre continued to sip his wine. The barmaid said with pent apprehension. "Now come on, come on, Jean Pierre, we don't want no trouble . . ."

Reaching out, McAndrew gripped a leg of the dwarf's stool and pulled it aside. Deliberately, as if expecting this, the little man neatly stepped away, frustrating the attempt to unseat him. Removing his hands from the bar-counter, he slowly turned and faced McAndrew. His small, obscene face wreathed up into a smile. He said, with a fine French accent: "She is right. We want no trouble. You pay, and then you go, eh?"

As the other scrambled to his feet and lunged towards him, the dwarf moved away from the counter. The Scotsman crashed against it, instantly turning.

The two men faced each other.

The navvies shuffled in a mass to make a ring, their calloused hands gripping their mugs, their eyes intent. The dwarf, scarcely four feet high, watched his opponent, one over two feet taller.

McAndrew rubbed his face, grinning.

"Well, well, I give you credit, Frenchy. What do ye want, for God's sake – going over me knee?"

A man's voice rang out from the navvies, "Watch him, Scotsman. He always picks the big 'uns."

"Reckon we'll call it a day if he pays for the ale," said McAndrew.

For reply Jean Pierre turned, seized the nearest glass and flung the contents into McAndrew's face. Instantly, the other reached for him; the dwarf seized one outstretched arm, leaped up, turned in mid-air and back-kicked McAndrew in the face. Staggering back, he fell with a crash and rose, fists bunched.

"By Christ, man, you've asked for it!"

The two circled one another, the customers pressing back to the walls to give them room.

McAndrew rushed. The dwarf side-stepped again. The big man crashed headlong into the navvies, and as he turned again, Jean Pierre folded his arms behind his back, crying aloud: "*Savate!*" and leaped high. Falling, face down, he gripped the back of a chair, and, as McAndrew rushed him again, donkey-kicked with both feet, striking him full in the chest. The Scot went headlong. With acrobatic agility the little man regained his feet, momentarily danced prettily, crossing his toes as in a ballet, then sprang in as McAndrew rose on hands and knees and kicked him again, sending him spinning against the bar-counter.

The men roared. The landlord, now in the public bar, shouted:

"Now stop this. *Stop it!* Fight outside if you want to!"

"First I kill 'im in 'ere," said Jean Pierre, and backed away, seeking room as the bigger man tore in, his fists swinging in vicious, hooking arcs. The dwarf dropped like a stone at his feet, screwing his tiny body into a ball over which his adversary stumbled, then pressed his palms on to the floor and kicked upwards. His boots caught McAndrew in the middle of the back and he was rammed, as if power-propelled, against the bunched navvies, who momentarily held him and then flung him off . . . into a double hind-kick by the dwarf. The left foot caught him in the chest, the other clipped his jaw. McAndrew sagged at the knees as Jean Pierre sprang upright, dancing daintily around him, planting kick after kick into the Scotsman's face and body.

58

"Savate! *Savate!* Savate! *Savate!*"

"I'll give you bloody savate," bellowed McAndrew, and crouched, following the dwarf relentlessly.

Jean Pierre was now prancing before him, pirouetting like a ballet dancer, his arms locked behind his back. But, when McAndrew neared him, his thick arms out seeking a hold, the dwarf leaped away. Now his body arched in mid-air. His small hands gripped the edge of the bar and he levered himself up, glancing over his shoulder for deliberate aim. McAndrew took the double donkey-kick full in the face. Yet the impetus of his own rush took him onward, and Jean Pierre ducked as his opponent again crashed into the counter. Now with his little arms held horizontally to maintain balance, he kicked yet again as McAndrew staggered up, his face covered with blood.

Through a film of blood McAndrew saw the dwarf; a tiny, dancing ballerina whose mincing steps kept exploding into blows of astonishing power. They came from nowhere, these crushing kicks, delivered from an opponent who was never still. Plodding on, hooking, swinging wildly, McAndrew tried everything, but succeeded in nothing.

Running into an avalanche of kicks, he now slipped to his knees, blindly trying to identify his enemy from among the swaying, cheering mass of navvies. And every time he found him, his reward was a stunning back-kick delivered from one who appeared to be floating in mid-air – or a sweeping side-kick from an expert hand-springing off the ground or the nearest obstacle – the back of a chair, a navvy's shoulders; anything would do for Jean Pierre to increase the leverage of his blows.

But still the big man came on, crouching, uppercutting nothing, feinting and counter-punching the air.

The navvies were laying odds now, roaring with savage excitement; blood was criss-crossing the saw-dust covered floor, and the landlord, fearful of being caught in the mêlée of kicks and punches, was darting around the edge of the contestants begging them to stop.

Jean Pierre leaped for the last time, cartwheeled over the

intervening space, jumped high and caught McAndrew as he lumbered in. The double-kick, delivered on the twist, took the Scotsman clean. He fell, face down. Instantly, the dwarf was upon him in a series of running kicks that felled the big man as he sought to turn. The navvies, fists raised, protested in violent explosions of sound. McAndrew tried to rise, then fell flat upon his face.

Jean Pierre stepped over him and went to the bar. Lifting his glass, he finished his wine. To the landlord he said, "Two pints he drinks, and do not pay. Twopence he owes you, yes?" He dropped the money on to the counter.

There was no sound now but McAndrew's breathing, his big body shuddering to his gasping intakes of breath. Blood trickled into the saw-dust.

Navvies were standing across the public entrance. The dwarf faced them. His hands crept to his hips and he stared up into their hostile faces.

Slowly, reluctantly, they broke ranks. Reaching out, Jean Pierre gently pushed them aside and swung open the door.

Caesar, the bull-terrier, rushed in, and licked McAndrew's face.

5

McAndrew wanted the sea.

The sea was calling to him with a disregard for his own wishes. In its freedom it was captivating his every sense. As the land called him in its seasons, so there was within him an ache, constant and growing, to be a part again of a great, wide expanse. His ancestors were of the sea; in their blood had run the salt of Culross and Kirkcaldy. It was because of the sea that he had come to Barry.

The dog followed McAndrew as he wandered in the clear sunlight. With one eye still shut tightly, the other bruised, he went in search of the schooner *Marie Prey*, in which Jean Pierre, the dwarf, served as a deck-hand; this he had learned from the navvies.

Here, within the area of Number Two Dock, thick wedges of navvies were thronging in from their billets in the village; three thousand men from all parts of the world, it was said, invading the Welsh country, drinking its ale and chasing its women.

Here, heard McAndrew, was being born the greatest coal port of the world. Carved out of the virgin soil by the brawn of these men, the face of Glamorgan was changing.

All this had happened a hundred times before in Britain, and now was happening to Barry, a village, the sister of nearby Cardiff.

Once peaceful, its farms browsing in the sun, the little port awoke to a savage invader who came, not with swords and fire, but with spades, picks and buckets. The labouring masses who earlier had built the railways that now snaked over Britain; who had dug the canals, excavated the tunnels. Into the quiet Welsh community had come the strangers with their home-bred laws, the drinking and fighting they called their randies.

Mostly from an impoverished Ireland, there were hundreds from the northern towns; tough, wiry little men, many accompanied by their camp followers – their even tougher women who jumped over a broom and called it marriage: who laboured side by side with their menfolk on the barrow runs of the Stockton-Darlington, and died in the sludge of Blackwall and Woodhead.

Now three thousand of them obeyed the Barry Railway hooter at Two Dock; thronging in shoulder to shoulder down the lanes and tracks in a clanking and chinking of shovels.

McAndrew, standing in a ditch, watched them on their way to work.

He could have joined them and signed on, he had been told this. But he did not want the captivity of the gang, the discipline of the army and its regimentation being still upon him. One of the navvies, a hulk of a man with a wheelbarrow on his shoulder, recognised him and called from the marching ranks: "That's a good shiner you got, marrer!" His comrades, north-countrymen mainly, shouted approval, and McAndrew yelled back:

"I didna see the coming and goin' of the bastard."

"Nor me, but he's lent ye a fine puffer!"

McAndrew grinned, delicately touching his swollen eye. "Where does he lodge, the wee chap? The *Marie Prey*, did they say?"

"Aye, the French schooner. She's coalin' down on Two Berth."

"Where's that?"

The navvy pointed. "Get on to Number One Dock and they'll tell ye, but shall I tell ye somethin' first, Scotsman? You'd best steer clear of Jean Pierre, for he'll have ye again and next time worse."

"Will you bet on it?"

"Ach no, I'd be betting on the lid o' ye coffin. Go home. I'd rather fight John L. Sullivan."

The navvies marched on. Beyond their bobbing heads and ragged shoulders McAndrew could see the sun breaking over the sea in wide, golden flashes, and the morning wind blew with an intoxicating freshness: his world of sea and sun was suddenly filled with smells of seaweed and tarred hulls.

A young woman, oblivious to the vulgar shouts of the navvies, watched the big Scotsman as if magnetised. She was dark-haired, a slim wench but with a well-filled bosom; her bonnet was on the back of her head and her hair flying in the wind. Bowing low, McAndrew swept his bowler hat in the gutter, crying, "Be patient, me lovely girl, I'll try to get round to ye!"

Later, he was down on Number Two Dock watching the workers.

Here was the leviathan of modern construction, a thousand yards long by two hundred yards wide: thirty-four acres of excavation, every cubic yard lifted and thrown by pick and shovel. And the navvies were swarming over it, an army of ants in a hundred different teams, throngs of men digging, carrying, lifting and hoisting down intersecting railway lines where engines and wagons hauled the loads. It was incredible activity, and McAndrew stared, marvelling at the industry.

This was the work that had lifted Barry's imports from sixty thousand shipped tons in 1890 to over four times as much six years later.

Labouring on the concrete quays were engineers in their hundreds; erecting hydraulic cranes and traversers; bonded stores for wet and dry merchandise, grain stores, transit sheds, cold stores, with ten high-level fixed coal tips to pour the coal wealth of the Rhondda. A foreman, wandering hands on hips among the labouring mass, stared at McAndrew on the quay above, his broad, wind-burned face turned up. He sized the man, his expert eyes discerning strength.

"You wanting work?"

McAndrew held the dog closer. "You build it, Foreman. I'll help fill it from the sea."

"Please yourself. But change your mind and you've got a berth, sailor."

McAndrew nodded, then walked through the piled debris of the workings to Number One Dock.

On his way through the caisson he saw the girl again and her smile was gay and charitable.

McAndrew arrived on Number One Dock as the *Marie Prey* slipped her hawsers.

She was a fine topsail schooner, built at Porthmadoc, he learned later, but bought by the French for trade between Brittany and the Welsh mainland; coal from Barry, slate from Port Penrhyn. The gap widened between her bulwarks and the quay.

McAndrew saw, of a sudden, a small, squat figure appear in the shrouds; the dwarf, Jean Pierre stood unmoving, staring at the Scotsman as the sea divided them, his eyes of impenetrable blackness unmoving in his flattened features. McAndrew shouted: "I'll see ye next time, eh, matlow?"

For answer the little man raised his face, and spat. The other cried, his hands cupped to his mouth, "Next time, Frenchy, it's the Battle of Waterloo. The name's McAndrew, and I'm goin' to kill ye!"

The dwarf laughed. Leaning against the ratlines, he laughed and it drifted across to the quay. "Non non, mon ami. Next time, my friend, it will be the same! Exactement!"

McAndrew turned away. The sun blazed, shedding instant light; the sea danced in diamonds, gulls cried. The dog stared up into his face with liquid eyes.

"The wee bastard," said McAndrew, grinning.

He was about to turn away when he saw the girl for the third time.

*

64

Number One Dock was filled with barques and schooners, mainly plying the slate and coal trades; smaller ketches and sloops, wet boats at sea. With boats like these the crew worked from a cock-pit abaft, and mostly they carried a twenty foot beam trawl.

These were the little shrimpers who combed the sea up and down the Welsh coast, carrying in their sterns a copper vat for boiling the little innocents the moment they gasped out of the waves. Dee salmon boats were there, too, McAndrew noticed, whose crews went out in the ancient coracles of the Severn and Conway. Now they dipped into the booming port of Barry to sell their catches to the navvies who paid in silver, and the prices were high.

Mumbles' oyster skiffs were there, also Tenby luggers, and anchored in mid-stream were throngs of Morecambe nobbies, who fished as far south as Cardigan Bay, though based as far north as the Solway Firth.

Shipping of every size and description was flooding into Barry, their silver cargoes feeding the tables of a village that had become a town; one threatening to grow into a city.

From all corners of the compass working men and women were converging on to the new Klondyke. Roads were being built with frantic haste to take the new traffic; cottages leaning shoulder to shoulder were being flung up by speculative builders anxious for new profit; cargoes of slate were being loaded as fast as the quarries of North Wales could hew and trim them; slates for the roofs of the new labouring population.

It was a time of speculation on a vast scale and the First and Second Parliamentary contests, when bills were forced through by the persistence and genius of men like David Davies, Insole, the Cory Brothers and Archibald Hood, the Tonypandy coal owner.

The refusal of the Marquis of Bute to expand his Cardiff empire sufficiently had forced an opposition, and the decision to open the port of Barry to the world trade had at last met with success; the preamble to the Parliamentary Bill being passed in June 1884. It was the greatest event that had happened to the little seaside town for half a century.

Two months later the Royal Assent was given and the planning for the reconstruction of Barry Docks was begun in earnest. Five million cubic yards of soil was excavated; three thousand men and thirty locomotives laboured round the clock: giant stones from the shores of Sully were brought to construct the massive quay walls; mountain limestone was hauled from the Alps Quarry, five miles distant by horse and cart.

Now McAndrew listened to the labour thundering in the empty basin of Number Two Dock, for the first dock had proved a gigantic commercial success. The black wealth of the Rhondda pits was already flowing into the holds of the big cargo bummers. New railways were built to accommodate the port whose first dock alone had become a world wonder.

A man was sitting on one of the quay bollards as McAndrew strolled along in the sun. He was a little man and wore thigh boots and a black jersey. On the back of his head, perched at a jaunty angle, was a faded blue sailor's cap. Trimmed neatly around his face was a white beard, and his hair, flowing out on to his shoulders, possessed the whiteness and sheen of an ancient patriarch.

The old sailor took his pipe from his mouth and spat, as McAndrew approached with the dog under his arm; the blue eyes twinkled and he winked at the younger man's swollen face.

"Aye, son, Jean Pierre was in form, all right."

"You were there?"

"Ach, no – in that drunken place? I were patting your dog and saw you come out."

The other grinned down at him. "Sunderland?"

"Good guess, marrer – Newcastle. The little fella did ye fine, you can't complain."

"It'll serve till we meet again." McAndrew narrowed his eyes at the sea.

66

Barry Sound was alive with ships and tugs fussing about them.

The older man pointed with his clay. "Meet him again and he'll hand ye worse. It's the French *la savate* – the leg is eight times stronger than the arm. Is it true you didn't have the price of a pint?"

"What's it to you, old man?" The Scot stared about him again. "I'll say one thing, the ale was good."

"O, aye? Just look at your face. 'They eat the bread of wickedness and drink the wine of violence.' Proverbs four, verse seventeen."

McAndrew raised his eyes to the sky. "'Give strong drink unto him that is ready to perish, and wine unto those that be of heavy heart.'" He pushed past the man. "Try thirty-one, verse six. The trouble with the Book is that God botherers like you can find anything in it to suit them. Didn't Jesus himself approve of a little bit of nose-varnish?"

"That, my son, is sacrilege! God forgive you."

"It's not, it's a living fact. Like the water into wine. Give Him a rest old man, ye blame Him for every bloody thing, so ye do."

They stood together in momentary silence.

"Are you looking for work?" The old sailor jerked his head towards Number Two Dock where the navvies were labouring. "Doesn't hard labour suit? I saw the foreman offer ye."

"I'm sick o' the land, I'm wanting the sea," said McAndrew.

Below the quay level an old Clyde Puffer was tied up and her for'ard hatch was filled to the top with coal; by her simmering he guessed she was ready for sailing.

Because he was from north of the Scottish border, McAndrew knew the Clyde Puffers.

In the mid-nineteenth century the Clyde was shallow in her upper reaches; sea-going ships had to discharge their cargoes on to smaller ones like these at Glasgow.

As a boy he had wandered the city docks and watched this process, and the little Puffers, full to their gunwales, chugging along the Forth and Clyde canal. But he was surprised to find one as far south as this. The old man noticed his interest.

"You wantin' a berth?" His blue eyes shone in his wrinkled face.

"Could be."

"Seaman's rates all found?"

"Och, no! Keep it. Not in that tub!"

"Up the Welsh coast to Port Penrhyn with coal, then back down here with Welsh slates. The wee puffer's all right, I tell you. You been to sea before?"

"I come from Glasgow, mun."

"Then the *Sarn Helen* will be no stranger. It's hard mind – and there's only me and the daughter."

"Count me out. I'm after an easier ride."

Then McAndrew glanced down on to the deck where a girl was standing.

It was the girl he had seen earlier. She was wearing a black apron over her homespun skirt now, and on her feet were clogs; she had a red scarf over her black hair and the ends were knotted under her chin. The sailor said: "To date we've worked contract labour, but the men come and go."

"Ay ay."

"What's your name, son?"

"Jim McAndrew."

The girl stared up; he stared down.

"What you done before this, then?"

"If I tell you that you'll be as wise as me, marrer." McAndrew grinned into the old man's face.

"Are ye on, then?"

"Do ye know something, Captain? Me and the dog have changed our minds. Now, isn't that strange?"

The girl below suddenly turned away.

Now that he was on the spot she didn't know her own mind, thought McAndrew.

He was not unused to sea-going women. He had known many of them during his younger days, the canal bargees; brown-faced women with babies at their breasts, women with bodies as hard as their men, raucous and hard-drinking, who would fight for their rights with the ferocity of meat-fed tigers.

He had seen them along the Forth and Clyde canal driving their horses with lusty shouts and blows, with less pity for dumb creatures than had their menfolk.

Their daughters were pretty in a hardened way, and he had steered clear of them.

The people of the road, the tinker and gipsy travellers, he thought, bred kinder children; girls like Rosa, who were in touch with the earth and had its gentleness.

The sea-women appeared cured by life, their characters stiffened by sea salt and wind. They knew where they were going.

"We'd best get aboard then," said the old sailor. "Mind you," he said, on the ladder, looking up, "first we got to ask Ellie. O aye! Whatever we do on this old crate, mind, we got to ask Ellie."

6

There was a song in the wind as the Old Man took the *Sam Helen* out of Barry Sound into the swim of the Bristol Channel. Spindrift flew from the combers, spraying McAndrew's face as he stood braced at the fore-rail; the little steamer's stern lug-sail took the wind and her bow swung starboard as she dug into a blue, perky sea.

McAndrew remembered the big ships of his youth and the winds of St. Andrews Bay on which he was raised. With Caesar held against him, he sang, his bass voice booming tunelessly. Ellie Kendall, the Old Man's daughter, cocked an ear above her accounts in the aft cabin and listened. Then, in a small, round hand wrote in the log:

13th April 1896
Today we departed Barry with forty-two tons of coal for Port Dinorwic. Documentation at Dock's Office less difficult. Mr. Henry Wendon's influence is apparently spreading to the lower officials. The dividend on ordinary stock in his Barry Company still stands at six per cent per annum. It is worth noting that after the opening of Number One Dock the share capital stood at over two million pounds. By the end of this year it is expected that this will grow to four million, a fine prospect. Yesterday we ceased contract labour with the Port Authority and signed on by gipsy bargain one James Alexander McAndrew: to say the least of him, he appears to be anything but a sobering prospect.

McAndrew continued to sing.

Shovelling coal in the tiny engine room, he remembered, with a nostalgia that touched him, other engine rooms up on the Clyde.

He had been three years old when his father first took him to sea; in the sounds of the old *Sam Helen*, the creaks and groans of her, McAndrew heard again the cabins of the sloops and ketches, the fisher trawls of distant Kirkcaldy; the silver harvesting of the nets as the herring came spilling over the gunwales, the big seas of St. Andrews.

And then, one day, his father did not return to port and he recalled, in snatches of his song, a tolling bell, his mother starched in bombazine grief, and three bodies lying side by side on the sand. The smile hadn't left his father's face, he remembered, although he had been in the sea for a week.

He was firing the boiler when Ellie Kendall appeared in the doorway, and he didn't spare her a glance, although he had seen her.

It was the engine.

He was a Scot and the sounds and smell of an engine were meat and drink to him.

Now, stripped to the waist, McAndrew swung the shovel and the firebox flared and lit the dingy stokehold, shining on the sweat of his body.

Ellie Kendall, the daughter of the Old Man, stood at the door of the engine-room and watched, unspeaking; McAndrew, with his back to her, swung the shovel again and bit into the coal heap and the coal rattled and shone to the bucking roll of the ship and the smoke billowed up momentarily, before dying into sheet flame and the belching of the firebox: the valves steamed. The little compound, double-cylinder engine chugged and hissed, its Stephenson's link motion and Joy's valve gear spitting and spurting.

McAndrew knew the names by heart – Top steam port, exhaust port, valve chest and slide valve; stuffing rod and gland, junk ring, restriction ring and crosshead: these were the names of his childhood, the music of his youth.

McAndrew went to the door, dragging the shovel behind

71

him, and Ellie shouted above the chattering machinery:

"Will ye come aft, Mr. McAndrew. I want a word, if ye please."

"What's that, lass?"

He had heard, but he wanted a shore-side sight of her. Draping the sweat rag over his naked shoulders he leaned towards her in the thunder and chinking of the engine. The sea roared, swilling combers down the shanks.

"I said I want to speak to you – *come aft!*" Ellie yelled the words, hands cupped to her mouth, and the old steamer heaved, and the spray lashed the engine-room door. McAndrew cried to Caesar, who raised his head in a corner:

"Would ye believe it, son, we're signalled into the captain's presence. By the left, who's the skipper o' this old bummer?" He opened his hands and the dog leaped into them.

With the shovel in one hand and the dog under his arm, he entered the tiny aft cabin.

It was the first time he had been in the cabin, for they had not sailed on the yesterday tide as originally intended. His daughter, Ellie, having some stocks and shares to attend to in the Docks Office, the Old Man whispered with confidential pride . . .

Therefore McAndrew had slept under the stars. Wrapped in a blanket for'ard, he had watched the moon rise over the sleeping earth and the wastes of the Channel were struck by moonlight into a flat, unfettered calm.

"I'll trouble you to put ye shirt on, Mr. McAndrew, when next I call ye to the cabin," said the girl, writing at the desk before him. Her dark eyes lifted with hostility.

"O, aye. Sorry, Missus." McAndrew touched his forelock. "Aye, certainly I will, beggin' ye pardon, Captain."

"And don't refer to me as that. If you must call me something, call me Miss Ellie."

"Ah! Thanks very much, Miss Ellie." He beamed at her, making large eyes at the dog. But then his smile faded because, beside the starboard porthole, above the well-scrubbed tiered bunks, was a bunch of wild flowers.

"Look! Wood anemones, isn't it?" He peered over Ellie's head.

Wood anemones never failed to charm him. They grew with delicacy and grace, he reflected, in all the secret places. Each flower possessed six petals (these he always counted), although he had found a worl in a Welsh valley down Swansea way, and that was growing five . . .

Ellie was writing vigorously. "Now then," she said, "your full name again, if ye please." She raised a pale, oval face to his, the pen poised.

"James Alexander McAndrew." He clasped the dog closer. "And this wee chap's called Caesar, being me brother, so to speak. Caesar, will ye kindly meet Miss Ellie, the skipper o' this old tub."

"Don't be facetious. My father is the captain."

Jake, her father, now that they were at sea, had spent the first morning playing hymns on his harmonium in the for'ard cabin.

McAndrew bowed with a fine male grace. "Ah yes, no offence intended, Miss Ellie."

He watched while the girl wrote his name in the log. The tramp heeled suddenly, taking a sea and he leaned on the shovel, the woman before him forgotten, for a finger of crimson light had entered from a vermilion sky, and was crossing the cabin from the starboard porthole; the wood anemones gleamed.

Aye! Between Grassington and Threshfield he had seen them last, McAndrew reflected; it was incredible! Clumps and clumps of wood anemones with their hundreds of tiny, white, star-like flowers. He recalled how he had lain upon his back beneath a row of poplars on the road to the dales, and listened to the rushing of a wayside brook.

"Are you registered?"

For the first time he noticed her pronounced geordie accent; it was her father's tongue. Vaguely he wondered if his daughter was doing her best to lose it.

"Registered?" He repeated it dully.

"Aye – come on – registered. Your Certificate of Discharge."

"Christ, I haven'a one of those."

"But you've been to sea before this – you told my father so."

"Aye, I did. Man and boy. But I lost me father to the sea, ye understand, and at sixteen I started as a fair weather soldier."

"And you didn't stick that, either."

McAndrew returned her cold stare with a grin of friendship.

She was a pretty wee thing, he decided, provided she could lift the droop of her mouth. The tramp was rolling to the tide now and Ellie steadied herself on the table as she rose and slammed shut the log.

"Listen, Mr. McAndrew. I'll treat ye with respect and bother you to treat me the same aboard this ship, but I think we'll part company soon, for I know your sort. It's a trip up the coast and a bottle o' booze, and at the first sight of a skirt you're overboard head first . . . are ye listening?"

"I've no option, Miss Ellie!" He stood smartly to attention and whispered something to the dog which stiffened under his arm. Faces up, they listened.

"I want no drinking, I want no fighting. Fight ashore, and you're out. Fight on the *Sam Helen* and I'll call the police." She was gripping the table now, her knuckles white. "I'm building a shipping line, and I'll brook no interference from anyone, least of all you.

"When we get to Menai I want a quick turn-round on slates, because I'm due back at Barry on the tide for a Chamber of Trade meeting. Any delay and you're out quicker than I took ye on." Turning away, she added bitterly, "But no doubt you'll be away a deal quicker'n that."

"I won't be, Miss Ellie. I signed on wi' ye father, and . . ."

"You did not."

"I smacked his hand, t'is the same thing for men."

Ellie slowly raised her face. "You mean you'll come back to Barry with us to unload?"

74

"I'll do more. I'll stay with ye till I've served ye. It were a gipsy bargain and we slapped on it, and that's enough for Jake and me." His smile faded. "But shall I tell ye something more, Miss Ellie, or whatever they call you. I'm here on a man's word, not yours, and I'm taking no lip from you, ye stuck-up wee cat . . ."

She made to go past him, but he gripped her shoulder and gently pushed her back into the chair. "Och, no – you hear me out, lady. Where I come from the place for the likes of you is in the kitchen or the bed, where you'd learn how to serve a man. So meanwhile, away wi' dandy manners whether me shirt's on or not. And I'd be obliged if you'd keep out of me engine room in future lest first ye knock on the door. Do ye understand?"

Ellie watched him coolly, her face lifted, her narrowed eyes unmoving. A smile touched her mouth.

"Then bloody remember it," said McAndrew.

7

Merrily along the Welsh coast puffed the little *Sarn Helen* in a sunlit, happy sea, her raised quarter deck for'ard breasting and washing up the big combers.

"Eighteen fathoms by the cast o' the lead!" yelled McAndrew, and the Old Man up on the tiny bridge waved a brief reply. On the lee side, away from the sea wind, Ellie Kendall watched him.

She could do with such a man, she reflected. Better had he been educated, but one could not have everything. His was a natural, self-made independence; also he was possessed of a fine male arrogance that would carry him far in the field of commerce.

From worse beginnings better prospects had been grown, thought Ellie Kendall. The uncoordinated strength of McAndrew issued its own challenge to her. She braced her legs to the roll of the ship, and watched him.

Certainly, she thought, he would provide protection. Little fear of physical assault with such a bodyguard. The burglars of the board rooms, the high priests of business would show a newly formed company a natural respect rarely afforded to beginners . . . once McAndrew was seen around: his bulk would do much to allay suspicions of home weakness.

Recently, Ellie had listened to a Barry Railway Company speech. The oratory was not of a high standard and conducted with a Welsh hwyl that perplexed and annoyed her. But one speaker – Mr. Thomas Webb, she thought it was – had said that he preferred raw material to the finished article.

In the van of business activity, said he, one must project an aura of simplicity and honesty; this sprang naturally from an unspoiled working man.

Ellie watched McAndrew cross the quarter deck and climb swiftly up the short iron ladder to the bridge where her father was at the helm: she smiled.

Mr. Thomas had also suggested that, in matters of profit and loss, it didn't pay to act undemocratically towards one's creditors.

She had the sudden impression, and it arrived with impassioned conviction, that James Alexander McAndrew might have come to Kendall Associates at an appropriate time.

The Old Man said, "The trouble with these puffers is that they skim sea. With a barque or a lugger she sits deep in, but with a tramp like this she skims, as I say; puts her head down and her prop comes out o' the water, so sometimes she breaks her shaft."

"Depends what you got in ballast, Old Man," answered McAndrew.

Jake spun the wheel. "When I first took her she was with stones, but then I loaded out. A tramp rolls, stones roll, too. Now I got her ballasted with water tanks, but the tanks are too small, especially when the glass goes back." His brown face creased up into a smile.

"You own this old crate?" asked McAndrew.

The other grinned hugely. "My brother Jason left her to us. O aye, we own most things we got, our Ellie sees to that. Got a good head for business, ye know." He munched his white whiskers on the stub of his pipe.

Gulls were wheeling and crying above them now. The Old Man said, with fine poetic fervour, looking up, "Always remind me, they do, o' a flock of kids coming out of school."

McAndrew was wiping his hand on cotton waste. "You were talking of your daughter."

"Aye! Well, I cherished my woman for a boy, see, and all I got was Ellie." He pushed his cap on to the back of his head. "Ellie's all right, but I wanted a son – a big lad who'd come

77

wi' a shovel and take things off me – we're sea-trade folks, ye
know, bone and blood." He measured the compass and
swung her a point westward. "When Ellie come, me wife
died. We were working the Clyde about then, in the timber
trade, which makes safe running, as ye know. You need safe
runnin' with a woman and kid aboard. Anyway, me little
missus died."

"So you raised a son in skirts. It doesn't work."
McAndrew cupped his hands to the flare of a match and
sucked at his clay. "Put daughters in trews and they come
sly."

"Oh dear no, our Ellie ain't sly," came the answer. "She's
just that hot with figures and things I canna keep pace wi'
her." Jake knuckled his beard. "It . . . it's just that
me and Ellie are so far apart, if ye get me? Me brother died
nigh two months back. He were a different kettle o' fish to me,
I mean, he was a business man, d'you know he left our Ellie
over ten thousand in stocks and bonds – Barry Railway
Company – and this old tub, and a deposit on another who's
due down from the Clyde. And me just an old Bible-
puncher."

"It's your life, Jake. Every man to his fancy."

"I'll never make a seaman, not in a month of Fridays. I've
got a Master's Ticket, but I'd be better saving black souls in
the missionary places, says Ellie."

McAndrew gripped Jake's shoulder. "We've all got weak-
nesses, Old Man. Me, you, even Ellie. I'll start on mine
directly and we'll be here all night."

The tide took them strongly as they rounded Burry Port
into Carmarthen Bay.

Going aft, McAndrew looked at the log. It indicated sixteen miles in the past two hours; not bad going, he thought.

Ellie Kendall was standing near the door of the engine
room when he got back to it, and he stood aside, looking
down at her as she passed him without a word. The lug-sail
was well filled and its effect was to stabilise the ship's rolling.

With Caesar watching him, McAndrew went round with
the oil-can and brushed tallow on to the tails of the pistons;

78

he knew this had to be watched. If the engine temperature rose too high, the tallow charred and the pistons seized; anything above four hundred degrees was asking for trouble; this he knew by experience.

Vaguely, he wondered when she was last blown-down; she took her boiler water in straight from the sea, and the salt precipitated. She was rattling away at about a hundred and ten, not bad for an old girl like this one, he thought. And just as he decided to blow down – his hand was actually on the valve – the Old Man put his head through the door. "Stoke her and we'll simmer," said Jake. "Ellie says dinner."

When he was at the bridge door Jake added, "She'll feed ye well, mind, our Ellie."

"O aye?"

"Oh yes, she'll feed ye. With most women the way to a man's heart is through the stomach, but Ellie's got the agricultural approach. You only get out of the soil what ye put into it, says she." The Old Man scratched his ear and made big eyes at McAndrew. "Ye'll find, McAndrew, that every mortal thing the wee soul does is aimed at output; if fourpence goes into ye, sixpence comes out."

"It's your own daughter you're talking about, remember."

"Aye, it is, and she's an endearing darlin', but everything she lays hands on, including herself, is entered on a graph of production. The man who lands our Ellie will land at the top for sure."

"She sounds an unattractive proposition."

The Old Man smiled. "It's speaking against me own, but these are the treasures of darkness. Isaiah forty-five; three. Be warned."

"I'll bear it in mind."

"Meanwhile, eat and be thankful. She'll have ye shovelling six hour shifts directly she gets you to Menai."

At the door of the pantry McAndrew looked for'ard. Ellie Kendall was standing on the bridge staring out on to an empty sea.

She looked, he thought, like the loneliest woman in the world.

79

8

The Menai Strait came up out of a sea-mist at three o'clock next afternoon and the Old Man swung the *Sam Helen* in with the tide, carrying her over The Bar.

The day shone, the banks of the Strait were lined with wild flowers; past Caernarvon castle they rode on the tide, and the little town was gay with its market day; the cries of its stall-holders from the square echoing over the sea. Off Dinorwic they anchored and awaited their turn to go in.

McAndrew was up on the prow with the lead hawser, and his voice boomed out, "Stand by port!" The *Sam Helen* slid towards the lock gates.

"Give way starboard!"

Hand on hips in the waist of the ship, Ellie watched him.

"You down there – stand by to fend off – lend a hand, damn ye!"

And he flung the lead rope, crying, "Catch it, you whore's child! Take a turn. That's right! Hold her, man, *hold her!*"

Jake joined Ellie in the waist. "Aye, he's a sailor's son right enough, but he's no fit for what you have in mind – board rooms."

When the ship was wharfed and tied, McAndrew came down to the waist.

"Twenty tons of coal off here," said Ellie. "Twenty-two tomorrow up at Port Penrhyn, and there we pick up more slates. The wagons are due down tonight." She gave him a look to kill and wandered away.

"Twenty tons, woman – do I shovel the lot meself? I'll do meself a bloody injury."

"We've a contract team o' navvies, but shovelling might cool ye, mister. It's high time you knew the meaning of work."

"You've had your dinner, what did I tell ye?" whispered Jake.

Here was a sight that took McAndrew's eyes.

The labour teams of Dinorwig slate were here, come down from Ashetton-Smith's empire up in the mountains.

Here were stacked the greens, reds and mottles of every size, brought by train from the mills where they were split and squared by the old slate craftsmen; slate for the roofs of Europe, then some, said the Old Man when the *Sarn Helen* was tied.

But first the coal had to be unloaded, and Welsh navvies came in a team of ten, kicked out the wedges, flung off the tarpaulins of the hold, and the coal came out. Stripped to the waist, these men, knee deep in coal, their sweating bodies already encrusted with coal dust: and McAndrew worked with them, heaving up the filled bags by ship's derrick and swinging them over the side into wagons.

Little engines steamed and fussed, shunting from one turnout to another, dragging filled wagons up to the main line, the turntable that sped them up to the higher line, the new four foot, and from there they were hauled to the Welsh towns: coal from the south in exchange for slates from the north.

Ellie Kendall worked, too, with a band between her legs to tie up her skirt and her hair scragged back with string. By McAndrew's side she laboured, bending to the swing of it, one knee forward, shovel, swing back and throw, keeping the navvy time, while her father controlled the derricking of the bags.

"I give ye credit, I wouldn'a believed it," said McAndrew.

"You should see her when she gets warmed up," cried her father, and the Welsh navvies leaned on their shovels and saw her, nodding, and spat on their hands.

As he worked, McAndrew sang lustily:

> "From Benton Bank to Benton town
> There's not a pitman's raw
> So when ye get to the Moor Yate
> Play footy ag'in the wa'.
>
> Then hie footy, and how footy,
> And footy agin, the wa';
> So when ye get to Moor Yate
> Play footy ag'in the wa'."

The Welsh navvies, born to singing, tried to join in, and McAndrew leaned on his shovel, beating the time, crying, "Altogether lads, come in for the chorus!"

> "Then hie footy, and how footy,
> And footy ag'in the wa';
> So when ye get to Moor Yate
> Play footy ag'in the wa'."

A big raw navvy shouted, delighted, "You tell us, Haggis, what's all this about the 'footy'?"

"It's the same game ye play in bed, ye numbskull, save that up in geordieland they play it against the wall."

Bending, Ellie Kendall loosened the band of her skirt and dropped her shovel, disgusted. The men roared, hooting and cat-calling.

McAndrew bellowed after her. "For God's sake, woman, are ye forgetting ye own people? T'is a fine old song from Stotty Cake Row. Or are ye losing ye love to the snobby Principality?"

Ellie strode away, climbed the rail of the *Sam Helen* and disappeared below decks.

Standing in the aft cabin she smiled. Yes, she thought, he was good material if ale and women didn't get him, which was likely at his present rate of delinquency.

The trouble had started, of course, when Uncle Jason died two months ago. Things would have been all right, thought

Ellie, had Uncle Jason lived. Now all she had was Jake, her father. She would have to handle things herself unless a better prospect appeared.

But only temporarily could she handle it, Ellie knew this. Kendall Associates, with a share capital of over ten thousand and two ships on its books, could never permanently be handled by a woman. Female representation was impossible in a male dominated world, this she realised.

Socially, her fellow shareholders in the company – Kendall Associates was a subsidiary to the main company – were charming and thoughtful of her; they paid her the deference that was her due as a female, but at the board meetings they ignored her views with almost studied intent.

If the worst really came to the worst, thought Ellie now, representation by James Alexander McAndrew might conceivably prove better than nothing, if she could teach him, before the next board dinner, to pick up the right knife, fork and spoon.

Dusk came, then darkness, and still they laboured. And when the Old Man washed and changed and went off to his Bible class, Ellie entered the cabin of the *Sam Helen* and boiled kettles of water, poured them into a hip bath and washed herself clean.

Later, after a few pints at the Half-Way House in Dinorwic village, McAndrew came down to the lock again.

With the dog watching, he stripped off his clothes and dived naked into the sea water of the lock, and Ellie Kendall heard the splashing of him, which was like a man drowning, and the deep-throated barking of the bull terrier. Pulling a chink in the porthole curtain of the cabin, she looked aft.

Other ships were moored along the quay, blanketed by night. There came to her the sweet, savoury smell of galley cooking, the raucous laughter of men, the higher voices of chattering women.

Soon, she knew, the navvies would come down from the Half Way House: this always happened when they came into Port Dinorwic: the navvies would come down on one of their randies and there would be drinking and fighting; men rolling splay-legged along the wharf trying to find their ship, cursing the foreign men, as they called them, looking for trouble.

Naked now, she pulled a blanket closer about her and stared at the locked cabin door. Fear momentarily swam within her, and she was glad McAndrew was in the vicinity, though probably there was as much to fear from this stranger as from the navvies.

Vaguely, she wondered when her father would be back. He always promised he would come before darkness, but when salvation called him there was no saying what time he would return.

Ellie dressed with slow, meticulous care. One thing was certain, McAndrew would want a meal. She didn't relish sharing the table without the presence of her father, but decided that she had little option; it was part of the bargain and wages. When he was washed and clean the Scot would come, expecting food. Unless she provided it he would probably leave, not to return. A man such as he could get employment anywhere, especially in slate, where a *rybelwr*, a labourer in the industry, was always in high demand.

When she was dressed Ellie examined herself in her small, cracked mirror.

The sounds of the night had died within the confines of the pantry where the stew she had prepared was on the hob.

Beyond the porthole here lay blackness, save for a solitary naphtha flare that burned at the entrance to the steps leading up to Dinorwic. She listened for sounds of McAndrew, opening the pantry door, but heard nothing save the faint noises of navvy revelry coming from the village.

The mirror, as she held it this way and that, told her that she possessed a small, complacent face. Her eyes, she decided, were the best features she owned, her black hair a garment that she wore with pride, and tonight she had unplaited it, allowing it to fall naturally in loose waves about her neck and shoulders.

The full silk blouse and dark skirt she had brought out especially for this occasion enhanced what she knew was a good figure; small, true, this she contemplated, turning to look over her shoulder. But it would compare, she thought, with anything to be found north of Corris. And, as she busied herself around the pantry, laying the small table with care, she began to wonder why she was taking so much trouble over so minor an affair.

McAndrew, she reflected, was but another in a long train of crew members, who came and went on the *Sarn Helen* without incident or drama. They were as much a part of the irresponsible era as she herself; a come-day-go-day trade of the sea likely to cease without warning, either by death or defection.

It was a significant accident of the time that labour was transient; new empires were being built by men of vision, and the demand for labour was total, armies of strangers flocking into the booming trades of slate, coal or dock construction.

Therefore – and Ellie thought this as she smoothed away lines under her eyes – one like McAndrew should be encouraged to stay.

She hoped she was not sowing dragon's teeth.

The night was now garlanded with silence; Ellie could hear nothing but the simmering of the pot on the oil stove and the gentle lapping of lock water. She stirred the stew; the action in itself appeared logical; the performance of even so small an office gave a new meaning to their relationship; she was cooking for the first time, for McAndrew.

Ellie had never known the love of a man. True, there was once a gentleman of repose and apparent good manners who had courted her, but his ethics (his one asset in Ellie's eyes, since he possessed neither money nor good looks) had died in his malicious demands for sexual satisfaction within moments of finding themselves alone. Now this man had gone, leaving behind him nothing but the melancholy memory of his lust.

And so, until the appearance of McAndrew, she had

85

managed to maintain within herself an element of self-sufficiency; suppressing her natural instincts with a show of virginal surprise at the faintest suggestion of impropriety. And now McAndrew had arrived to attract her, she had built in herself a bastion of hostility behind whose turrets she was hiding . . . to save herself the indignity of desire.

Beyond the pantry porthole lay a black embroidery of night branches; a spidery trace that moved on the glass with stark fingers. The oil lamp on the beam above the stove burned lower, and she turned up the wick, banishing the etched shadows of the tiny room.

She began to wonder where McAndrew was. The hands of the compass clock, brass bound and severe, said ten: vaguely, she supposed he was probably still drinking up at Half Way House. And then, overcome with a sudden wish to learn more of him, Ellie opened the pantry door.

The moon was high, burning the foredeck into a salted whiteness; the little donkey engine spiked the moonlight with ears and hooves. She saw behind it on the quarter deck the narrow door of the ship's chain locker and the for'ard bunk where McAndrew slept.

Earlier in the day he had left the locker door open and the roll of the ship had swung it wide, exposing the bunk within and neatly rolled blankets. In a jam jar on the table was a bunch of snowdrops; she had seen them growing along the banks of the Menai when coming in; presumably he had gathered them from there on his arrival. His love of flowers perplexed her; it was out of character with the barn-storming gregarious man he had so far revealed.

Curiosity took her across the deserted deck; a white wraith moving against a black, silken sea. The air was still and Ellie heard the tide of the Strait booming and reverberating from the distant Swillies, probably the most dangerous water in Britain.

Conscience wagged a bony finger at her as she opened the locker door.

A candle burned on the small table within.

McAndrew, naked, was towelling himself down after his swim. Seeing Ellie in the doorway he stood motionless, hands on hips. Legs splayed, his big body leaned towards her, and his grin grew wider as Caesar, in an ecstasy of delight, was hurling himself at her feet.

"'Evenin', lady," said McAndrew, and patted the bunk beside him. "Bide yourself on here for a bit, I'll be with ye directly."

Clutching at her dress, Ellie turned and fled.

Booming laughter followed her across the deck to the pantry.

The big Scot's hair was golden in the light of the pantry lamp.

He was growing a beard and the young hairs were already curling on his chin and up the sides of his face, merging with bright curls that covered his head. His teeth were white and strong against the fullness of his lips. Still in his ragged shirt, he ate the stew she had prepared, and Ellie watched.

He looked, she thought, like some elemental giant spewed up out of the Menai's Roman and Phoenician past; and ate like a man long starved, spooning up the broth, breaking the bread in his huge hands with an unconcealed lust.

Ellie did not speak and there was no sound but his gasps of hunger and the thunderous noises he made with the spoon; sucking up the broth, pausing only to pick out pieces of bone with his finger and thumb and toss them before him on to the table. It was an exhibition of gluttony that appalled her. He was acting as one alone, unaware of a watcher who was assessing him.

McAndrew, Ellie concluded, lived in a shut dream; a man incapable of acting a façade. The stew was his; she had the impression that, had she reached out a hand, he would have growled at her like a dog. No niceties belonged to him; he was vulgar and uncouth, yet through this his honesty prevailed.

Veracity, Ellie concluded, was an essential quality for the kind of service she had in mind; table manners were something which could be learned by the most unpropitious pupil.

McAndrew belched and patted his stomach, flashing a white smile at her.

"Good stew."

His face raised, his jaws slowed and he stared at her with sudden, unrefined desire, as if she were edible and awaiting him as afters.

"Got any more?"

"No, you've eaten the lot."

He looked at her unused knife and fork. "How about you, then?"

"I . . . I didn't want any."

"And Jake?"

"They always feed him at the Bible class."

He did not lower his gaze. His blue eyes burned into hers.

It was something more than invasion of her privacy; it was as if he were looking into her soul.

Ellie lowered her face. She could feel the colour moving into her cheeks, as if he had kissed her mouth. When she looked up a small, taut smile was playing mockingly upon his lips.

"You should have stayed, girl," he said, and winked.

"Stayed. . . ?"

"Just now, up for'ard. You should have stayed. You'd not have regretted it."

"Mr. McAndrew, please . . ."

"Why did you come, anyway?"

Ellie rose, not answering.

Despite herself there was humour in the situation, and she badly wanted to laugh. His arrogance was impossible, yet his directness was a moving compensation. At least one knew, she reflected, where one stood with McAndrew. She began to gather up the plates. He rose, too. Leaning against the bulkhead he began to fill his clay pipe, a nicotine-stained stubby affair into which he was screwing uncut tobacco. He said: "Don't get much of a time of it, I expect, do ye? How can ye, with a little God-botherer of a feyther like that one? Was Uncle Jason any better?"

"Uncle Jason was a fine man, and I'll trouble ye not to slander me father, Mr. McAndrew."

He spoke to her again as she washed the dishes in the little canvas bucket; she did not apprehend the context of his words; they acted only as a bass accompaniment to her thoughts.

Probably, she considered, this man would not suit the task she had in mind. Clearly, he did not possess even the basic qualities of uncut material.

One might shape him, sharpen him with promises of reward, fashion him into some semblance of social behaviour. And he might, for a time, repeat parrot-fashion all his schooling . . . to revert to his own datum the moment her influence was removed.

At twenty-five – and this, she guessed, was about his age – he was already too mature, too far gone for change, she thought. He was unperjured by life, true, and he did own certain qualities that could be of use in an emergency.

Cajolery and flattery, she considered, for instance, would probably never penetrate his consciousness, such was his enormous ego. He was articulate yet ungrammatical; but this, with care, might be remedied.

McAndrew, she thought as she dried the plates (and she was aware that he was carefully watching her) was one of life's tumblers, a posturer whose unrefinement would shatter the equanimity of the most catholic of board rooms. Men such as he, she thought, lived with their elbows on the table of life; they blundered onward, unaware of criticism in total, oblivious confidence.

A week before she had taken delivery of a kilt and trews for McAndrew, sending for stockings, boots and jacket to complete the outfit; wondering, even as she wrote to Edinburgh for them, whether he would grace her gift with acceptance. To her pleasure he had done so with thanks, and Ellie was pleased. But to date he hadn't troubled to wear them. Then, to her astonishment, he had asked for a set of bagpipes, and she had sent for these also.

Ellie had actually met men like McAndrew at the Cardiff Chamber of Trade meetings, to which, as a minor shareholder, she and her father had been invited, though Jake never went.

They were the artisans of commerce, such men: they sweated while gentlemen perspired. They dug the fields of industry while their betters, the white-gloved aristocrats of wealth, did the hoeing – breaking the soil into a fine tilth, for personal aggrandisement.

In such a system of class, McAndrew would only be tolerated, but was anything more required? she wondered. One thing was certain, he would be feared, therefore respected. And wives would be charmed by his animal magnetism; this would prove a distinct advantage. His personality was forceful, his appearance magnificent. In evening dress he would dominate every man in the room.

Ellie wondered what the famous Lord Windsor would think of him, he who was the chairman of the company. The opinion of Mr. Henry Wendon, vice-chairman, brilliant engineer and entrepreneur, she had already assessed. Because he was closer to the ground, McAndrew's basic earthiness would appeal to him. Did the others really matter? Ellie considered this. She herself had been little impressed by the personalities of the rest of them – mainly sleeping directors – men who were run-of-the-mill.

But one thing was certain, she reflected as she sat again at the table; it was necessary that Kendall Associates, with ten thousand pounds worth of first preference stocks, should be properly and forcefully represented.

The highest price quoted for the undivided ordinary stock last year was over three hundred pounds. With further judicious buying such a yield might eventually buy a seat on the board. It was quite impossible to assess the final outcome, but according to Uncle Jason, the people in first were sitting on a fortune.

"You're pretty quiet."

"Aye," said Ellie, and smiled. "To tell you the truth, I was wondering if you like my dress."

"Is that a fact?" said McAndrew.

9

Come June, the old *Sarn Helen* was still on the Barry to Port Penrhyn run, up and down the Welsh coast. The earth grew warm, the sea kind, the winds were gentle from the west, the little ship's business thrived.

McAndrew came out of the engine-room, went up to the bridge and took the wheel. Shielding his eyes from the burnished topaz of the sun, he stared eastward where the land shimmered. The sea reflected light, the little compound engine chugged merrily, the old tramp knifed the flat, fettered sea, leaving behind her a foaming wake.

"Have ye heard about the new coaster Ellie's getting?" asked the Old Man.

McAndrew wanted a drink and Jake, the Old Man, knew it. At times like this, thought he, the Scot exuded an air of frightening infamy; as if he might explode; touch-paper to a flame.

"She never mentioned it," replied McAndrew, his fingers deep in his bright beard.

"O aye! She'll be comin' down from the Firth within a week or so, says Ellie – a thousand tonner; two hundred feet and a fourteen foot draught, an' she's going to take some handlin'."

"Then ye precious Ellie can count me out," said Mc-Andrew, and he took from his hip a gin flask and tipped it high, gasped and wiped his mouth with his hand, while Caesar, at his feet, watched him with unquiet eyes. "Ay ay! She can count me out. I've me belly full o' this old crate already, so if she's after crewin' for this new bummer she can look the other bloody way."

"Then I wasn't so wrong about you, was I?" asked Ellie, coming up. "And I want a word with you, anyway, Mr. McAndrew, in any case."

"Help ye'self, lass – fire away."

"In the aft cabin, if you don't mind . . ."

"Ach no!" He opened his arms to her. "Ye sweet thing, you've come to it at last!"

For reply, Ellie walked away, and Jake said, softly, "You've been called to the Supreme Presence, young fella – best you pad the seat o' your trews."

"That'll be the bloody day," said McAndrew.

Sitting in the aft cabin at her chart table, Ellie opened the log book and pushed it towards McAndrew. Caesar, in his arms, stared down at it.

"Did you draw these, Mr. McAndrew?" asked Ellie, and flicked over the pages.

In the unused blank spaces, beneath every log entry, was a drawing.

Beautifully executed, and in the most intricate detail, each drawing covered one of the last six days of May; and every one was of Ellie aboard the *Sarn Helen*.

There was one of Ellie Kendall playing the lady, clearly trying to be something she was not; an ironic and cruel representation of ambition . . . Ellie in an evening gown carrying a lap-dog while watching, aristocratic ladies aped her feeble attempts at refinement.

"And this?" Ellie flicked over another page of the log.

This was Ellie the duchess attended by a tiny blackamoor carrying a cushion, and on the cushion was the head of Jake. An Ellie half naked in the bath came next, flatteringly proportioned, happily playing with a little fleet of floating freighters: then came an Ellie shovelling coal at Dinorwic, her hair scragged back and her bottom up to the swing of the shovel, showing her bloomers. There was an Ellie down and out, in rags and clogs, begging on a drab street corner in the snow, and, finally . . .

"This one I find the most insulting," said Ellie, and turned another page.

This was of Ellie doing her hair in the cracked mirror of the cabin, smiling provocatively at a reflection in the glass, which was not her own reflection, but the face of McAndrew. Even Caesar looked shocked, turning in McAndrew's arms to stare into his face, for behind his master's reflection was an unmade bed.

Ellie said, slamming shut the book, "I suppose you know, Mr. McAndrew, that it's a Trinity House offence to deface a ship's log?"

"Aw, come off it, woman – who gives a tinker's cuss for stupid officialdom!"

"And that all these drawings are not only extremely rude, but are very unflattering?"

"Ach no – be fair. The one of ye in the bath anna so bad."

"Ye realise, I suppose, that's there's no berth for ye aboard the *Sam* after this?"

"Ye darlin' thing, don't take on so – look, you're upsettin' yourself over nothin', and . . ."

Ellie rose. "I mean it, Mr. McAndrew – you can take your dirty little drawings elsewhere. There's not room for two of us aboard this ship, and I think I realised it from the moment ye set foot aboard!"

McAndrew was grinning: Caesar looked worried to death.

"Ye're taking' it all too strong, Miss Ellie. I was only wondering, you see, if in the thirty or so years ye've been alive, nobody's troubled to tell ye the truth of yoursel' – and that's where you're goin' wrong, ye see. . . ?"

"When I need psychology, Mr. McAndrew, I shall not come to you. And I'll trouble ye to remember that I'm not yet thirty – so away wi' you and the pesky dog . . ."

McAndrew grinned wider. "Ah, ye dear thing, you're beautiful when you're mad at the world, like now – with ye little hot face and red twisted mouth, and all the lines and frowns of you. Dear God, woman . . ." and he leaned a thigh on the chart table, bending closer, "would ye be doing that

93

for twelve hours a working day if you could only see yourself smiling?" Reaching out, he tilted up her chin, but Ellie snatched her head away.

"I'll bother you to leave at once, Mr. McAndrew. Not only do I find ye too personal, but your presence is becomin' objectionable!"

"Leave ye? Just now? Ach No!" He cajoled her, his handsome face wreathed in smiles. "Jesus, we're only just beginnin' to understand each other, girl – come on, gi' us a kiss and make it up . . ."

"Mr. McAndrew!"

"An' I'll promise never to do another drawin' of ye except when you're in the bath – or smiling. Dear me, Miss Ellie! Do ye realise how beautiful ye look when you smile? The clouds all go and the sun comes out – and do ye know somethin' more? There's a rare loveliness in you that I've never seen compared – and I've seen some women in my life . . ."

"That becomes patently obvious, Mr. McAndrew, and I'll bother ye not to start your ambitions in this department. I've got a job to do and I intend to do it – build up Uncle Jason's shipping line – and that doesn't include perambulatin' wi' you or any other man till the time and mood suit me. Now please go, for I've got work to do." She pushed past him and threw open the door.

"Wee tyke," said McAndrew into Caesar's questioning eyes, "we're being given the order o' the boot, for the captain's got her bloody rag out." He sprang to attention and saluted, with Caesar rigidly in his arms.

"Certainly, Skipper. Good day to ye, sir."

After they had gone, Ellie sat down again at the chart table, her expression changing.

She began to smile, then chuckled. Then, flicking over the pages of the log she came to the drawing of her in the bath. Ellie's expression changed again, and she closed her eyes and raised her face to the ceiling, until the old *Sam* shifted in a trough of green sea, and brought her back to earth . . .

*

94

Out on deck now McAndrew saw her again: she was dressed as a woman for once, he thought, with her hair done up in a bun at her neck and a white lace shawl over her shoulders.

"What's all this about a new coaster?" he asked, with the lead in his hands, and Ellie replied,

"She'll be down in a week or so – a hundred and sixty feet and a thousand tonner – cheap at three thousand."

"Three thousand won't buy ye a Whitby collier, woman!"

"And she'll be running coal and slate; north, south – same as the *Sam* – that's where the real money lies."

"Is that a fact? If you're makin' money, Missus, I've seen no sign of it. I could double me rate by diving overboard. There's quarrymen wanted up in Bethesda, you know, and Penrhyn's payin' over the odds, they tell me."

"Perhaps," replied Ellie, "but that's because it's summer. Come cold, he'll cut ye to the bone, and besides, there's a strike on at the moment, or perhaps ye didn't know? If you're set on quarrying – and it's harder than shipping, mind, ye'd best get moving on a private contractor, for men like Penrhyn and Assheton-Smith will starve ye to death for fourpence."

A little sea-wind swept the deck, blowing her hair over her face and McAndrew suddenly saw her in profile against the sunlit sea. He was at the wheel and she leaned against the binnacle, steadying herself to the ship's roll. "Anyway, if you're bound on leavin' us, you might have the good grace to mention it."

McAndrew stared at her. "Christ, woman – not an hour back ye put one on me arse!"

"I merely suggested you'd have to leave unless your behaviour improved, and please do not be vulgar."

He said, "Does a fella know how he stands wi' you from one minute to another, Ellie Kendall?"

She strolled away, smiling over her shoulder. "Keep 'em guessing, McAndrew – two can play your game. Are ye leaving us or not, then?"

He swung the wheel. "I'm always leaving; I'm the fella who keeps his hat on, lest he intends to stay."

'Rock of Ages' drifted to them – Jake was on the harmonium. Ellie made a strange little face, as if she were crying inside.

The Menai Strait was sliding past them now. On the near bank they could see bluebells and cuckoo-flowers; also, through woods, a faint blue haze of dog-violets.

"They're early this year."

Ellie looked. "The dog violets? Aye, I've seen them earlier, though. You like flowers, don't you?"

"It's all of your own making, woman," he said, "Ye deserve all that's coming to you. How did your Uncle Jason run it?"

"He had help, but they all left when he died. He had the pioneer spirit, too, but it didn't pass on to me feyther." Ellie wandered across the deck.

On the starboard side the luxury yacht of the Assheton-Smiths was coming up; her upper works shining white in the sun; blue-jacketed sailors were scrubbing her decks. McAndrew said, "That's your trouble, isn't it? Money."

"Money?" Ellie turned to him.

"Aye, woman – money. But a million pounds don't buy a baby's fingernail."

Ellie shrugged. "No, it isn't just that."

"Ambition will get you hung. The power of malevolence and the power of joy. Give me a good sky and a road beneath my boots and you can keep all the rest of it." He nodded towards the anchored yacht, now abeam.

"Look at that thing. Slate dust and dying. The thing's a floating coffin. The sum total of a mad man's ambition. But I say it again. If you're determined to own a shipping line, then you need a man to run it." He stared doggedly over the wheel.

"So they keep telling me. David Davies said more. He said it needs a family of men, with a Georgian house overlooking the bay, servants doing the chores and a clerk on the books. My Uncle Jason, I reckon, did a thoughtless thing in dying and leaving the firm to me."

Ellie joined him at the wheel. They stood in momentary

96

silence, staring at the sea; gulls were wailing against the moaning incantation of the harmonium.

"Christ," said McAndrew, "he's inside the bloody thing."

He smiled down at her; her eyes, he thought, were astonishingly blue, as if reflecting the gentian-coloured sea. She said suddenly in a small, lifeless voice:

"What about you. Would you take it on, Mr. McAndrew?"

He started like a man with pepper in his veins. "Me, woman, ye must be mad!"

"No, I'm not. I've thought about it. I've thought long and hard about it. You could do it."

He laughed. "I've no more self-reliance than a magpie!"

"With me behind ye, you could. It does need a man, I'm finding that out." She snapped her fingers. "Anywhere in the shipping office it's the same – a woman talks and men start jabbering. Ye raise a hand for attention, and nobody looks; you get up and walk out and nobody notices. You need two fists as well as a brain in big business."

"You can say that twice."

"Sometimes I wonder if it's all worthwhile. Other times I just feel I could fold up and die."

"And this is what you want me to take on? Go and jump in the sea." He turned his back upon her and strode away as Ellie took the wheel. At the port rail McAndrew tipped the flask to his lips again.

Suddenly, he shouted above the noise of the engine. "I tell ye what, I'll give ye a hand with the coaster – look over the technicals, I mean, that sort o' thing."

The ship lurched. Smiling, Ellie clung to the wheel.

"I'd be obliged to you," she said.

"Likely it'll cost ye something, you realise?"

She lifted her skirt and went aft to the companionway.

"I wouldn't be at all surprised."

It was pay night in Bangor and the quarrymen had thronged in from Penrhyn, Dinorwic and as far afield as Bethesda, bringing with them their six weeks wages. And the Nelson on Bangor shore road was crammed to the doors and the ale flowing; Irish fiddles were going, hymns being sung in one corner of the bar and bawdies in another, to which an old lascar was playing a melodeon. Dressed in his new kilt, up on a table and beating time, McAndrew was in form.

"What are you doing down in this part of the world?" cried a quarryman.

His face was lined with sun and wind and his ears pinched thin by the frosts of his years; this, the seal of the rock-face quarryman.

Stamping with his big boots McAndrew swung a quart pewter in his direction. "God knows, but I tell ye this, I've been down here before."

"You didn't show yourself, then, big fella!" The Welshman and Irish navvies clamoured around the table on which McAndrew stood.

"When the Blue Bonnets came over the border, son – don't you read your history. When the Romans had ye building roads on slave labour, we came down and chased 'em off."

"Tell me another!" This from a giant quarryman in a corner.

"Aye!"

"Is it a military fella ye are, then?" asked a navvy.

Wider than a door, this one, with blue eyes dancing in his mud-stained face and he lifted his glass and killed his pint at a swallow.

"I'm a Scot who's lost his way, me son. What the hell I'm doing down here among you bloody Sassenachs is somethin' I'm keeping from me children." McAndrew swayed, fighting for balance on the table. "But I tell ye what. While we're here, me and my tyke will sing for ye," and he opened his hands, clapping them, and the bull-terrier leaped into his arms.

The men roared; the landlord, fat-faced, screwed up small eyes in his puffy cheeks and peered in McAndrew's direction. "No messing with that drunken pug," he warned. "He shouldn't be in here, anyway . . ."

"Ach, to hell, the dog's entitled to a pint like the rest of us," cried McAndrew. "Will somebody toss me the melodeon, for he's a queer pooch, and he won't sing without music."

The men pressed in from the other rooms; ragged men, their faces lined with the labour of the tumps; men from the Irish counties, Welshmen, Spaniards and Lascars off the ships from Bangor to Porthmadoc. McAndrew had got them going, and he knew it; the landlord watched with apprehensive eyes. Head cocked to one side, McAndrew tuned the melodeon, trying for a note, and then began to play and sing bassly, and out of tune:

> "Hey for the buff and the blue,
> Hey for the cap and the feather.
> Hey for the bonny lass true,
> That lives in Hexhamshire."

And Caesar howled. Sitting up on his hind legs he howled at the ceiling.

"That's fine, wee dog!" cried McAndrew. "Now all join in the chorus," and the quarrymen and navvies, who had heard it all before, sang while the bull-terrier, face up, howled on.

> "Through by the Saiby Syke
> And over the moss and the mire
> I'll be going to see me lass
> Who lives in Hexhamshire . . ."

"Do ye know any more of that?" cried the landlord. "The dog's drunker than you, Scotsman. Get the animal out of it."

"Are ye from Hexhamshire, then?" asked a navvy, and he was wearing a moleskin cap with a feather in it; a cap he had taken from the head of his brother who was killed on the barrow runs of the Stockton-Darlington. "What's your name, for if ye a Scot you're not singing the true haggis songs."

"Me name's McAndrew, lad," McAndrew waved his hands for silence. "But they call me Mac for short – would you care to have the history of that?"

The men pressed around the table, slopping their ale; the room swirled with smoke and the smell of unwashed bodies.

They had laboured on the face of the quarry, pushed the rock rubbish trams, and the refuse of slate; now their pains diminished in the amber slant of old and mild, they clamoured, hands raised, for silence.

"It's a wonderful tale and as true as I'm here, if I never move a yard again. For I'm Scotland born and bred, and I'll sing ye a Scot's bawdy at the end for the proof of it. Listen . . ."

The men muttered into silence, grinning up. "The real name of me, you'd be astonished to hear, is James Alexander P. Quick-McDangler – did ye hear that?"

"We'll have no bad language!" warned the landlord, "we've got a barmaid here, remember!"

"Ach, sure to God, she'll enjoy it more than you – let the wee lass come closer . . ."

The men shouted joyously, stamping their feet for order, and McAndrew cried, "But I wasn't goin' out into the world with a handle like that, you understand? So I decided to put something fore and aft on it, so I studied and took the cloth up in crofter country." He drank again, guzzling at the ale. Caesar watched him with worried eyes. "So now I could call myself the Reverend P. Quick-McDangler, Doctor of Literature, and people started to pay respect, me being a priest, ye see?"

"A priest?" cried the landlord. "You a parson?"

"Aye, but I still wasn't content." McAndrew swung his pewter in front of the faces of the grinning men. "So I joined the army to hide me dreadful name the more, and now I was Captain the Reverend P. Quick-McDangler, R.A.O.C. Then they posted me to India and I won the M.C., and I reckoned I'd covered up me terrible name . . ."

"Now now. . . !" cried the landlord, "there's ladies present, I tell ye!"

The men surged about the table, bellowing up. Flushed faces, eyes watering with unshed ale, and these were the navvies. The faces of the quarrymen were more sober, disapproving. On their hardwood seats lining the walls they watched, unspeaking.

They did not blaspheme, these men; if they swore at all, it was in a minor way; their jokes, and there were few of these in the Penrhyn empire of slate, were filled with ironic humour and vast understatement.

They did not like strangers, and McAndrew in particular. His brashness grated on their sensitivity. And the Nelson was their pub in any respect.

They were not given to drinking and violence: there was enough blood on slate already, they said, but they were quick to anger if the tone of the place was wrong; in the pub, the chapel or the home.

So now they raised hostile faces at McAndrew and glanced apprehensively at the young barmaid polishing glasses in the tap. The Irish navvies were bellowing, knowing what was coming, and McAndrew cried:

"Then one night I spent out on the tiles wi' a little Indian whore, and she were the colour of brown chocolate. 'That'll have to come off,' says the doctor. *Obsairve!*" cried McAndrew, and he pulled up his kilt. "So now, for short, I call me'self Mac."

"Crimes, he's well shod!"

McAndrew, his kilt held high, paraded in a circle, his ammunition boots stamping the time on the table. The navvies roared; the Welsh quarrymen moved uncertainly. McAndrew, waving his jug, bawled, while Caesar accompanied him in howls of anguish:

> "Oh, her feyther loved her well
> Her mother loved her better
> I love the lass mesel'
> Alas, I canna get her!"

"He's a lovely bloody comedian, this one," said the big Welsh quarryman, "Flashin' his luggage in public like that. I say shift him."

"He'll need some shifting, Idris."

"I've shifted bigger."

The quarryman rose, put down his glass and pushed his way to the table on which McAndrew was standing.

"Down, you big cow," he said, "and I'll hand you more than you'd have from a Caernarfon slaughterer – exposing yourself in front of a child."

McAndrew stooped and patted the other's cheek. "Och, don't worry yourself, son – like as not she's seen it before. Don't ye know that stone lions roar when a virgin walks down Port Penrhyn?"

The quarryman swung his foot and kicked the table from under McAndrew, who toppled and fell in a crash of glass and breaking wood.

Lying on the floor he heaved himself on to an elbow, and the dog rushed to lick his face. "Ach no! Just look what he's done, tyke, he's spilled me beer . . . and it's dearer than blood these days." He staggered to his feet in grunts and groans.

The big quarryman measured McAndrew and struck. The Scotsman neatly slipped the punch, stepped in, frowning up, and hit short: the man slipped down the front of him to the floor.

Silence.

There was no sound but the quarryman's snores. McAndrew rubbed the knuckles of his hand, saying, "Aw, come on, we're people of peace, the little dog and me. We want no bother. Will ye not give a welcome to a stranger in a far country?"

The customers rushed.

One moment jollity, with the ale swimming under the doors, next moment bedlam, with every Welshman in the place trying to belt me, said McAndrew afterwards, and failing that, belting each other, with Irish navvies joining in; peace and friendship one minute, said he, and violence the next, and there's very funny people these Welsh, taking umbrage at nothing; shouting ancient war cries, yelling abuse and cursing flashes, and Caesar tearing the backside out of every pair of Irish trews in sight, and you've never heard such a commotion since the Israelites got into the Philistines at Shochoh, he told Ellie afterwards.

The door of the Nelson went back on its hinges and McAndrew went out, with Caesar following rapidly. And they sat there together in the moonlight, listening to the sounds of peace returning to the gentle strains of the lascar's melodeon.

McAndrew took out his hip flask. "Do ye fancy a nip of the hard and hot, Tyke?" he asked, and unscrewed the stopper and offered it to the dog who sniffed at it and sneezed. "In the name of God, these are very strange people, these hospitable Welsh. Why is it that everyone here wants to hit hell out of us?"

Tipping up the flask, he drank and gasped. "Dear me, son I've just remembered. There's poor little Ellie . . . sitting all alone in that rusty old tub. Would ye imagine, for instance, that she could handle a bit o' company?"

The landlord of the Nelson said, "That's got rid of him. There's always trouble when that mad Scotsman's in port. Jake Kendall ought to keep him chained up, I say."

"He'll be down the road to the Castle now," observed a quarryman.

"Or back to the *Sarn Helen*, more likely," said another, lifting his glass.

"To Ellie Kendall?" asked a third, looking at nothing.

The landlord was polishing glasses; his hands paused. "What about her?"

"Just wondered. With old Jake out at his Bible class, I mean . . . Alone, isn't she?"

"Ellie Kendall can take care of herself," said the landlord. He glared at the barmaid. "What's wrong with you, Purity?"

The girl was standing with her cloth stilled on a glass, her red lips curved in a smile, eyes vacant, a woman transfixed.

"That's the effect he has on 'em," said the landlord.

Ellie was sewing in her cabin when she heard McAndrew coming; her fingers slowed on the dress she was making. She felt the *Sarn Helen* lift gently to the incoming tide, straining her hawsers; the bulkheads creaked.

Ellie glanced at the clock. The hands said ten: she wondered when her father would be back.

Meanwhile, McAndrew was coming nearer; in her mind Ellie traced his stumbling, swaying steps. The little port was wrapped in night mist coming in from Menai; earlier the fog hooters had been moaning dismally, like injured gulls. Now she heard McAndrew's bawdy barrack room ballad, to the tune of 'The Church's One Foundation':

"We are Paul Kruger's Army
No bloody good are we.
We're Nancy boys who cannot fight,
We cannot do C.B.
And when we get to Capetown, old Kruger, he will say:
'Mein Gott, mein Gott, what a bloody fine lot,
For Gott's sake go away!'"

There was more. Ellie made a face and put her hands over her ears.

She heard the bull-terrier singing, too, something McAndrew had taught it to do. They were worth each other, these two, she thought; one of them wanted for murder in three countries, the other making ground in the same direction.

Ellie had had complaints from the publicans of Bangor. Apparently the Scot had been flung out of every public house between the Castle in Town and the Wellington in Bethesda, and the dog was fighting everything on four legs in sight. It would be bad for trade if it carried on, she reflected, now stitching again.

People like Lord Penrhyn were powerful, and already the agent of Assheton-Smith had complained about her crew's behaviour. Earlier, Ellie had wondered at the advisability of transferring McAndrew to the *Elida*, the big coaster she'd just taken delivery of in Barry, but had decided against it. He could do less harm here on the *Sarn*, she thought, where he was under her eye.

Nevertheless – and the thought was a retrospective aspect she had not considered before – an irresponsible McAndrew might be better than none at all . . . Though the major difficulty would be to keep him in one place as long as possible. Find the remedy to this, thought Ellie, and she might still have a man in charge . . .

Now Ellie could see him.

McAndrew was stumbling along the stone edge of the quay with Caesar staggering at his heels: even the dog was drunk. Impatience spilled within her. No, she would not get him supper. If he wanted food he could get it himself. Swiftly, she ran to the pantry, unlocked the door and returned to her cabin.

It was strange, thought Ellie, that she was now enduring a sense of insecurity: this had never happened to her before and she wondered if it were some unwarranted premonition. Whatever his other faults – and she neither knew nor cared about his exploits with other women (she had heard of these in Town) – McAndrew had never, to his credit, made a move towards her.

There was the young barmaid up at the Nelson, of course; her name, astonishingly, was Purity . . .

She opened the door of the cabin. The quarter deck leaped into light, the moon was brilliant, the stars burning with majestic fire. There was a sweet and magical odour about the night; this would soon be lost, no doubt, in McAndrew's beer-laden breath.

In drink, she thought, men such as he possessed unusual talents for evil, so one never quite knew when lust might commend itself . . .

It was an arresting and disturbing revelation . . .

Reaching out, she locked the cabin door.

Stiffly, Ellie sat at the cabin table with the dress held against her.

10

"Miss Ellie!"

McAndrew was closer now. Reaching out, Ellie turned down the wick of the lamp. The whale oil smoked, the air of the small room was suddenly acrid. Then a footstep slurred the quarter deck and she heard the terrier's pattering feet; the moonlight lying beneath the cabin door was scarred by shadow. Faintly, between quick buffets of the wind, she could hear McAndrew breathing.

"Miss Ellie?" It was a question now.

She did not reply. The door-handle turned.

There was growing within Ellie a self-revulsion. It was foreign to her nature to sit thus, awaiting the pleasure of any man's mood. Never before had she been dominated and it expressed itself in a nagging impatience. She wanted to fling open the door and face McAndrew, yet deep within her moved a warning.

This in itself was unusual. On other nights he had come back drunk to the ship; roaring his bawdies, mumbling his incoherent fancies he had stamped for hours along the quarter deck, yet no fearful premonitions of disaster had discomfited her then.

The men knew her in Barry and McAndrew now knew these men; presumably her reputation for virtue had preceded her. Once, much earlier, he had told her of the women up in Stirlingshire, presumably his home, though he had never enlarged on this. They were high-breasted and robust women, he said, and with one of these, in his youth, he had fallen in love.

In the telling he showed this woman scant respect, and Ellie remembered it now. He had taken this girl's comforts, apparently as acts of homage, and with the casualness of a drunkard taking a drink. Even Jake had mentioned McAndrew's obvious disrespect of women.

"Open the door, Ellie." The Scotsman's speech was slurred.

Ellie had turned the wick of the oil lamp too low; now, just when she needed light most, the flame spluttered and died, leaving the cabin in blackness about her. Nor did she move to relight the lamp, for the vow of silence was now difficult to break; the light would also betray her presence. Then the humility of her position again assailed her.

The cowardice of the situation was suddenly appalling. She was sitting in the dark like a scared servant girl awaiting the intentions of her master. With a quick movement she flung away the stitching, rose, went around the table and opened the door.

McAndrew was standing within a yard of her, gently swaying on implanted feet. The effect of the moonlight was to increase his immensity, taking away shape, leaving him etched in a black silhouette, like a bear feasting. He, for his part, saw her face pale and startled in the moonlight, the eyes falsely shadowed, the lips black; her eyes were shining with a brilliance he had not seen before. Ellie appeared, to McAndrew's reeling brain, even more dimunitive than usual; a faint perfume touched his nostrils and he looked over the top of her head into the room.

"The . . . the light went out," she said faintly. "I . . . was about to open the door when the lamp went out."

"You . . . you wouldn't keep me out, would ye, Miss Ellie?" He put a big hand upon her shoulder and gently pushed her before him into the cabin.

Ellie's hands were sweeping the table for matches. Her fingers were trembling and she hated their weakness; her heart began to thump with such insistent panic that she

107

thought it must betray her. The moon faded; the cabin came to blackness again as McAndrew shut the door behind him. She heard the lock click faintly.

"Have you got a match?" She was surprised at the clarity and calmness of her voice.

"Do we need one?"

"Don't be ridiculous . . . Give me a match."

"Not good enough for ye, am I?"

"Mr. McAndrew, please open the door. Stop this at once."

She spoke with casual gaiety, as one in control.

He said, moving towards her, "You're watering last year's crops, little Ellie. This is today. You want me as much as I want you, so why the hell don't you accept it. It's got to happen some time, woman, why not tonight."

Ellie retreated, stumbling backwards. He said, with a smile in his voice, "Why treat it as tragic? Lovemaking is a sublime activity of the mind; ye canna shut it out for ever, however hard you try. Come now, be reasonable, I'll treat ye gentle as a kitten."

"You touch me – just touch me, McAndrew and I'll scream . . ."

"Ach, woman, you're right to play the rules. Carry on and scream, I'll enjoy ye the more. 'Tis the eternal comedy of pursuit and forbid, ye know, so ye'll like it all the better for acting reluctant."

In the dark there began a blind man's bluff; McAndrew reaching for her, Ellie slipping away, and his boots were heavy on the boards. Cornered, with his big arms sweeping about her, she dropped down the front of him, leaving him to snatch at air. But she was breathing heavily now and he was following the sounds, and as she continued to elude him so he moved from impatience into a sudden great black rage, grunting furiously as he floundered after her in the dark.

Her nimbleness at first outmatched him, but the longer it continued so the confines of the little room shrank; Ellie's white blouse revealed her retreat as his eyes grew accustomed to darkness. In the farthest corner beside the bunk he suddenly trapped her, now chuckling bassly as she fought him, twisting away, seeking the door.

The key, she thought; first the key, turn it, then flight into the open quarter deck. Somehow, gasping, she levered her body under his tightening arms and lurched out of the corner. The table impeded her; striking it, she fell, over-turning it with a crash. McAndrew followed, tripped and fell headlong.

"Ye damned little bitch!"

Ellie no longer knew panic; it was now a fight against outrageous strength. Nor did she particularly fear him because she instinctively knew that, despite his mood, he would not seriously harm her. Amazingly, and afterwards she re-membered this emotion with reluctance, she was experienc-ing invigoration. She had lived closely with this man, too personally to know absolute hatred; so the chase, lusty and exhausting, yet contained an element of seedy humour. And as she stepped aside again, nimbly avoiding a bull-like rush, Ellie wanted to giggle.

Amid the smashing of the cabin furniture as McAndrew floundered after her, she suddenly shouted in triumph as he tripped over a suspended table leg and went down again, emitting soldier's curses. For, despite her predicament, she had the inner knowledge that an appeal, were she finally trapped, would save her. She could not believe that he would take her against her will. Meanwhile, to play the game to the end, one must seek escape.

Somehow, despite the groping hands that tore her dress and skirt, Ellie managed to reach the door. Clutching the key, her back to it, she turned it the wrong way. Instantly McAndrew was upon her, bearing her down. He was mutter-ing incoherently now, some Gaelic imprecations she did not understand, and in his strength at capturing her he hurt her and she cried aloud.

"Quiet, for God's sake! Nobody's goin' to eat ye." His hands sought her body, their coldness taking her breath.

"May God forgive ye, McAndrew."

"Och, I doubt that. He and I anna on speakin' terms. Now quiet, Ellie, be reasonable, I've wanted ye for weeks."

She fought, but his strength was beyond her; he held her one-handed with ease, and she knew the weight of him; seeing, for a moment as the moon flooded out again, the outline of his head and great width of shoulders against the curtained fanlight of the door.

"Please . . . McAndrew, in the name of ye mother . . ."

"If I ever had one, Missus, I don't recall. I'm a signed up member o' the vulgar-tongued classes, ye see, and some of us are parentless."

"Please don't do this, please. . . !"

His lips touched her face and moved slowly to her mouth; despite the strength of him, Ellie sensed in him a tenderness.

The cabin was returning to them both after the exhaustion of the chase; light and darkness, sounds and silences, began to take their place within Ellie's disorientated mind. She said, while he rested above her:

"Soon my father will be back. He'll kill you for this. D'ye realise? He'll tell the men and they'll come down from Bangor, and kill you."

"Sure, it'd be the first time a crofter's been killed by a Bible class."

"If . . ." and she stiffened in his arms, sensing escape. "If ye let me go now I'll not tell anyone. I swear it, I'll not tell."

He muttered, his voice suddenly cultured. "When the wine is from a grocers, woman, it tastes accordingly. God, Miss Ellie, ye lose your charm when ye beg." He laughed softly. "Let ye go and ye won't tell? That's a rational for a school-girl's argument. Lie still and be obedient, damn ye!"

"*Listen!*" whispered Ellie and tensed against him.

Footsteps on the deck.

They came closer.

She could hear them plainly. He heard them, too, and raised his weight, staring beyond her face towards the locked door. The footsteps stopped.

"It's my father!"

McAndrew whispered against her cheek. "Shout, then,

and let the men come down and bloody kill me. Ach, dear me, I'd be prepared to die for what I've had already, to say nought of what I'm about to receive, ye soft wee thing. Shout, will ye? I doubt it."

The Old Man whispered through the door, "Are you all right, Ellie?"

She lay rigidly in McAndrew's arms: formed her lips for the cry, but no sound came forth. McAndrew saw her lips move soundlessly and lowered his face and kissed her cheek.

"I heard a noise. Are you in there, Ellie Kendall?" whispered Jake.

Sometimes, when she was a child, he would call her this. McAndrew lifted his body to allow her to reply. Ellie said:

"I . . . I was asleep. Yes, I'm all right, feyther."

"Is McAndrew aboard, then?"

"Who cares?" the reply came instantly. McAndrew grinned, his fist against his mouth.

"He's fightin' drunk. He's damned near wrecked the Nelson tonight, they tell me."

"God alive, mun, who's afraid of McAndrew?"

"Then good night to ye."

"Good night."

They listened to Jake's footsteps going for'ard.

"That's better, lassie," muttered McAndrew. "Now lie still and I'll make a woman of ye." He gripped her and lifted her hard against him. "What you're hearing now is the thunder, bonnie girl, the lightning is about to come."

"Dear me," said Ellie.

"What did ye say? I didn'a catch it . . ."

"You talk too much," said Ellie.

The moon was coming up again, the fanlight glowed.

He was intent on her, as a tiger at prey; therefore did not see Ellie smiling in the dark.

For two months more they did the Barry-Penrhyn run and a sickness came to Ellie Kendall in the mornings, and a thickening of her waist.

"Is there something amiss with ye, sweet girl?" asked Jake,

III

and came to Ellie and took her hands and looked into her face.

"I am with child," said Ellie.

Jake started, momentarily transfixed.

"God grant ye forgiveness! I don't believe it. Say it again!"

Ellie said, "I'm with child, Feyther, and no amount o' biblical palaver will alter it."

"And the parent?" Jake gripped the rail for support. "Oh, holy God, protect us from the infidels, the fallen women and the fornicators!" And he put his hands together and sank to the deck in prayer. "What will I tell the Bible class?"

But Ellie was not listening. They were between Worm's Head and Tenby and they ploughed the silver sheen of the sea in strickening light; the sun burned in the azure sky, the distant shores flashed greenness.

"I asked ye who was the father, woman! Answer me!"

"McAndrew – who else do you think?" Ellie raised a pale face.

And Jake held himself kneeling there on the deck, then clapped his hands together like a priest at a Shinto shrine trying to evoke the Deity. He shrieked, "That Scotsman is the Devil's instrumental!"

"The damage is done, Feyther – it takes two to make a baby, so do not blame it all on to McAndrew."

"Shameless hussy!"

"It were loneliness, you see," said Ellie at the sea. "Him and me. Nobody has discovered the trick of making perfection. He was there, you understand, and for us it were the loneliness."

"By heaven!" cried Jake, getting to his feet. "A primitive and fiery glare will rise from Hell, for you, daughter, and all seducers."

"Perhaps. Meanwhile, we've a man to carry on the trade. A man married and part o' the family. One I can lean on for a change, for I could never lean upon you."

"Ah, yes," answered Jake, his anger cooling. "I never thought of that. He wouldn't be able to leave us, you mean, if he was sort of signed for, sealed an delivered?"

"That's the general idea. Now you can act the outraged father and bring down the wrath of the Bible class."

"For marriage, you mean – done proper and official?"

"That is what I mean," said Ellie.

"You're a business woman if ever I saw one,"

Fanning his wrath to keep it warm, Jake went aft in search of McAndrew.

"I decided it was worth a try," said Ellie after he had gone.

And so, on the twentieth day of August 1896, Eleanor Alicia Kendall took the name of McAndrew in Seion Chapel in William Street, on a hill in Bangor.

She wore a full white dress pleated at the waist and down to her ankles; upon her head was a mantle of lace and lace was at her wrists and throat.

McAndrew, towering above her, was resplendent in tartan trews, a fine lace jabot and a cap with an eagle's feather; on his cap was pinned a silver brooch of the Stewart clan and printed thereon were the words, '*Nemo Me Impune Lacessit*,' which, being translated, means, 'No One Threatens Me With Impunity.'

The sun burned down and the leaves were falling in the distant forests; the mountain of Snowdon was lying on its shoulder in the fine, crisp morning; the sea glimmered and shone.

And the elders of Jake's Bible class, men and women dressed in black, walked in double file on to the deck of the *Sarn Helen*; the labourers of the port stopping to stare, believing this to be a funeral without a corpse.

In bowler hats and wing collars, starched and stitched in worsted homespun went the men, their boots creaking. Their women, hands delicately on their escorts' arms, walked in bombazine black, their wide-brimmed hats inclining right and left to friends and strangers.

Up the hill from the quay they came in double file, taking the road to the chapel where the minister waited in the sun.

On McAndrew's arm, went Ellie; in elegance and purity, bowing this way and that to the assembled villagers, smiling up into McAndrew's face, while he, gaunt with the cares of captivity, walked hunched and forlorn, with Caesar, head down, slouching behind him.

And in the rear, in his role as official gaoler came Jake, to give the bride away: stiff-legged went Jake, with the key of the ship's armoury in his pocket and a twelve-bore down the leg of his trousers.

In this manner proceeded Ellie Kendall to the chapel on the hill; knowing, as she gracefully swayed along, that her future was assured; that the partnership of Kendall Associates, fortified now by a man on the board, would soon be legally ratified.

Later thought Ellie, the partnership might be legally consummated, but strictly according to the dictates of her mood; this part of the bargain, as McAndrew was soon to discover, Ellie considered to be singularly unattractive.

Later, with the wedding guests departed and Jake at his Bible class up in Bangor, Ellie locked herself in the aft cabin and awaited the coming of the groom.

McAndrew, after fruitless knockings, abandoned the nuptial chase, and, going to his fore-cabin, fetched out his bagpipes.

Sitting on a bollard on the quay he played 'The Black Bear' to the moon, and people stopped their activities in Snowdonia to listen. So did Ellie, smiling thinly as she lay in her narrow bunk.

When he had finished the melody, McAndrew bellowed down to the *Sarn Helen*'s deck, "Did ye hear that, woman? That was a black bear dancing, but I'm tellin' ye this for free – you're not gettin' me dancing to any of ye bloody tunes, so hang on to ye hat till the mornin'!"

Tomorrow, thought Ellie, was another day.

It might take time . . . but he would learn.

He then began to play 'MacCrimmon's Lament'. With her eyes closed, Ellie listened . . . it was quite beautiful . . .

11

McAndrew's son, Thomas Jason McAndrew, was born in March of the following year, on the *Sarn Helen* and in a storm off St. Ann's Head, near Skokholm.

The glass was falling even as Ellie went into labour, and McAndrew looked at the sky and said: "God, we've got nothin' in common, you and me, but think o' the bairn. With old Jake useless and these clumsy hands . . ." and he held them out before him while the little ship dipped her bow into a rising sea and the wind came howling in from starboard.

When the glass fell further he ran around the hatches with a sledge-hammer, swinging lustily and driving home the wedges, fearful that the slate cargo would slide and cut a way through the hatch covers like razors.

White breakers were building up from the east and the *Sarn Helen* took a heavy drift to windward, losing her course. And Old Jake, fighting the wheel, peered through the spume-swept glass of the bridge while the little ship rolled and plunged beneath him in a pea-green, furious sea.

At noon, with sight of land lost to them on the port bow, the wind rose to greater anger, whining through the masts and rigging; a giant swell on a following sea lifting the ship stern-high and foam-topped waves slid down the after-deck, deluging the waist. Half submerged, she rose and rose again, shaking herself in a vibrating thunder of her freed propeller, putting down her head in a threat to plunge to the bed of the ocean.

A premature darkness fell at four o'clock and, with Jake still at the wheel, McAndrew staggered along the port rail and across the deck to the aft cabin. Timing the plunge and roll of the ship, he swung open the cabin door and stood with his back against it momentarily; the hurricane lamp hanging from a beam before him assumed a perplexing angle, then swung in the other direction, flashing over Ellie's face.

McAndrew had spent the storm rushing up to the bridge to lash the ship on to a new course, dragging Jake off the seat of the harmonium and scrambling back to Ellie. Somehow, in his pitching, bucking world of wind-scream and waves, he managed to warm a saucepan of soup in the pantry; this he spooned gently to her lips, first blowing on it, his feet braced to the roll of the ship. Back then, wading through the wallowing deck to the bridge ladder, and the strains of 'Nearer My God to Thee' drifted to him above the shrieking of the storm. When this was over, thought McAndrew, I'll kill that bloody Jake.

Now Ellie lay as he had left her, lashed to the bunk. Her hair was tangled with sweat, her face white with the shock of the labour: her eyes opened and she lay mutely, at first disregarding McAndrew, then raised a hand.

"It's all right, I tell you."

For answer he leaped across the space dividing them and knelt, gripping her hands.

"Oh, Holy Jesus, oh Ellie!"

She stiffened in his arms. "I tell ye I'm all right. Now come on, get a hold of yourself, mun, you're worse than Jake."

"Is it bad wi' you?"

"Ask me tonight, it'll be a couple of hours yet." She held him away; the ship bucked and heaved, her hull thumping and reverberating like cannon shots as the floating lumber swished and battered in the hold.

"Is she taking it fast?" asked Ellie.

"It's nigh two foot of sea water in the hold just now, but the donkey-engine's checking it. Christ, do ye know it's coming down the vents?"

Ellie raised herself. "Aye, I can hear it. If this keeps on you'll be needing a sea-anchor. Have ye ever rigged one?"

"I have not." McAndrew wiped the water from his eyes. Ellie smiled at him. No fear was in his face, though she was discovering that he knew less about the sea than he made out.

"You'll find it in the chain-locker. Lash the wheel and get Jake to help you. You've got to get her head to the wind, then we'll sit and ride it out," Ellie raised herself on her elbows. "Get to the ship, understand, Jim? Forget about me. Is the lug-sail up?"

"No, I took it down."

"Get it up – half-reefed, it'll keep us on to the sea." She jerked her head at the porthole. "By the look of it it's coming sou-sou-west now and we'll catch it on the change o' the tide. All hell will come loose. What's Jake up to?"

"Up on the wheel singing 'Abide with me'."

"Get him down, like I say. Rig the drogue and throw it over the prow. Do it now, it'll get worse before it gets better."

McAndrew rose, hanging on to the beam above him. Stripped to the waist he stood there, the water running down his big body. "I've stuffed the vents, is that right?"

"Aye. But she'll like three feet of water in the hold – it'll stop her rolling; just keep the donkey goin', if ye can, for we mustn't ship more." Her voice faded in a sudden bluster of the wind; Ellie laid back, her hands clasped over her stomach.

"Christ," she said, and closed her eyes. Sweat sprang to her forehead and she wiped it into her hair.

"Me sweet woman . . ." said McAndrew and bent to her.

"I'm all right, I tell ye," said Ellie. "It's a kicker, but it'll be all right – see to the ship."

Reaching out, she held him as the *Sarn Helen* bucked and shivered; the hold echoed dismally as the cargo shifted. They felt the ship tremble as the slates slid in great bellowing crashes. When the tramp came upright she pondered there, then took to a list, momentarily wallowing in a trough of the sea. McAndrew rose again. "What's that?"

"The slate has shifted."

117

"I'd best get down there." He lunged for the cabin door.

"No ye don't!" Her hand went out.

"Woman, we canna' just sit and hope . . ."

"Ye've got no option. Leave it, I say. If you're down there and she rolls like that again, it'll cut you to pieces on the slide. How's the engine?"

"Healthy enough."

"Keep it going. Keep her head to the sea, ye understand? And don't trust me feyther. If it steps up higher he'll likely be on the harmonium."

McAndrew looked at her. Never before had he seen courage in a woman and the thought suspended him, confining all his actions into insignificance. Her calmness astonished him, and he realised his own shortcomings. Her composure suited her, he thought; she was as much a part of the elements here at sea as he was to the land. The *Sarn Helen* heaved again, then heeled, hung momentarily in the lee of the gale, then leaped onwards, shaking herself like a terrier.

"Can I do anything for ye?"

"Aye, ye can get the drogue out like I said. Where's Caesar?"

"I've got him in the pantry."

"Is the galley fire out?"

"In. I've got more soup comin' up for ye."

"Forget the soup and douse the fire. Keep at the engine. If the engine stops we're sunk."

Braced against the cabin door, he looked at her.

"You're all right," he said.

"That's what I told ye. Meanwhile get Jake to rig up a riding-light amidships. There's a lot o' traffic off St. Govans round about now."

"I'll treat ye decent after this, Ellie."

She patted her stomach. "Right now I'm wishing ye'd never treated me at all."

The steamer rolled and then pitched; a double action designed, it seemed, to take McAndrew off his feet. "She's a bitch in this sea," he said, and cursed.

"She's not, she's a dream of a girl. I'd rather be in this old

118

puffer in a force ten than an ocean liner. She was built on the Clyde, like me.''

"I'll be back to see you directly.''

McAndrew ran out into the wind again and raised his face to the storm-swept sky. With both fists high he shouted above the howling of the wind:

"I'll never forgive ye for this, do ye hear me? Ye damned old thing – the woman's having a baby, or don't you care? I'll never forgive ye!''

Dusk found the *Sam Helen* wallowing in a gentle swell, her sea anchor out, and on her best behaviour, said McAndrew. The stars came out and Ellie called; it was the only time she called in the labour, he remembered.

"Will ye come to me?'' she asked from the bunk. "There's things to be done and I can't face me feyther with nakedness. Hot water, cloth, and a clean bucket?''

When McAndrew had got these things and returned to her, his son was already born, his thin cries drifting across a requited sea.

"God forgive us,'' said he, and knelt, staring at the bundle in Ellie's arms. "Jesus alive and reigning – it's a baby . . .''

"A boy,'' said Ellie. "Where's Feyther?''

"Och, the sweet wee thing,'' said he, and put out his hands. "It's a son, is it? Me, Jim McAndrew, a son!''

Ellie pulled aside the blanket. "Aye, and the spit an' image of you, Mr. McAndrew. Take him, then – and careful, remember. Do not squeeze the life out of him.''

McAndrew took the baby and held it against him, whispering, "Sure to God, he's one o' the clan, look! He's got bags under his eyes like all of us. You'll like ye pint soon, lad, unless I'm mistaken . . .''

"If he follows your blood, God help me,'' said Ellie.

"And his name, woman? His name?'' He glanced up at her.

"Thomas Jason McAndrew,'' said Ellie. "Shift away,

mister, I want to make the bed. Will ye fetch Feyther, I say? It's his child, too, you know."

McAndrew said, going to the open door of the cabin, "Tom Jason McAndrew. It's a heaven of a name . . ." He stroked the baby's cheek upward with a big finger. "Wouldn't me father be proud just for a glimpse of ye?"

He turned, his back to the door. "Oh, Ellie, I'm grateful in my heart. A son. . . !" and he reached out and swung the door wide and ran out on to the gently heaving deck. Along the quarterdeck he went and up the port rail and Ellie stood at the cabin door shouting warnings, but McAndrew did not heed her.

The sun had come out now and the *Sarn Helen* wallowed in a pink-clad sea.

It was a warm, breathless, bare-footed sunset that threatened to banish the night; the wind was quiet from the west like a child that has cried itself to sleep, whispering its tonic solfa in the rigging as the little ship rode the swell. And McAndrew lifted the baby high. With his legs braced to the roll, he lifted it high above the bow rail and shouted at the sky:

"Look! A son. Thomas Jason McAndrew! A son by me, out of Ellie! Ah, ye sweet thing for preserving her. Look, look! It's another McAndrew! I tell ye this, I'll never forget you. Thank God for ye, I say!" And he held the baby higher, shaking it at the sky. He turned away, then back again. "One good turn deserves another. See ye in Kirk on Sunday!"

Ellie appeared at the port rail. Gripping it, she shouted, "Mr. McAndrew, don't be a fool! Come back here with that baby directly, ye hear me?"

Returning, he put the child into her arms. "I wouldn'a harm him. Him nor you, little love . . ."

"You don't know your own strength, ye fool!"

"Aye, may be, Ellie girl, but I wouldn'a harm him."

"I ask ye again," said Ellie. "Go and fetch my feyther."

"The wee scoot! That I will. And break his neck into the bargain. Feyther!" McAndrew ran to the bridge. "*Feyther!*"

12

Ellie said, "Table manners and correct deportment are necessary when one's dealing with our social superiors, Mr. McAndrew."

"If it's you sayin' so, Miss Ellie."

"The rules of etiquette are simply applied, they're only common decency when you get down to it. When you're at the table, for instance, don't start eatin' till the hostess begins – this will be Lady Jane Windsor, the wife of the company chairman."

"The big woman in the big black hat I saw in Church last Sunday?"

"That's her. You'll be introduced to her soon after we go in. Don't talk, just bow like I said, and hold yourself decent, like ye can."

"Is the wee fella abed yet, Ellie?"

"No, he is not."

"Can I see him before ye put him, Ellie?"

"If ye listen." Ellie sighed like the well of life going dry. "This is your trouble, you won't listen, will ye? Now your napkin – don't flap it about." Taking one off the table, she seated herself and spread it on her lap. "Like so. Everything graceful, everything slow."

"The thing's always slippin' on the floor."

"Well if it does, don't scramble about for it. Just sit and wait until a servant picks it up. Don't talk with your mouth full; don't, I repeat, don't sit chewing wi' your knife and fork up in the air, like so," and Ellie sat, chewing nothing, the knife and fork held up.

"I'll behave real dainty. Can I see the boy. . . ?"

"The spoon, Mr. McAndrew. The spoon. It is not a screwdriver, so don't hold it like one." She swept around the small cabin with a professional air. "The Trade Association dinner is an important function and I want your best foot forward. One thing more – no drinking."

"God, won't ye allow us to wet our whistles?"

"One, then – for the loyal toast. The toast-master will give it. Just follow exactly what the other people do – oh, and the soup. The soup plate should be tipped slightly away from ye, or the soup might land in your lap. And drink from the side of the spoon, don't suck it with a noise of thunder."

"*Och*," said McAndrew, "you're a wonderful wife, Miss Ellie. In the name of heaven where did ye learn such things?"

She faced him, staring up into his face. "I'll have you remember, Mr. McAndrew, that there wasn't a trick of business nor a social grace that Uncle Jason didn't know. And the fingerbowl's there for dipping in your fingers."

"Aye, well you're expectin' a lot of a vulgar fella like me to follow in that chap's footsteps."

On tiptoe now, she kissed his face, her small, slim hands expertly brushing away specks of dust from his evening dress jacket. "I'll say one thing for you, ye'll have no equals. No man there will hold a candle to you, Mr. McAndrew. And on the face of it you're a truly exemplary character, having not yet been discovered in crime."

"I'm as innocent as a babe."

She turned abruptly away, her smile fading. "Tomorrow's a great day for me. To be sitting on the top table at the Trade Association dinner is an honour indeed, and I'm not having it spoiled." Ellie wandered about, her hands clasped before her. "The top table, remember – even Uncle Jason never got on the chairman's right. Mr. McAndrew, we're on our way."

"Can I see wee Tommy now, then?"

Ellie's smile suddenly radiated. Head on one side she put out her hands to him.

"My God," said McAndrew deeply. "When you smile you're beautiful!"

"You're happy here?"

"Aye, so I am!"

"Really happy, I mean, now you've got your boy. And ye'll stay with me?"

"Though the seas run dry, woman." He came round the table to her, hooked his arm around her waist and drew her hard against him; he would have kissed her, but she put her fingers between their lips. McAndrew said, "Since me son came I've been dying inside for ye, Ellie."

"Aye. Then come and see him, you've a right. Put a golden beard on him and he'd be the spit and image of ye."

"Don't trifle wi' it, Ellie. I'm as dry as a desert. When, for God's sake?"

"All in good time," said she, and pushed him away. "*Come.*"

The log of the old *Sarn Helen*, in Ellie's hands, became akin to a diary.

In those early days she recorded, in her small, precise hand, every item in their daily round which she considered of interest.

She noted, and in the greatest detail, her sending to Edinburgh for McAndrew's clothes. She dealt postally with the best tailor and she supervised their fitting with meticulous care.

In the log (a prize for later historians of McAndrew) was recorded the date of their marriage and the birth of Tommy. The arrival of the *Elida* from Barrow (where the ship underwent repairs prior to Ellie taking delivery) is recorded as June 1897, a brief note. But to the appointment of the *Elida*'s master, a certain Ross Bolton, Ellie gave enlightening prominence. She wrote:

24th June 1897. Barry Port, South Wales.
The *Elida*, my new ship, sailed in from Barrow today, thanks be to God and Uncle Jason. She is a fine girl and will prove worthy of the Kendall line: as indeed, I consider, will Captain Ross Bolton, her master. Naturally, I

made searching inquiries at Trinity House concerning him, discovering him, despite his youth, (at twenty-two he is eight, years my junior and makes me feel quite old . . .) to be a most excellent master, having served on the *Elida* in her earlier years, mainly on the China Run.

Mr. David Davies, once the company vice-chairman, advised me that the body of a ship is its iron, its engine its heart, but its master its soul.

It appears my fate to surround myself with handsome men. But Captain Bolton is also possessed of excellent manners and his social education is apparent. At four hundred pounds per annum – the salary Uncle Jason proposed – this addition to the fleet I consider some'at more than a bargain.

My husband, however, is not of my opinion, which is understandable: they are as fire is to water, these two, as chalk is to cheese.

Today, with the arrival of the *Elida*, is perhaps the most important one in the history of Kendall Associates. Not only have Mr. McAndrew and I been invited to attend the Trade Association dinner, but I, as the only lady owner in Barry, have been asked to reply on behalf of the guests. It is a signal honour, but I am terrified. Never before have I been called upon to make a speech. Further, I can only hope that my husband comports himself with reasonable dignity. For such one can only pray. He, incidentally, has been asked to propose the loyal toast, God help us!

Barry was alight with activity and sun as the tug pulled the *Elida* up to her berth.

From Number Two Dock came the clattering of the diggers and the clashing of shunting engines; the navvies, mostly stripped to the waist, were singing their bawdy songs of labour.

A group of gentlemen, presumably businessmen, top-hatted and frock-coated, were standing on the quay as the *Elida* came in. Ellie guessed they had arrived for the Trade Association function. On McAndrew's arm she came down the gangplank of the *Sam Helen*, leaving her father standing in the waist.

"Me little Ellie," cried Jake, "you look fine! If your Uncle Jason could see you now you'd warm the cockles of his heart!"

"You take care of the wee one, Jake," called McAndrew, "or you'll never hear the end of it!"

The gentlemen made way as she and McAndrew approached.

Ellie was dressed for the evening celebration in a white bodice and skirt: her hair, in tight curls, was held at the back with an ivory comb. McAndrew walked as a man embalmed; upright and straight he went, his left arm by his side, his right arm rigid, and upon this Ellie had placed her hand; inclining her broad-rimmed summer hat to the gentlemen as she passed.

"Mistress Kendall, I understand . . ." One, white-haired, came from the group and bowed. "Allow me to introduce myself – Sir Henry Lever." He indicated his friends. "These are my company directors. We offer congratulations upon the addition to your line, ma'am."

Ellie nodded acceptance. "The *Elida* is a fine ship."

"I had the privilege of knowing your uncle. Kendall Associates continue to be on the right lines. And, if I may say so, in the right hands." He glanced at McAndrew.

"My husband," said Ellie, simply. "The name's McAndrew now, sir."

"My congratulations to you both, Ma'am, and I beg your pardon."

His faded blue eyes moved over them both.

The *Elida* came on; her bow towering above them. Ropes were thrown. McAndrew started forward, but Ellie gripped his arm. "Leave it," she said, softly.

They stood, watching. Ellie raised her face, suddenly seeing Captain Bolton on the bridge.

He brought her in, said McAndrew later, so gently that he wouldn't have cracked an egg, but I never liked the beggar from the start, no I didn't, with his fine fancy airs and graces.

But then he was lost to the beauty of the evening.

Gulls were crying above the *Elida* as she berthed along-side, to the bawled commands of the dockers. Kingfishers and dippers – and he identified both immediately – were playing over the sea. He glanced at Ellie. She was still staring up at the ship's bridge with a profound radiance of expression. Captain Bolton's hand rose stiffly to the salute. Ellie, smiling, acknowledged him.

"He's a good looking young scoot, I'll say that for him," growled McAndrew.

"It's the start of a wonderful year," said Ellie. "The second ship – we're on our way, you know – you, little Tommy and me."

"Shall we be seeing you tonight at the Trade Association dinner, Mrs. McAndrew?" asked the old gentleman.

"Without a doubt, sir."

"I look forward to it. Also to the prospect of a little business talk with your husband?"

"If its business you're talking, sir, you'll do it with me."

"On the subject of possible investment, perhaps? We of Barrow Yards Ltd.," and here he gave McAndrew his card, "have come south . . . and, if I may be bold, with money to spare. Your line is looking an attractive proposition."

"It'll cost ye, remember," said Ellie. "We're on our way up. You'll excuse us now, sir, while I greet my new captain."

The men lifted their hats as she walked away, their eyebrows raised in mute surprise.

The gangplank of the *Elida* was coming out now; the sun burned down in smells of seaweed, tar and hot cloth. McAndrew was staring beyond the ship's bows to distant fields.

The early harvest, ready for reaping, was standing golden, straight and tall, waving in quick swathes of the wind: sheep were bleating fitfully, and he heard the oyster-catchers calling from the Sound. This he heard, and saw beyond the docks to the distant rim of the mountains where bedsheet clouds were running like white-gowned monks before the sun.

"Aye, it'll cost 'em, right enough," said Ellie. "Shall I tell ye something? When their hats came off the brass drops through their pockets – Uncle Jason used to say that, and he's right. And once ye get them going, you kick their behinds."

The dockland began to lay at their feet all its activity and noise, as together they climbed the gangplank of the *Elida*, to meet her captain.

"Thank God for Uncle Jason," muttered McAndrew.

The foyer of the Angel hotel was crowded with guests; distinguished, said Ellie, and not only for their money.

The best blood of the county was there, then some, said she. They arrived in style in a brougham, as she had planned; their pair high-stepping it, hooves clattering, before the entrance.

Ellie nudged McAndrew. "Hand me out, walk me up the steps, and for God's sake mind ye manners. Bow to the women, shake hands with the men, and don't thank servants for anything."

An urchin at the hotel steps regarded McAndrew, thinking that he had never seen anything so splendid. With his bright head taller than any man there, the Scot stood in his tartan jacket and kilt, wide-shouldered, bearded, his chest bulging and its buttons in agony.

Frowning into the chandelier lights, McAndrew mounted the steps. Behind them the lights of Cardiff Castle blazed. Music sounded faintly as they went over the soft-carpeted floor of the Angel foyer. Ellie, her figure regained after the birth of Tommy, walked with a confidence she did not feel.

The Barry Railway Company, since its inception, had earned a name as a lively advocate of mixing business with pleasure. Its directors were as forthright in play as in business; entertainment, when undertaken, was on a lavish scale.

These were the pioneers who had challenged the Marquis of Bute's authority, refusing to accept the growing congestion of Cardiff docks which, since 1882, was being overwhelmed by a meteoric growth of the South Wales coal trade.

The growing prosperity of the Rhondda alone had risen to a flood-tide of coal that threatened to sink the Welsh seaways for generations. So full were the Marquis of Bute's Cardiff docks – twenty million tons of coal poured out of the valleys in the year 1882 – that it was possible to walk from one side of his port to the other without wetting one's feet, said David Davies. Yet the Marquis stubbornly refused to expand, preferring restriction of output to capital expenditure, until growing economic pressures finally forced him to act.

In 1882 Parliament sanctioned Lord Bute's proposal that a new dock should be constructed at Cardiff and his shipping charges raised, but David Davies, founder of the Ocean Coal Company, became impatient at the continual delays. He and his associates, he said, represented collieries with an output of five million tons.

As freighters seeking a coastal outlet, they would, said he, appoint an engineer of repute. Under the chairmanship of Lord Windsor they decided to build a competitive dock at the village of Barry.

Thus the Barry Railway Company, in the year 1884, came into being: the first sod of the Dock construction was cut that same year; a new railway system laid that made the freighters independent of Cardiff.

Five years later the main coal trade switched from Cardiff to Barry. By the summer of 1889 came the culmination of the vast commercial enterprise; ships were queueing up in Barry Sound to carry South Wales coal to the ports of the world.

A new town sprang up; fortunes were lost, but the fortune of the Barry Railway Company increased. And the wealth of small subsidiaries, freighters like Kendall Associates, formed early by men of vision like Uncle Jason, was assured.

In on the ground floor, as Ellie put it. Firms which specialised in steam, when steam was at a premium, would flourish as shareholders in the new Barry Company, and Ellie knew it.

Despite her inner fears, she therefore entered the Angel

hotel for the fourth annual ball of the Trade Association in the knowledge that as owner of Kendall Associates, she was held in high regard.

With the impassive McAndrew beside her, this regard grew into respect and from respect into a growing welcome in sound.

"Mr. and Mrs. McAndrew!"

The toast-master's voice cut through the buzz of conversation. All heads turned, and mainly, Ellie noticed, to her husband.

This did not disturb her. Her own looks, she knew, were not outstanding, and beside McAndrew they suffered by comparison. The women, especially, were aware of him; Ellie heard a few whispered remarks behind white-gloved hands.

All the young women there, with few exception, were beautiful; the elderly made graceful by their jewels. Girls chaperoned and unchaperoned, showed a vital interest in the proceedings as she and McAndrew approached. From a knot of elegantly dressed men in evening dress, Mr. Henry Wendon cried:

"Ah, Ellie! I'm delighted you could come! Your husband?" He smiled up warmly.

"Pleased to meet you," said the Scot, offering a huge hand.

The other looked about him with kindly patronage, "Where's the chairman? I'd particularly like you to meet him before he's completely overwhelmed. We've had a deputation down from Barrow today, you know."

A waiter came with a tray of glasses. Ellie took a sherry.

"Whusky," said McAndrew, and stared around the ornate room. Ellie said:

"The Barrow delegation? Yes, I know. James and I met some on One Dock today."

"They're particularly interested in Kendalls, I understand." Mr. Wendon sipped a drink. McAndrew grunted:

"Aye, and they know what they're about. It's for setting up a workshop down here in Barry, so they are."

"You approve of that, sir?"

"I do not. We'll do our own repairs."

"In the usual manner of the engineering Scot?"

"Ah so, sir. What Barrow knows of ship repairs she's learned from across the border, though I canna claim to be a qualified engineer. Besides, there's a poor margin of profit, don't ye know? A good skipper will be keepin' his repairs to a minimum."

"I hope you've got a good one in Captain Bolton." Mr. Wendon smiled up at McAndrew. "We met your new captain this afternoon, and I'm very impressed."

"Ach, it's early days," came the reply. "Ye'd best give him time to wet the baby's head, so to speak. For it's one thing to berth a ship wi'out cracking her skull, but another to keep a coupler-flange bolted and a spindle-guide floatin'. 'Predestination in the stride o' yon connectin'-rod,' Mr. Wendon, thank God for Kipling."

"*McAndrew's Hymn!*" The vice-chairman nudged Ellie. "As Sassenachs we're in wicked company. Are you sticking it here, Mr. McAndrew?"

"With the wee woman here and a bairn, where else would I be, for God's sake?" McAndrew took another whisky from the tray he was offered, tossed it back and lifted a third, while Ellie watched with disapproving eyes. "Ye've paved our streets wi' gold, Mr. Wendon, and Ellie's obliged to you and your directors."

"Ellie is the darling of those in power – don't thank me."

"The president, ye mean? Lord Grey-Cambourne?"

"For one." Mr. Wendon nodded.

McAndrew sipped at the glass. "You pay your wages decent and treat your navvies fair. What more can be asked of any commercial enterprise which does its work in dirty places." He leaned down, smiling, tugging at his beard. "It's a change to discover a commercial proposition wi'out the distinct smell o' prostitution, or is that too hard a term?"

"Mr. McAndrew, for God's sake . . ." whispered Ellie.

"It could be so considered. Big business, McAndrew."

"But not by you! For you, if me memory serves me, are more an engineer than a vice-chairman or a sleeping director – they come ten a penny. Like this bloody fella arriving now." He nodded.

Ellie said quickly, "I . . . I think this is Lord Windsor coming over . . ."

"Before he comes – the speech . . ." said Mr. Wendon. "Is it all cut and dried?" Clearly, he was ignoring McAndrew's remark.

"She'll do it fine, never fear."

"You'll reply for the guests? We're grateful to you."

The room was filling now, the toast-master shouting famous names. The Barrow contingent entered from an anteroom with bluster and drinks, shouting greetings to Lord Windsor, and this delayed him.

Women, Ellie noticed again, were watching McAndrew in the exchange of unspoken secrets; the young ones with furtive intent, wandering near, whispering behind their fans; bejewelled women, their bosoms pushed up to the tight restriction of their stays, something that Ellie could not personally bear, because of the discomfort, and more, decorum.

They appeared enamoured of everything, these girls, the daughters of success who walked with the grace of hunting tigers, consumed by a precocious, amorous excitement.

Their beaux, the sons of enterprise, moved in schoolboyish limps of boredom, old before their time, thought McAndrew. A waiter, preceded by a tray, went past and McAndrew lifted another whisky, examined it in the chandelier light and then gulped it down.

Mr. Wendon had now gone in pursuit of Lord Windsor, leaving Ellie and McAndrew momentarily alone. The people swept about them; an orchestra struck up. Strains of 'The Blue Danube' drifted across the enormous parquet floor.

Hung with chandelier light, the room blazed. There came to Ellie's sensitive nostrils the pleasurable scent of cigar smoke and the clash of expensive perfumes. On McAndrew's arm again she crossed through the clustered people, acknowledging their greeting.

It was an appalling remembrance that soon, from the top table, she would have to address these people, mostly of .

131

superior education and station to herself. Out of its unusual doomed habit her misery uncoiled into a sudden outrageous apprehension.

Her youth, thought Ellie, had always been ordained into perplexity; there had been always one mountain higher to climb, yet another ocean of endeavour to cross. And now this.

When the invitation, gold-edged and delivered by hand had arrived – a formal request for her to speak as guest of honour – no frail timidity usurped her courage then. Indeed, she had accepted the new challenge with alacrity. But now, the gallows built, Ellie measured the heart-beats pounding in her throat.

"Are ye all right?"

Ellie straightened. "Of course."

"You're as pale as wheaten flour," her husband said.

"It . . . it is nothin', it will pass."

"T"is the speech thing you're doin', isn't it?"

"Of course not, do not be ridiculous."

Even as she replied Ellie smiled, encouraged by her chamelion ability to alter her speech to the colour of her mood or the quality of her audience. It sounded gentile, and she was glad.

"Ye shouldn't have taken it on, it's too big a thing." McAndrew sighed, turned away. "Dear God, who's this arrivin'?"

Ellie fussed and patted herself to see if she was still there. "It . . . it's Lord Grey-Cambourne, the president."

"The fella wi' the money, did you say?"

"They've *all* got money. Stand decently, Mr. McAndrew. Please this one and we're made – it's Uncle Jason's life-long friend." With her dress held wide, Ellie curtsied low as the old gentleman came up.

But five feet high, pinned on a stick, he regarded McAndrew with baleful eyes.

"Is this the one you married, Ellie?" Reaching out, he gripped the Scot's arm, the better to examine him. "God alive, girl, would your Uncle Jason approve? A Scot, I hear.

Did ye have to pick a border raider when you could have taken your pick of the English aristocracy?"

"I'm over thirty, Uncle Teddy. I have to take what's going."

"Are you an engine man?" The old gentleman eyed McAndrew.

"Aye, sir."

"Then will you tell me something. Did you have a hand in the buying of the *Elida*?"

"I did not."

"I'm delighted to hear it." His lordship turned to Ellie. "Jason was in his next childhood when he paid a provisional deposit on that barnacle crate, and you'd have been wiser to cancel it." He swung back to her husband. "Did you look over her?"

"I did. She's due for the breaker's yard, and I told ye so, Ellie."

The old man nodded. "She's a sea-ponce and her skipper's a woman-killer. You've got trouble there, little Ellie. Next time hearken to the advice of your man." He frowned up at McAndrew. "You say you're an oil rag?"

"We've been Scots engineers since the year dot, and lairds on me mother's side."

"Then they don't call you Viscount Loon."

"Nay. We leave the chinless wonders to the English aristocracy."

His lordship chuckled in his goatie beard. "Well said, for I'm of Welsh extraction myself. Do you hear all this, Ellie girl? He's got a sense of humour under his steel bonnet, for all he's a thick-headed Scot. You've chosen well. For you've got to go north of Hadrian's Wall before they know a differential from a bilge pump." He added to McAndrew. "How's she treating you?"

McAndrew was grinning now. "Fair to middlin',"

"And this Ocean sea-coal? Does it fire on the shovel?"

"T'is a step better than Dunfermline's."

"But the men who hew it are the same, eh, lad?"

The old man pushed McAndrew against Ellie. "Take

him – your uncle would have approved, though I expect he'll have you and the brains on the China run before he's done with you. Do you pick 'em for brains or for size, woman?" He crept away. "Good meetin' you, McAndrew, ye'll sit next to me at dinner."

Ellie, glowing now, stood watching. All heads in the ball-room were turned in their direction. The orchestra struck up. She said, "Yes, Mr. McAndrew – that's where the money lies. I'd not have the Barrow consortium snapping at me heels with Uncle Teddy's thousands behind me."

"Do ye know him well? He treated you like a daughter."

Ellie lifted the hem of her dress and moved away. "He and me Uncle Jason were practically blood-brothers, but he can't stand me feyther. I tell you this, Mr. McAndrew, play your cards right and we'll land on the right side of the death-bed. He's got no wife now, no blood relations. When the box goes down we're likely in the money."

"You're a ghoul, so ye are, Ellie Kendall."

"I'm not, I'm a businesswoman."

"It's a bitter irony of Fate that ye weren't born fifty years earlier."

He saw beyond her the open window of the room and beyond that to where the stars were glowing with a strange, roseate light.

McAndrew was thinking of the open road and the kick of the wind in the hedgerows, the pounding of boots, the night-screams of barn owls; other summers returned to him, when the world dozed in the sun with a handkerchief over its face.

His sudden silence brought Ellie to a mild consternation, for his temperament at such times was nevertheless that of a man feverishly alert, a paradox of mood.

Raising his glass, McAndrew sipped his whisky, then swallowed it, his eyes unmoving as he put down the glass.

"Do ye dance?" asked Ellie.

He emptied his hands to her in a sad resignation. "Ach, yes. It's a pansy business for a grown man, but I will if it'll please ye. As long as ye smile, for it spreads honey on your grasping nature."

134

She was not offended, but stepped into his arms. The music quickened. He danced well, with the grace and assurance of a man well versed, and Ellie was a little surprised. "Perhaps Lord Grey-Cambourne was right," said she. "I'd know where I stood with a member of the aristocracy."

A younger woman was watching, her face expectant, staring at McAndrew with unrefined interest. She was beautiful, tall, slim, and dressed in pink; her hair was piled upon her head in a chignon style, her jewels glittered.

McAndrew saw her, Ellie did not. Later, he heard that she was the common law wife of Captain Ross Bolton of the *Elida*; meanwhile, he bowed, saying to Ellie:

"What are ye doin' tonight, gorgeous Mrs. McAndrew."

Ellie replied, bowing as she walked, "As Mr. McAndrew should know by now, sir – nothing in particular."

"Jesus," said McAndrew, "I'd be better off as a *Castrati* in the Barry Ladies' Choir."

13

"Pray silence for the guest of honour, Mrs. Eleanor McAndrew of Kendall Associates . . ." The Master of Ceremonies bawled it behind Ellie's head and positioned himself behind her chair.

Ellie thought, Oh God, let me die . . .

The banqueting hall, until a moment before filled with a hubbub of chinking glasses and conversation, slowly settled into silence. A silence that shouted in pent breath. Menus were lowered, opera glasses were raised.

Ellie rose to her feet to face a small sea of white tables. Around these, slowing into immobility, liveried waiters padded, their buckled shoes soundless on the thick-carpeted floor.

Now nothing moved. Ellie's thudding heart was the only sound in her world. And as she stood there, unspeaking, men lifted their heads in mute enquiry.

It was an era of audaciously beautiful women and the occasion had taken its choice of these. Safe in their seats they raised painted faces: a lid slammed on Ellie's coffined world. Glancing down at McAndrew she sought courage in his presence. He, motionless, seemed stolidly removed from her predicament. She heard herself say:

"Lord Grey-Cambourne, Lord Windsor, my lord Bishop, ladies and gentlemen . . ." Her voice diminished into nothingness: heads inclined to hear the better, fans were lowered. Ellie continued,

"A certain vicar, the incumbent of a church not far from

here, received at a celebration of his ninety-second birthday a letter from his bishop suggesting that he might now consider, after seventy years in office, of retiring to make way for a younger man . . ."

Ellie smiled about her, fighting the threat of her trembling legs. "The vicar . . . replied, 'My lord Bishop. I received your letter with pronounced misgivings. Had I known, sir, that this was but a temporary appointment, I would never have accepted it in the first place . . .'"

Silence again.

It beat with baffling wings about her. A stony-faced silence, not laughter, greeted her small attempt at humour.

With an effort, Ellie continued. "There is an analogy here. Could . . . could it not be said that we, the major shareholders of the Barry Railway Company, would not have invested in such a living had we not been assured of a fair return on capital? But now I say . . ." and here she addressed Lord Grey-Cambourne, "that there the analogy with our unfortunate vicar ends. Thanks to the genius of men of commerce – such as their lordships, David Davies – aye, and my much lamented Uncle Jason – the Barry Railway Company will enjoy not only the fruits of its courage, but its preaching of the gospel of wise investment – long after the demise of less gifted encumbants."

She was losing them. Ellie sensed it. The participation of the audience, until now one of moderate goodwill, was slipping into disinterest. Feet began to shuffle. Menus were raised, glasses lifted. Men were craning their necks, looking at the doors, the ceiling. She cried, raising her voice in pitch:

"The construction of Number Two dock will make it plain to the Marquis of Bute, that Barry is not a leaner but a leader in our new world of commercial enterprise. Since that day in April, fifteen years ago—the first meeting of the House of Commons appointed to discuss the Barry bill – vast decisions have been taken and great strides made towards a self-supporting port that has no relationship with and no directive from the lords of Cardiff . . ."

Again the shuffling of feet; a small but audible buzzing of conversation began which threatened to rise to flood.

A man rose, tipsy but not drunk, and called from a distant table, "My respect to Lord Grey-Cambourne. But may I point out that this is a male concern? Has the time come for men to be represented by a woman? This is a male prerogative, sir."

"It's not a prerogative," cried McAndrew, getting to his feet, "it's a presumption. And your presumption, I take it, is that Eleanor Kendall isn't good enough to delineate ye views? Yet you voted for your committee and your committee invited her, am I right?"

"Right, sir?" said Lord Grey-Cambourne, wearily.

"Then shall I tell ye something also," said McAndrew, "I reserve the prerogative, which she canna, being a lady, to come out into the body of this hall, and fling ye into the street, sir, for this is a meeting of gentlemen and we want no truck with upper-class hooligans."

"And who might you be?"

Ellie whispered, leaning over the guest beside her. "Sit down. And *shut up*, Mr. McAndrew."

"I'm the lady's husband, son, and I strongly advise you to put your seat on your rear before I consider meself personally affronted." McAndrew turned to the chairman. "I apologise for the behaviour of my sex. May I carry on where my wife left off, for it's clear that she won't get a hearing."

"Kindly do so. Accept the chairman's apologies for the interruption, Mrs. McAndrew." Mr. Wendon rose, bowing, and resumed his seat. A small smile flickered on his handsome face.

McAndrew continued, "Can I make it clear that I'm speaking for myself, because my wife and I may differ on fundamental issues. Though that doesn't deny her right to speak, even in the diluted democracy of what some call Big Business." He glared around the room.

Ellie, initially lost within her embarrassment, came slowly to life.

She became gradually aware that McAndrew was speaking in a new, refined accent. She lifted her face to his, and heard him say:

"The fundamental issues we differ on is not the firm's benevolence. Give credit to the working classes, they know their friends, and those who are not.

"Nor do we differ on the meteoric rise of the Barry Railway Company. The rise is more than meteoric, it is a phenomena in every respect – labour relations, Parliamentary representation, and engineering planning . . ." and here he bowed to Mr. Henry Wendon . . . "And financial and industrial foresight, the like of which I have never seen before. But there's good engineering foresight farther north than this – it's not confined to south of the Pennines . . ."

Men muttered bass approval, women smiled.

They sat enthralled, contained by his authority. McAndrew cried,

"But there's a legendary tale in Wales that the Welsh should learn, and there's a few Welshmen sitting on this board, unless I'm mistaken, who are a mite short on excuses. When God made Wales, you know, he was running a bit short of the requisite material. His planning, this suggested, had come a wee bit adrift . . ." Fists on his hips now, he grinned happily around the room. "Having made the Universe in six days, he hoped for a rest, ye see, and retired to a couch in his workshop."

They sat in total silence.

Ellie's eyes were riveted on her husband now: it was as if she were listening to a stranger; a man of new articulation and substance. She heard him say,

"But the wind which God had created moved over the world, and it blew ajar the door of his workshop. And God saw in a corner a small barrel of clay, a larger barrel of enterprise and a great barrel of vision. And he knew, did God, that his task was not yet finished. Rising from his couch, he said, 'I will make another nation.' And because he was getting to the end of the alphabet, he called this people *Welsh*."

McAndrew deliberately lifted his glass, drained it, and put

139

it down. "Because they were of small stature, he made more of them – a dark-skinned people, fashioned from the bottom of a barrel. And God filled these people with vision and enterprise; put them down into the fields of the earth and bade them mate and multiply. This they did right readily, because they were Welsh." McAndrew paused, staring about him. "Yet, strangely," said he, "they did not prosper, but stayed stunted and uncultured. And, watching them over a thousand years – which, for him, is a moment of time – God realised that he had made his first mistake. 'How', he said to himself, 'can a people of small stature, though filled with vision and enterprise, see into far places when standing on plains?' " McAndrew paused again, "So he made their country with mountains . . ."

Ellie narrowed her eyes.

The quiet was such that she heard people breathing. Her husband added:

"The thought will not have escaped ye that there's mountains in Scotland, too . . ." He turned to Lord Grey-Cambourne. "So I say with the greatest respect, my lord, that, after that parable, you're on the wrong horse.

"Maybe Ellie Kendall would have got round to it, maybe not, but I tell you this. Your company was conceived as an act of genius and it's being run by men o' the same salt as yourself. But you're standing on the plains, the lot of you. You're filled with vision, but ye canna see beyond the mountains, and I'll tell you why."

McAndrew made a fist of one hand and raised it. "All your eggs are in the coal basket, and if the coal-house door slams shut, your dreams are bankrupt.

"As Ellie says, you exported five million tons of coke and coal in the past twelve months and of general merchandise, a mere eight thousand, so will ye tell us what happens to you – money bags an' all – if the South Wales coalfields die overnight?" He pointed to the back of the hall where the gentlemen of the Barrow shipyards were sitting together. "Yon sits the men of the Barrow company, come down today

140

with suggestions about opening up ship repairs. Has anyone heeded them? 'It'll cost 'em,' I've heard say. 'Keep out,' say you. So I'm telling you this, my lords.

"The Barry company is hell-bent on its own destruction. We shareholders are lemmings running for the cliffs. *Diversify!* D'you hear it – that's the word – *diversify!* Encourage new capital, build shipyards, support heavy engineering; export coal and coke, aye, but also timber, wool, meat from Welsh cattle – agricultural machinery, slate on a vast scale – not the piddlin' bits and pieces you're running now from Port Penrhyn and Porthmadoc.

"Grasp the nettle. Do ye realise that there's a war coming? It will sink Welsh coal and Barry with it down to the tenth generation! You've an authorised capital in stocks, shares, loans and debentures of four million pounds. The money's there – *diversify*, or twenty years hence these docks will be finished and you'll be dead, too – sitting in a town wi' grass growing on its streets." McAndrew's voice rose to a shout. "What names you have! Listen to them – David Davies, the founding genius of this company, Lord Windsor, related to Clive of India; Louis Guéret, one of your most assiduous directors; gentlemen such as Lord Grey-Cambourne! These are the magic names, aye, and many more. In God's grace, gentlemen, spread your wings and fly! And generations of Welshmen will hallow these names and build them into the stones of Welsh posterity!"

In the silence McAndrew said quietly, "Ladies and gentlemen, the chairman has granted me the privilege of proposing the loyal toast . . ." Bending he lifted his fingerbowl and raised it high.

Ellie's eyes opened wide in horror. She whispered:

"Oh God, Mr. McAndrew, no! Your wine glass, man, not the fingerbowl!"

But McAndrew, unhearing, cried, swinging the bowl to every corner of the hall. "Aye, the loyal toast. The Queen, God bless her!"

Faces lifted in mass astonishment.

"On your feet now. The Queen!" shouted McAndrew.

141

Beside Ellie, old Lord Grey-Cambourne rose shakily to his feet, lifting his fingerbowl.

"The Queen, God bless her," he said, his expression vacant.

Staring in disbelief, the top table followed suit, and the example was followed by the people in the hall.

Fingerbowls raised, the banqueting hall echoed:

"The Queen, God bless her!"

Ellie, now up beside McAndrew, tugged at his sleeve. "But not in fingerbowls. Oh God, McAndrew! After all I've told ye. . . !"

"Aye, in fingerbowls – what's amiss wi' that?" he demanded. "D'ye think I'd be toastin' the old bitch in anything but water? I'm saving ma whisky for Mary Queen o' Scots."

"Oh God," said Ellie.

14

The pages for the month of August 1897 are absent from Ellie's *Sarn Helen* log.

The log – in effect a personal diary – was kept for many years in the vaults of Trinity House, being brought out for the inspection of approved historians, as occasion demanded.

Requests to view the diary were many and varied and included the name of Professor Ratza Spielman, a native of Vienna.

Spielman, as a German, was presumably interested in McAndrew's link with Constanze Mozart – this, by the year 1920, having been firmly established.

The missing pages, the professor asserted, must have been removed by students in his absence, but fortunately for posterity, Spielman had earlier translated these pages from the English into German for his own convenience. The following is his version in English. There is no reason, the experts say, to doubt the verisimilitude of the translation.

25th August 1897. *Sarn Helen* berthed at Barry. Today we received sad news. Lord Grey-Cambourne, our respected friend, died on the 20th., my first wedding anniversary, alas. According to his solicitors, who contacted me by telegram, he went peacefully in his sleep. Mr. McAndrew and I are required to attend tomorrow the reading of the will, which, unless my woman's intuition has deserted me, should certainly be of benefit to Kendall Associates, the firm his lordship floated in my uncle's name. We are required, it appears, to travel to Cambourne, which is his lordship's country house. I have, of course, been expecting this, but why the solicitors insist that Mr. McAndrew should also attend is quite beyond me. The *Elida* is in berth again after charter service along the Brittany and North Wales ports. It is a pleasing thought that her master, Ross Bolton, is coming to dinner tomorrow. Until we obtain a house ashore, however, we shall have to dine him out. I pray that this inconvenience will not long continue because Mr. McAndrew now seeks immoderate reasons to excuse his absence. It becomes increasingly obvious that these two do not like one another. Such are my husband's outrageous manners that I think Ross's attitude understandable.

Ellie left Tom, now toddling, on the *Sarn Helen* in the care of her father. Though showing little interest in anything but his Bible readings, Jake adored the child, and never let the boy out of his sight. McAndrew levelled a finger at him. "He's into everything, Jake, so watch him. No psalms, no readings. Guard him, or I'll skin ye, man, as God's me judge."

"Oh, come on, come on," said Ellie.

Cambourne House was no attempt by a rich old widower at Victorian ostentation, but a small Georgian manor set in six acres, a retreat to which Lord Grey-Cambourne could fly when harassed in his London home, a splendid house in Duke Street.

Sully, Glamorgan, in which county Cambourne was situated, was conveniently close to Barry, to which his lordship (once an engineering apprentice in the works of Cambourne and Nicholson) travelled most weekends with the lady of his choice: talk having it that, when he didn't bring one down in freight, so to speak, he moved a lighted lamp three times across an eastern window.

This brought a young housewife for reward, and such was his bachelor ability and charm that they quarrelled, it was said, for the privilege.

The house itself was of Georgian simplicity, a typical squireen's house and elegant of the time. It stood on gently sloping ground and dominated the surrounding fields with pastoral benevolence, rather like an old lady concerned to see that people attended church. Its entrance was guarded by Roman Doric, of the eight orders the most simple, and to many the most refined.

It possessed a terraced garden decorated with fountains that worked; at the back a walled garden supplied the occupants of the house with produce.

It had shooting-sticks standing in an elephant's foot in the hall of mosaic and marble; on either side of the main staircase, which was the pride of nearby Sully, aspidistras in china pots decorated with Chinese dragons stood in disconsolate greeting. The staircase wound upwards in teak and ironwork to the balcony landing above.

Hands in his pockets, McAndrew surveyed it with a wanton air.

"So this is it," he said.

"Pity me," replied Ellie. "This, after my mother died, was where I spent my childhood."

McAndrew thought that this explained a lot.

A servant in black skirt and starched apron rustled her way through the hall. "I'm Megsie, ma'am. Don't suppose you'd remember me. You was only a little one when I saw you last." She waved a plump hand. "Mr. Sandford, the master's solicitor, is in the library – shall I show you in?" Her Welshness then betrayed her and her faded eyes filled with tears. "Can't believe it still, none of us can't. One moment he was here, next moment gone . . ."

"I will see you afterwards," said Ellie. "How's cook?"

"*Diawch!* She's fine. Don't change a whimper, do she? The moment Miss Ellie comes you tell me directly, she says."

McAndrew followed Ellie into the library, a large, ornate room lined with books of gilt and leather.

"Ah, Mr. and Mrs. McAndrew." The solicitor rose from behind a desk. "I'm Sandford, his lordship's legal rep-

145

resentative." He stared up at McAndrew. "Pray be seated. Since you are the only beneficiaries likely to be present, this shouldn't take long."

Beyond the window birds were singing. One by one McAndrew identified them. Earlier, he had heard an occasional harsh croaking from the marshes and he saw, in his mind's eye, a cormorant winging across the estuary, and heard the unmistakable gobbling and bubbling of a red grouse, the startled clatter of pheasants.

It was good game country, and he knew it. From the duck pond, which he could clearly see through the latticed window of the library, came the chirricks and quarks of resident moorhens; a lapwing called plaintively. Ellie nudged him and he awoke to the droning voice of the solicitor:

"He's reading the will, man. For God's sake pay attention."

"The man's a bum-faced Pharisee."

"Aren't ye interested?"

McAndrew moved his big body with testy reserve. The solicitor read:

"To my cousin, William John Grey of the town of Adelaide, New South Wales, I leave the bulk of my fortune, in the hope that he will use it wisely and well in the advancement of his four children, Alicia, Arthur, Henry and Gwendoline, on the understanding that his wife, Gertrude, receives from this arrangement no personal benefits; to Gertrude I leave my compliments . . ."

Mr. Sandford said apologetically, "Truly, we will be here for hours if I read all this. Shall I confine myself to bequests affecting those present, Miss Ellie?"

A little startled, Ellie glanced up. "Please do."

The solicitor shuffled the papers, and read again;

"I bequeath to Mrs. Eleanor Alicia McAndrew, the niece of Jason, my life-long friend, my fleet of freighters – *Turk*, *Serb*, *Celt* and the *Cambourne*; the *Kaffir*, the steam-coaster

146

Collin, also the *Ben Reed* and *Mary Dale*, – together with all yards and equipment appertaining thereto at Maryport. I make this bequest in the hope that Mrs. McAndrew will change the name of the firm of Kendall Associates to Cambourne Freighters, in memory of me."

Mr. Sandford looked up momentarily. Despite her good fortune, Ellie discerned a slight apprehension upon the solicitor's face. He read, tonelessly:

"To James Alexander McAndrew, the husband of the aforesaid Eleanor, I leave the sum of five hundred thousand pounds . . ."

Ellie gasped aloud, rising slowly out of her seat. McAndrew was staring at the latticed window, for blackbirds were calling from the shrubberies of the garden. Earlier, he had heard a lark singing above the Big Wheatfield, of which Ellie had spoken. The solicitor said, "Mr. McAndrew, pardon me. Are you listening?"
"Ay ay! Every word."

". . . this sum to be spent exclusively in the interest of his wife for the direction and growth of her shipping firm, which, I am convinced, needs a man in control . . . Therefore, holding the financial reins of Cambourne Freighters, its destiny will be directly in the hands of the aforesaid James Alexander McAndrew."

"The . . . the old devil!" whispered Ellie, slowly sitting down again.

"Coming more to domestic affairs, the province of women, I leave Cambourne House, together with its land, fixtures, furbishings and appurtenances to the aforesaid Eleanor in the hope that it may prove a home wherein she may raise her children and care for her husband in wealth and comfort . . ."

147

Ellie interjected, white-faced, "The town house? What about the town house?" And Mr. Sandford replied.

"The town house in Duke Street has been left by his lordship to a lady . . . a lady whom . . . shall I say, is not of my acquaintance . . . shall I read the clause?"

"Don't bother."

Ellie was on her feet again. Giving McAndrew a look to kill she pulled on her gloves with fussy anger, and swept past him out of the library.

The solicitor lowered the will and removed his spectacles. "Is . . . is your wife all right, Mr. McAndrew? She . . . she had gone extremely pale."

"The poor mite," said McAndrew, rising. He went to the library door. "Excuse me, if you please."

The sun was cascading over the fields: bright green, they swept away to a purple horizon. It was a keen, beautiful air and McAndrew momentarily stood beneath the columned portico taking great breathfuls of it, cleansing himself of the musty and repressive atmosphere of the library. And then he saw Ellie standing by the pond within the terraced garden, and swiftly crossed the lawn towards her.

She turned a puffy, tear-stained face to his. He said:

"Dear God, don't cry. I canna bear you cryin'," and held her. "The fella's dead and gone, girl – ye canna do nothing about it."

"The old skin-flint." Gasping, Ellie turned herself out of his arms. "Last will and testament! He'd strip a bloody dog-fish . . ."

"Don't swear. Not you, Ellie, please don't swear . . ."

"Aye? Well, it makes me sick. I ran this firm, ye know, long before you come, Mr. McAndrew!" She raised a red, wet face. "An' I did it despite 'em – despite Uncle Jason, because he were past it, despite me feyther, because he isn't in this world . . . How the hell am I expected to run a fleet o' freighters without capital? Cambourne, he says – who wants bloody Cambourne?"

"It's your friend you're talkin' of, Ellie . . ."

She tore herself free of him. "*Domestic* affairs, eh – and I

148

run Kendalls for the past two years. What kind of woman does he think I am?"

"Friends are there to be loved, Ellie, not judged."

"And you playin' the holy righteous. Half a million! My God, ye stepped yourself lively, didn't you, McAndrew? Never in my life have I seen cards played better." Her fingers were twisting in repressed anguish.

"Half a million? Is this the trouble, then?"

"Aye, *five hundred thousand*! Or weren't ye even listening? I get the Cambourne freighters, but you get the control. What will ye do now, start up on your own?"

McAndrew said, "My God, Ellie, ye don't take prisoners, do ye?"

"Aye no!" She thumped herself. "Because my blood is Uncle Jason's blood, and the guts of shipping lies in the banks. In this business you're either in or out . . . It's eat or be eaten . . ."

"Come now." McAndrew's arms went about her and he drew her against him. "Settle ye'self. The money's yours, the old man meant that plain. And the control of it, too, if you want it, for I dunna . . ."

"God," she whispered, "you make me feel terrible!"

"It's you I want, me love." He held her away, grinning down. "I'll pay ye all that half a million for a smile. Ach, that's better. I tell you, Ellie, you're a lovely thing when you smile. It's . . . it's just that your amiss with ye priorities."

"It can make a successful shipping line!"

"Then, that's what you'll have. The money's yours. Now smile again?"

Afterwards, he went back to the library. Mr. Sandman, the solicitor, rose as he entered.

McAndrew said, "We'll come round to your office later, sir; just now you'll have to forgive me wife. His lordship was a darling friend of the family, if ye get me, and . . ."

"I understand, Mr. McAndrew."

149

15

Ellie's entry in the log of the *Sarn Helen* for 10th March 1900 was her final one, because it was the day she and McAndrew came ashore and settled in Cambourne House, leaving Jake, with a crew of three, to captain the little Clyde Puffer, the source of Uncle Jason's wealth. She wrote:

Today, a bright spring morning, saw us tie up in Barry Two Dock and move into Cambourne House after its extensive redecoration. This, and the refurbishing of the main rooms, I have left entirely to Mr. McAndrew, who has spent much time ashore recently, supervising it. To my surprise he shows a quite remarkable artistic taste, and where this comes from in one so unscholarly is quite beyond me. True, his little drawings, done occasionally either to annoy me or entertain Tom, seem to possess some ability in this direction, but clearly he has employed art-decorators at Cambourne because my rooms are adorned with truly beautiful murals. Tom is three years old today, and is being quite ruined by the servants; my husband is already engaged in the process, promising the child barbaric adventures in the coming year.

Now, at last, I have a centre where important guests can be received in a manner worthy of Cambourne Freighters, the capital share issue of which continues to thrive. And so, a house-warming is afoot. I shall entertain all my captains, an excellent opportunity to discuss the Company's future.

Meanwhile, I have my own suite of rooms in the west wing of the house while Mr. McAndrew (after protest) has the equivalent in the east wing that faces the sea. We are therefore now self-contained, so to speak. The onset of the Boer War has immeasurably increased our profits of course, and Mr. McAndrew, to his credit, has gained the respect of all our associates; technically, therefore, our partnership has proved a wise investment.

Ross Bolton is coming to dinner on Tuesday week, when the *Elida* is in port. It is too much to hope that Mr. McAndrew might learn from him gentlemanly deportment and social grace. It will be refreshing to dine with a man who knows the sequence of table cutlery and the difference between Burgundy and cooking sherry.

"Left, right, left, right, left . . ."

Ellie was standing by the french windows of her study when McAndrew's voice came booming over the Big Wheatfield. The spring morning, premature with warmth, was filled with birdsong and the tragic cooing of doves.

Earlier, Ellie had been making up her accounts, something she continued to do despite McAndrew's protests that they should be handed over to qualified accountants. There was an interim shareholders' meeting due at the new Barry Dock Hotel, and, according to Uncle Jason's philosophy, it was necessary to keep your boots on the necks of your debtors and your fists around the outgoings. One knew where one stood, persisted Ellie, if one did the adding up.

Keeping track of her ships, their cargoes and their ports of call (though she left technical details to their individual captains) was a task she performed daily, simultaneously with the Cambourne Freighters' Graph of Production . . . a complicated scroll of red and blue lines which covered the whole of one wall in her study.

Now, by the windows, she raised her face as McAndrew and Tommy came into her view; marching single file, the boy leading, around a bend in the Cadoxton River: this ran along the bottom of Cog Hill and formed the southern boundary of Cambourne's acres.

"Left, right, left, right. . . !"

The wind moved over the duck pond before her, bringing her husband's voice.

Ellie smiled faintly, clutching at a small lace handkerchief.

"Look to your front there! Keep your head up!" McAndrew's voice boomed on. "Ye might have broken your mother's heart, but you won't break mine. Company, *halt!*" All being interjected by Caesar's furious barking.

Tom, aged three, with a broom at the slope, came to a stop, his small face puckered up to the sun while McAndrew, towering above him, stamped slowly around him on a tour of inspection.

"Get ye hair cut! We're havin' no weekend poets in this mob. Stand closer to the razor. And stand still, mun! *Look to ye front!*"

With his paper hat sideways on his head, Tom stood rigidly.

"Right. Order arms! Stand at ease. *Fall out!*"

Tom dropped the broom and went headlong, giggling, and McAndrew fell to his knees. They rolled together, instantly at war, down the slope of the river bank and were lost to view; only the small white body of Caesar could Ellie see, and hear his barking on the desultory air.

Ellie envied the affinity McAndrew enjoyed with Thomas.

There was a masculinity about their man and boy companionship which her feminity could not enter; it transcended the normal relationship of father and son, and this perplexed her.

From the moment he opened his eyes in the morning the boy went in search of her husband, scrupulously accepting his mother's presence in his life as something to be tolerated, but clearly not enjoyed.

Standing there, Ellie listened to the birds, aware that a belated dawn chorus was in progress. One by one she identified the songs – the kittie-needie of the sandpiper, the twittering of sand-martins . . . to the full-throated shouting of blackbird and thrush. And, as McAndrew appeared again, with Tom in his arms, so the singing increased in beauty and sound – stricken now by the harsh cawing of rooks and crows in the tops of the poplars, as if in a frenzy of delight at the sight of him, he who spent hours mimicking their songs; clearly, thought Ellie, they thought him a bird.

This knowledge of his acceptance, and Tom's devotion to McAndrew, brought to Ellie a thin, sad loneliness: self-expression cried for air within her. She wanted to open the windows and rush down to the river. And Tom, as if sensing a watcher, climbed to his feet and stared in her direction. Straightening, McAndrew waved. Ellie briefly waved back, and the child, in a stumbling, swaying run, suddenly raced towards the house. Now he stood, breathless and bright-haired, laughing as she opened the french windows.

Ellie wanted to kneel and snatch him into her arms.

"Daddy's the sergeant, Mamma!" Tom fought for stuttering words that would not come. Then, "We . . . we've got a secret. We're going to catch a fish and cook him on a fire, and . . ."

Caesar was leaping excitedly about him.

"Come in," Ellie commanded, and caught Tom by the wrist. "Just look at ye feet, they're soaking!" She lifted a taut face to McAndrew. "The grass is wet, don't ye know? D'ye want the child to catch his death?"

"We . . . we're going to catch a fish . . ." said Tom. His eyes, bright blue, and close to tears, searched her face.

McAndrew, banished for marital reasons, was discovering that the east wing of Cambourne House possessed advantages over Ellie's suite on the other side of the building.

Hanging on the wall of his capacious study was a small, gilt-framed plaque with a poem thereon in French. Interwoven with naked cupids, complete with bows and arrows, were the words:

> The dear old *Droit du Seigneur*
> Is the joy of the local gentry.
> It came from France
> With the minuet dance

In the days of wealth and plenty.
And it's here to delight me and you, dear boy.
It's here to delight me and you.
For birth's not a matter of chance, my love
But a perk that's a gentleman's due.

Although reasonably certain that Ellie had no knowledge of French, McAndrew nevertheless decided to play safe. Removing the plaque from the wall he put it in the bottom drawer of the writing bureau, an immense affair of solid mahogany and capacious black and red inkwells. In this drawer was an envelope. Taking it out, he read:

Private to James Alexander McAndrew of Cambourne Freighters – from Lord Grey-Cambourne (temporarily deceased)

Opening the envelope he read the letter within:

Duke Street
London W.

My dear McAndrew,

Firstly, let me make it clear that I, like you, have an entry in the *Dictionary of Rogues*. Had I not sensed that we are kindred spirits, I would not be writing this.

Ellie did mention that you would be occupying my private suite of rooms, therefore, as a new occupant I greet you.

Consider what I have given you – wealth and power is yours, granted on a whim. The moment you denounced Jason's stupidity in buying the *Elida*, I knew that the future of my beloved freighters would be safe in your hands. Your speech castigating our policies confirmed this view.

Thank God I shall not live to see the Barry Railway Company's demise.

Secondly, do not assume that my gifts will go unrewarded. Did you know that I am a believer in the Occult?

I have decided to live on in you, McAndrew; your manhood having sufficient virility for the pair of us, though one be a ghost. Men are essentially polygamists; I advise you not to give our beloved Ellie a second thought; wives are as fickle as lusty husbands, given the chance: of this I assure you.

You will find in this drawer the key of my cellar, certainly the most elegant part of my *Saturnalia*; I was much impressed by your knowledge of vintage wines during our table conversation. The *plaisir* bottles from Bordeaux you mentioned – I have these in plenty; again, our taste is identical. Cigars come by running contract; a small firm in South America meeting all demands, the cost being paid by banker's order.

Husbandly duties apart, you will find it necessary to extend your hospitality to the village. Ellie, I suspect, is not all she should be, and, even if she were, would scarcely suffice. Women of meagre attractions, aware that it is their sole possession, are inexplicably loathe to part with it. Therefore, a midnight candle moved horizontally across the easterly window (of the room in which you are reading this) will bring response within the hour.

The rate of payment at the moment is a sovereign and a bottle of Moselle, though any person below the age of sixteen naturally doesn't qualify for the latter. On the other hand, should you find yourself in London, my house in Duke Street (at the moment tenanted by Princess Maria Joseldon, late of a royal house in Bavaria) will be as free to you as it has been to me, princess included.

She is about your age and is highly appreciative.

At the bottom of the *Saturnalia* will be found Recommended Reading – Sir Richard Burton's translation of the *Kama Sutra* being a somewhat hot favourite, if I may put it that way. Incidentally, my Barry accountants keep financial records – one book for the single births, another for the twins – dealing expeditiously with every claim; have no fear, therefore, that any indiscretion might reach the objectionable stage of an affiliation order.

Meanwhile, James Alexander McAndrew, be assured that, within your embrace of the bottle and dreams of fair women, I shall never prove an encumbrance: there I shall also be, but only, alas, in spirit. Enjoy yourself to the full, being prepared, as I, to weep at Satan's funeral.

May he grant that we meet again, and soon, and bless us.

Yours fraternally,

Lord Grey-Cambourne (Teddy)

19th August 1899

"Well, I'll be damned," whispered McAndrew.

16

Captain Ross Bolton, the master of the *Elida*, came to Cambourne within the month, to dine at Ellie's invitation.

"Do we have to have the fastidious fool tonight?" asked McAndrew.

"We do," replied Ellie, fastening her pearls.

"Can't ye handle him yerself, woman? I'm due down at the Chain Locker for a quart or two wi' the lads."

"You will stay here and do your duty as my husband – Captain Bolton is our newest captain and ye'll show him due respect."

"Aw, Christ," said McAndrew, and raised his hands to the ceiling. "Obsairve me situation. I'm due to dine wi' a stuffed shirt parakeet, and me wife's insisting on it."

"Kindly get yourself dressed, Mr. McAndrew," said Ellie.

Ross Bolton was good-looking, and knew it. Rumour had it that he had a wife in every port; one thing was certain, he kept a common law wife in the Barry Dock Hotel, and McAndrew knew that too: he had seen her before – at the Angel reception, when he first met Lord Grey-Cambourne; she was a high-flown piece, he thought, and said so.

Ellie was adjusting his collar-stud. "You've no proof of that."

"Does it even matter, woman? How are you concerned?"

Her hair – Ellie's hair – was the most beautiful he had seen; he thought this, too. Dressed in a long, white gown, she moved with lithe grace, and her demeanour, like her make-up, was perfect. Desire is all anguish, thought McAndrew, all anguish is desire. His need of her obliterated his total world. Two months now he had been at Cambourne and had not yet drawn a candle over a darkened window.

"Aw, do ye really have to pay pretties to this pansy bugger?"

"Mr. McAndrew!"

"Well, I canna help it, Ellie. Wi' anybody else I'd be fechtin' mad. You're basing kindness on a false assumption. What's he got that I haven'a, for God's sake?"

She raised a pert, pretty face to his, smiling with fake brilliance. "One day you might know, Mr. McAndrew." Raising a hand she delicately flicked a speck of dust from the jabot at his throat. "Aye, one day. Can we leave it at that?"

"You needing me to change some, ye mean?"

"They'll never change you, Mr. McAndrew, that's your trouble." She swept past him across the room to answer a knock.

"Captain Bolton's arrived, Miss Ellie," said Megsie, at the door.

Ellie nodded, and turned. "Coming, are ye?"

"I'll never change, Ellie. There's an old saying – ye canna take the breeks off a highlander."

"And there's a fallacy in that, too. They all wear breeks, including you. Except, of course, when you're exposing yourself in the *Nelson*."

"Ach, gi' us a break."

Caesar, sitting at the foot of the stairs, whimpered as they went past.

"Away, ye murdering tyke," said Ellie. "The police'll be arriving. He's just killed another one in Cadoxton – the biggest Alsatian I ever did see."

"It's only when he's in the drink, mind," said McAndrew.

"A good skelping with the tawse, that's what he needs."

McAndrew knelt. "Away, mun. Tonight they're talking violence to the pair of us. God Almighty, look what's arrived."

*

Captain Ross Bolton was in his master's uniform; tall, blue-clad, brass buttoned. With his peaked cap held across his chest, he bowed, came into the drawing-room and kissed Ellie's hand.

"Good evening, Mr. McAndrew." His voice was classically English.

"'Evening." McAndrew went to the sideboard. "What pleases ye, Bolton? Whisky?"

"Port, if you please."

"Christ." McAndrew poured two ports, one being for Ellie. Gulping down a double whisky, he poured himself another, saying:

"When did ye get the *Elida* in, then?"

"The evening tide."

"Oh dear," said Ellie. "I hope you had sufficient notice, Captain . . ."

"Weren't ye due last midnight?"

Ross Bolton replied, "I got caught in the Sound and laid off. They had a dredger in Number Six."

"Loading coke this time?" asked Ellie.

"Timber, Ma'am. It appears that the company is heeding your husband's advice. Diversify – that's the latest slogan."

"They're already too late," said McAndrew gruffly. "The war's upon us and there's nothin' in trooping." Glass in hand he ponderously crossed the room.

His bulk, thought Ellie, dwarfed the captain; his movements contrasted with the latter's athletic grace, which was almost feline. She felt Bolton's dark eyes moving over her with slow assessment. And Ellie, although acting with obvious unconcern, yet felt depressed and frustrated by the presence of her husband.

Captain Ross's scrutiny, brief but efficient, seemed to release her from the bonds of life.

The game was dangerous; this she knew. McAndrew was talking now, some gibberish about lack of amenities in the town for workmen, but clearly Ross wasn't listening, and the fact pleased her. She had heard from other women that his ardour was untiring and that he was possessed of the principles of a jackdaw. This in no way diminished him in her eyes; indeed, the prospect excited her.

At their initial meeting his eyes had betrayed neither shame nor delicacy; this challenge Ellie now accepted. It was as inevitable as the coming of day that soon Ross would make love to her, this she knew.

Inwardly, though now smiling brilliantly at McAndrew, she was cursing herself for snatching at him when, after a brief wait, she could have had this new and exciting man, whose attentions would make her the envy of Barry. McAndrew, bearish, boorish, was, she considered, like a wild animal in prudish company; she was astonished that he was still getting away with it.

"How's the ship behaving?" she asked.

"Well enough. Jason surveyed her, and he was no fool." Ross smiled.

"She'll hammer out her boiler if ye get her in a squall," said McAndrew over his shoulder. "Grey-Cambourne said she was a sea-ponce, and I agree. Your troubles are yet to come, bonnie lad." Joining them with a new glass, he added, "How did she behave on the Porto run?"

"She melted a gland."

"Where?"

"Propeller housing. I had to take her down to Gib – no workshop facilities on the big double-compound."

"With slate aboard? That'll cost ye, Ellie!" McAndrew grinned hugely.

Ross Bolton said, "Not so much. I know the trade. There was no demurrage; the fitters and chandlers came out in an engineer's boat."

"Loss of time?" McAndrew smiled over the rim of his glass.

"That wasn't important . . . But . . . we lost a man. Frankly, I've been raking up the courage to tell you."

McAndrew started. "Ye lost a man!"

The captain nodded. "Albert Horton's boy – a grease monkey."

Ellie, pale, said faintly, "Oh God, I know the lad. I took

him on. What happened, for heaven's sake?"

"He was greasing on the propeller shaft and we were taking a bit of sea. The prop came out and she raced; the bearing over-heated and spattered over his hands. Third degree burns. The doctor in Gib said he died of shock."

"You brought him back?"

"No. We buried him at sea, off Cape Ortegal. This is what his father wanted."

"Jesus," whispered McAndrew, turning away. "He were no more'n sixteen."

They stood in silence. McAndrew added, "She's cursed, ye know. Nothing's gone right aboard that bloody *Elida* from the moment we bonded her. She's nothin' but bad luck!"

Ellie said, a woman removed, "That . . . that's the way I'd like to go, you know . . ."

Ross whispered, "Ma'am, for heaven's sake. . . !"

"Aye, I mean it."

McAndrew snorted: "Ellie, spare us the damned homilies. Now's not the time or place for amateur dramatics – a child's dead, or didn't ye hear it?"

"I only said I'd like to be buried at sea, that's all. What's wrong with that, for God's sake?"

McAndrew gulped at his whisky. "Don't listen, Bolton – she gets it from Kipling – *The Mary Gloster*." He glared at Ellie. "Must ye always be talkin' of dyin', woman? What about staying alive for a change?"

And Ellie said, as if to herself,

". . . By the little paternosters, as you come to the Union Bank,
We dropped her – I think I told you – and I pricked it off where she sank.
Tiny she looked on the grating – that oily, treacly sea –
'Hundred and Eighteen East, remember, and South just Three . . ."

She smiled brilliantly. "Do you know something, Captain Bolton – I've checked the latitude and longitude – Kipling did his research all right, they're actually there – a tiny group of islands. Isn't it marvellous? Do you know Kipling well?"

"No, Ma'am." Bolton sipped at his glass, his eyes on McAndrew.

"The old ship owner buried his wife at sea, you understand . . ."

McAndrew exclaimed, "Woman, gi' it a rest!" He slopped more whisky into his glass. "Have ye been to see the lad's mither, Bolton – that's the important thing . . ."

Ellie laughed, but it was false laughter, and all there knew it. Turning, she swept gracefully across the carpet towards them. "Captain Bolton understands, even if you don't. . . ?"

He bowed. "Of course!" Ellie continued:

"It . . . it's just something I've always wanted – burial at sea. You know – and I'm telling the most important people in my life – if Mr. Horton's son had to die, I could think of no better place for him to rest. I'm not making a lot of it – only that I'd like the same thing to happen to me."

"I asked ye, mun, if you'd been to see his mither yet?" demanded McAndrew.

The whisky was getting him and Ellie knew the signs. Earlier in the day he had been drinking hard and she didn't want trouble in the presence of Captain Bolton.

"Have you been yet, Captain?" she asked kindly.

"Certainly, and given her the usual ten sovereigns."

"See her again and make it fifty," growled McAndrew. He brushed at his eyes. "Sixteen years!"

Whisky has two ways out of a man, thought Ellie, and one way is through the eyes; she said with forced gaiety:

"On a happier note, we'd best go in for dinner. Are you ready?"

Megsie, the maid, was standing by the dining-room door. "Ready Ma'am."

She was plump and forty and McAndrew stayed to spare her a look of pleasure.

His mood, in seconds, had changed; the whisky was now making shock attacks upon his head. Last in, he paused, saying, "You're a sight for sore eyes, Megsie. Serving fodder to us? You should be in some fine foreign place with the moon that big you can pull it out of the sky, and in the bed of some young eastern potentate!"

"Oh, go on with you, sir," said Megsie, very pretty and flushed.

"Mr. McAndrew!" called Ellie. "If you please!"

Caesar, like a pariah, slunk in behind him.

Ross Bolton said, over his soup, "I've taken the liberty of bringing you back a small present, Miss Ellie."

"Why, that's wonderful!"

McAndrew glanced up. Ellie opened large, delighted eyes.

"I was bazaar shopping in Gib and came across a painting by Seurat. It was one of six canvases, and I don't think the vendor knew the value of any of them. Do you know Seurat's work?"

"I can't say I do," said Ellie simply.

The captain broke bread with slim, dark hands.

"I got the painting for a few pounds, but I venture to think it would fetch more. The new school, you know. He lays a claim to fame – he was present, they say, when Van Gogh cut off his own left ear. . . !"

McAndrew, ladling up his soup, grinned. "You're sure o' that, Bolton? You're not mixing him up with St. Peter? Matthew twenty-six, verse fifty-one?"

The captain continued, ignoring him with studied intent:

"Are you informed about the Impressionists, Miss Ellie?"

"Er, no, Captain."

"I ask, you see, not to air my knowledge, but because art is of greater interest if one possesses even speculative appreciation."

McAndrew drank, his eyes shining. "Continue, mun, you've got the floor."

Bolton said, while Megsie served him, "This happens to be my particular hobby, you understand?"

"Art? Oh, how *wonderful*!" cried Ellie.

"Explain about these Impressionist people . . ." interjected McAndrew, with his mouth full.

163

He was eating with gregarious pleasure, hauling huge amounts up to his capacious mouth, and chewing lustily.

Bolton sipped his wine. "To simplify it for you, the Impressionists sought expression in bright colours, rejecting coherent shape."

McAndrew drank, smiling faintly. "Is that a fact?" He picked his teeth with gusto.

"You're interested in art, Mr. McAndrew?" The other peered across the table.

"Well, shall we say I'm a seasoned warrior in the business of living – put it no higher than cartooning. Please go on, Captain, don't let me interrupt."

Bolton nodded. "One of art's tragedies, you know, is that artists invariably live in obscurity. So my small Seurat painting is probably worth little; he hasn't been dead long enough." He smiled around the room, flickering a secret eye at Ellie.

"Also," added McAndrew, "he made the mistake of being an intellectual. The painter-theoretician's a dangerous animal, ye know. Myself, I prefer the instinctive man. Gauguin. . . ?" Making a face, he pondered this. "But preferably Toulouse-Lautrec."

Ellie said, "Are you trifling with us, Mr. McAndrew, or merely trying to be funny?"

"Tell ye the truth, Miss Ellie, I'm out of me depth. Jack of all trades . . . I can play the tuba, too, but I'm best on the Irish fiddle, with the pints goin' round – let me fill your glass, Bolton." He leaned across the table with the wine bottle. Ellie said, swinging about:

"Oh Tommy, no! What are you doing out of bed!"

McAndrew, bottle in hand, turned in his seat. His son was standing in the doorway in his night-shirt, hair tousled, his eyes heavy.

"Hallo, wee fella . . ."

Ellie said, "Tell us what you want, son, and then go back to bed. You know you're supposed to be asleep."

"Are you taking me, Papa?" said Tommy.

"To the woods wi' the fish? Aye, I will. Didn't I promise?"

164

"You promised before, but you didn't come." said the child.

"Aye, so I did." McAndrew rose and gathered the boy against him. "So now I'll tell ye something, lad. I swear by me honour bright that I'll take ye down to the dell on Tuesday week, the night before I wheel meself to London." He turned to Ellie. "Wednesday's the meeting, isn't it, Mither?"

"The meeting of the Import Trade Association, ye mean? Aye, Wednesday the fifteenth. Tuesday morning we've got all the captains in – for heaven's sake remember that."

"Then Tuesday's the great day, son, for I'll be home."

"You promise, Papa?"

McAndrew, with Tom held against him, swung to Bolton. "Now tell the livin' truth, Captain. Have you ever known me to break a promise, second time round?"

"Never." Bolton smiled. "Hallo, Tommy."

"Hallo, sir."

"Bed now," said Ellie, and got up from the table. "I'll take him."

"Ach no. Leave the wee thing to me. Come on, son."

McAndrew took the boy through the door and up the winding stairs.

"Papa, will you do a drawing for me." asked Tom.

"Aye, I'll do a drawing of a big, bad bear eating up a princess."

Ellie said, "I hope you don't find my husband too elementary, Captain."

"In connection with art? On the contrary, I find him passably well informed."

They sat in silence, no words between them.

After the meal they went to see the painting. Captain Bolton said, "I took the liberty, Ma'am, of asking your maid to hang it for me. Seurat is best seen at a distance."

In the reception room the three of them stood together.

The painting was about twelve inches square: the pale,

oval face of a young woman stared out at them from the canvas. Ellie said, clapping her hands together:

"Oh Captain, I think she's delightful!"

"It's a Seurat right enough." said McAndrew.

"I'm quite sure it is!" cried Ellie. "Oh, Mr. McAndrew, look!"

Her husband said, "He was a remarkable fella, this one. I remember seeing his *Sunday Afternoon on the Ile de la Grande Jatte* . . ."

"Really?" answered Bolton, flatly.

"Ay, ay! One of the earliest scandals of the Neo-Impressionists. I saw it in Italy, somebody had it on tour." McAndrew waved a big hand towards the portrait. "You can see Lehman's influence there, and Ingres. But he was less inspired by Classicism than Delacroix's Romanticism – that's in every damn stipple. You've done well, Captain. You're aware, I take it, that you might be handing Ellie a fortune, fifty years from now?"

"I think he is very, very generous."

Ellie was frowning thoughtfully at McAndrew, Ross Bolton was plainly disconcerted.

"I'm glad you're pleased, Ma'am." Bolton took out his fob watch. "I must go. I didn't realise it was so late, I'll be locked out of the Dock Hotel."

"As long as they don't cut off your supply in the Chain Locker," added McAndrew. "I'll see ye to your carriage – did Megsie call it?"

"Aye, it's waiting outside." answered Ellie.

"Good night, and thank you both for a marvellous evening." Bolton kissed Ellie's hand.

"Good night."

Their eyes met momentarily. McAndrew nodded and winked expansively, saying jocularly, "Well, well, it just shows ye – there's more to some sea-dogs than compasses and reciprocators." Putting a huge arm around Bolton's shoulder, he steered him to the door, opened it, and closed it behind them.

They stood together within the columned entrance. The

night was black in glittering immensity; the carriage waited, the horses stamped.

McAndrew said speculatively, "Seurat, you know, played on decomposed light. He had depth, but never true perspective – only the contrast of light and shade, ye realise that?"

"Of course," answered Bolton.

"He worked, ye see, on a basic principle of optical law – colour, and colour alone, was his controlling factor – through a superpositioning of differing planes. Would ye agree with that theory, Bolton?"

"Why yes, but . . ."

"This being so, he was without perspective lines."

Bolton made to go. A hand delayed him.

"But that portrait's full of perspective lines, and you know it, don't you?" McAndrew was smiling into the other man's face.

"I . . . I must say, McAndrew, that I've had some recent doubts . . ."

"Your portrait's a fake, and so are you. You picked up a copy of Seurat and put his signature on it. So now I suggest ye get back to your floosie in the Dock Hotel and stop coveting my wife. She's the only thing I've loved in me life, so you're walking on hallowed water."

"Mr. McAndrew! That's a preposterous allegation!"

The other slammed the carriage door. "*Away!* Show your arse around here without a business invitation, Bolton, and I'll kick your moving parts from here to bloody Cardiff. *Out!*"

McAndrew slapped the nearest horse, then stood watching as the carriage left by the eastern gate.

He laughed, softly at first, then louder. With his hands on his hips he turned up his face and shouted laughter.

Ellie, already in her bedroom, raised her head to listen.

When the house was quiet, McAndrew, having bathed and put on his new dressing-gown (purple and white and elegantly tailored under Ellie's supervision) went down to the cellar Lord Cambourne had given him.

167

There, amid the dusty racks of claret, Sauternes of 1855 vintage and expensive Barsac, he chose with care a bottle of the famous Lafite. Cleaning it, he went back to his bedroom, found two glasses and proceeded along the corridors of Cambourne to Ellie's suite in the west wing.

"*D'une élégance, grâce et bouquet merveilleux, goût délicieux,*" said he as he went, rolling the French on his tongue. "If this and my new gown dunna persuade the sweet creature, nothin' will."

Ellie was sitting at her dressing-table brushing out her hair. It lay in black silken waves to her waist.

"Who is it?"

"Megsie," said McAndrew, soprano, entering when Ellie opened the door. He put the bottle on the bed. "The choicest wines of France," he said, "together with your ever loving husband, bathed and powdered. The intention, ye lucky thing, is to sleep with ye."

For answer, Ellie closed the door.

She thought he looked magnificent in the gown she had bought him. The cork of the bottle popped. "It's a libation I'm offering you, Miss Ellie. After long and serious consideration, I've come to sacrifice myself on the altar of womanhood."

"Oh, God!"

"Think of your situation! You're running a successful shipping company, you've a house in the country and capital of half a million: a son, ye've got, the sweetest mite, and a portrait by Seurat. What else do ye need, if it isn't me?"

It was forced gaiety; both of them knew it.

"I'm tired, Mr. McAndrew." Ellie walked past him and sat at the dressing-table again.

"God Almighty, woman, are you always so tired?"

"I'm tired and I've got a headache. Please, haven't you got a bed?"

"I have, girl, but it's coming mighty lonely. Do you realise I haven'a consorted wi' you in months? What do you take me for, for God's sake?"

The brush suspended, Ellie lowered her face from the mirror.

"This part of marriage I find unattractive."

"You make that plain enough. But it was in the contract, woman, or didn't ye read it? Tonight I come to worship the mother o' me son; soon I'll be away to find myself a woman."

"Please go, Mr. McAndrew."

"There's other addresses, ye know. A fella with the need o' mine anna all that choosey." There was a stricture in his voice: he was finding it difficult to breathe.

"Then go to them. You were sharp to do so before."

There was a silence.

"I wasn't in love with you then, Ellie."

She turned in her chair.

"Look – tomorrow? Will you come tomorrow? Any time, but for God's sake not tonight."

"Why is tonight so different?"

Lowering her face Ellie loosened her tears.

Instantly he was beside her.

"Ach, don't cry, Ellie." He bent above her, his big hands in her hair. "Please don't cry, Ellie. Are ye ill?"

"Can't you guess what's wrong with us, Mr. McAndrew?"

"I haven'a any spy-glass to see into your soul, girl, I can only hear your sounds."

She raised a tear-stained face to his; her look was an act of contrition. McAndrew said:

"Ellie, what's wrong with us? Canna ye do it with me any more? For the trouble is that I'm loving you, can't ye understand?"

They were silent within a strange, perfidious quiet, save for Ellie's sobbing.

"I ask ye again. Please go, Mr. McAndrew." She added brokenly, "You see, you didn't turn out the way I prayed. It's no good beatin' about the bush, husband, ye just never will."

"Nor you, come to that," said McAndrew. "Though I thought we were taking us for better or for worse." He sighed. "I must have been mistaken."

At the door, he said, bottle in hand, "I'm one for dramatic

exits, you know. Legally this leaves me free for cricket on the side. Is that what you're wanting?"

Turning at the mirror, she stared across the room. "It's your life, Mr. McAndrew – do as ye please. But don't you shame me. Think of the company. I'll never forgive ye if you shame me."

He bowed. "Good night to ye."

First, McAndrew returned to the little cellar and brought up half a dozen bottles of Latour '93. Returning to his bedroom he examined his watch.

It was a few minutes to midnight.

Lighting a candelabra on the dressing-table, he went to the eastern window of the room and drew the heavy, velvet curtains. Instantly the night was flung across the room, the window bisected by stars.

Nothing moved on Cambourne's lawns. Faint yellow lights winked from the village.

Lying upon the bed in his room, McAndrew drank steadily. The drinking of wine never failed to remind him of Henri Toulouse-Lautrec, his artist friend of the days of Montmartre. And the sense of emptiness that now assailed him, kindled within him a sadness at Henri's loneliness.

McAndrew grinned in the moonlight, remembering that very first army desertion that took him to Paris, and friendship with Henri, so soon to be his mentor.

Before he had formally met the famous artist, McAndrew had often seen him entering or leaving the Cabaret Mirliton in the Élysée-Montmartre. And one day in summer he had followed Henri on the arm of his latest flame, Rosa la Rouge (from whom, according to Henri, he had 'caught the curse' as he called it).

Amazingly to McAndrew, their journey took them to the main gate of the infamous Bicêtre Asylum: later, he had learned that Henri had ostensibly gone there to visit a sick friend. In fact, forever seeking new subjects, the artist was in search of new aspects of humanity.

The venture was to prove a sad mistake.

McAndrew, hungry, with his clothes in tatters, had stood by the asylum railings, and watched.

Within the hospital grounds small, scattered groups of abnormal children were happily playing. And, seeing the dwarfish Henri approaching, had assumed him to be a new playmate, rushing towards him with fiendish cries, catching his hands, snatching at his clothes to bring him into their game.

Their total acceptance, said Henri to McAndrew later, had brought its message of total rejection. And imperishable love, McAndrew thought now, was treated exactly the same.

Such love, in itself (he now reflected) was a form of abnormality, a sickness which nurtured familiarity in the loved one . . . and brought discountenance, and eventual rebuff.

And so a longing, sudden and immense, came upon him – the necessity to unshackle himself from this commitment – the wish to be free of it beset him with embracing force, and he slowly sat up on the bed.

Staring into the moonlight he tipped the bottle high and guzzled at the wine, and Atopia House . . . vital and free, rose up before him like an obliterating light. As the old house had beckoned him before so it called to him again . . . Atopia, presided over by the demented and god-like Uncle Dumb – the lonely family of imbeciles on the Yorkshire moors within whose enclave true sanity was retained – yet a total and accepted lunacy. To this place he had gone before, to this freedom he had deserted many times.

McAndrew grinned to himself, gripping the bottle.

Think of it! Old Vicar Groper might even still be there (God, if he was, he must be over ninety . . .) preparing to dance the lead in *Giselle* at Covent Garden. Brunel, the mad inventor, would still be pouring over his higher calculus in his dreams of perpetual motion; Conrad (who sat on gravestones reading Byron, being a failed vampire) would certainly be alive – when last seen he was comparatively young: Marie Antoinette would be at table with her entourage, Lord Effington-Smythe shop-lifting from his own store, Miss Pan would be sitting on her earth closet in the middle of the hall and Ferdinand the anarchist still exploding his bombs in the cellar.

There'd be hell to pay, of course, for the great mural in the banqueting hall was still unfinished, and Uncle Dumb was not easily cajoled: Mama Meg, too, could be a virago if upset . . . But more, the open road was calling, and the hay was flying in the wind.

Meanwhile, there was a certain item that demanded his attention.

The ostler had forgotten to turn off the fountain and beyond the yellow drive white water descended in a myriad light sprays, flung up from the mouths of petrified fish. For a moment McAndrew watched this, glass in hand, then moved the lighted candles across the window.

Back, forward, back.

Minutes passed, and nothing happened. He drank, filled the glass and drank again, seeing, for the first time above the little window, a small gilt-framed portrait of Lord Grey-Cambourne.

Strangely, this brought him faint annoyance.

McAndrew moved the candles again. Almost instantly a light blazed from the west side of the river. He watched as the light degenerated into a lantern's flashing beam: it came closer, closer . . . then moved westward along the river to the bailiff's footbridge. It crossed the bridge, an errant glow-worm dancing in suspension.

The moon, as if in contrition, suddenly blazed, lighting the scene. McAndrew doused the candles.

A woman was walking over the footbridge. He could now see her clearly. She walked swiftly and with confidence, and he knew she was young. When she reached his side of the river, she momentarily stooped; the lantern went out.

McAndrew unbolted the french doors. Bottle in hand, he lay on the bed. Slowly the moon faded, to blaze again, violent and uncouth, lighting the lawns, even the room. And in this new light Ellie seemed to call to him from the distant tranquillity of her dreams. Come drama, tempest – Ellie slept the moment her head touched the pillow and McAndrew envied the inviolate serenity of her mind. Suddenly a footstep, slurring the gravel outside, brought him back to the immediate. A shadow moved on the glass of the door.

McAndrew sat up. Night perfumes entered as the door came ajar; spring garden flowers of impenetrable sweetness filled the room. Fingers moved on the catch of the door.

A girl stepped into the room, her clogs silent on the thick-piled carpet.

"'Evening, Mister."

McAndrew, unmoving, watched her. "Come in," he said.

But she was already in, snapping the door locks with a professionalism born of practice. McAndrew saw the slimness of her body as she reached up to draw the curtains. This done, she crossed the room, pulling down her dark hair as she went; bending, she turned the key in the bedroom door.

"Shall I get the claret?"

Her voice held the lilting song of the Welsh; from her voice alone McAndrew assessed her age, since he could not clearly see her.

"Claret?"

"His lordship always reckoned on the claret, see; a toddy or two of the red stuff makes the man, he used to say. But you're the new master; perhaps you don't need it?" Her voice held a hint of mockery.

"Carry on as ye did for Lord Grey-Cambourne, woman."

For answer, she lit the candelabra. Holding it high, she approached the bed, looking down at him.

McAndrew saw her face for the first time; in that wavering light it possessed the pallor of a disembodied ghost. Her eyes, glittering in the candlelight, shone with a strange fire, as if from an unsubstantial world.

"*Diawch*, Mister," said she, "you're a man and a half. His lordship were only a cock bantam of a chap."

"Ye'll discover it has major advantages," replied McAndrew.

He drank, tipping up the bottle. The girl moved as in refracted light, the room momentarily swam.

"What's ye name, sir?"

"McAndrew." He drank again.

She said, with sudden joy, her hands together as if in prayer, "His lordship always let us call him Teddy."

"Refer to me as Viscount Loon," said McAndrew, and struggled up the better to see her. "And yours, child?"

"I'm Tuesday."

"What kind o' name is that, for God's sake?"

"I'm Tuesday. There's six of us, d'ye see? One for each day of the week, except Sunday, because of the Pope. Today's Tuesday, so it's me."

"Well, I'm buggered," said McAndrew under his breath. "Are ye single?"

"Aye."

"A virgin?"

"*Diawl!* What do you take me for!" She was outraged.

"I apologise. You've been up here before?"

"Ay ay. Been coming since I was fifteen. His lordship had me first, in a manner of speaking."

"So what's happening now is no shock to your system."

The girl pouted prettily. "His lordship used to say I were the joint of the week."

"Then get yourself undressed, I've a crying need for ye."

"And the claret?"

"Forget the claret, haul yourself into bed."

Tuesday set down the candelabra and went to the dressing-table.

Before the mirror, with an elegance McAndrew didn't expect, she removed her clothes. Up with the plain grey domestic's dress; down with two petticoats, the last one flannel, and she was there in whalebone stays. Down with red bloomers, roll down black stockings.

Drinking, McAndrew watched. Tuesday undid her stays and draped them over a chair; sitting now, one leg up, she examined a bare leg.

She looked beautiful, he thought; it was a bare, prim and

instinctive loveliness made the sweeter by her very harlotry: Tuesday unlocked her hair and shook its black waves down to her waist.

In a moment, on an instantaneous stroke, she became Ellie.

McAndrew sat forward on the bed, staring at her; the girl, without artifice, had assumed Ellie's symmetry and grace.

"God Almighty," said McAndrew.

There was neither shame nor delicacy in Tuesday; as naked as when with the midwife, she approached the bed. McAndrew, bottle in hand, stared up at her in the candle-light; her vitality and warmth crept over the bed and into him. She said, with an assurance past her years:

"You're young, Viscount Loon. Down the village they said you was older than his lordship." She opened empty hands at the room in total resignation. "At the end, ye know, he reckoned that this love business was worth no more'n a good winter's sneeze."

"Aye, well, when ye get as old as his lordship the activity's incongruous. But don't tire me with your philosophy, woman, you're paid by results. How old are ye, incident-ally?" Hand poised, he held up the sheets.

"Nigh twenty."

"Pop in, then. You qualify for the Moselle as well, for I'd hate to be breaking the law. Will ye drink it now, or later?"

"I'd prefer a dish of pickled onions," said Tuesday getting in.

"I'll give ye pickled onions," said McAndrew. "Stay in one place, damn ye."

The girl cried out in panic for breath, laughing as his arms went about her.

Later, before she left him, Tuesday said, "Two sovereigns, Mister? I reckoned on one."

"You pleased me."

"Aye. And you me. D'you know something? I'd come up here for nothing, for my heart's sad and sore for you." She took his hand and held it against her throat. "Some men cry, ye know. I had one who called for his mam. But the sounds you made I never heard before. It came from deep down in you, like something goin' mad . . ."

"That's why I call meself Viscount Loon."

"And me name isn't Ellie – it's Tuesday, you know."

McAndrew opened the french doors for her. "You talk too much, get going."

"Next Tuesday? I'll be waiting . . ."

Standing by the window he watched her lantern cross the bailiff's bridge, then, turning, he sat down in the middle of the floor.

After a little while he began to rock himself to and fro: with his hands over his face he moaned in bass discord. In that manner, for many minutes, he rocked and moaned, and Caesar came out from under the bed and sat beside him in trembling agitation.

Then McAndrew reached out and gathered the dog against him and moaned and cried, and Ellie, lying in the canopied bed of the west wing heard this and raised her head, listening, and thought that it was an animal in pain.

17

Ellie's captains were coming to Cambourne House.

From midday they started to arrive from different ports of England. From Captain Galli, the Italian skipper of *Turk* to John Barnard of the *Celt*, the five thousand tonner which was running grain between Gibraltar and Amsterdam, also the *Kaffir*, which was on charter to a Greek company trading in the Adriatic.

The *Ben Reed*, named after her skipper, oldest captain of Cambourne Freighters, had arranged to put into Barry for the convenience of her ancient master: he, stricken with rheumatism but still afloat, as Ellie put it, arrived in style in a two-horse brougham. By the time they were being served tea by Megsie (and Cook, who had come from the kitchen especially for the occasion) nine captains had presented themselves, including Jake of the *Sarn Helen*.

Only Captain Ross Bolton of the *Elida* was absent.

"I wonder where he could have got to?" asked McAndrew.

Resplendent in tartan coat and trews he greeted the men with expansive pleasure, claiming that there were enough blue jackets and braid present to rig out the British Navy.

"Mind you," observed old Captain Ben, "he were always a late starter, were young Ross; wi' a missus like his, it's a job gettin' up in the morning, beggin' your pardon, Miss Ellie, for she's a right ducksie is Ross's wife."

"What port is he?" asked Ellie absent-mindedly. The fact that Ross had a wife was news to her.

"She's stowing in the Dock Hotel, isn't she?" asked another. "Sure as life I saw her steppin' out this morning."

Ellie said, "Ye must be mistaken, Captain Bell."

Bell was a lanky man with thin, aesthetic features; more like a booking-clerk than a sea-captain, and it was Ellie's intention to rid herself of him. She added:

"To my knowledge Captain Ross isn't married. If he is it isn't in his contract." She turned to McAndrew. "Where's the *Elida* berthing?" she asked, although she knew this perfectly well.

"Liverpool." McAndrew consulted the wall chart. "On the two o'clock tide this morning."

"Then he'll likely be down on the three-thirty from Cardiff. It will take him an hour, so we'll wait a few minutes more."

The men stood in chatting groups, with McAndrew the centre of attraction, as usual, thought Ellie, and she knew the loneliness of social isolation. And so she stood on the fringe of their male camaraderie, accepting polite glances of recognition, greeting new captains as they arrived, but never accepted within the orbit of discussion. Automatically, she found herself looking out of the window, waiting for Ross . . .

More, the drink was going down, and Ellie didn't like it: it was a tea-party degenerating into a beer garden, and McAndrew, she thought, was responsible. Joining her, he said, "Och, this is a grand reunion this, Ellie, and we should do it more often." He peered at her. "What ails ye? Come and join the fellas."

"I don't want this to become an orgy, Mr. McAndrew. The tea, the sandwiches – nothing's been touched." She nodded towards Megsie who was waiting with patient reserve, Cook having long ago retreated to her kitchen.

"These are sea-dogs, Missus. What did ye expect, a vicarage tea-party?"

"You are responsible for conducting this with decorum, and please don't call me missus!"

"Hasn't the darlin' Ross come, then? Is that what's up ye apron?"

"Please don't be ridiculous!"

Ellie's face flushed. She was dressed in a black, velvet gown, full at the hips and, for Ellie, low at the bosom; he

178

thought she looked beautiful. Now, gripping the dress, she swung about impatiently:

"How can we possibly start until everybody's here? I'm getting worried . . ."

"About Bolton? His common law wife's down at the Dock Hotel, don't ye know? So he won't be far away. Any minute now, Ellie girl, he'll come steamin' over your horizon." He gave her a knowing wink.

Ellie waved him down, saying, "It's churlish the way you men scandalise each other – you're worse than women!"

The conversation swelled in sound as the men, in a body, came strolling towards them over the Chinese carpet, and Captain Ben, senior Captain of the Fleet, overhearing, cried:

"Aye, but Mac's right, ye know – he's a right Randy for the girls, is Ross." He tossed back his whisky. "Teddy Cambourne used to say that we had to wait till Ross got his leg out before a meeting could start. Did ye hear what happened to him on the China run, lads?"

The men clamoured about him, and Captain Ben shouted laughter, and said, "Well, it seems he got married once – official, ye know – some fresh-faced youngster whose people lived in Hong Kong. And after the honeymoon – they spent it in Macao, I think, he brings the lass back to his ship – indeed, I think it was the old *Elida*, and they bunk down in his state room for the night. Next mornin' in comes his faithful old steward wi' the mornin' tea, and before Ross could explain, he shakes the lass by the shoulder, waking her up, and says, 'Tea now, Missy – time you go home.'"

McAndrew bawled laughter, going double: the men stamped about, spilling their drinks: Ellie, pale, played nervously with the cornelian necklace at her throat.

And yet, secretly, she was experiencing a strange sense of elation.

The old sea-captain cried, "God knows what they see in him, even his ducksie down in the Dock Hotel must know what's goin' on – but women're queer cattle, ye know – the cheese is often sweeter when nibbled by another mouse, beggin' ye pardon, Miss Ellie," and he waved his arthritic sticks. "Meanwhile, I've got another date . . ."

"Will ye be taking those sticks with ye, Captain?" asked McAndrew.

"Only to keep her on her toes, son. Ye know, Ellie, if your man had a heart instead of a swinging brick, the beggar would heave to more often. But I'll be back on the *Ben Reed* this time tomorrow to catch the Thursday tide to Boulogne wi' coal and slate for Brittany. For these days my ladies come one night at a time."

Ellie blushed, the others laughed, and old Ben continued:

"I mind the times in the old days when I used to come here for the meeting wi' Lord Teddy . . ." He put his hand on Ellie's shoulder. "You're descending from good stock, takin' over from him." He nodded at McAndrew. "And it appears to me you've chosen the right blutty Pharaoh to lash the slaves o' Cambourne Freighters. Are captains' salaries on the agenda?"

All laughed merrily, pushing closer. Old Ben continued:

"I recall our very first meeting – there was only the *Turk* and my *Ben Reed* at sea then, wi' more coming down the slips. Lord Teddy was building up, if ye get me. And I pledged to meet him at the Three Bells here in town.

"As I got out of my trap a bear comes loose – ye recall the big Siberians who danced in the streets in Barry?" The old man sipped his rum.

"Aye, well he comes loose, this big bear, tame no more, being sick of the indignity of chains. And he goes roaring down High Street, having mauled his trainer, and everyone rushing helter skelter! Navvies wi' clogs up and women wi' skirts up, and he arrives at the Three Bells, this big black chap, just as I was going into the pub. So there's only me and the bear, ye get me? With him foaming at the mouth and bellowing to raise St. Cadoc's . . ."

They were silent, anticipation on their faces. Ellie cried:

"And then?"

"Then, out o' the Three Bells comes Teddy Grey-Cambourne wi' six pints aboard and the froth still on his whiskers, and he hadn't a leg under him. Up he goes to the mad Siberian, and says polite, 'My dear man, pray, what *is* all this noise about? Why all this confounded commotion?' I tell ye, I stood petrified. 'Stop it at once, please,' says he. 'Do you realise you're causing a breach of public order? I arrest you, my boy, under clause four of *Defence of the Realm.*' And with that he pulled out a little scented handkerchief, and tussled it under the animal's muzzle . . ."

"*No!*" bellowed McAndrew.

"He *did* – ye mind the size of him – five foot one? Up he went on tiptoe and dangled that lace handkerchief under Siberia's nose.

"So there was his lordship staggering about and the seven-foot bear following him, sniffing at the handkerchief. 'Come and have a little toddy with me, my friend,' says he, and takes him through the door of the Three Bells, with the clients going head first through the windows, their quarts still in their hands. And shall I tell ye more? He had that bruin sitting in the tap when the trainers came with nets and ropes – sitting there with a quart o' Guinness in front of him, sniffing at the scented handkerchief."

The men shouted laughter, bantering, pushing their way to the table for more drink. Megsie lifted dismayed hands at Ellie, who raised her eyes and nodded. The maid cleared away the tea, and Ellie, taking one last look at the empty drive of the western gate, said, clapping her hands:

"Gentlemen, gentlemen. It is nearly five o'clock. We really must get started."

"You're right, Miss Ellie," shouted a wag. "I'm seeing her at six."

"With the size of this agenda I fear she's in for a wait," said Ellie. "Mr. McAndrew, kindly open the meeting."

When all were seated, McAndrew said, "Gentlemen, the meeting's informal, as you can see. The idea, mainly, is to get ye ashore once in a while, for the welfare of sea-farers is dear to the hearts of all owners, as you well know . . ."

The captains laughed.

"For God's sake get on with it," whispered Ellie.

"To give a detailed run-down would take all day," continued McAndrew, "so I'm restricting the report to basic facts. And, the first fact is this one – Cambourne Freighters, thanks to you, is on the way up. It may not be news to all of you, but we are now no longer a subsidiary of the Barry Railway Company, but a limited company with a paid up capital exceeding half a million – and another quarter of a million in stock."

There was applause at this. McAndrew continued, "From the beginning of next June we're offering three per cent debenture and four per cent first preference, with a standing capital of a hundred thousand pounds ordinary undivided stock. And this, mark me, after all outgoings have been accounted for and accountants' signatures are obtained.

"The profits – and since Miss Ellie has made you all shareholders, you've a right to know – are up by two per cent to eighty thousand in the first three months of this year. But, of course," and here McAndrew lowered his voice, "there is a long, long way to go. Yard facilities, major repairs are not available here in Barry. Yet this is the centre point, the fulcrum of our trade. We will press, as a management, with everything in our power to get full port facilities; while you keep us at sea, gentlemen, we will keep you on land.

"A break with the Barry company was inevitable. In trooping, they tell us, lies profit. Is that a fact! I tell you this – there was never any profit in transporting men and equipment, to South Africa or any other place. The War Office, gentlemen, is too skilled in the art of cutting transport throats for there to be profit margins worth having in war. Boots, guns, cloth, ammunitions, manufacture – yes, but not trooping. And the day we broke affiliation with the parent company was the best day of our lives; one which the grand old bear-baiter, Teddy Cambourne, would have celebrated."

McAndrew raised his glass and drank. Ellie, he noticed, was staring through the window to the drive beyond, like a woman lost. He continued:

"Now, to come to the ships themselves – the major tools of our trade; the reason why you're here . . ."

His voice boomed on. Ellie sat, apparently intent upon every word, yet with the demeanour of a woman who was listening out of loyalty.

Normally, it was her delight to listen to McAndrew. He had the magic to grasp and hold an audience, rendering it captive. But Ellie's mind had flown beyond the jargon of the sea and its business.

Sitting there, with McAndrew's voice thundering above her, her own internal silence seemed to narcotise her, inducing sleep.

The sun was already darkening on the lawns beyond the window and still Ross Bolton did not come. She began to wonder if she had sent him an invitation, and then remembered that McAndrew always took care of those. The tiny painting signed by Seurat, now hanging near her bed, seemed the only link between the now enchaining life of Cambourne Freighters and the romantic freedom offered by Ross.

"For God's sake, Ellie, don't doze off," whispered McAndrew, and she heard him say:

"And now, gentlemen, to the main subject – the business of buying. Money that isn't working is dross, and ships are at a premium. Therefore, it's the board's intention to buy another three freighters, which will bring the Cambourne fleet to thirteen." He straightened. "These, gentlemen, will be based on the Clyde. Provisional deposits – subject to contracts – have already been paid, and . . ."

His voice diminished into silence. A hand crept to his beard and he grinned wide as he gazed over their heads.

"Tommy lad," he said, "Now what the heck are ye doing here?"

Tom was standing in the doorway to the hall. He was dressed in oilskins, with a sou'wester set sideways on his head; in one hand he held a bucket, in the other a fishing-rod. He said, simply:

"I'm ready, Papa. If we go now, we'll catch the tide, remember?"

Ellie was on her feet. "Tommy! Leave here this moment. Your father's busy . . ."

183

"No, no . . . hang on," said McAndrew.

"Mr. McAndrew, I insist that he goes. . . !"

The captains were chattering now, turning in their seats for a sight of the child. Shouted greetings and waves greeted Tom's appearance. Ellie made to go, but her husband gripped her wrist.

"No, wait, Ellie. He's the son and heir of the place, don't ye know? One day he'll be standing here addressin' these same men, perhaps. Don't you make him small." McAndrew beckoned. "Aye, son, come here! The captains are delighted to see ye."

The small figure wound a path through the chairs to where McAndrew and Ellie were standing. Man and boy faced each other. Tom said,

"Unless we go now, Papa, we'll miss the herrings . . ."

There was a silence; the mettle of its importance was apparent: most there were fathers. Tom said,

"Half-past-five it is, says Megsie. We're late already, Papa. We . . . we've got to catch the herring, and . . ."

McAndrew explained to the men, "The herrings come in on the tide, as perhaps ye might know. And the tide is slippin' in half an hour from now . . ."

"You must go, McAndrew. You've no choice," called a man.

Ellie said, coming round the desk, "Oh no, I'm not having this. A child of three and he breaks up a company meeting?" She made to take the boy's hand. Smiling, McAndrew restrained her, saying:

"Och no, it's a reasonable request . . ." He turned to the men. "I've promised the lad twice before, so he's within his rights," and Captain Ben Reed called from the back seats, guffawing:

"If ye let this financial nonsense break a promise to a child, McAndrew, you're not the fella I took ye for. Away fishin' with the pair of you, and give Miss Ellie the floor."

"I'll never forgive ye for this, McAndrew," whispered Ellie, as, hand in hand with Tom, he left to the cheers and laughter of the captains.

*

Dusk fell, then darkness.

"Got him!"

McAndrew hauled out the fishing-line and the mackerel shone in wriggling phosphorescence, flapping across the concrete of the Two Dock caisson. The still waters of the dock were shafted with the yellow lights of moored ships and drooping hawsers.

Amid the labouring activity of the docks, the chugging of donkey engines, the deeper grumbling of the giant cranes, they knelt, McAndrew and Tom; a stone came down. The fish died, its iris eye glinting at the moon.

"That's put an end to his capers."

"Is he a herring?"

"O, aye, he's a herring." McAndrew held the mackerel up by its tail. "Have ye got the biscuit-tin lid?"

"Aye, Papa, under me coat."

"And the matches?"

"Cor, no! We're rubbing sticks together. Remember you said?"

"God help us," said McAndrew in his breath, and seized Tom's hand. "*Come!* Away to the woods!"

A group of soldiers lounging nearby beneath the gangplank of a troop-ship bound for South Africa, watched them go.

The woods were sombre around the Cadoxton River.

From here, surrounded by elms, McAndrew could actually see the lights of Cambourne. Tom knelt before him in a jubilation of excitement. To have deserted him this time, thought McAndrew, would have been a major crime of indifference.

The fire McAndrew had surreptitiously lighted with a match in Tom's absence gathering wood – after frantic efforts to make fire in boy-scout fashion. Now the red flames leaped up between the stones, lighting the intent faces of man and boy.

A little wind blew through the new spring branches; the whole earth, thought McAndrew, was coming alive with smells and perfumes: the lesser celandine and his favourite, the wood anemone – its faint scent contrasting with marsh-marigolds from the nearby river and the pungent smell of burning elm. He knew them all and could identify them.

Barren 'strawberry he had seen growing earlier, in the undergrowth of the woods; early sorrel entangling the common chickweed as he and Tom came running to this spot.

Now the crescent moon lay on its back on the tops of the Cambourne elms and the night was filled with the chirping of birds. A barn owl, worried by their continued presence, rose from his perch and flapped lazily into the night: earlier, it had caught and eaten a mother dormouse, then raked out her nest and devoured her young.

Tom was watching the fish sizzling on the tin; McAndrew was listening to the night, its wildness calling him.

"Is it done, Papa?"

"*Eh?*"

"Is he done? Can we eat him?"

"Och, you scavenger, give the fish a chance!" With sticks they turned it. Steam arose, tainting the forest air with fishy smells. A Cambourne cat, eyes closed in an after-meal, ginger siesta, twitched its nose to a little wind from the river, and slowly raised its head.

"Are ye hungry?"

"Aye, Papa!"

"We're goin' to get topped for this, you know. She'll have the pair of us wi' the same fist, for sure."

"Me, too?"

"You more'n likely, unless I speak for ye. Your mither's right, ye coot, ye should be abed. And d'ye realise I'm due on the ten o'clock from Cardiff? At this rate, I'll be in London on the blutty milk train."

Tom's eyes were bright in the firelight, his small red hands screwing together. Staring about him, he said: "Being out late in the woods like this, d'you think monsters'll get us?"

"Likely so, if we hang about." McAndrew turned the fish again. "See, he's as brown as a Welsh cake. Have you some stones to eat from?"

"Here!" Tom pushed them up.

The saliva was wet on his red lips, his small face puckered with a tremulous delight. McAndrew stripped off the flesh and forked it on to the stones.

"And mind ye mouth. It's as hot as Hades."

They ate, kneeling, gasping at the steam, oohing and aahing at the scald of it; holding up the bones and sucking them through their teeth.

"Never, never did I taste the like of that," said McAndrew. "Sure to God, it was a meal for a king."

They lay together in the refuse of past autumns, while the moon sailed above them on the scudding clouds of night. Hand in hand they lay, and for McAndrew life was suddenly timeless; a timelessness of nothing, soundless save for his son's rhythmic breathing beside him and the sigh of the wind in the elms.

A night-bird called, its mate replied: both rose in clattering branches for a safer destination, away from the smell of humans. McAndrew saw them, and longed . . .

He longed again for the sound of boots striking the road: for the cold, white meal of the frosted fields, the aching of long-numbed fingers, the blaze of a roadside fire. He slept, but did not know for how long; to awake stiff and cold, instantly turning to his son.

The child breathed against him; his small, cold face in the folds of his father's coat.

"Ah, ye sweet wee thing." McAndrew rose, with the boy in his arms.

In this manner he carried him through the woods, along the river and over the bailiff's bridge to the duck-pond, taking the path that Tuesday had taken.

Ellie, white-faced, was standing in the hall.

"You damned fool! D'you realise the time? It's nine-thirty and you're due on the Cardiff train at ten. Are ye raving mad these days?"

Reaching out she took the sleeping child. "The trap's waiting. Get going, for God's sake, or you'll miss your connection. Your case is in the hall."

McAndrew smiled, kissing Tom's face.

187

18

McAndrew arrived at Barry station as his connecting train with Cardiff was steaming out. In his cloak and top hat he stood watching as it disappeared around a bend.

"Sorry, sir, I did my best," said the driver.

"Think nothing of it. Take me to the Dock Hotel. I'll wet me whistle and stay the night."

"You're not going home, sir?" The man lowered the overnight case.

"Oblige me by explaining to me ever-loving wife. I'll stay the night and catch the milk train."

The trap stopped outside the Chain Locker, the bar of the Dock Hotel. McAndrew, rising in the trap, could see above the rails into the bar: the place was crammed to the doors with navvies.

Sitting on a high stool at the gaudy bar, with his back to the door, was Jean Pierre, the French dwarf.

"Shall I wait, Sir?" asked the driver.

McAndrew rubbed his face with the back of his hand.

It was a situation that demanded time and coolness.

Entering the hotel's main entrance, McAndrew went to the reception desk.

"I'll stay the night," he said.

The pasty, frightened face of the clerk stared back at him.

"Yes . . . yes, Sir."

"What time's the milk train?"

"For Cardiff? Three a.m. Sir . . ." The man looked about him like something trapped. "Will you sign your name, Mr. McAndrew?"

"Certainly."

"I . . . I'll take your case . . ."

"Leave it. I tell you what, you can hold me coat." McAndrew took off his cloak and draped it over the desk. "Excuse me."

Pushing past the clerk he went down to the Chain Locker.

In the pin-drop silence as he opened the door, all heads turned slowly in his direction.

The high stool at the bar was empty.

The navvies stared in silent consternation. One, cursed with double chins and ribald humour, shouted, "We ain't seen arse nor hair of you these years back, Sir. Come in, come in . . ." His voice tapered into the vacuum of the room, his eyes switched nervously to the vacant stool.

"Where is he?" asked McAndrew.

"You really is a man and a half, ain't you! I remember . . ."

"And you're a son of a bitch," said McAndrew, pushing past him. "Where is he? He was here just now."

"You know dwarfs," said a barmaid, polishing, "they go up blutty chimneys."

She was new, bright-haired and pert and her blouse was undone.

The men laughed with surly banter, grumbling, unafraid but uncertain. The barmaids drew away in mock alarm and astonishment as McAndrew dropped half a sovereign on the counter.

Pinta, Rosa's tinker relative, sat unseen in a corner behind a pint pewter.

"Make it a quart," said the Scot. A foot on the bar rail, he gazed around the room. One of the barmaids poured the ale. She was new to McAndrew, possessing a nymph-like beauty, reminding him of Tuesday. He said, out of context:

"Ye wouldn'a be putting me on now, would you?"

Of a sudden he knew a sad, drag-net loneliness. He saw the

room in the golden tip of the ale. The noise was thunderous now, the tension lost in beer swilling and shuffled saw-dust. A man in a corner began to play a Jew's harp, stamping the time. McAndrew listened, his eyes switching about him: Jean Pierre, he sensed, was in the vicinity.

The talk was mainly of the new railway Rhymney branch line, due to be opened for traffic in the following year.

Many of the men were building the new valley viaduct behind Castell Goch, and the working height over the Taff was a hundred and twenty feet.

"Did ye hear that, gentlemen?" said one, confronting the Scotsman. He was a huge man with a merry Irish face and shoulders on him like a barn ox; McAndrew's eyes drifted over him.

"Hear what?" He gulped at his ale.

"That we're working over a hundred feet above the river."

"So what? Ye can kill yourself by falling ten."

"So you don't give credit for working at height? For that's our claim. We reckon to be paid over the odds."

"That's right and fair. But what's it to do with me?"

The man's blue eyes danced in his face. "Jesus, I worked on the Menai Bridge, you know, up in Anglesey. And the little rivet-baggers – they was no more than bloody kids – used to climb to the suspension wires with the bags. We lost four in the Menai – dropped into the Swillies. Two shillings a day. Bad cess to the bosses. The same bloody thing's happening on Walnut Tree Viaduct, you see. Is it right you're an employer?"

"Aye, God help me." McAndrew frowned into the light.

That dwarf must be laughing his head off, he thought.

"The Barry Railway Company?"

McAndrew idly leaned backwards, trying to see over the bar. "Not now."

"But you're a boss, still, is it?"

"Aye." On tiptoe now, he tried to see out of the window.

"Then will ye speak for us? For it's a crying shame to see the young boys up at height – Christ, some are no bigger than leprechauns." The navvy took the pewter McAndrew slid towards him and drank, gasping: jagged, slack veins at the man's temples began to bulge ominously. McAndrew said:

"Sink a rye to settle your nerves, mun, and I'll speak to someone in the morning. Walnut Tree Viaduct, ye say?"

"Aye, just that we're wanting over the odds for height."

The navvy drank again, looked past McAndrew at the bar and made large eyes in his face.

"I know," said McAndrew, "the wee bastard." Taking his quart he bent over the bar and threw the contents under the counter.

"Now then, now then. . . !" cried the barmaid. "What the hell are you up to?"

"I apologise for spilling me ale, woman."

"Oh, for God's sake, Dada!" cried the barmaid. "He's splashed my new dress. Just look at my dress!"

"What's all this, what's all this?" cried the landlord, coming up.

"He's tossed his ale over me dress," said she, plaintively. "Call him a gentleman?" She eyed McAndrew.

Beneath the bar counter Jean Pierre sat in soaked misery, one hand over his absinthe.

"It was an accident, landlord," cried the navvy. "Mark, Mary and Joseph! Would you have the gentleman's life-blood? D'ye think he did it on purpose?"

"Fill 'em up," said McAndrew.

"Right," said the landlord, "but no funny business, mind. They had trouble with you 'afore I took over, I heard say."

"It's a slander!"

More navvies were coming in now, the late shift off the Walnut Tree Viaduct, and most of them lodging in Barry, and the great Chain Locker bar was as tight as a barrel of herrings, with men halloing left and right.

Big men, most of these, with their clothes in rags, their breeks yorked at the knees with leather or tied with string: grimed and mud-caked, their faces were lined with weariness.

"Who's this coon, then?" A big one elbowed his way up to

McAndrew at the bar. "Tell him to remove his bloody top hat when he comes in here."

"You try removing it," said McAndrew.

"Now now, mind your tempers!" The landlord had his barrel-tapper now, his face as red as a turkey's wattle.

"Me temper's fine," said McAndrew, "it's saucy people raising it." He drank, grinning, and bought the big man a quart.

"Will ye speak for us, then, sir?" This from the earlier navvy.

"Aye, I will. I said so, didn't I?"

"Employers! They've more under the floor boards than Protestant bishops."

Pinta, the Gilwern Fair tinker, safe in a distant corner, watched McAndrew over the rim of his mug, and did not speak.

With a big farmer on a chair in the middle of the floor, blindfolded, McAndrew gave him a glass of water.

"Taste that, and tell me," said he.

"Water," said the farmer.

"Now this. And it's pints all round, mind, if you fall by the way," and he gave him a pint of stout.

"Stout," said the farmer, sipping it.

"And this?" McAndrew gave him beer.

"Beer," said the farmer.

"And this," and he was given a mug of water to sip.

"Stout," said the farmer.

"Drinks all round," said McAndrew.

The navvies guffawed, raising their pewters, and the language coming up was enough to singe the tail off Satan said the landlord, and what the hell's the use of puttin' a lady behind the bar. McAndrew, getting tipsy, cried:

"Now I'll try ye on this one – though by the look of you there isn't a glimmer of intelligence among you, to say nothing of art."

He raised his hands for silence in the ensuing uproar. "I'll lay ye – a whisky for every man in the room, that I'll do you a drawing – a fine drawing of an African village with palm trees and a river and a sugar-cane plantation, and a boat and a fella catching a fish, and the moon shining through the clouds – and a pair of bloody cannibals thrown in – all in ten seconds."

"You'll draw all that in ten seconds."

"In ten seconds or less."

"And if ye lose?"

"A whisky for every man here, like I say."

"The gentleman's cuckoo," said the barmaid, and a navvy asked, softly:

"A drawing of Africa, is it?"

"Aye, of darkest Africa. And the landlord'll be the judge."

They crowded closer, their faces alight with interest.

"And what's it to you, then?"

"A bottle o' whisky, for I'm as parched as a desert."

"You're on."

"You're sure, now, because ye going to lose, the damned lot of ye."

"Bets laid, gentleman! Start drawing."

"Bring me a box of matches, a candle and a saucer," said McAndrew.

The barmaid brought them, handing them over the bar.

They were intent as McAndrew lighted the candle and smoked the back of the saucer.

As intent as children, they watched, breath pent.

Suffering was in their faces. Their cheeks, pock-marked by the frosted winds of the Stockton-Darlington, were now the humps which held their sunken eyes. Their ears were bloodless and thin, bitten by cold; under the grimed and whiskered faces were the tell-tale lines of ravaging hungers, the childhood scavenging in the bins of Derry, Newcastle, Liverpool and the Clyde. The vein-nosed old and the peak-faced young, all craned their necks for a look at the drawing, their faces split in white grins of youth or red, gummy age. But all bones ached to the breaking and dumping, the bar-rowing, boring, lifting and packing, the drilling and wedging; the shivering of wet working.

They fought hard and beat their women, these men,

cherishing their children by sending money home to the little North Country houses sitting shoulder to shoulder against the wind, or the mud-walled cabins of Londonderry and Cork. They possessed deep prides, and the foremost of these was comradeship. If a Newcastle marrer was down on his hunks, you put him up an Irish leg. So they thumbed their mugs or drank or blew off the froth, and stood silently like scolded children, watching, and there was no sound but their breathing and the scratching of McAndrew's match.

He, grinning, with the saucer held up to the light for all to see, drew away the soot with the tip of the match and the African plantation, the village, the palm trees, the boat, the man fishing, the cannibals, the river and the clouded moon, sprang into life.

"Finished," said McAndrew, and flicked away the match.

"*Well!*"

"Seven seconds," said the landlord. "Would you credit it."

"Is it the picture I promised?"

They moved, in bass acknowledgment and acclamation. It was fair. Their smiles were wide, their hands reaching for their money.

"Make it Johnny Walker," said McAndrew, and cried, "Now shall I tell you who taught me that? It was a little French dwarf. The finest artist I ever did see. Aye, in Montmartre I saw it done, and I've been drinking on it since. It's not what ye draw, gentlemen, it's what you leave out, d'you see?"

Jean Pierre, the French dwarf, dripping under the bar, lowered his absinthe and pricked up his ears.

McAndrew shouted, putting the saucer on the bar, "Aye, gentlemen, to my mind the world's greatest artist. The man who paints humanity as it is, shorn of its conventions and facades. Now watch this!" and he staggered to a wall, bottle in hand, and the navvies moved aside, shouting for room.

"What you up to, Mister?" called the landlord apprehensively.

Dipping his fingers into the nearest navvy's ale, Mc-

Andrew drew on the distempered walls. Ten strokes . . . and the profile of a man appeared. Near-bald, bespectacled, thick-lipped, prod-nosed, he grew into shape. His straggling beard came next, then the small, bespectacled eyes that peered into the room through pince-nez spectacles. The navvies gasped. And Jean Pierre, unable to contain his curiosity, raised his head and peeped over the bar counter.

"Get down, ye fool," whispered the landlord. "Down, or he'll have ye!"

But Jean Pierre's eyes opened wide in his flattened face and he rose still higher, staring in disbelief as the caricature appeared like magic on the wall.

"Any guesses?" asked McAndrew, standing back.

"*Lautrec!*" shrieked the dwarf. "The Little Treasure! Henri-Marie-Raymond de Toulouse-Lautrec! Wonderful! Magnifique! *Sacrebleu!*"

"Got you, ye little sod," shouted McAndrew and dived head first over the bar.

The dwarf kicked out. In the confined space behind the counter McAndrew took it full and staggered, tripped and fell, taking a barmaid with him. In a tangle of black stockings and petticoats he fell, and down came the wall shelves with the casks and bottles in a crashing of glass and splintering wood. In the screams of the barmaid and the doleful cries of the landlord, Jean Pierre leaped up, vaulted the bar counter, scrambled through the navvies' legs and disappeared through the door, with McAndrew in wobbling pursuit.

Standing on the steps of the Chain Locker he heard Jean Pierre's falsetto laughter as he fled into the night.

"Next time, Jean Pierre. Next time, my friend!" he called. "I thought that would fetch you!"

"Next time – the same!" came the reply.

McAndrew began to laugh. Hands on hips, he raised his face to the moon and shouted laughter.

Almost instantly he was aware of a watcher.

A small girl – he guessed her age at about four – was sitting on the top of the Chain Locker steps.

She was well clad, with strong little boots and white stockings, and the sight of her shawl-framed face pleased him. Her eyes, great in her small, brown face, stared up. The rag doll she held was hard against her.

"Ach, you sweet thing," said McAndrew, and bent to her.

She smiled and he saw in that smile her tinker beauty.

"What's your doll's name?" He touched her hair with the tips of his fingers. A voice said:

"Leave the child alone."

McAndrew straightened. "Is she yours?"

"Aye."

"And is she sitting out here, while you're pubbin' it inside then?"

"My business," said Pinta. "Get going."

McAndrew said, "Haven'a I seen you before some time?"

"Likely so, but I ain't seen you. Get going, I said – interfering with the child."

"Christ, man, I've one of me own . . ."

McAndrew closed his eyes. When he opened them again the eyes of the little girl were full upon his face.

"Likely so," said Pinta. "Get going just the same."

Turning, the Scot went, to save himself the sin of murder.

Lying fully dressed on the bed of his hotel room, McAndrew awoke to a touch on his shoulder.

Sober, drunk, he slept in the manner of the vagabond, one eye open in his soul, when the slur of a foot in leaves, the snap of a twig brought wakefulness.

A woman was standing beside his bed.

In the light of the window moon he saw her and raised himself on an elbow.

Getting out, he struck a match: the gas mantle glowed.

The woman was dressed in a white gown that reached to her feet. She was young; her hair, bright fair, was tied with white ribbons; she possessed in that soft light, the air of a sleeping-walking nun.

"Good evening, Mr. McAndrew."

The Scot knuckled his eyes. Fumes of alcohol were sweeping over his numbed brain in psychedelic colours, and he focused her in vain. Then the vision of the woman made shape again.

"What the devil do you want?"

"Oh yes, you're running true to form, McAndrew. They told me you weren't a gentleman."

He had seen the woman before. Spectres out of the past invaded him, nagging him with querulous insistence; faces on pillows, faces in straw. Making love, he always thought, was merely a graft of loving; the lost faces became as unsubstantial as their kisses. He just couldn't place her, and said, to gain time:

"What do you expect? It's a stuffed shirt community, of rags. It's short on grace and good manners. Nobody here has even heard of Homer, Goethe or Galileo, so why should I be different?" He rubbed his face. "I asked ye who you were."

"The common law wife of Captain Ross Bolton."

He was at the window. This turned him.

"Well?"

"It should mean something to you, I hope."

"It does."

He had placed her.

He had seen her before at the Angel Hotel, on the night he had met Lord Grey-Cambourne. She looked older now, he thought; more used by life, but still vitally alive.

"Does your husband know you're here?"

"No."

"Then what do you think I can do for ye, girl?"

"I'm a miserable woman, Mr. McAndrew. You have the ability to lift the load. There are times . . ."

"Man trouble?" McAndrew wandered around her. "Then we've something in common, for I've got trouble with me woman." He turned his back upon her. "Forgive the bowels of compassion, but it strikes me we're all gagged, bound and executed at birth. What's he been up to?"

She said, sitting down on the bed, "He . . . he didn't attend the afternoon meeting at Cambourne today, did he?"

"No."

"Yet you expected him?"

"Yes."

"Do you know why he didn't come?"

"I've no doubt you'll tell me."

"He didn't attend because he didn't want to see you."

"That's reasonable. Only his mother considers Bolton a real contribution to humanity."

"That isn't your wife's opinion."

"Perhaps not, but we're all entitled to our views. Can I go back to sleep now, or is this a school for scandal?"

"It will be if the servants find out, Mr. McAndrew. Right now he's in her bed."

He took a deep breath.

"Ellie'd have the hair off your head for saying that."

"If you doubt me, go to Cambourne and find out for yourself. God, I'll kill him for this!"

McAndrew didn't move as her sudden fury beat about them both. He had misjudged this one, he thought. God help Bolton. She was a tough Lancashire girl, no milk-sop, and she added, furiously:

"You don't bloody care, do you!"

"Not all that much."

He stared about him with false vacuity.

"That's a pity, I hoped you would. It's been going on for a long time – their mutual attraction, I mean. But now it has come to a head. Some strange twist of fate must have brought you here tonight, do you realise that?"

He did not hear what she said although his brain recorded the sense of it, and the poignancy of it rose like a small sickness within him so that he swallowed it down. Then came anger.

The woman was speaking again, her voice anguished, like a woman on a cross. McAndrew asked faintly:

"What . . . what did you say?"

"I said that I'd stay here tonight if you'd let me. I'm not everybody's woman, and . . ."

McAndrew opened the door. "Go now. You'll feel better in the morning, and your position's stronger if ye keep yourself clean. And me?" He touched her hair as she passed him

198

and it was like worn gold in his hands. "Well . . . I've already had enough young lovers to satisfy my caprices."

"And them?" She nodded towards the window.

"Ach, be generous. Life's short. Let 'em enjoy themselves. Who knows, we'll all be dead tomorrow."

"You're a very strange man." She stared back at him: her eyes in that light were like the eyes of an animal.

"I'm that bloody strange that they say I'm mad."

"They're not far wrong, Mr. McAndrew. But I'm sane."

He stood watching her. Bolton, it appeared, was in for a rough passage.

Cambourne was in darkness when McAndrew reached it. The house stood like an empty sentinel guarding the ruins of his broken world. McAndrew entered the side entrance, using his key, and walked quietly down the corridors to the west wing where Ellie slept.

Earlier, from the east wing, he had heard Caesar whining softly, but ignored it.

Now he was in the main hall. The winding staircase leading to the balcony rooms faced him, their wrought ironwork of gilt and gold shining in the window light of the moon.

McAndrew could hear voices; the deep grumble of a man's, a woman's lighter replies. The door of Ellie's room was shut; he moved silently towards it, listened, then knocked.

In a night whisper, he said, "Miss Ellie, Miss Ellie! Quick, open the door!"

"Who is it?" called Ellie; fear, he sensed, was in her voice.

"Come quickly, oh, please come quick! It's Cook."

"Just a minute."

McAndrew heard Ellie's gasping haste within the room. She said something unintelligible, and he presumed it was to Bolton; now her feet were thudding on the carpeted floor. Her hands fumbled on the lock. The key turned.

"What's wrong, for God's sake?"

Ellie swung open the door. Her eyes widened with disbelief and horror as she recognised McAndrew and her hand instinctively flew to the top of her night-dress.

"What . . . what do you want. . . ?"

But McAndrew had already pushed past her into the room.

Bolton was sitting up in bed, rubbing his eyes with the air of a man awakened from deep slumber. He stared up as McAndrew reached him, yelled with astonishment as he was pulled out of the bed.

Naked, he staggered away and lay against the wall by the bed; the utter astonishment of his face was now replaced by panic. His eyes switched, seeking escape as McAndrew struck, but the blow was glancing and Bolton, shouting, lurched away.

Reaching out, McAndrew caught him and hauled him back, steadied his aim and hit short; Bolton took it full in the face, crashed back against the wall and slowly slid down to the floor, his arms outstretched in appeal, like a crucified doll.

Now Ellie was beside McAndrew. She cried, "Jim, Jim, for God's sake. . . !" Then rushed past him and knelt beside Bolton. She began hysterically to call endearments to him, stroking his face; kneeling, holding him against her.

McAndrew closed his eyes. He felt his soul crumbling. Ellie was saying, in broken sobs:

"Oh, my love, my darling! I didn't know he'd come. Oh God, I'm sorry, I'm so sorry. . . !"

Still on her knees she glared up at McAndrew. "You've killed him – look, you've killed him, ye great filthy bear – look at his poor face. . .!" With the tips of her fingers she wiped away blood from Bolton's cheek. "Ye'll never part us, Mr. McAndrew – not now we've found each other – never! D'ye hear me?"

For answer McAndrew reached down, caught her arm, lifted her up and threw her across the dishevelled bed. Stooping, he dragged Bolton upright, bent, and flung him across his back.

"Put him down! Put him down!"

"Aye, I will. After you've woken the servants and they've seen what you're worth, ye little whore."

"And you – what about you, you damned hypocrite?"

200

McAndrew kicked open the bedroom door. "I only took mine when I couldn't get you, woman!"

With Bolton, still as naked as birth, sagging on his back, the Scot strode off.

"I'll call the police. Put him down!"

"Call 'em, and we'll tell the whole of Barry. What would they say about this in the Chamber of Trade? Or don't ye care any more now I've built the thing up for you?"

Reaching down, he opened the main entrance door and ran down the steps into the night, while Ellie, lifting the hem of her night-dress, ran beside him, alternatively fuming with anger and begging forgiveness.

"Where are you going? What are ye going to do?" she wailed.

"I'm goin' to cool the bugger down. You, too, if ye don't watch it."

The duck-pond was coming nearer in the moonlight. Ellie was hanging on to Bolton's legs now, her bare feet skidding on the wet grass as McAndrew towed her after him.

"You wouldn't dare!"

"We'll see, bonnie lass!"

"Mr. McAndrew! I am ordering you . . ."

"Those days are over, Ellie. Act like a whore and you'll get the biblical treatment."

"Please, oh please!"

He saw her face white and startled, and her eyes were filled with terror, and his pity for her, and his love, seemed to wander away from him at that moment of begging, like a down-at-heel man he had never known.

Bolton, recovering consciousness, was stiffly moving, his strength returning and McAndrew gripped him.

"Jim, in the name of our boy, please listen to me. Please let me explain. . .!"

"Don't you mention him, ye set bitch."

Suddenly McAndrew felt the sadness we feel towards another's tragedy; deep within him some lost thing was crying aloud with its hands over its face. This, he thought vaguely, was perhaps the essence of love.

Now Ellie was tearing at Bolton's limbs in an effort to dislodge him from her husband's grip, but McAndrew freed a hand and pushed her away.

On the edge of the duck-pond he raised the man high, and Bolton lay for a moment in a posture of naked sacrifice, his arms and legs feebly moving, before McAndrew threw him. The pond splashed. From the bulrushes rose ducks in a commotion of wings and squawks. Frogs awoke and began their interminable croaking. The slumbering water burst into a cacophony of life.

Ellie cried, "You swine, McAndrew! You damned swine!"

"Now you!" said he, and reached out, snatched Ellie against him, lifted her and threw her in beside Bolton, who was slowly raising himself, weed-covered, like some emerging prehistoric monster.

McAndrew turned away. "Now carry on from where you were interrupted."

19

"Where is he?"

Jake replied, "In his study, as usual. This is a hell of a house and I'll be glad to be at sea again. How does he think a man can sleep?"

"Hush," whispered Ellie. "Listen . . ."

Jake peered at her in the faint moonlight. "God, one moment I was in the arms of Morpheus, next there were trumpeting elephants. What's happening?"

"He's on the bottle again."

"Aye, and making enough palaver for a madhouse."

And Ellie said, her eyes steady: "That's because he is mad, and I've only just realised it." They crept together on bare feet over the cold mosaic floor.

Unknown to either of them, Megsie and Cook, side by side in sleeping-gowns and lace-frilled night-caps, were peering around the door of the servants' quarters.

"Heaven help our poor mistress, I say," observed Cook, and she wiped her double chins with a large red handkerchief, and wept.

"Don't take on so, my love," replied Megsie. "Six of one and half a dozen of the other, I always say, but if I was a man and had her for a missus, I'd never be sober. She's been carryin' on with that Ross Bolton chap, you know?"

"Stop that at once. The very idea!" said Cook.

McAndrew roared anew; a drunken brawl of a song that battered off the east wing study and echoed through the house.

"If this continues I shall send for the police," said Ellie with finality. "I shall . . ."

"I wouldn't do that if I were you, my love," said Jake.

Towards dawn the drunken revelry died. There was no sound now but a faint dawn chorus of awakening birds and the sighing of a little wind from the sea.

Ellie awoke stiff and cold in her armchair. Rising, she went to the window of her room and listened, her face taut. She swung about as a faint knock came on her door.

"Yes?" Her hand was on the lock.

"It's Jake. Let me in."

Her father said as she opened the door, "He's gone, Ellie."

"Gone?" She searched his face for truth in the half light.

"Aye, woman – gone. I've searched his rooms, there's no sign nor smell of him. I've been upstairs to Tommy's room. He's safe, his door's still locked." Jake peered at her. "But he has left some'at behind him, woman, that you ought to see."

Ellie followed her father down the long corridors.

The door of the study was wide open. One side of a wall-case had been pulled down and had spilled its contents over the parquet floor, the room was littered with empty wine bottles. The inkwells of a writing desk had been overturned. On the wallpaper behind the broken wall-case was a drawing that stretched from floor to ceiling, commanding the room in its enormity.

It was the life-size drawing of a woman in black underclothes. Half naked, her back to the viewer, she wore black stockings and money was scattered at her feet: more had been tossed upon the end of the rumpled bed. And the woman was looking at her reflection in an unheld mirror. Ellie saw the blousy, painted face, the false beauty spot upon the cheek.

"'The Whore at Toilet,'" whispered Jake to himself, and slowly sat down, assimilating the shock. Turning, he stared at Ellie with frightened eyes. "For heaven's sake . . . do ye see the title? Such a thing as that – here, in this house?"

Ellie's hand crept to her throat; a board creaked and it swung her about.

Cook and Megsie were peering around the half-open door.

Ellie shrieked, leaping up, "Get out! *Out*, d'ye hear me?"

The footsteps scurried into silence. Jake was now standing motionless, staring up at the painting, a man without words. Ellie said, softly:

"But who . . . who's it supposed to be, for God's sake?"

Jake did not reply.

"Who?" She shouted the question. Jake answered faintly: "It . . . it's got your face, Ellie . . ."

She thumped herself with a fist. "You mean it's supposed to be me? What, in God's name, have I done to deserve that? Just Ross Bolton? Talk sense! He calls me that – he paints that of me – after McAndrew's own behaviour?"

The last recorded knowledge in the year 1900 concerning James Alexander McAndrew (again, according to Professor Ratza Spielman, his biographer) is an entry in the log of the S.S. *Turk* which left Barry on the dawn tide of that morning bound for Cape Town with the 14th Dorsetshire Regiment aboard. An entry in the captain's own hand, reads:

The owner of Cambourne Freighters, James Alexander McAndrew Esq., came aboard (plus one small animal) for the voyage to Cape Town. I received his instructions that nobody ashore was to be informed.

Book Three

20

1905

There was more happening than in a Bedlam mad-house.

The Ridings of Yorkshire, come April, lie round and cold under the moons of spring, but summer came early to the dales that year. The winds blew warm from the south, the rocks and scars were soft buttresses to the night, not threats; the sun booted wailing winter out of it.

So the winds of this pretender summer came gentle, said McAndrew, all perfumed with the smells of an awakening earth. Moles and badgers burrowed and swept with new vigour, new generations of rabbits ran bob-tailed to the snares and guns of the tinker poachers.

And an early nightingale, which he saw before, was singing in the high branches of elms surrounding the forest clearing, especially arrived, said Mrs. Tinker Bob, for the Travellers' Orgy. McAndrew watched it with tears in his eyes. Saliva bubbles from its upturned beak were drifting against the crescent moon.

After a bit, when the orgy got going, McAndrew, Raver-in-Chief, was singing, too, with Caesar in full blast at his feet.

"Up, up, *up*! Pick 'em up, Mrs. Bob," cried McAndrew, "by the bloody left, we'll show 'em!" and he armed the old girl around the bonfire, his size elevens stamping the ground, one arm waving, his clothes in tatters.

And she, knocking seventy, her rags fluttering, pulled up her skirt to show her pink bloomers – lifted off a gentry wash-line last spring – and kicked up her match-stick legs with her boots at a quarter-to-three.

Round and round the bonfire they went in the reel, while the tinker band thumped out the rhythm, with Irish maids and young bucks cavorting, and wizened old grans following them on sticks.

A hundred or so travellers were dancing, bottles waving, scarves flying, with urchin children doing cartwheels around the edge of the fire. And you've never heard such a commotion, said Mrs. Tinker Bob, since I paid the rent to the policeman with me father's Irish shillelagh. The bonfire blazed, lighting the faces of the dervishing dancers in a medley of flying skirts of every colour.

"So it's up and up and up and round and round we go," yelled McAndrew, and he flicked up the tail of the tinker's skirt and the clearing rang with hoots and jeers.

"Ach, McAndrew, you're a darlin' fella!" cried she. "Will you dance with me all night, for all you're a Scottish heathen?"

"Christ woman, no!" gasped he. "I'm saving the rest of me for the drinking and loving – loose me, ye old prune."

"Can I lay soft with you, then?"

"That you can, lady," and he knelt and smoothed the forest leaves for her. "Fifty years back, if I'd cornered ye then, you'd be beggin' for mercy."

"Ye dear sweet soul! You're the best thing that's happened since original sin."

As they lay together hand in hand, old woman, young man, the dancing slowly stopped and the people sat huddled and cross-legged around the bonfire. Save for crackling flames the night was silent in the nightingale's song. And Vladimir Timoshenko, a vast, Rasputin-like figure, began to play 'Tom Bowling' on a melodeon, singing in a tuneless, bass voice while tears ran down his riven cheeks.

McAndrew, with Caesar lying against his throat, listened with his face turned away. Mrs. Tinker Bob listened also, her face in the grass. Lover Alf, who could charm any housewife from his rags of gentility, cleaned his fingernails with scrupulous care, smiling at the stars. Blind Jack, who waited at bus stops for old ladies to cross, rolled his opaque eyes around the clearing, seeing all, missing nothing. Nag, the horse man, who could make a devoted slave of a horse by a single whisper into its ear, stared his round, impish face upwards at the moon.

"You believe in God, McAndrew?" asked Mrs. Tinker Bob.

"No."

"Nor me. But I reckon, were he activatin', he'd be playing the melodeon. You ever give him a thought?"

"Aye, once."

"What stopped you since?"

McAndrew said, "One day recent, outside Newcastle, I saw a pair of rooks dropping a baby hedgehog – on stones, you know, to open him up." He smiled at the memory. "Well, I put him in my pocket and took him to a pub I was hitting at that time, and laid him snug in a nest of sheep floss beneath a wall in the garden. 'Seems I just come along in time,' I said to God, and that night the wall fell down and killed the creature and that wall had been standing four hundred years, they told me. I never believed in God after that."

"That's a good enough reason for anyone," said Mrs. Tinker Bob.

There was a smell of burned pines and smouldering wood-ash, and the old woman came up on an elbow. She possessed a face of nobility once, thought McAndrew, but it had died in service to men.

"You seen the Florence people lately?" she asked.

"The Florence people?"

"Rosa Florence. Weren't you and her thick one time?"

"To hell, that was years back." The Scot folded his hands under his head and stared up through a tangleweed of branches. He sighed. "Rosa was sparking that Tam Shenks, if I remember."

"Sparkin'? She were for marrying him. But she didn't."

"Good for Rosa."

"She didn't 'cause she died."

"She died?" It sat McAndrew up.

"In child."

"By Tam Shenks?"

"Could be. I never asked her." Taking a clay pipe out of her rags Mrs. Tinker Bob tapped it on a stone, filled it with herb tobacco and lighted it with a faggot from the fire, aware, as the yawning blaze struck her face that McAndrew was watching her. "Was it your'n, Scotsman?"

But he had bowed his head. The tinker said, "'Cause, if it were your'n, they'll bloody come after you – you and yours down to the third generation. Them's blind people, perhaps, but babies come important and fathers more so. Six I've had in my time, and God, they stretched me, but I always knowed where they come from. 'Where did that come from?' asked my youngest when the last was born – the vans are small, ye know – ye get no privacy. 'Ye papa put it there,' I told him, so he says, 'If she takes all that time getting out, why did she go up there in the first place?' Jesus, it's a life, isn't it?"

"Jesus," said McAndrew, screwing up his hand.

The old woman smiled at the fire. "'What you doing to my mama?' he once asked my old man, and I had no reply for him, but my fella had – a right poetic chap he is. 'The storks get tired flying in from Finland, son,' says he over his shoulder, 'so poor folks like us make the babies in the caravan.' What's wrong with you, Scotsman?" The old woman peered.

"Nothing you'd understand."

"What you want is a drink."

She handed him a bottle of gin and he tipped it high, swigging at it, his eyes clenched, and handed it back.

"Jesus forgive me." He wiped his mouth with the back of his hand.

"Settle yourself, lad," said Mrs. Tinker Bob. "It takes two storks to carry a baby, remember that. But remember, too, that they'll come after ye – you and yours."

Later she said, when the stars were bigger, "Are you an authority on women? I heard tell so."

"I'm an authority on pigs," said McAndrew.

"Because there's a fine set-up young piece watching ye now." Mrs. Tinker Bob jerked her thumb. "Bangle earrings and hair to her waist, look," and McAndrew looked and saw a little way off a young girl standing on the edge of the clearing. She wore a red skirt and yellow dancing bodice, and as he looked so she drew herself up with a fine dignity.

"East Riding tinker – same as Rosa. She's been throbbing like a festering thumb for ye, I heard say, but you'd best keep clear, for Pinta sent her."

McAndrew nodded. "Pinta, eh?"

"With ten young bucks behind him for a rumpus. For all my love for you, son, you've been here too long. Get going."

"That'll be the bloody day!"

"I won't tell ye twice, McAndrew. Get going."

"I go when I please, woman."

"Try it on one leg, then," said Mrs. Tinker Bob, and rose and spat on the earth at his feet and went away into the darkness.

McAndrew slept until dawn, with Caesar watching. Later, with the wind taking a boot to the sky, they were on the road between Fridaythorpe and Wetwang and the sun was coming up and the day was splendid.

At the regulation pace of a hundred and twenty to the minute they went, with Caesar hopping on three legs behind, and at midday came to a great stag elm under which a little wizened man was resting.

"Good day to you," said he.

From a branch above the little man's head three rag dolls were hanging, their necks grotesquely twisted, their tiny faces upturned into the sun: on each doll's chest were the letters R.I.P.

"You've got a major tragedy there," observed McAndrew.

"Murder in the first degree," answered the little man, and indicated Caesar. "You've a fine wee tyke there, unless I'm mistaken."

"He is if he fancies you."

"But he's only got three legs. What happened to the fourth?"

"The Boer War – Relief of Mafeking," replied McAndrew, "but he's not keen on discussing it, so lay off. Who are you, anyway?"

"Toppam, the official hangman – Shanghai gaol."

"And you're still at it?" McAndrew nodded at the dolls.

"I'm a pro, sir, and a professional has got to keep his hand in. I've done over a hundred, you know."

"Really!"

"Oh, aye. St. Peter's got a high regard for me, I reckon, for I send 'em up with the best cranium knot in the business – as clean as wash-days, every one. Chinese, mainly, of course – two Lascars, a Turk and an Irishman. In ten years of trading I never swung on a leg."

"You're a craftsman, without a doubt."

McAndrew squatted beside him under the elm. On a carpet of oxlip he sat, cowslip coloured, their throats opened to catch the sun, and he smelled them, taking deep breaths of their scent, and their heads of peach-like perfumes fell on to his hands like bunches of hanging keys. Their beauty was new to him and he momentarily forgot the stranger.

Caesar was urinating at the bottom of the tree. Mr. Toppam adjusted his bowler hat on the top of his near-bald cranium and examined McAndrew through red-rimmed eyes; corpse eyes that shone hunger from the caverns of his sunken face. Yet there was an elfin beauty about the man that drew McAndrew, and a suffering that stamped all the people of the road; a cleanness despite the grime of his face, and his rags.

It was right and fair, thought McAndrew, that Mr. Toppam, even in his madness, should epitomise nostalgic sincerity.

"What's your name?" the little man suddenly asked.

"James Alexander McAndrew."

"And you are on the road?"

"I am."

214

"Then you're as mad as me, Mr. McAndrew?"

"Quite possibly, Mr. Toppam."

Later that day, striking north, they were in the country of Wintringham, and with the coming of dusk, made camp. Picking up Caesar, McAndrew pointed down the hill to a farm in a distant valley.

"Chicken," he said.

"I used to order my meals like that," announced Toppam.

"And likely got what ye ordered," growled the other. "But this tyke's short on brains. Last time he came back with a turkey."

The sun was sinking over the earth in redness; the trees were pink-tipped, the light soft brown: beside them a brook was splashing its way to the Derwent; the dusk flung up strange perfumes and the evening star came out while Toppam hanged his dolls.

Earlier, while on the road, he had fashioned a new one, a girl. Her body was of reed, her limbs of rushes, her face he planted with daisies and her bonnet he made of barren strawberry.

McAndrew, after making and lighting a fire, lay back against a rock with his boots cocked up and his clay pipe in his mouth. "When's she taking the drop, then?"

"Tomorrow dawn."

"You're a splendid original, d'ye realise that, Mr. Toppam?"

"Her name," said he, "was Chang Su-la . . ."

"In fact, I'd go so far as to say you're a collector's piece, mun."

"She was eighteen years old."

"Uncle Dumb would be delighted with ye. How long have you been on the road, did you say?"

"All your sins remitted, this time tomorrow," said Toppam, kissing the doll, then he smiled up with a naked mouth, answering:

"I don't know how long. Since they shipped me back from China, perhaps? How long, I wonder, is that?" And he began

215

to hum a plaintive oriental tune while his deft, grimey hands positioned the flowers. The other said, sucking at his pipe:

"Would ye like to live in a house, Mr. Toppam? A fine, big house where ye can do as you please – hang your dolls, hang yourself, if ye like. I'm not promising anything, mind, but I'll speak for ye. Your chances are fair, I'd say, for you've got a marvellous potential for absolute innocence."

"As long as they'll let me hang my dolls."

"That," replied McAndrew, "is your finest credential."

In darkness now, McAndrew turned the spit over the fire and the chicken spluttered and hissed while Toppam dozed.

Caesar, however, was wide awake, staring westward down towards the farm.

From the other side of the brook a ferret watched both men and the dog, its nostrils flaring to the smell of the chicken; nearby a rabbit watched the ferret. The men saw neither ferret nor rabbit; Caesar saw both.

He saw, but ignored them: also, he ignored the smells of the roasting chicken, because earlier he had eaten his fill from the farmer's pigsty, nipping the rump of the mothering sow to move her over.

Coming out of the pigsty, he had seen a hen which was moving windward of a fox.

Caesar was killing the hen when a bitch bull-terrier came from the house into the shippon.

Unlike Caesar, she was well-fed and in her prime, and she came silently, head down over the cobbled yard, and Caesar did not know of her because of farmyard smells. She came swiftly, in a low, swerving run, attacking in a flurry of squawks and feathers, fastening her teeth into his rear leg. She would have killed him had he not yielded, and this he did because she was a bitch. Raising his paws in submission, he lay below her, and she had one paw on the hen and another on his chest. She was muscled and strong, but he did not fear her.

Never before had she seen one of her kind; the sight of him kindled within her a strange, foreign desire. The fact that he

216

possessed but three legs merely excited her curiosity; perhaps, she considered as she held him down, mates were made like that. And yet his infirmity bred dominance and she might have killed him for this alone, had she not been in season.

"Are you all right, son?" asked McAndrew, turning the spit, but the dog made no sign that men existed.

This was a good master; Caesar acknowledged it. He of the large hands and feet was gentle, and his voice, though deep and authoritative, held a strange and wild music.

Two former masters Caesar had known; one was a child who wielded a stick. The other, earlier, had been put into a box, and men had carried him away.

But now the stick had gone, and there was nothing but love, and an occasional painless threat.

True, thought Caesar, this was a lazy master. One had to hunt for him, and this, on four legs had been difficult enough; on three legs it was proving nearly impossible. Indeed, many things were proving difficult on three legs; this Caesar was rapidly discovering, because after a little while the farmer's bitch, tiring of his efforts, bit him on the lower jaw and left him. And he was there in the middle of the shippon with the dead hen, the grumbling cattle and the grunting sow.

The failure had been total and iniquitous.

Now he sat in an angry, discordant silence and his body ached in that silence, and he smelled again the smells that brought visions: visions of soft fur and red tongues and milk. But the marvellous dominance that he had known, when he had risen in the shippon and backed down that bitch, faded slowly into his knowledge of utter defeat.

Now Caesar licked his bloodstained lip and did not turn when McAndrew called to him yet again, but turned his back on the fire and crawled away into darkness.

"All right," said McAndrew, smacking his lips, "so ye don't want any bloody chicken."

21

Atopia House, called by biographers of McAndrew as 'The House of Eccentrics', stood deep in Pickering Forest on the North York Moors; a gaunt stone pile that reared up a single battlement tower against the stars, for it was dusk when the two men and the dog reached it.

A fortified manor house built before the Wars of the Roses, it stood in crumbling dereliction, its surrounding walls, breached by Lancastrian artillery, still unrepaired.

Within the great hall of vaulted timber roof and Gothic carvings were the coats of arms of a dozen ancient families. These stared down on to a minor sea of Italian mosaic, the biggest hall in the county, it was claimed; the floor still stained at the place where the young countess, Yvonne Hilair of Rochefort, was burned to death.

Behind this stain stood a great chair most beautifully worked in teak and red velvet, the only furniture in the room. Before the chair, in attitudes of ragged veneration, stood McAndrew and Mr. Toppam, with Caesar sitting bolt upright between them.

They were awaiting the coming of Uncle Dumb, the owner of Atopia House.

"Is he God?" whispered Mr. Toppam.

"Damned near," said McAndrew.

Nine years earlier when McAndrew was a regular guest in Atopia House, bets had been laid as to who was the bigger, he or Uncle Dumb; the latter, perhaps because of his regality, winning by a short head – in the parlance of the trade.

Vicar Groper, who collected the bets, however, never paid the winner – being arraigned the next day for an improper suggestion to a waiter on the L.N.E.R. But that was years ago and things had changed drastically in Atopia, and for the worst, thought McAndrew as he watched Uncle Dumb approach them on the arm of Mama Meg, his devoted housekeeper.

The man, too old to die, it was said, came in a shuffling gait. Over his gigantic frame was a gown of flowing white that reached to his feet: bare-headed, his white hair hung upon his shoulders; above his spade beard, snow-white, his face was grey; the skinned face of the once badly burned, pouched and wrinkled.

Seating himself in the chair he regarded McAndrew and Toppam, and his eyes, bright blue, were the eyes of youth.

Now Uncle Dumb's long, tapering hands moved in the sign language of the mute, and Mama Meg, with an earlier brilliant smile of greeting to McAndrew, watched them. Once she had been a London barmaid, slim and beautiful; now her body was of layering grossness, yet her face, thought McAndrew, was unravaged by years of service to her master. She said, at the old man's hands:

"So, you have come back!"

"If you will allow it," replied McAndrew.

"After nine years? Life must indeed have been hard. Explain it."

The Scot straightened, his hands clasped. "The army – but you knew about that. Dismissed for desertion – coming to Atopia too often, they said. Then to the sea and making money. Married to a social whore and became a merchant prince."

Uncle Dumb replied and Mama Meg said, "That kind of money!"

"I gave employment."

"In drinking and whoring too, no doubt."

Caesar glanced up at this. McAndrew made no sign that he had heard it. The old man's fingers moved and the woman said:

"And now?"

"I want to paint."

"There was a time that I, too, wanted you to paint, but you left me. The mural you promised me is still unfinished."

"I will finish it now," said McAndrew.

"My God, McAndrew, is your world so bad?"

"It is cleaner here, in Atopia House."

Uncle Dumb raised his face, smiling faintly. "In the business of phrenology, McAndrew, you've got all the right bumps and you've a tongue of the Devil's Advocate. How do I know you'll keep your promise?"

"You don't," replied McAndrew.

"Your friend looks cleaner. Introduce me to him."

The Scot did so, explaining his meeting with Toppam, who stood in silence, his dolls in his arms, and the old man said;

"To you, McAndrew, I give this message. 'It is not the beginning of any great matter, but its continuance until it be thoroughly finished, that yieldeth the true glory.' Leave me again without permission and Atopia House is closed to you for good." He turned to Mr. Toppam.

"You, Sir, are a welcome guest here – indeed, I am bound to say, a truly exciting theorem. Never before have we possessed a public hangman, and the prospect delights me. But before I sanction your entry, listen carefully to what I have to say. You appear removed. Can you hear me, Mr. Toppam?"

"Yes, Sir."

Uncle Dumb said with his hands, "It is necessary that the rules of Atopia House be explained to you, as they are to everybody who comes to live under this roof. Are you listening, Mr. Toppam, you do not appear to be doing so."

"He is listening," said McAndrew.

"Nearly a hundred years ago I was born in this house," continued Uncle Dumb, "and, in 1831, when I was twenty, I took to myself a bride from France; a young and beautiful woman whose name was Yvonne Hilair, a countess of the House of Rochefort. Her family, rich and famous, tried to insist that we be married in France; Yvonne herself pleaded with me, but I was adamant that our wedding should take place here." The old man raised his head and stared past them to a distant window, saying:

"After the wedding, a great ball was held in this very room. Even a royal prince attended with his entourage. The occasion was splendid. Yorkshire, it was said, had never seen anything like it before. But, although everybody else was happy, my young wife was in tears, because she was not in her own country and her relatives had forsaken her. My mother had even to bring her from her room, to lead the dancing.

"We danced together. Because the floor was congested, I waltzed her clear of the other couples, and this took us to the edge of the floor, and her dress caught fire from niche candles. It flared. The flames enveloped her."

Uncle Dumb's fingers slowed in the telling; Mama Meg's voice faded to a whisper:

"We burned, both of us. We became like whirling torches, a dance of shrieks. She died in my arms near the place where you are standing now. The loss of her, the pain, took my speech, and for seventy years I have been dumb. And so I changed the name of this house to Atopia House, proclaiming that all who henceforth lived within these walls did exactly what they pleased without interference from men, and if possible from God. Tremendous happiness has been known here since then, pure freedom has been unleashed, marvellous things have been achieved . . .

"Ask in Levisham, the nearby village, and they will tell you I am mad; that this is an asylum for the deranged, a county hall for the bewildered. But is it madness to bring serenity to the perplexed or genius out of the lunatic?" and here he glanced at McAndrew.

"Many strange people live here, Mr. Toppam; compared with some the hanging of dolls is the activity of a pastoral mind, but you can do it, oh yes, if you so please. For in this house lie the extremes of liberty and concord. Great, great things have happened in Atopia – Ibsen himself visited this house while working on *Pillars of Society* – oh yes, my friend, yes, yes!

"Here, in this very room I discussed with Nietzsche the philosophy of self-assertion and the 'will to power' – he who died insane not six years back . . ." Mama Meg's voice rose as the hands worked faster.

"The great and famous have visited me – Browning and Barrett have wandered in these grounds, here Richard Jefferies finished *The Story of my Heart*." The old man rose to his feet and flung wide his arms and Mama Meg shrieked:

"I have read the sacred writings of the Sanskrit, I have studied Brahmanism and have lectured on its political and religious supremacy over the Kshatriyas. . . !

"The great historian von Ranke treated me as an equal because of my infinite patience in research into ancient Rome. . . !" And Mama Meg, at the end of her resources, clapped her hands before the old man's face and he slowly subsided back into his chair, his fingers moving but feebly:

"I apologise to you, Mr. Toppam. But is it madness to be carried away by one's intellectuality, when the mind is a saturation of all knowledge? Listen to me! Live here in quietude and peace, cause no controversy, no discord, be kind to all and accept their kindness. In return, you will be clothed and fed, working when you are instructed, resting when wearied. But cause a single objection to your presence, and you are out. *Out*, you understand?"

"No," said Toppam.

Uncle Dumb smiled at McAndrew with empty resignation, saying to the smaller man, "Well then, is there any question you would like to ask me before you take your place in this community of friends?"

"Yes," replied Toppam. "When can I hang me dolls?"

The old man smiled warmly, taking Toppam by the hand. "Yes, my friend," he said, "you are truly excellent material. You will cause no conflict or animosity here, for the world has taken from you all power of understanding."

With this he led the hangman to meet the other guests of Atopia.

22

Summer came in perfume across the moors with mouse-ear chickweed on her feet, a gown of violets and a hat of wild strawberries, and the woods in Atopia's fifty-eight acres bloomed with willow-herb and dog-roses.

Lakes of foxgloves, springing from the death of fading bluebells, painted up the heated days, and the chops of Atopia's cows were smothered with gold-dross.

Blackbirds cocked up their ears to the rich, brown earth; larks were nesting, swallows building. And the great green country from Whitby to Thirsk and Redcar to York, lay on its back and dozed in a pot-bellied, bee-humming June.

But Vicar Groper, the oldest occupant in Atopia House, was not dozing. In his black tights and sweat-shirt he was adopting the five positions of the classical ballet (as propounded by Michel Fokine) when McAndrew entered the music room.

"'Morning, Vicar!"

"Ah, my young friend McAndrew – you are home again. Welcome, welcome! Six years it must be, surely?"

"Nine, sir."

"Of course. Three years are lost to me, you understand." In fragile old age, the vicar approached. "Defrocked and incarcerated during Her Majesty's Pleasure. Indecent exposure, they called it. A trumped up charge, of course." He pranced suddenly and spun on one foot. "Not bad for ninety, you agree?"

"Have ye seen Constanze, by any chance?"

"You've heard, I take it, that I've got the lead in Covent Garden this year again?"

"Aye, mun, I heard. Warm congratulations!" McAndrew stared about him. "She was last seen coming in here, they said."

"But indecent exposure, my son. Consider the shame! And in the window of a third-class carriage – Waterloo, of all places."

"Wrongful conviction. You should have appealed." McAndrew went to a window and stared out on sunlit fields and the river flashed light in a mirage of heat. Caesar, waiting outside, saw him and barked.

"Fortunately, it will not affect my engagement to dance *Coppélia*," said Groper, "the contract having been signed. *Giselle*, of course, is my particular role. I danced it with Taglioni under Diaghilev. She was the first ballerina to dance en pointe, did you know that? Constanze, did you say?"

"Tell me where she is and I'll be away," said McAndrew.

Groper clapped his hands in a little delight. "Is it love you seek, my young friend? Then mime it – look, place two hands over the heart, like this. And with the aid of Constanze? Then she is but a motion with both hands in the air, like so," and he did it. "Your intentions towards her are honourable, McAndrew?"

"Ach, Padre, there's not a cleaner fella in Yorkshire."

"Of course, of course. I apologise for questioning it. Our darling Constanze has just gone down to the river. Charming, charming creature."

"Dear me, she's like a pound o' fresh-poured cheese."

"Meanwhile, are you aware that we are alone, my man?"

"Being thoroughly aware of it, I'm off," said McAndrew.

"Oh dear, what a pity. But you promise to come and see me in *Coppélia*, don't you?"

"Get me a ringside seat," said McAndrew.

Such a performance, thought he, could be a doubtful starter. The vicar's practice of standing at the window of a first-class door and beckoning to terrified passengers with a leer and a long, bony finger, would soon ensure him something more private than a carriage to himself from London to Redcar.

*

224

Constanze Mozart, the wife of Wolfgang Amadeus Mozart, dressed in Atopia's long white gown for runaways, was lying on the bank of the river when Caesar discovered her. McAndrew sat down on the grass beside her.

"You're new to Atopia, they tell me," said he.

"Yes. I came in last night."

He examined her in profile against the bright sparkle of rushing water: she was small, her body delicately fashioned, and her fair hair hung in tight ringlets to her shoulders. There was about her an air of aloof disassociation; even Caesar, McAndrew noticed, was doubtful about making up to her, and ingratiation was his stock in trade.

"Where did ye come from, woman?"

Her eyes were vacant. "I do not know."

"Then how did ye get here, for God's sake?"

Constanze smiled at him, and in her smile was nothingness. She was beautiful, McAndrew thought; certainly she was the most beautiful woman he had yet seen in Atopia.

"I don't know that, either," she replied. "What brings anybody to anywhere, when all of us are as nothing moving in emptiness?"

"Aw, Jesus, girl, it isn'a as bad as that!"

A silence fell between them. The alders were turning up their leaves at the sun. From a distant spire a bell chimed midday on the heated air.

"D'ye think you'll settle here?"

Constanze replied, "It will suffice until Wolfgang comes. The important thing is the children, of course. And they do so miss him when he is in Vienna."

"I didn't realise you had children, mind," said McAndrew, weakly.

Turning her face away, she replied, "I expected you to be well versed in knowledge of my husband. You are an artist, they tell me. How is it possible that an artist would not know?" She moved testily, quietly outraged. "I have four sons and a daughter – Raimund, Karl, Johann, Franz and Theresa. True, three are dead, but since we are all dead I consider them to be living."

"That's not unreasonable."

"You are ill-informed, sir," said Constanze. "I suggest you read the Nissen biography. I prefer it to Otto Jahn's, though I was not alive when I read that. My husband would have approved of both. Each conveniently omits a list of his lovers. When we were married we went to live in Zum roten Sabel, Wipplingerstrasse, did you know?"

"I did not, lady."

"We were happy there, and woman would be foolish to tabulate a list of indiscretions, like a clerk keeps a ledger. The Countess Josepha Pálffy was one, as you probably know – the niece of Archbishop Hieronymus – a politically dangerous affair. But it happened before I came on the scene, so why worry?"

"Why, indeed."

She shrugged, emptying her cares. "I recall thinking once – he was playing at Eszterházy or Galitzen, I forget which – that the audience which cried '*Bravissimo!*' never knew the man called Mozart. Only I am privy to that."

"You didn't do so badly, from what I've heard." McAndrew lay back and Caesar curled up on his chest, watching Constanze with the whites of his eyes.

"Don't you worry," said she, "I didn't go short. Scandal soon turns a swan into a goose. While writing *Don Giovanni* he was living with the daughter of his housekeeper, treating himself to her cakes and coffee between scenes and bedding her between acts."

"Come on, come on," said McAndrew, sitting up, "He wrote *Don Giovanni* long before you met. I've read his biography too, you know. You had affairs on the side, while he was treating the world to genius!" He and Caesar stared at her with plain hostility. McAndrew said, "You've got your dates wrong, too, and you're conveniently forgetting your own sly romances, while accusing Mozart to salve your conscience." He laughed at her.

"Untrue!" Constanze defiantly lifted her face. "I was a good and virtuous wife!"

226

"O aye? That's not the impression here in Atopia. Antonio Salieri, for a start!"

"Salieri. . . ?" Her hand crept upwards to her throat.

"Yes, among others I could name. Historical personages, girl, sleep, not *a*sleep with historical facts – don't assume that the world's entirely daft."

White-faced, Constanze stared up, getting to her feet in growing panic. She whispered, "Salieri is dead – dead and gone, you understand?"

"Ach no, love. He's here, in Atopia."

"Here?" She began to tremble and the trembling spread from her hands to her body.

"Why not, woman? D'ye think you're the only one re-incarnated?"

Caesar watched from a respectable distance because of the madness. McAndrew said, "Jesus, this place could send ye over the wall were it not for a spot o' romance."

She wept when he left her, her hands over her face.

23

In the banqueting hall of Atopia House McAndrew had restarted work on the mural for Uncle Dumb.

Many years ago he had begun this project, stripping one wall of the vast room free of pictures and ornaments and painting direct, after fixing with isinglass, on to the plaster.

Working on lime-and-haired plaster, McAndrew clearly thought, would mean the eventual destruction of the painting through crumbling. Unfortunately, he took no account, say his biographers, of modern methods of preservation, which could sectionalise, peel the paint free, and reback.

There existed between Uncle Dumb and the Scot an acceptance of his ability. McAndrew never claimed it, the older man merely spoke of it as an artisan's gift – in return for services rendered at Atopia. So, if Uncle Dumb recognised the mural's genius he never mentioned it, nor did he enlighten successive biographers through people like Mama Meg, the longest living member of the Atopia family.

And biographers like Ratzman, because Constanze (of whose murder McAndrew stands accused by history) came to the house as late as 1905, knew little about the period before her occupation. Even McAndrew's original visit there is only known through the barrack-room characters who first invaded the canvas – detention guards in full uniform on the barrack square at Hendon; a hussar cashiered, his gold braid torn to rags; a regimental sergeant-major of bucolic countenance: these, and a small, frightened-looking drummer-boy standing by the barrack gate . . .

So the precise date when the great mural was begun is still unknown, and probably will never be discovered.

Gunner Jenkinsop was there, also Rosa Florence and her family – her mother and step-father, Pinta, Evan Kinto and Brookie, Rosa's brother; these were sitting around a bonfire, or on the steps of their caravans.

McAndrew's later Montmartre experiences complimented the work of Toulouse-Lautrec, but this early painting owes nothing, it is claimed, to the influence of the Impressionists; the lines were formal, the proportions precise.

But, with the inclusion of Tuesday into the right-hand side of the canvas – the little courtesan of Cambourne House – McAndrew appeared bewitched. Lord Grey-Cambourne was there, frock-coated, drinking at a bar: Tommy, his son, took a prominent position; strangely, Ross Bolton was standing behind him, his hand on the boy's shoulder. Megsie, her back to the viewer was serving at table; Jean Pierre, perched on a high stool, stared out with sad, luminous eyes.

These subjects, painted within the first month of McAndrew's return to Atopia, seemed to translate the artist's attempt to free himself from Nature and convention. His colours here were brighter, his shapes became slight caricatures, only features were precise. As Gauguin's wavy lines betrayed the onset of brain damage, so McAndrew's depiction of those in Cambourne House made comparison with the lunacy of Fatu-Iwa.

Was *La Javanaise* – the lover who ran off with the contents of Paul Gauguin's studio – was she, the critics later asked, the Ellie Kendall of McAndrew? And did the environment of Atopia House lay the basis of McAndrew's torment of the mind? One thing is sure, they claimed – that Ellie Kendall subscribed to this, laying upon his brush an advocacy of madness.

In his delirium, apparently, he painted Tuesday's face with the face of Ellie. And, at the back of the canvas, insignificantly placed, her mirror raised high, was a whore at toilet.

Constanze, whom, because McAndrew was working almost round the clock he had not yet seduced, arrived in the great hall to sit for the canvas.

She arrived unheralded and after many requests by McAndrew, and sat in Uncle Dumb's great chair with her hands folded in her lap, a white-gowned virgin bidden to sacrifice.

McAndrew ignored her, and went on working. And as he worked he sang, a bawdy barrack room harlot of a song that battered itself off the crested walls and echoed in the vaulted roof above. With his trousers in tatters and halfway up his hairy legs, he worked bare-footed, as ragged and torn as a Southern State grandpappy, the bright hairs of his chest sprouting up through the rents in his shirt to meet his unkempt beard.

He was thinner than when at Cambourne, his features gaunt and cadaverous and his eyes burned red-rimmed in the hollows of his cheeks.

"Mr. McAndrew . . ." began Constanze.

"Aye, aye woman. Bide yourself there till I give ye a call."

"It would be helpful . . ."

"And I'd be obliged to ye if you didn't interrupt."

Two things McAndrew demanded from Uncle Dumb in return for the mural – artist's material and whisky; the former was obtained at intervals from York by Vicar Groper, and, if not forthcoming, production was delayed; when a bottle was empty production stopped. Food was of secondary importance; its table formality meant interruption and was therefore rejected. And so he ate while he worked, supplied with hunks of cheese and loaves either by Mama Meg direct or Toppy, her new assistant in the kitchens.

A workhouse waif, lanky, freckled and ginger-haired, Toppy was discharged to Uncle Dumb on signature; the poor duck not being quite a full pound, said Mama Meg, and she ain't goin' to the bloody looney bin, bless 'er little socks.

Every midday saw Toppy tiptoeing into the great hall; here, behind the big chair she laid down the food and fled, followed by McAndrew's curses and with Caesar in barking and shrieking pursuit.

Never had Toppy felt more at home than within the friendship of Atopia.

Earlier that day, before the arrival of Constanze, Miss Pan had come to the banqueting hall and sat on the chair where Constanze was sitting now, her face held high with childlike expectancy.

"Good morning, Miss Pan."

For reasons known to himself McAndrew accorded to Miss Pan's three-feet-ten inches the respect he reserved only for Mama Meg and Uncle Dumb; setting down his pallet, he bowed to her. She, aged seventy and dressed as a child of seven, slipped down off the chair, curtsied prettily and climbed back on to it.

"Good morning, McAndrew. It is your intention to put me on canvas, I understand."

"With your permission, lady."

She gestured towards Rosa and family. "Providing, of course, that you do not include me with your gipsies." The airy gesture she made told him to get on with it.

Miss Pan, next to Vicar Groper (today shopping in York, Uncle Dumb having officially notified the county police) was the oldest guest in Atopia.

Her real name – Lady Elizabeth Brownlow – Miss Pan kept to herself, and, although Uncle Dumb knew her antecedents, of this he made no mention, having saved her from a careless gentry determined to 'put her away'.

Miss Pan lived apart from the other guests, an entity surviving within a self-constructed world of French cuisine and mainly Beethoven. She dwelt alone, in a bell tent at the bottom of the garden in summer; in winter pitching it in Atopia's vast reception hall. She rose early to work in Uncle Dumb's fields, a milkmaid who knew every cow by its name and every pig by its grunt.

Daily, after work, she would bathe and dress for dinner, sitting outside her tent at a little card table upon which she had set a lighted candelabra; dining off Royal Albert and attended by devoted but mythical servants, whom she scolded or appraised with a gentile autocracy.

Usually, after dinner, she would smoke a Havanna cheroot and, more recently, play 'Death and the Maiden', Schubert's

String Quartet in D Minor, on an aged phonograph: since it is nearing the hour, she used to say, when children even as young as me must go to the final party . . .

Miss Pan, so named comparatively recently by Uncle Dumb who delighted in the fame of J.M. Barrie, contributed generously to the upkeep of Atopia: at least, her relatives did. But Mama Meg, the antithesis of all she stood for, had reason for complaint – Miss Pan's habit of sitting on an earth closet in the middle of the jarrah wood block flooring being a continuing source of difficulty. But, as Uncle Dumb gently pointed out to Mama, Miss Pan was, after all, essentially an out-of-doors person.

Now she said, "You are aware, McAndrew, that not only are you invariably drunk these days, but your appearance is dissipated?"

He was working swiftly, brushing her in at the foot of the canvas in wide, deft, sweeps of the hand.

"Yes, lady." He gestured carelessly. "Would ye mind standing now?"

Miss Pan obeyed. In a white, frilly party frock, ankle socks and brogues, and with her greying bobbed hair tied with pink ribbon, she stood in demure obedience, saying:

"You do not eat properly, they tell me. This inspirational nonsense can go too far, you know. You will dine with me tomorrow night, do you understand? And if you are fortunate, we will share a bottle of Asti Spumante – a sweet Italian I usually reserve for the attentions of Uncle Dumb. God help you, McAndrew, I intend to feed you."

Miss Pan glanced over her shoulder at the approach of Constanze. "Good gracious," she added, "look what's coming." Confidentially, she said in a whisper, making big eyes, "She's not quite the ticket, you know. She believes herself to be the wife of Mozart. Seven-thirty sharp tomorrow, then?"

"I shall be delighted," said McAndrew.

"And McAndrew . . ."

"Yes, lady?"

"Be kind to her."

24

With Constanze watching from the big chair, McAndrew put the finishing touches to his depiction of Vicar Groper, placing him centrally in a position of importance: dressed in a black, female leotard, the vicar was doing his five positions in front of a mirror.

Next to Groper on the mural, leaning on the bonnet of his latest Rolls Royce was the plump, convivial figure of Lord Effington-Smythe, or Bugsie, as he preferred to be called in Atopia, to which he made periodic visits.

His lordship, owner of Effington's, the famous store in York, was chairman of the local Tory party and a member of the Chamber of Trade, therefore incorrupt. But, like Vicar Groper, he suffered a minor cerebral complaint, as Uncle Dumb put it: Groper from social maleficence, Bugsie from kleptomania.

This expressed itself in shop-lifting from his own store in the High Street.

His practice was to enter in morning dress (with his Rolls waiting at the kerb), raise his top hat to the staff, and proceed to appropriate unguarded items.

Vicar Groper, for his part, had never been a sitting duck, as McAndrew called his posing subjects; and he worked happily from memory.

Indeed, at that very moment, Groper was shopping in York, having successfully eluded a following policeman and made his way to the Rainbow's End, a public house in the vicinity of the Minster. There, after three brandies and sodas, he had put a shilling each way on Ardent Lady, a filly running in the three-thirty at Redcar.

From there he had repaired to Effington's perfumery, where the exotic nature of the products had an unusual effect upon him; the eyes of a female assistant opened wide in apprehension.

"Is something wrong?" asked Groper submissively.

"You dirty old devil! You touched my leg!"

"Dear child, I assure you I did no such thing."

The under-manager drew himself up. "You realise, young woman, that you are accusing a man of the cloth?"

"Excuse me, ladies, excuse me please," said Groper, pushing his way to the exit; here he came up against a fat lady proceeding in the opposite direction. She cried:

"You ought to be ashamed of yourself, my girl – he's a respectable clerical gent," and she shook a large, red fist.

Groper raised his black Stetson to her, struggling to get past.

"Dear lady, quite so. I'm deeply obliged . . ."

"What's more, he's nicked a bottle of *Paris L'Aimant*! Look, he's got it under his bowler!"

"An item which I intend to purchase," cried Groper. "Really, upon my soul. . . !"

Then the fat lady's jaw dropped. Outraged, she wriggled.

"Put my dress down, you dirty old sod!" and she began hitting Groper with her handbag.

Meanwhile, on the other side of the store, Lord Effington-Smythe, taking advantage of the commotion, was shoplifting with a technique that left his store detectives gasping. With his rubicund face wreathed in happy smiles, he purloined a box of cigars for Uncle Dumb, buttons from the haberdashery for Mama Meg, the poems of Byron for Conrad, and six toilet rolls for Miss Pan.

With his top hat raised and his waistcoat bulging, he made his way out to the street.

"Oh God," said the under-manager, "he's at it again."

*

234

The policeman who had been following the vicar came through the door as Groper sped out, pursued by lady shoppers.

"You can't do this," shouted Groper, apprehended. "I'm dancing *Giselle* at Covent Garden tomorrow."

"You'll be dancing, son, but not at Covent Garden."

"Make way, make way," cried his lordship, and climbed into his Rolls. "Atopia House, if you please."

A valuable contribution to the economy of Atopia, it was Bugsie's boast that he'd never been caught.

"Yes yes, I know, Officer," said Uncle Dumb when interviewed later. "I do accept the fullest responsibility, but like the accusations made against our dear Lord Effington-Smythe, they are unfounded, and it is unpardonable. I remain convinced that our vicar couldn't do such a thing."

Mama Meg's cockney lilt became accentuated by the frantic working of her master's fingers:

"You must 'ave dirty minds, you lot down at the Station. Either that or you're round the bloody twist."

McAndrew said to Constanze, "Now stand, woman," and she obeyed, letting her long white runaway gown fall to her feet.

He saw her against the languorous, quilted beauty of the dales, through the hall's latticed windows, and the little cottages and farmhouses were glowing the colour of cream. The morning was hot. Sheep were bleating plaintively on the heated air. He murmured, "O, land of cool water, heather and the lairds . . ."

"You're drunk," announced Constanze.

"Probably."

"Miss Pan's right. You're always drunk these days, McAndrew."

He said, "Drink no longer water but use a little wine for thy stomach's sake and thine other pestilential bloody infirmities – Timothy five:twenty-three. Aye, drunk with your charms, my lovely Constanze. No wonder Mozart died young."

235

With the bottle tipped high he drank, gasped, and wiped his face with the back of his hand, and at that moment the room shook to an underground explosion; wavers of whitewash flaked off the ceiling and drifted down.

"Well done, Ferdinand. Blow the bloody place up."

"Oh God!" whispered Constanze. "They're getting bigger and bigger."

Unknown to either of them, Mama Meg, in her kitchen, caught her Wedgwood speciality as it fell, and put it back on the mantelshelf. McAndrew said:

"How to tell of you, Constanze, with only paint to use?"

"Clearly, I'm wasting my time," said Constanze. "Do you want me here or not?"

"My love, I want you everywhere. By the river; tonight, in your bed; here, this moment, on the floor."

"I think you are disgusting. My husband would have found words for you – a man without a sense of shame or delicacy."

McAndrew said, coming closer, "Do ye happen to know, my beauty, how long it is since I had a woman?"

"Another step and I'll call Uncle Dumb!"

"O aye?" He moved his paint-stained hands before her. "Playing God, me love, is a tricky old business. Who's the more shamed of the pair of us, sweetheart – you or me? When Mozart died, what part did you play? Not, I think, that of the adoring wife, oh no! No witnesses at his funeral, not even a cross to mark his grave!"

Constanze turned away, screwing at her fingers. McAndrew said, "Even the skull they found twenty years later could have been the grave-digger's. The wife of genius, eh? Christ, ye did him well!"

"Please. . . ?"

"And ye didn't even dispel the local rumour that your husband was a libertine."

She turned her tear-stained face to his. "Who are you? I came to this place for peace. What do you want from me. . . ?"

He held his head at a marvellous angle of conceit, saying,

"Ah now, ye don't know, do you! So that's one up me sleeve, Mrs. Mozart. I'll just tell ye this – I need you sore. I need you sore, but the phantom pipes'll be playin' 'The Flowers of the Forest' before I beg it off any bloody woman!"

Later, after Constanze had gone, McAndrew went to the mural and painted in the right-hand corner the name 'Salieri'.

Atopia House, when its budget allowed, provided its inmates with one meal a day; a main meal of giant proportions cooked by Mama Meg with help from Toppy and other available females on a roster system. The men, playing their part in the household economy of vegetable growing and general husbandry, were banned from entry into Mama's kitchen: the breaking of this female preserve was allowed only to Mr. Toppam, who, from the moment he entered Atopia insisted on helping with the washing up. In this he was not dissuaded, otherwise Mama Meg ruled her kitchen with fearful authority.

On the occasion of Vicar Groper's release from prison (six weeks on both charges of indecent assault) both McAndrew and Miss Pan presented themselves at the dinner table with the other twenty-three guests; this was at Uncle Dumb's request, that all should be present to give a welcome to one of the family falsely accused and now returned to the bosom, so to speak.

Many were present on that early August evening who have never been listed by the McAndrew historians; nor, indeed, are their names to be found in printed editions of the official bibliography. Only by Mama Meg are these people recorded, and then only by passing references she made in her many letters to a Lady Grace de Maid, at a date long after McAndrew left Atopia for Montmartre.

Conrad, a recent acquisition to Atopia, was one of these, also Ferdinand de Silva, the Santiago revolutionary: Brunel, the failed inventor of perpetual motion, a morose and silent man, was one who could quite naturally be overlooked since he played no part at all in McAndrew's eventual descent into oblivion.

But the haunted Conrad and the volatile, disruptive Ferdinand are shown by the mural itself as clearly affecting McAndrew's subconscious. Both are granted eminent positions on the canvas, both are depicted as the essence of Atopia's sadness.

There were many others present at table in celebration of Groper's homecoming, of course; some who are known to posterity only by name and not for any outstanding aberration, physical or mental.

For instance, there was Mr. Leonard, a lean and pallid man with ambitions to be an undertaker, but, who later, after years in Atopia, left to become under-manager of York's Wholesale Co-operative, subsequently moving to somewhere in Chile with the funds.

There was Banker, who wrote love letters to Miss Pan on paying-in slips, and hid a scheming, quick-witted cunning behind his puffed-up grandiloquence. And Porky, he of the dolorous expression on one side of his face, the other side being that of a merry pig: hunched in his poor, blighted body, he held Mama Meg's hand under the table. Dribbling, awry, he was the only idiot there.

"Stand, please!" called she, and all rose in a clatter of feet and scraping chairs as Marie Antoinette arrived, waiting for silence before she took her place. She came, not in the full regalia of the Tuileries, but in the simple execution gown she wore at the Place de la Révolution, her face stricken with the brutalities of the Conciergerie, yet possessing a profound radiance; she inclined her head to McAndrew.

"Monsieur . . ."

Ragged, gaunt, he bowed to her, adjusting her chair.

Groper arrived last, seeking full approbation, coming through the door in pirouettes and jumps to thunderous applause.

Mama Meg then raised her arm for silence, and Uncle Dumb, sitting opposite her at the end of the long refectory table, moved his long bony fingers before his face like a man speaking to a cobra, and Mama cried:

"O bounteous Grace that provides our protection, grant us serenity of mind, and food."

"Amen."

Ferdinand de Silva leaped to his feet, crying, "A toast, a toast – to our most excellent vicar, falsely accused, wrongly imprisoned!" But McAndrew sat motionless, staring at Constanze farther down the table, who sat with an averted face. Ferdinand cried:

"Long live the *Uspallatas*! Long live the Republic that is suffering equal injustice under the hated General Appariz!" and he brandished his fist.

"Yes, all right, my duck," said Mama Meg. "Sit down now, there's a good lad," and with Toppy's help ladled soup into bowls from a giant tureen and passed them down the table.

Uncle Dumb, his white hair flowing over his shoulders sat rigidly in his muteness, the accepted god of Atopia.

All were equally muted; it was a silence of switching eyes and tinkling plates. McAndrew was watching Constanze, seeing her not at table but spread-eagled in a bed of tumbled clothes. Groper was trying to catch his eye. Ferdinand was lost in dreams of assassination, the shattering of General Appariz into a haze of blood. Conrad, recently returned from his pilgrimage to Transylvania, sat with a taloned hand around his goblet of red wine, his eyes burning in the yellow parchment of his face . . . at the neck of Marie Antoinette.

"It's the phenomenon of friction that is the enemy, of course," whispered Brunel the inventor, to Miss Pan, who smiled appreciatively at the confidence.

"A nice little bit of underdone for you, my ducks?" asked Mama Meg, serving Conrad with meat, and she cut lustily at the joint and wiped stray hairs from her sweating face. "Lean for Miss Pan, fatty for Banker and the bone for little Porky. What about you, Mr. McAndrew? Full moon tonight, ye know."

"None for me, woman." McAndrew raised his whisky and gulped at the glass.

239

Fearing little in the world, he yet feared Conrad, for the Occult in any form induced in him fearful dreams. Thoughts of even a failed vampire would bring him upright in his bed. Talk had it that Conrad kept a coffin in his room, others whispered that he slept in it and prowled the grounds of Atopia on nights of full moon. Yet, withal, he knew a small, felicitous comradeship for the other's troubles.

The mural was going badly, its colours were wrong, the shapes and positionings congested idiocy, and Ellie's face kept rising before him.

He saw her laughing in the little cabin of the *Sarn Helen*, he saw it sweating in the coaling labour of Port Dinorwig; he heard her voice faintly disapproving, or whispering in the pillows: with Ellie beside him, he thought now, he could paint the wind, yet without her he was lost.

McAndrew glanced up from his reverie. Mr. Toppam, at the other end of the table, was smiling at him with a naked mouth, and in one arm he nursed Chang Su-la, the tiny effigy of the child he had hanged. Porky, now being fed by Mama Meg, grunted and leered at him; Ferdinand, his hands over his face, was sobbing. Conrad, Banker, Constanze, Miss Pan – McAndrew thought – Vicar Groper and all the others . . . He himself was the nut within this kernel of lunacy from which, somehow, he must escape.

Suddenly Brunel leaned across and said to him:

"Uncle Dumb tells me that you wish me to sit tomorrow. Is that correct, Mr. McAndrew. . . ?"

"If ye please."

The man smiled from the benign beauty of his face. "Do place me insignificantly on your mural. I am a failure, and do not wish to be seen too prominently, you understand?"

Miss Pan interjected warmly, "Mr. Brunel was once a great engineer, you know!"

"Oh aye?" McAndrew raised his great head. "How come he's in this daft place now, then?"

Brunel said, "Briefly, I designed an aqueduct for the Argentinian government. It was the longest waterway in South America. It's finished proportions were as beautiful as its calculus – mathematics is also an art, are you aware of this?" The little man stared about him, disconcerted.

"Please continue," said Miss Pan.

"Well . . . on the day of its opening it was decided that a person of royal blood should cut a ribbon on the middle span – standing on the prow of the first barge through, you understand? The barge weighed over a thousand tons, and, when I saw it approaching my nerve failed me and my mind began racing over my calculations . . . do you know what I mean, Mr. McAndrew?"

"Of course."

"In my hysteria I recalculated the girder bending moments and moments of resistance, sectional modulus and shear – you see, I had realised something terrible . . . I had not allowed for the weight of the barge."

"Dear God," whispered Miss Pan.

Brunel said, his eyes betraying his agitation, "The crowd was cheering and everything was gay, I remember. Flags and coloured bunting was draped over the barge and it came nearer, nearer to the centre span. A band was playing some gay tune . . . and I was in agony. My brain photographed the coming disaster; the sudden buckling of the transoms and load-bearing stanchions, the cracking masonry, the thundering cascades of released water as the whole complex collapsed, and I saw the barge dip and the people spilling out . . ." Brunel closed his eyes. "I fainted, you know."

"And then?"

"When . . . when I returned to consciousness many people were bending over me, offering congratulations. The barge had safely passed over the aqueduct, and all was well. The royal person was asking to see me."

"Well then?"

Mr. Brunel shrugged vacantly. "I realised then that the barge, in water, weighed nothing; displacement, you see, is not weight. But it was too late. Overwork . . . my brain was damaged.'

McAndrew stared at him, finding no words.

"So put me in some insignificant place on your wonderful

241

mural, Mr. McAndrew. Somehow or other you have hung
on to your genius – never, never have I seen such astonishing work – except, perhaps, in the Louvre – the New
Expressionists. Toulouse-Lautrec comes especially to my
mind."

McAndrew, now disinterested, was looking at Constanze.
She was eating with delicacy, her blue eyes lowered, but he
knew that she was aware of him.

"We've all got our crosses, mun," he said to Brunel.

When the meal was finished, Mama Meg first took Porky up
to bed and then went to Uncle Dumb's chair and stood
behind it. Watching his sign language, she said to the room:

"As all here know, this small party is being held to
celebrate the homecoming of our beloved vicar, free at last
from the hands of those who falsely arraigned him . . ."

Hurrahs and whoops at this, with those who were nodding
off waking up.

"And I begin with some excellent news. Within a few weeks
we will be joined by Monsieur Jacques Collard, a fine sculptor from Paris – a friend of a friend – who is in need of the
serenity and peace that only Atopia can offer . . ." At this
McAndrew raised his head and interjected:

"Montmartre community, sir?"

"I understand, Mr. McAndrew, that he has certain con-
nections in the artists' quarter." Uncle Dumb continued and
Mama Meg translated:

"I know that you will give our foreign friend a particular
welcome to the house." The old man paused, then:

"Spring and summer this year have proved most successful. The farm has flourished under the expert guidance of
Miss Pan, the men are to be congratulated upon excellent
results in agriculture and market gardening. Do you know
that we are now self-sufficient in wheat and vegetables?
Happily also, the relatives of our beloved Miss Pan have this
year proved unusually generous; we are, ladies and gentlemen – as the world of economics puts it – out of the red . . .

"Therefore, it has proved possible to widen our horizons,

242

and I herewith welcome Mr. Toppam, our new intake – begging all to ensure that, following the creed of Atopia, he is allowed to carry on his profession without let or hindrance – provided, of course, that he restricts his activities to dolls."

Clapping and laughter now, with Toppam being patted and congratulated and he not knowing, said McAndrew later, if he was in Atopia or the Arctic. And Uncle Dumb continued while Mama Meg shrieked it out:

"We also welcome the return of our old friend Conrad from his pilgrimage to Romania, and are excitedly anticipating his forthcoming lecture on Elizabeth of Bathory, who bathed in blood to restore her youth. There is enlightening discussion, I understand, on boiling, roasting and skinning alive!"

Oohs and Aahs at this, with people holding themselves and shivering, while Uncle Dumb, delighted at the effect, smiled happily around the table.

"However," he continued, "even on such happy occasions as this, there are usually grounds for complaint, and it is necessary to air them so that this house be kept clean.

"Miss Pan, for instance, has been receiving letters from a male guest which are of a somewhat amorous nature. Miss Pan says that she is no longer young, and requests that such letters immediately cease."

People looked crestfallen at this, with Banker appearing glum; rumour had it that he enjoyed a romantic hope of marriage to Miss Pan.

"There is also a general request to Ferdinand de Silva, our most volatile anarchist, to keep his bomb experiments down to reasonable explosions. We are able to sleep safely in our beds because Ferdinand is in charge of security here, but cracks are appearing, I am told, in the walls of our cellars."

Now Uncle Dumb's fingers moved faster in obvious agitation and Mama Meg craned her neck to read them:

"Another lady guest has made complaint to me. This person, long widowed and with children lost to her, is being pursued persistently by one who should know better. Atopia is not an abode of love. Its women are not available at

243

another's whim. If affection is reciprocated, then all is well; unions of great happiness have been made within these walls.

But nor are we savages to pursue and outrage. The lady concerned is not of an age when physical love becomes incongruous, so her morality is under strain."

Uncle Dumb raised a fist. "I will not have her pestered, is this understood? Tears have been shed and they, as you know, are outlawed in Atopia. And so, whatever the standing of the man involved, he will leave Atopia if his pursuit continues." Now he glared down at McAndrew. "Does he understand? Even those who love him will hound him from this place!"

McAndrew sat glowering, chin on his chest, one fist on the table gripping his bottle and his eyes were fixed on Constanze. She sat motionless, her face low, and the people nudged and murmured, fearful of the wrath of Uncle Dumb, their eyes switching to McAndrew and back again to Constanze.

"Meanwhile," added the old man, ". . . and it may now seem a reasonable time to ask – how is my mural going?"

McAndrew did not answer; ragged, unkempt, he was staring at Constanze.

Uncle Dumb continued:

"Last time I saw it, it was possessed of towering energy, its dark solemnity silvered by a rich vein of humour. I have not expressed an opinion on it before, Mr. McAndrew, but I am not without knowledge of Impressionism. It has tonality and bravura – your soul is in it.

"You tell me, sir, that you are calling it *The Feast of Madness* – an apt title professionally, perhaps, but one which I abhor. The inference is clear – that all depicted there are insane. May I tell you, and your world of art, that we in Atopia are the sane ones, in a world of total lunacy. For does not peace and serenity exist in us. Is this not a house of love, when all without is bridled by reins of hatred." Uncle Dumb smiled. "But that is my only criticism. When will it be finished?"

McAndrew rose, clattering back his chair. Seizing his bottle he strode from the room. Caesar, emerging from under the table, trotted after him.

"Tell that gentleman," said the old man with his fingers, "that, when he is cooler, I would like to speak with him.

"And finally, ladies and gentlemen . . ." added Uncle Dumb, and Mama Meg's hands moved faster in excited expectation, ". . . may I make yet another small appeal? *Buttons*, ladies and gentlemen. Buttons! Buttons of infinite quality, variety and description – nothing will be rejected, nothing will come amiss. This lady, Mama Meg, is in constant service to us, you know this. Therefore, it would be less than ingenuous of you; more, insincere – were you to conceal upon your persons a button of any description after I have made this last appeal on her behalf. Give generously, I beg of you, to Mama Meg's collection."

Uncle Dumb bowed to the room. "That will be all."

25

Conrad, as Miss Pan always put it, was night-prowling again, it being a hunter's moon, and Ferdinand was on guard in Atopia's grounds. Dressed in his uniform of a Bolivian partisan (one made by Mama Meg) – with Uncle Dumb's ancient twelve-bore at the slope and a bandolier of cartridges across his chest – Ferdinand marched with precision, hoarsely singing *Uspallata*, the battle song of the New Republic.

Earlier, despite Uncle Dumb's entreaties, he had set off his new fertilizer bomb in the cellar, shaking every window in Atopia House and smashing Mama's Wedgwood speciality on the floor.

Now Conrad listened, and watched: perched high on a gravestone in Atopia's cemetery – ground consecrated by Vicar Groper before his defrocking – he saw Ferdinand pass along the perimeter wall.

Later, wandering among the tombs of Atopia's generations of deceased, Conrad had seen McAndrew walking slowly in the moonlight towards the north wing of the house.

McAndrew, with Caesar hopping like a dog's ghost behind him, saw neither Ferdinand nor Conrad, his attention being otherwise engaged; this being his chosen night for the seducing of Constanze, the wife of Mozart, by Antonio Salieri, the composer's contemporary.

History does relate, making it clear that it relates only through rumour, that such an attempt at seduction occurred; it makes no mention that the act was condoned by Constanze; nor has it been proved that Salieri poisoned Mozart out of a fit of jealousy, as has been alleged. Likewise, history has no evidence of the state of McAndrew's mind on the night he went to Constanze's room, or that he left Atopia by wish or through expulsion.

Only one fact is known – that the mural was left, at that time unfinished.

Constanze could not sleep that late autumn night. She sensed that Conrad was abroad, for it was a hunter's moon, and this she always found disturbing, and therefore locked her door.

Earlier, while walking in twilight along the river, she had seen Toppam hanging his dolls, which he did with full observance of an executioner's ceremony; the sight had sickened Constanze, and, when she found sleep, was awakened almost instantly by Monsieur Jacques Collard, Atopia's new arrival; his interminable sculpting, the new music of Atopia, chinked and hammered into her consciousness.

It had not taken the Montmartre Frenchman long to find his niche in Atopia.

Discovering a rocky scar of monumental height near the west gate, the sculptor sat himself upon it; diminutive and sad-eyed he perched himself there and laboured incessantly night and day, rain or fine, seemingly with no purpose, said McAndrew, and certainly without art, and the two men clearly had nothing in common.

But it is possible that Collard might have mentioned the death of Toulouse-Lautrec, which had occurred four years earlier in 1901, and it is known that, at this time, McAndrew was unaware of it.

The effect upon McAndrew was traumatic; this in itself would have been sufficient to make him leave Atopia.

Constanze Mozart's room was situated in the north wing of Atopia House; all the women guests slept here, their presence presided over by Mama Meg as matron in charge, and her bedroom was the last at the end of a long corridor.

Toppy slept on the first floor; two more and Marie, their

247

rooms either side of Constanze's, looked out, like hers, on to woods; a tree-fringe of young elms whose roots were spreading under the foundations of the old house: slowly, inexorably, Nature was taking over.

Ferdinand, making his midnight rounds, saw a light burning in the banqueting hall and looked through one of its latticed windows. The guard was not surprised to see McAndrew working on his mural; latterly the Scot had been working well into the small hours. According to evidence he later gave, the artist was unusually drunk, and, even as Ferdinand watched him, he suddenly fell to his knees, and, began to tear at his clothes, as if in a sudden paroxysm of rage or pain.

Ferdinand watched, he said, for over half an hour, during which time McAndrew was lying flat upon his back, with Caesar bending over him and whining.

It was the last time he set eyes on the artist, said Ferdinand later, under oath.

Conrad's evidence, however, was of a differing kind.

He was taking a stroll in the garden, said he, because he could not sleep. The time? he was asked.

"About one o'clock, I think."

"And you saw the man McAndrew go past?"

"I did."

"Where were you at this time?"

"Alongside the cemetery wall – it was bright moonlight and I saw him clearly."

"Did you speak?"

"I did not speak. He was drunk and I feared him; also the dog was growling."

"The small white dog he called Caesar?"

"That is the one."

"And then?"

"Then," replied Conrad, "I saw him go to the north wing of the house. The door was open and he entered. The small white dog sat waiting outside."

"What did you do then?"

"I went back to my room in the attic."

"This man, you say, was drunk. You saw him enter the women's quarters. You knew that he had no right to be there, and yet, although you could have told the guard who was in the grounds, you returned to your room?"

"I did."

"You gave no heed to the safety of the women?"

"The women of this house, Sir, are not my affair," said Conrad.

Toppy said, "Oh no, Sir, I never talked to Mr. McAndrew. I reckon he was ravin' mad, Sir. I used to take his food in while he was painting and he would swear and curse with the most horrible language, and his dog used to see me off."

"When did you last see this man?"

"Day 'fore yesterday, Sir."

"When you took his food into the banqueting hall?"

"That's right, Sir."

"Where were you, young woman, on the night when this poor lady was attacked?"

"In bed, Sir."

"But before that – say round about midnight?"

"Don't know, Sir."

"Oh come, child, you must!"

"Down the village, Sir."

"Seeing a boy – am I right?"

Toppy bowed her head.

"You are not allowed to go to the village unaccompanied, are you?"

"No, Sir."

"But, when you did return, you came in the door of the servants' entrance, and left it open, I'll be bound . . ."

"Oh no, Sir!"

"Are you prepared to swear on oath that you locked it, then?"

Toppy raised a tear-stained face.

"The fact is that you can't remember if you locked it or not, is that the truth of it?"

Toppy wept, her hands over her face.

"That will be enough," said Uncle Dumb, through Mama Meg.

McAndrew entered the north wing by the servants' entrance, the door having been left open by Toppy who had come in from the village but ten minutes earlier.

Marie Antoinette replied, "This is not a court of law, it is a rabble and I refuse to be accountable to it."

"Madame . . . Your Majesty, you are right, it is not a court. There is no legal jurisdiction here. This is merely a provisional enquiry into the death of this unfortunate young woman. Later, perhaps, certain charges may be laid, meanwhile . . ."

"Meanwhile, Sir, you may continue your enquiries at your leisure but I shall take no part in them. I was in my chamber, and happily, it appears, was asleep. Now please go about your business, I am concerned with deeper issues, the affairs of State."

"Your . . . your Majesty, please . . ."

"You may go now," said Marie Antoinette.

Ferdinand said in evidence that he was patrolling the woods around Atopia House when he heard a small splintering sound coming from the vicinity of the north wing; this, he also said, could have been caused when the lock of Constanze door was forced – it was such a sound.

"And you saw no person in the vicinity, Guard?"

"Only Conrad – he was walking along the cemetery wall, but he didn't see me."

"Did you notice the direction this man took?"

"Oh yes, Comrade. He was already walking towards the women's quarters."

"And you followed him?"

"No, Comrade, I did not. This is a strange house. At every

hour of the day and night they are wandering about. I watch, but I do not follow. It is my wish only to go to Bolivia, for this reason I make the bombs, to kill General Appariz."

"Did you . . . did you admire the lady Constanze?"

"Admire her?" Ferdinand kissed the air. "She enchanted me. Just to be near her was all a man could desire. It was a tremendous pity that she was sick in the head; without this sickness she would have made a wonderful wife."

"You had no wish to harm her?"

"Harm her? Kill her, you mean, for she is dead! I had no such wish. In death I would love her. Now I kiss her hands, her feet."

"But you went to the house – to the north wing?"

"Of course. It is my duty to guard such beauty."

"Did you, by chance, see Mr. McAndrew's dog – the small white dog – sitting outside?"

"Comrade, I did not see the dog. The last time I saw this dog he was in the great hall. The painter was drunk, did I not tell you this? And the dog was whining and licking the painter's face."

"That will be all," said Uncle Dumb, through Mama Meg.

Constanze, fearful of Conrad who was walking under a full moon, sat up in the ancient bed of her room; a room bare of furniture save for this and a single high-backed chair. Earlier, she had pulled the curtains and the room was in darkness.

On one occasion, when she had first arrived at Atopia, she had left the curtains wide, and Conrad, with his hands on the sill, had slowly raised himself on the flower-bed outside and looked through the window.

Now a footstep slurred the boards of the corridor outside.

"Who is it?"

Constanze had seen the handle of the door turn.

"Is that you, Mama Meg?"

No reply. Constanze sat up in the bed. Sweat flooded to her face.

251

She was getting out of bed to light the oil lamp when the lock suddenly splintered and the door flew open. It seemed an explosion of sound that detonated into her growing consciousness, and she flung herself back on to the bed.

Someone entered. Because the room was in total darkness she could see neither shape nor being, but heavy footsteps told that it was a man. Constanze shrank away, her hands moving to her throat. She heard the door quietly shut; the blackness about her tingled with silence.

The intruder did not move. Vaguely, in her growing terror, Constanze wondered if he had gone out into the corridor, but then she heard faint breathing and the sound of naked feet slithering on the boards of the room. Against the faint glow from the edges of the curtain something moved; as her horrified eyes grew more accustomed to wakefulness she could discern shape more clearly, and the man was coming around to the other side of the bed, where she was lying.

Raising her hands she put them into her hair, clutched and screamed; mouth wide, eyes clenched, three times she screamed, her face turned up, but made no sound; no sound she made in those screams, and, as she lowered her hands the man reached out, seeking her; touching her, his hand slid down to her wrist and he gripped it. Constanze, her body now shaking, heard herself say:

"Who . . . who are you?" for the man's touch in some strange way was the comforting touch of humanity, and Conrad, whom she did not consider a human, had constantly invaded her dreams.

"Salieri." The reply, a whisper, instantly came.

"McAndrew!" The knowledge sat her up and she peered, straining towards him.

"Ah no, Constanze, that's the whole point. The name's Salieri."

"How . . . how can it be?" She had found her voice. "Salieri is dead!"

"Risen from the dead, Constanze – the same as you." He sat upon the bed. "Or have ye forgotten so soon what hap-

pened in the apartment in Schulerstrasse when I came before? If ye play a role, woman, you've got to accept the defeats
as well as the victories." Gripping her arms he pressed her
back into the pillows.

"Please . . ." her voice begged. "In the name of my husband. . . ?"

"In his name? God alive, woman, except when he wanted
you he didn't give a damn for ye! If ever there was a damned
Lothario he was one, and I wouldn't have trusted him with a
pet goat. Didn't I tell ye that before, and didn't you agree?"

"That was before! Now he's dead and I revere his
memory!" She fought to be free, but his strength was greater
than hers and after a while she lay back, gasping, her face
averted. McAndrew said:

"Aye, and that's the trouble, isn't it! The rest of the world
enjoys the canonising while Mozart goes free of the taint –
the double-dealing. God Almighty, I couldn't have copied
the score of the *Requiem* in the time he's supposed to have
written it. Ask your sister-in-law – ask Nissen, and ye'll get
the truth of the pupils who worked for him. Jesus good! How
can ye go wrong, Constanze, with genius like Beethoven
knocking on your door? Half his work wasn't his and you
know it, yet people like Sussmayr and I took a back seat at
Court while he took the glory!"

Constanze said faintly, unhearing, "You . . . you are a
painter. Salieri was a musician. How can you be reborn as
Salieri?"

McAndrew chuckled bassly. "As you are reborn as Constanze, yet the wife of Mozart who died ninety-six years ago
was dark, as dark as you are fair. Nor do you resemble her in
form or face."

She lay silently and he leaned above her, his voice a faint
whisper now. "And if, like me, you claim rebirth, then you
lay victim to ills as well as health, grief as well as joy. Stain as
well as purity become yours, me lovely wee thing – now
haven't I done a fine body on ye for the mural? So come on,
lassie – were ye so reluctant when I lifted ye skirt in Schulerstrasse with your old man out singing Papageno? Aye! And

me doing the bird-catchin' in his own bedroom! Surely you remember?"

"I do not . . ." She beseeched him. "Oh please, Salieri!"

"Ach, that's good, you've got me name right at last. Didn't ye notice I've signed the canvas by that name in respect of ye?"

Now he was beside her on the bed, bringing himself to nakedness and he pressed his body against hers so that she felt the heat and strength of him.

"Salieri, please, please don't tell my husband!"

"Rest yourself, lass, that's the last bloody thing I had in mind."

Constanze cried aloud with the pain when he went into her, dividing her body, making her as one with him, and this was an agony to her because she had not been used before. And so, within the rape she lay with clenched hands and averted face; it was a fraud of death, a play on dying within the knifing thrusts.

And while this went on in an eternity of defilement there came to Constanze a sense of dedication that seemed to purify the obscenity: she would dedicate this degradation, she thought, to a remission of the pain of her conscience. Could she, she wondered, lighten her sins of betrayal . . .? the betrayal of Amadeus, at the time when he needed her most – not in life, for in life she had never betrayed him – but in death?

Perhaps, she thought now, within the rhythmic thrusting of a rapist's body . . . perhaps it was possible, through this pain, that the world would no longer condemn her as heartless, but understand and forgive?

This realisation came into her consciousness like a bright exploding light, and within a sudden surge of relief Constanze lifted her hands and caressed the bearded thing that was a face. And when the rapist quickened she knew in his strength an act of expiation that removed her from the room's darkness and the floundering grunts, and in her relief she heard herself whispering words of pity; later, even those of consolation and endearment, as a woman speaks to a child.

254

"Ellie, Ellie, Ellie!" whispered McAndrew.

Constanze listened, her eyes opening slowly.

McAndrew was now kissing her face, her hair, her lips, and he gasped:

"Oh God, *Ellie!*" And he groaned like a man on fire. "Why? Why?"

Constanze would have asked the meaning of this but could not, because his hands had fastened around her throat.

Next morning, Mama Meg said, during the interview, "I think I heard Constanze cry out and this woke me. I listened, then thought I must have been dreaming . . ."

"You heard a cry, you say? What time was this?"

"Don't know, sir. No idea, really speaking."

"Did you hear anything else suspicious last night, ma'am?"

"Oh yes, I heard Ferdinand singing the *Uspallatas*, but he's always singing that, ain't he?"

"Is he? I am not aware of it. What is this singing?"

Uncle Dumb spoke and Mama Meg interpreted, "It is the revolutionary song of the Bolivian freedom fighters. Actually, although Ferdinand is unaware of it, it is Chilean."

"What are his political aims?"

"Ferdinand's intention is to assassinate General Lopez Appariz, once the head of Bolivia's ruling junta – he is unaware that the general died in his bed three years ago. To this end he makes bombs and explodes them in the cellar."

"You allow this?"

"Of course."

"But why?"

"Because here everybody does that which pleases them."

"And have you any reason to suspect this man's violence in other directions?"

"Good gracious, no. He is the gentlest of creatures."

"Madam . . . Mama Meg . . . you found the body of this young woman, I understand?"

Mama Meg replied, her face lowered, "She didn't come for breakfast, see. I was goin' to send young Toppy for her, but I was glad I didn't. I found her behind the door, hanging from a bedsheet."

There was then no sound but that of Uncle Dumb sobbing.

"What time was that?"

"Half-past eight, thereabouts."

"You cut her down, I'm told."

Mama Meg raised a tear-stained face. "Christ, yes. What do ye take me for? She was mine, weren't she? How could I leave her hanging?"

"And then?"

"Then I called Uncle Dumb."

"And when you checked the other bedrooms the man you call McAndrew had not slept in his bed, you say?"

"No, but that don't mean to say he done it."

"Madam, I am not inferring that. I am merely trying to establish the movements of people in this house . . ."

"Well, it ain't anyone here, I can tell you that!"

Uncle Dumb interjected, "This is a house of peace and love. It is not possible that any of the family . . ."

"Madam, what, in your opinion, was the relationship between the deceased and the man McAndrew?"

"Now look," said Mama Meg, getting up. "Don't you start that bloody caper – begging your pardon, Uncle Dumb – this was a respectable house . . ."

Uncle Dumb moved his hands. "It is possible that they were in love . . . but nothing more than that of affectionate relatives, you know? I have seen McAndrew looking at Constanze with something akin to reverence."

Uncle Dumb said, before the Inspector left, "Yes, McAndrew has gone. The paw marks of a small animal were found outside the door of the servants' entrance – all right, I accept that Mr. McAndrew could have been there at some time or other. But I tell you, Inspector, it is just not possible that he could have done such a thing. Look for an intruder, I beg you. If our beautiful Constanze was murdered, as you say, it was by nobody in this house."

*

256

After the Inspector had gone Uncle Dumb said to Mama Meg:

"Will you discover for me what Mr. Toppam was doing last night, between the hours of darkness and dawn?"

"Oh, Sir, for Gawd's sake, Sir. You don't suspect our poor little Mr. Toppam!"

"My dear lady, of course not. Do compose yourself. It is only that . . . how shall I put it . . ." His big hands moved more slowly, and with affection. "That our Constanze – in miniature, you understand – would look so very much like a charming little doll."

26

It was a morning of benefaction, of cold air and brown, autumn light, and the wayside trees of the road to the south were exultant in the wind.

With Atopia House far behind him, McAndrew walked with a fine swing to his military pace, his boots thumping on the tarmac and Caesar, in a hopping trot, was six feet in the rear.

McAndrew had breakfasted at dawn, tickling from a brook two dumb, compliant fish; these he had gutted and skewered over a fire of twigs, then ravenously bolted them down; now specks of their white flesh clung to his lips. He went bareheaded, his golden hair vegetating in bright curls down to his shoulders and his spade beard chafed the nakedness of his chest: ragged, disreputable, he went in lusty singing one moment and infuriated curses the next, shaking his fist at the sky.

Caesar evinced no enthusiasm for the journey. At Atopia, being the only dog (and he had seen to it there were no cats) he had eaten three meals a day with relish under Mama Meg. Now, head low, he followed out of habit born of obedience, moody, showing the whites of his eyes at his master's ravings, not even pausing to savour wayside perfumes.

Nor had Caesar breakfasted, but dumbly watched Lazy One cook and eat the fish without the slightest reference to a hungry comrade. Now, as he followed McAndrew, he thought of the bitch who had rejected him in the farmyard – indeed, the only bitch he had ever wooed.

Bitches, his life had taught him, had to be watched. One

had emasculated a friend of his in Hendon by fighting her way through a gap in some railings; nothing was worse than such a mate – first showing desire and then reluctance. But the one he had known in the shippon was all desire, and now, trotting behind McAndrew, Caesar remembered the lithe quickness of her; he remembered, too, her litter-language and the smell of her and he lifted his muzzle to the wind in hope of her: but he smelled only ribes, which were growing by the way – a cat stink – tom-cat at that, and his nose infuriated him.

"Come on, come on!" shouted McAndrew. "Get goin', mun. What the hell's wrong with ye?" Fifty yards ahead now, he halted and raised a tattered arm.

Near Spalding Moor they rested. Caesar, lying on his side, panting in the midday sun, listened as Lazy One did his unfathomable shouting at the sky; much time had been occupied in this strangeness, he thought. And McAndrew was at it now, a big fist raised:

"Are you satisfied? He was thirty-seven, d'ye realise that? Did ye even give him time to make his genius?"

The dog watched as McAndrew stamped about on the road. "Chopin, Schubert – Mozart and Van Gogh. By Jesus, you let your useless bloody kings live long enough, don't ye? And still they call you God. Well, I say that you're a heartless beggar, and stupid at that!" Caesar cornered his eyes, showing their whites when Lazy One suddenly wept, knuckling his face with his fist. "Did you really have to have Lautrec? You've only just taken Seurat at the age of thirty-two!"

Then Lazy One fell to his knees and howled aloud, rocking himself and groaning.

Comfort of some kind appearing to be a necessity, Caesar rose and went to him, licking Lazy One's hand.

"Who do you take your troubles to?" asked McAndrew.

All that day they travelled, and the next, and on the evening of the third day the sky darkened and mist began to swirl among the brown-topped hills. South of a place called

Coneysthorpe they rested on the bank of a lake, but only briefly. And when McAndrew rose to continue the journey, Caesar did not follow. Therefore the man returned to where the dog was lying and said to it:

"What ails ye, for God's sake? You're a lazy old tyke if ever I saw one, get up off your rear," and he prodded Caesar with his boot until he rose.

Then Caesar followed again, but in his ribs was a great pain that neither the eating of herbs nor the drinking of water would abate, and this was a worry to him because he knew that with nightfall would come hunting-time, and Lazy One did not expect to hunt for himself. Perhaps, indeed, he would be angry if no food was obtained, and stamp about and shake his fist.

Most of that night they travelled and Caesar could not understand the reason for this. Never before had they gone at such speed, either; also, Lazy One was acting strangely, such as looking behind him, and sheltering when other people approached. And there came to Caesar an increasing weariness and he would have laid down to sleep, had this been allowed. But he laboured on, hopping on three legs behind McAndrew, and, on the evening of the fourth day, with the sun setting red in the Howardian Hills, Lazy One picked him up, held Caesar momentarily in the crook of one arm and with the other hand pointed, saying:

"Rabbit!"

There, not fifty paces away, with his nose snitching and his ears pricked up in the wind, was a big buck coney, the stamper of his tribe.

Fine and beautiful he looked with the sun scarlet on his coat, and, seeing him, Caesar hoped that perhaps he would have a doe about him because, were there a doe there would possibly be young, an easier catch . . .

"Go on," commanded McAndrew. "What's wrong with ye, ye big soft thing – rabbit, *rabbit*! I need me supper."

The wind changed in the valley.

The buck sniffed dog-smell, unbuttoned his tail, stamped the earth, and was off.

"After him!" yelled McAndrew.

Buck was fast, cool and strong. Nature, knowing a leader, had trained him well.

Often in the chase by dog, ferret or fox, Buck had laid the scent and run in great loping strides across the meadow, diverting them from his warren. And, in this confidence, even a rabbit is not without his sense of humour.

Only a glance at Caesar was needed – this dog was old, and slow, and might be led a dance – a dance that the other rabbits would see – and this would commend a leader. So, with his ears flat down upon his skull, Buck of Coneysthorpe went windward, while Caesar lumbered in pursuit. And, as the chase began so the evening grew red in sun-fire, bathing the hills in a roseate light, and for Caesar it betokened the end of the earth.

For Buck, with rabbits, ferrets, and a single dog-fox watching, it became the spirit of the chase with little chance of being caught. Therefore he leaped and cavorted, springing high over the boulders while Caesar staggered after him and McAndrew, now up on a wall, became an excited scarecrow of waving arms and laughter.

Caesar ran full pelt, tumbled head over paws, and scrambled up and ran again, and did not bark; for to bark was a waste of energy, and this, he knew, he must conserve. And once, when Buck, over confident, stumbled, too, Caesar was almost upon him, his steel jaws snapping an inch from his tail.

From Caesar's tongue the saliva streamed, his broken teeth rolled drunkenly in his mouth. Buck was now running with greater care, for the strength of his pursuer was proving greater than he thought. His lean body streaked across the meadow, gathering and expanding to his raking kicks: sail up and over . . . up over a rock-scar, swift cut and a swerve and swerve again, and Caesar, his lungs filling with heart-water, floundered after him, paws skidding, tongue lolling, his breathing now in gasps.

But the rabbit could not shake him off and there grew in Buck's ball-eyes a shine of fear. This became terror when he collided with a boulder and the dog was again almost upon him. And, with his terror came misjudgment, and it took him into a bog: instantly slowed, Buck waded out of the slime and turned; with a quarry crevice behind him he was instantly trapped. His eyes bulged in panic.

Caesar, sensing death by the kill, trotted to a halt and stood there, swaying; great gasps for air shook his body.

Dog and rabbit momentarily faced each other.

And in Caesar's fuddled brain, one limpid through oxygen decrease, the head and horns of a bull made shape in showering blood. Yet all the time the thought raced with his heart-beats – *Lazy One must be fed* . . . Now, in his ears he heard the baying of the crowd, and *Lazy One must be fed*: the rattle of the baiting-chain he heard, and *Lazy One must be fed*, and the cobbles of the bull-ring were slippery with gore. And he feinted as he had done once before a century ago, and darted in, for Lazy One had to be fed: Buck went one way, and Caesar went another, and he opened his jaws and shut them down on fur and bone, and the bull bellowed . . . while the sun rushed in redness over Buck's dilating eye, in death.

The sun went down, and the moon came up and the night glittered with stars. But still McAndrew sat, hunched black against the autumn moon with Caesar in his arms.

When dawn came, he was asleep on the ground with the dog against his face, and when the sun came red and raging over the earth he fashioned a tool and with this dug a shallow grave.

Laying Caesar within it, McAndrew marked it with a stone.

Caesar. Died August 1905. Age unknown.

After doing this McAndrew cooked and ate the rabbit.

27

Wales called McAndrew. It was as if his Gaelic blood reached out for the mountains, a second-best consolation for the loss of his distant Scottish home. And always, of course, in Wales there was Ellie.

With the loss of Caesar had come emptiness. The sound of pattering feet behind, now gone, echoed in his loneliness.

A week later found him south of Gloucester, and the end of the month on the road to Barry, and the sight and sounds of Ellie invaded his crazed mind. As he grew nearer to her there came to McAndrew the necessity for speed . . . to find her at the end of the tramp, arms awaiting him.

Then he remembered her as the tousled, love-sick libertine in the bed of Ross Bolton, but regret soon followed the untidy image and now he blamed himself for her betrayal. Ellie, said her father, who was always complaining about lack of heart in others, yet needed the skill of a surgeon to find her own. Yet, while the loins of any women would serve to abate McAndrew's need, from the loins of Ellie had come forth a son . . .

Therefore, through the clandestine years of other loves, he longed for Ellie Kendall with a hopeless, parched desire.

Often he wondered if she had ever loved him in return, for it had seemed that she could never bear to offer him affection, as if this might create a desire she could not fulfil.

Was this, he thought now, as he tramped along, the essence of love?

The very stillness of the night, as he lay in a barn outside Barry, was a balm to his insomnia, for the closer he came to

Cambourne the less the need for sleep. And so he lay awake, with his face a foot from the stark-black roof of the barn, and listened to mouse-cheep and the deeper rustling of rats.

Thinking of Ellie, his body moved, and he knew an ache for her that nothing could requite; not sleep, not rest, not work, neither the fumbling madness of the canvas with its bright colours and grotesque shapes.

It was raining. The trees dripped tearfully on to the corrugated-iron roof, the water-spouts of the farm were running full bore to the shippon. McAndrew listened, screwing up his fist to the rainbow colours of his mind.

Dawn came, violent and unkempt. Rain-squalls and blustering winds rent a sky of vermillion clouds. But in them McAndrew smelled the sea and the smell was good. So he lay there in the hay until morning died into the ghosts of cock-crow; this slowly filled him with a sudden and joyous conviction. *He was going to see Ellie and Tom again*, and they would take to the road with him. Amid the Welsh hills where the brooks ran like flooding wine, he would see them.

"Are ye there, Mr. McAndrew?"

He sat up in the straw and rubbed his grimy face; twisted, and looked down the ladder leading to the ground.

The farm-wife was standing in the barn with a pot of oatmeal in her hands.

"Aye, Missus!"

He wondered if he ought to kill her after all . . .

She was as thin as a Handel lute, with black broomstick legs, but she had a fine sing-song voice and was Welsh, she claimed, down to the third generation.

"Is it cold with ye up there, mun? You should have slept in the house, to hell wi' the neighbours!" Her wizened face smiled up.

McAndrew came down the ladder and took the oatmeal from her hands. "Ach, it wasn't the neighbours, girl. Sure to God, I wouldn't trust myself under the same roof with one so beautiful."

"Oh, go on with you! And me knocking seventy!"

"On the likes of you, girl, I'd play the sweetest music. Can ye afford this oatmeal?"

"Aye, I can. I've taken it off me old chap's dinner."

He thought: I could reach out and grip her throat with my hand and her neck would break.

He kissed her face. "If I was your old man, I wouldn't bother about dinner. Could you lend me a morsel o' bread for the journey? I'll pay it back one day, so I will."

"It'll down the pig, mind."

"Och, to hell with the pig. One day I'll come back, ye pretty little Welsh."

"Is it tears on your face, Mr. McAndrew?" She smiled up from his shoulder.

"No, woman. It's the rain. Good day to ye."

She was standing in the shippon, a shrimp of life hammered by people into skin and bone.

"Good luck to ye!"

"God speed, Mr. McAndrew!"

He was a fine and terrifying man to arrive on a doorstep, she said to herself, but we're on this earth with an obligation to others. She was glad she had fed him. The moon was still squatting on the roof of the barn as she went back into her cottage.

It was a wicked, bare-legged ghost of loneliness that stalked her kitchen after McAndrew had gone. Crossing the room the farm woman looked up at the portrait above her mantle.

"Thought it was you come back, Dai."

After a while she made herself tea, and sat there looking at her fingers.

In a public house outside Barry, McAndrew played his landlord's trick and got a free quart, though the barmaid gave him a whimsical glance.

She was a well set-up piece, with crocheted lace across a well-filled bust and a complexion of roses and cream.

265

McAndrew thought she looked like *La Poudreuse*, Seurat's ponderous mistress.

Possessed of wondrous, china blue eyes, the barmaid's voice was as dry as tinder, though he sensed in her an instinctive, child-like innocence, and warmed to her feminity.

Were he to lay his face against her breast, he thought, the manhood years would slip away and his mouth bring him the marvellous peace of infancy. Some time earlier in his life . . . although he could not remember his mother . . . McAndrew had known this peace. Now it touched him with no sense of time. Therefore the barmaid's motherhood called him, bringing to him a sweetness which his wandering brain defined; love in its unadulterated, purest form.

But room noise beat about him and he felt disturbed.

"What you blutty looking at?" asked the barmaid.

A farm labourer, big, uncouth, leaned over and dropped a penny down the front of her.

"I pays for what I gets, Missus," said he, "You got a pint o' that good stuff for me?"

McAndrew closed his eyes. The barmaid said, "O aye! This one's ale, see? This one's stout, and the one in the middle is bitter," so he went out into the night.

The sun arrived early over the sea at Barry, a light flower-pink. A breeze from the island wandered in over the calm, pea-green waves, and McAndrew remembered when first he had come to this place and been taken on by Jake. That was during his riotous communion of the streets and the navvy labour, the building of Number Two Dock and the Lady Windsor.

Now the navvies had gone, unsung, forgotten; the only token of their industry the metallic clatter of the winching cranes, the grumble of coal shutes, the whining of hydraulic traversers and grain elevators. It was a confusion of prosperity; a port of pulsating life – exporting eleven million tons of coal a year, more than her sister Cardiff.

*

Nobody noticed McAndrew; he was one of many, the ragged riff-raff of the waterfront looking for a berth or a barrel of ale. He went with his hands in his trews, his eyes missing nothing, and saw at the end of the dock the old *Sarn Helen*. Rusted, rejected, she was one of a score in a forest of masts – steamers, schooners and barques. She sat in still water, the old Clyde Puffer he had learned to love. And the old ship called him as surely as if she had beckoned.

With a glance around for watchers, he leaped aboard her and prowled her deck. The aft cabin door was swinging in the sea-wind, creaking harshly above the shrieking of gulls; McAndrew went within.

Here was the table where he had eaten with Ellie; there was the bed where she had borne his son in the storm off Skokholm: only eight years back? McAndrew rubbed his bearded face; it seemed a bloody lifetime.

He felt again the buck and heave of the ship beneath him, the smash of waves in the storm, he heard wind-shriek and the crying of a child . . . with old Jake playing 'Nearer my God to Thee' on the harmonium.

Vaguely, he wondered what had happened to Jake . . . Think of it, young Tom was eight years old now! He pondered this, believing it to be impossible. And he heard again Ellie's calm voice:

'. . . Now come on, get a hold of yourself, for God's sake, Mr. McAndrew. Tell Jake to rig up a riding-light . . . And a drogue anchor. Get her head to the wind and we'll ride it out, the bitch.' McAndrew heard himself say, 'I'll treat ye decent after this, Ellie . . .' and her reply as she patted her stomach, 'Right now I'm wishing ye'd never treated me at all . . .'

He stared around the bare cabin. The broken door slammed shut, bringing him to darkness. But a single ray of sunlight shafted on to the table, and in that moment he seemed to see Ellie by the magic hand of chance – momentarily, as part of the autumn.

Bright-eyed, dark-haired, as if authorised by Nature, she stood in sunlight.

"Och, me sweet girl!" McAndrew said.

Above him the gulls wailed their petulant grief; beneath his feet the deck grumbled to the throbbing beats of industry.

He had to see her. And Tom. If only a glimpse. The wish came upon him with enveloping force and he turned and kicked the door open, crossed the deck, handsprung the rail, and ran along the quay.

Jean Pierre, the French dwarf, from the hatches of the *Marie Prey*, watched him, unseen. Rolling a cigarette one-handed he put it between his thick lips.

"*Ah oui!*" The dwarf grinned, exposing big, yellow teeth. "*Returnez vous? C'est bon, mon ami!*"

McAndrew waited until darkness before he went to Cambourne.

28

It was Tom's eighth birthday: McAndrew had not realised this, he could never even remember his own. Now he approached the house with care, keeping to the Cambourne woods.

Earlier it had rained. Now the wind had a fine mist of wetness that mantled his hair and beard; he was soaked, and the night air chilled him.

He possessed no money but, even so, would not have gone into the Chain Locker for fear of being recognised. He moved slowly, a wraith of silence through the trees, and was surprised to see a little cluster of caravans and a bonfire burning at the top of the Big Wheatfield.

Ellie had apparently given the tinkers permission to camp there; the thought pleased him. The tang of the bonfire came to his nostrils, and he remembered Rosa.

Bramble and meadowsweet were growing on the banks as he crossed the river by the bailiff's bridge. He remembered Tom and how they had cooked and ate the fish on his last night in Cambourne. McAndrew paused on the bank now, hearing faint music.

Across the meadow the house blazed light, sending searchlight beams into the darkness, and above the orchestra he heard a nightingale singing. The sound pleased him. Raising his face he imitated its song. Immediately other birds joined in; these he imitated, too – a jackdaw flying above – its caw-caw harsher than the rook's: now a jay sang, and the rippling si si si of a goldcrest. The old days flooded back to McAndrew and he cupped his

hands and echoed the birds so that soon the river valley was
alive with their singing – thrush, blackbird, goldcrest and
linnet, night-jar, owl and jay.

Squatting on the end of the bridge, he got them
going, and all the memories of Cambourne flooded back so
that he could have shouted aloud with joy.

Ellie, in her dressing-room on the first floor, heard this
bird-song, which was like a night dawn chorus, in itself
strange. Opening the curtain, she peered out. The meadow
below her lay bright in moonlight. She saw, far away on the
ridge of the Big Wheatfield, the tinker bonfire, vaguely
wondering who had given them permission to camp there.

The birds sang on, a disputing chorus that encompassed
the whole of the Cambourne woods. It was a fanciful
thought, and frightening, that McAndrew might be
around; Ellie banished the possibility . . .

McAndrew did not see the light from the curtain movement, but stared about him, mimicking bird after bird while
the choir grew in pace and sound.

"Silly old buggers," he said.

Ellie closed the curtain as the bird-song ceased. There
was nothing now but the call of a night-jar. In swift strides
McAndrew crossed the meadow and merged into the
shadows of the house; here the oaks spread their verdant
branches over the yellow gravel of the drive. Carefully, he
crept around the ivy-covered walls.

The main lawn at the front of Cambourne was a panel of
yellow light. The music increased in sound as he drew
nearer. Peering around the jamb of the french doors that
led to the garden, McAndrew saw within a refurnished
drawing-room, one of amazing opulence, compared with
the one he knew. Surely not Ellie's doing, he thought, for
she penny-pinched when it came to the house.

The ornate ceiling blazed; antique chairs, exquisitely
carved and padded with velvet, lined the oak-panelled
walls; a bright yellow Persian carpet reflected the
chandelier light, and a refectory table, conveniently placed

to allow dancing, was laden with crested silver plate: a banquet of food and wine in ice-buckets spread the width of the room.

In the middle of it couples in evening dress were dancing; in one corner an orchestra was playing a waltz.

McAndrew moved closer, the better to see the guests.

Lord Windsor he instantly recognised, the Lord-Lieutenant of Glamorgan: talking to him with zest was the eminent Thomas Webb, a director of the Barry Railway Company, so soon to die. Louis Guéret, the Frenchman, was there, as was the company's solicitor, Mr. Downing. Unknown to McAndrew, Downing's presence was the reason for the celebration; his own portrait was about to be presented to him.

Many younger people were dancing, the dresses of the girls lending colour to the scene. And then McAndrew saw him – saw Tom and knew instinctively that this was his son. The intervening five years had changed him, bringing him from babyhood. Tall for his eight years, he was possessed of the same chunky strength of his father; little of Ellie, physically or mentally, lay in her son.

McAndrew rubbed his mud-stained face with the back of his hand, staring at the boy. Dressed as he was in his black velvet jacket and tightly-fitting tartan trews, he could have been the son of a laird; McAndrew wondered why Ellie had dressed him so . . .

Now the door of the drawing-room opened and Ross Bolton entered.

The years, thought McAndrew, had laid no mark on Bolton's face; he moved with the old athletic grace, inches taller than any man there, and his old imperious manner, akin to insolence, had not deserted him. Pushing the door wide he stood, hands on his hips, waiting. And through the door, in the arms of a manservant, came Ellie. Thin, pale, with her eyes shadowed, illness was written on her features.

An exclamation rose in McAndrew's throat, but he fought it down, automatically moving closer to the french doors. Faint clapping from the guests greeted Ellie as the servant set her down on to a settle, and McAndrew caught but a glimpse of her before the people gathered about her, obscuring his view.

"*Ellie . . .*" he said.

Then the guests drifted away from her as the music began again, and McAndrew could see only flash views of her through the waltzing partners. With growing apprehension he came closer to the glass, staring into the room. The music was growing louder in his ears, obliterating his consciousness. The predominant thought prevailed – Ellie was ill: it beat within his head with relentless force.

Now the dance ended and he could see her clearly. Tom was sitting on a stool at her feet; guests were greeting her, and she received them with the lethargy of one at the door of death.

McAndrew wondered what was wrong with her. In the old days, he recalled, she used to complain about her heart, but neither he nor Jake ever took it seriously. In the coal-loading, at Port Penrhyn and Dinorwic, she would shovel the hours of a man. Now, dressed in a white silk gown with a bustle, high in the waist and puffed at the shoulders, the effect increased her look of frailty; its whiteness drained her face of colour.

She appeared debilitated, thought McAndrew, as if by long illness: moved listlessly, her feathered fan sometimes covering her face. She looked bloodless, lost to the gaiety and sparkle about her. And behind her chair, feet astride, his hands locked behind him, stood the carrier, the man-servant. Bald, bullet-headed, of immense proportions, his gaze moved arrogantly around the room, clearly he was the family bodyguard, presumably employed to disconcert people like McAndrew.

Ross Bolton, with three young women, came up to Ellie, momentarily engaging her in some witticism, an attempt to cheer her. Ellie smiled faintly, and in that smile the old Ellie instantly returned for the watching McAndrew.

He saw again the brightness of the summer day when first he had come to Barry, and the girl whom he thought was a

272

fisher-girl with her dark, inviting smile. He saw her again in the coal-basketing: saw her sweating face in the cabin of the old *Sarn Helen*, when in labour.

The bite of the wind he knew, the sun-warmth of the Menai Estuary. And all the love he had ever held for her welled up within him, so that he could have cried aloud. Momentarily, too, Ellie's fan stopped moving and she stared directly at the french doors, her eyes opening wide in recognition, and then fear.

Slowly, she sat upright on the settle, staring at McAndrew whose massive form had now made shape. And he, as if magnetised, saw this recognition and shouted:

"Ellie!"

Ellie shrieked. Dropping the fan she put her hands to her face, and McAndrew heard the cry, his bemused brain interpreting it as a greeting.

With outstretched arms he barged against the glass; it held, so he kicked his way through it, punched it aside in shattering crashes, and gained the room. All heads swung to him. Women screamed; men cowered away from the tattered scarecrow appearing in their midst.

The glass had cut him; McAndrew was bleeding from a dozen gashes as he had barged his way across the floor; one slicing gash on his forehead had opened a vein and blood filled one eye, pulsating in streams into his beard, pouring over his chest.

Now he stood before Ellie in the moment before the bodyguard rushed; his bloodstained hands begged to her.

"Aw Christ," he said, *"Ellie!"*

The bodyguard, coming round the settle, crouched momentarily, then leaped. Gripping the Scotsman's arms he pinned them behind his back.

Men were gathering about him, yelling tonelessly into his face, women were shrieking as they bore him down. But he rose, his blood spattering the floor, and flung them off: turned and clubbed the manservant to his knees. McAndrew knelt then, his arms again open to Ellie.

"In God's name, what's wrong with ye? Are you ill?"

273

Ellie shrank away from him. He saw a flash vision of his son, his arms protectively around his mother as the men dragged him away, his bare legs trailing. But McAndrew was up instantly: hitting out, and they fell before him.

A woman broke her rhythmic screaming to shout:

"The police. Call the police, call the police!" Other women, their dresses clutched against them, were racing into the garden. McAndrew saw Ross Bolton's face before him, and struck it, sending it reeling away. And Ellie, her white gown spattered scarlet, rose weakly from the settle; in the mêlée of blows and shouting confusion, she stood there staring down. Her husband's blood-covered face was upturned, his clasped hands pleading.

"Get out, McAndrew!" she said.

He saw two faces, Ellie's and her son's; side by side in condemnation in the moment before the manservant pushed him headlong and swept Ellie up into his arms. The servant ran, weaving a path through the milling people. And over her shoulder as she was carried away Ellie shrieked, white-faced:

"Get out, you animal! Do ye hear me, McAndrew? *Get out!*"

The Scotsman rose. Blood from his right hand dripped monotonously on the floor within a sudden, stricken silence, and he turned slowly in the middle of the room.

Mouths were moving aimlessly in unspoken consternation; he saw the faces of Downing and Lord Windsor. Guéret, the Frenchman, was adopting a fine air of disassociation. Other men were standing in protective clutches, staring from one to the other.

"You'd best go, McAndrew . . ." said Downing, gently.

Then Ross Bolton interjected, "Oh no, he doesn't. He's staying here for the police."

Mr. Wendon came forward. "Go – go now, Mr. McAndrew. And never come back, do you hear me?"

McAndrew wiped blood from his eyes, peering down into the man's face. His old respect for Henry Wendon touched his brain, momentarily steadying it. He said:

274

"Have I killed anyone, for Christ's sake?"

"No. Nobody has been harmed. You are only killing yourself. Ellie will be all right, I give you my word. Leave now?"

Jean Pierre, the French dwarf, was sitting on the fo'castle head of the *Marie Prey* when McAndrew returned to the docks. With his eternal cigarette in the corner of his mouth, he said as the Scotsman came alongside:

"*Voilà!* The big savage! And fighting again, eh?"

McAndrew saw him in the moonlight; the squat body with its barrel chest, the thick arms, the crippled legs. The dwarf's eyes were gleaming strangely from the folds of his shattered face. With a cap on the side of his head, naked to the waist, the little man sized McAndrew.

"You fight me now, Monsieur? We go to the Chain Locker bar and fight again, eh?"

"You sod off, you and ye soddin' Chain Locker."

"I buy you drink, perhaps? I buy you drink and you draw for me *The Little Treasure* – Henri Toulouse-Lautrec? *Vive Henri!*" The little Frenchman kissed the air with his fingers.

"Don't you mention his name, you bastard."

Jean Pierre said, "You got trouble, Big Savage?"

"Not so you'd bloody notice." McAndrew wiped the blood from his eyes.

The dwarf shrugged. "A sailor has troubles? He takes them to sea, my friend – to wash them away. You got gendarme trouble, I think, with all that blood."

"Get buggered," said McAndrew.

The dwarf rose and stepped on to the quay. No higher than McAndrew's belt, he stared up at him. "Later I get buggered, like you say, but now I take you aboard, my friend, for the police are coming, can you see?" He pointed with a stubby finger across to Cadoxton. Three helmeted constables were coming abreast, truncheons drawn, their feet stamping on the concrete. Jean Pierre said:

"I speak to the captain and you come aboard? And

nobody has seen you, *n'est pas?* Who will look for you on the *Marie Prey?*"

"You got whisky in there?" McAndrew jerked his head.

"We have better – we have cognac, also black coffee." Reaching up, he felt McAndrew's bicep. "You sail schooner rig, Big Savage?"

"Before ye come up, mun – out of the Clyde."

"And the *Marie*, she sails in half an hour – on the tide. Bound for Brittany, and then to the east? What more could you ask, Big Savage?"

McAndrew looked over the basin towards Cambourne and there the stars were brightest.

Book Four

29

1911

It was mid-spring when McAndrew left Rouen, and the third mate of the *Kobe Maru*, a China run trader, called from the rail:

"You're coming back, did you say, McAndrew?"

Halfway down the gangway, McAndrew shouted back, "I told ye I'd be signin' on ag'in, what more do ye want?"

"Your brawn for the bales. We're away on the night of the sixteenth, remember? So can I depend on it? I'll keep open the berth . . . And ye can paint to your heart's content."

The sun burned down; Rouen shimmered in heat; it was a springtime to end all springs, the sailors said.

McAndrew waved a big hand, hitched up his rucksack, canvases and pallets, and went without a backward glance, rags fluttering in a hot wind from a mirrored sea. Into the cacophony of the crowded, dust-filled waterfront he went, the thundering cranes and swinging cotton bales, the cracking of the whips and the bawled commands.

The third mate tried once more, cupping his hands to his mouth:

"If I know you're coming definite I'll enter your ticket, see. . . ?"

"You know what you can do," said McAndrew. "If I'm sailin' east ag'in I'm doin' it in style. With ye stinkin' weevil grub and your high-handed owners, ye're a harlot ship, mun – a floatin' house o' the Pharisees!"

"Did ye say something, Mr. McAndrew?"

"Aye, I did so. The prostate gland and the shin are two freaks o' nature, Mr. Alehouse, and you're the bloody third. You know what you can do wi' your ticket."

He waved a cheery hand, giving the mate a happy smile.

"We'll be looking forward to seeing you, then!"

"Not if I see you first," said McAndrew.

In the market square of Rouen, McAndrew bought wine, fresh-baked French bread, and cheese.

The stalls were end to end here, with vendors crying their wares and the cafés spilling their customers out on to the pavements in the sun.

Peasants of the Seine river basin, from Duclair to les Andelys, were there with their carts; the women in gaily-coloured dresses, the tinkers and gipsies of the red and gold caravans McAndrew had earlier seen trundling in from the docks with young cobs for sale, and great vats of butter. And the Rouen housewives were now duffing this up on their slabs, their faces sweating red under their white, lace bonnets, and he loved the rush and tear of it all.

Normally his size attracted attention, but few noticed him now as he eased his bulk on to a café chair and thumped the table for wine: the attention of the people being riveted to the cross on the cobbles where Jeanne d'Arc died, for here a giant Negro was standing, staring down, within a retinue of bejewelled women and film cameras.

Now the big man strode across the square towards the café; on the end of a leash he held a young tiger: two white women were escorting him, one on each arm.

McAndrew drank his wine, watching.

The Negro, white-suited and boatered, was approaching McAndrew's table and a crowd was following him in delighted pursuit. The Scot asked of a nearby waiter:

"Who might this be?"

"He is a boxer from Martinique, Monsieur. François Descamps, the promoter, found him; he is taking him to America to bring back the heavyweight championship of the world."

"O, aye! His name?"

"Rufus Mambara, the Black Shadow. His training camp is at Acquigny." The waiter gave a sallow smile: the tragedy of being a French waiter, thought McAndrew, was serving food while being half starved.

"Does not Descamps manage Georges Carpentier, also?"

"The Flame of France? Ah, now you are talking! Yes, he is also training at Acquigny. But Mambara is large and short of sparring partners."

"Acquigny on the road to Chartres?"

The waiter nodded, collecting glasses.

The giant Negro approached; the tiger's claws were scrabbling the pavement and it was growling deep in its throat.

The women – Parisian actresses, McAndrew heard later – chattered vivaciously up into the black man's face, their gesticulating fingers dipped in blood, their high-heeled shoes clattering.

The Scotsman's eyes moved over their skin-tight dresses, their young, sensuous bodies. He rose, putting down money. The eyes of the Negro met his. McAndrew gave him an expansive smile. The boxer's smile faded. And the women, instantly perturbed, stopped; the retinue of cameras paused. McAndrew said:

"You needin' sparring partners?"

The other nodded.

"Then I'll be seein' you, black man."

Inches taller, Mambara stared at first, then his face broke into a white grin.

"You do that, Whitey . . . you just do that." Reaching out, he tugged at McAndrew's beard. "But you'd best get this thing trimmed, man, so Ah can see your chin, eh?"

The women shrieked, stamping about.

"You try trimming it," said McAndrew.

It was dusk before McAndrew was clear of Rouen.

Crossing the Seine south of Igoville, he made camp near

Pont de l'Arche. The night was dark, warm and intimate, like the inside of a womb.

Surrounded by bluebells, buttercups and cowslips, he rested, boots up in military style, within sight of a lovely red-brick château. Before sleeping he sprinkled along a farmhouse lane handfuls of grain soaked in whisky, for earlier he had seen chickens ranging free.

A badger watched him from its earth; a cockerel crowed over the forest of larch. McAndrew ate French bread from his rucksack, biting off huge hunks with his strong, white teeth, and stuffing in cheese behind it.

Earlier, he had reckoned his pilgrimage as being something over two hundred miles, and it was his intention to cover twenty miles a day at the regulation pace. He drank cheap vin rouge from a bottle; sat back in the refuse of autumns and stared up at a full moon rising over the crest of the forest.

Later, before the moonlight faded, he pulled out a faded catalogue of drawings by Toulouse-Lautrec. With this still in his hands, he slept, to awake at dawn, cold, and ravenous with hunger.

Two hens and a bantam cock, their gullets filled with the grain soaked in whisky, were sleeping it off in a ditch near the lane; they died, still unconscious. Farther up the lane he found a cock pheasant walking in circles.

With the chickens and the pheasant tied to his belt, McAndrew set off again in the blue, gold-streaked dawn, marching along the road to Evreux.

Farther south, two days later, on a hillock overlooking the village of Acquigny, McAndrew rested, looking down on to a picturesque bridge where a little river flowed in trout swims and waving bindweed.

It was midday. The sun slanted down on to verdant fields of rape and vineyards. And in the river two men were bathing, one being middle-aged, the other young. The elder, of jovial face and corpulent, had his loins decorously covered; the young man was naked; wide-shouldered and as slim as a girl at the waist, his bright hair shone in the sun.

The young man waded into the shallows of the river; the older one swam to the bank, dressed himself, and went away.

McAndrew watched.

For a time the young man lay upon the bank, then rose; pulled on a pair of white shorts. Picking up a rope, he began to skip.

He skipped magnificently, with the languid movements of the professional athlete, and his body, bronzed with sun, danced in the shimmering heat. The rope curved about him to the intricacy of his steps and his feet were silent on the grass. Soon he began to sweat and this wetness emphasised the beauty of his muscled body; it rippled and shone like dancing quicksilver.

McAndrew, now on his knees, stared down, entranced. Gathering up his charcoal and Ingres paper, he hurried down to the river.

The young man went on skipping, apparently unaware of McAndrew, even when the Scot sat before him on the river bank but a few yards off.

Swiftly, McAndrew drew; first sketching the outline of the athlete with firm, incisive lines, then filling in muscled shoulders and biceps, the narrow waist and loins, the long, beautifully proportioned legs and feet.

The boy – McAndrew considered him little more than seventeen years old – went on skipping, moving with the assiduous grace of a cat, and his eyes, dark-shadowed under his jutting brows, ignored McAndrew; they were fixed as if on distant horizons.

His skipping finished, he folded the rope with slow, meticulous hands, and turned away.

"Monsieur, if you please," the Scot called in French. "You are Georges Carpentier?"

The boy nodded and his eyes drifted over McAndrew; steel-grey eyes, amazingly light in his brown face, and of impenetrable depth.

McAndrew said, "Will you take this sketch as a present, Monsieur?"

"You are English?" The voice was deep.

"Scottish."

"Is it not the same?" A smile flickered on the Frenchman's handsome mouth.

"It is not the same."

"You come here to my camp – to draw this?" The eyes moved again, assessing McAndrew's strength.

"Yes."

Carpentier held the sketch up to the sun. "It is excellent."

"Ten francs?"

"If I sign it, it will be worth a hundred, will it not?"

"Thank God for you, Monsieur."

"You are down on your luck?"

"I am an artist."

"But wasting your time as an artist, when there is money to be earned at a better trade. Spend three minutes in a boxing ring with my friend, Rufus, and you could earn yourself five thousand francs."

"Rufus?"

"The Black Shadow. Have you not heard of him? – the new heavyweight about whom they are making a film?" He gestured. "Up the road in my training camp?"

McAndrew eyed him. "Why do you not do it?"

Carpentier waved nonchalantly. "Because it is side-of-beef boxing, and I am only a welter-weight. You and Rufus are well suited for beef. Listen. You hit him, he hits you. *Viola!* It is over! The film is made. Another sparring partner bites the dust. A little blood, perhaps?" He emptied his hands, grimacing. "What is a little blood to a hungry artist?"

McAndrew tugged at his beard. "You mean I do a dive?"

"That is what they call it in America. Here, in France, we call it good discretion. My manager, François, pays good money to philosophers."

"Perhaps he will kill me."

"Then," replied Carpentier, "there would be one less hungry artist in the world, which is all to the good."

"That makes sense," said McAndrew, reflectively.

*

Two days later the Carpentier training camp at Acquigny was a scene of activity.

From as far as Paris the reporters came, crowding in from the road to Rouen with their note-books and cameras; the Descamps publicity machine was in full swing.

An American film crew was there, especially appointed to record the Black Shadow disposing of six sparring partners within the hour, an event being supported by Carpentier giving exhibitions of the new craze, *la boxe anglaise*, now rapidly superseding *la savate*, the old French art of self-defence.

The crowds were coming in by train, charabanc, on horse, on foot; pouring in to the forest clearing, packing the inns and taverns, sleeping rough for just a glimpse of Georges Carpentier, the teenage French idol whose lightning punches had already subdued Young Joseph, the British title-holder, and later knocked out the heavyweight champion, Bombardier Wells, in seventy-three seconds.

But this time public interest was not centred on the Flame of France, as the French called Carpentier, but on François Descamps' new sensation – the Black Shadow, the giant from Martinique.

All the paraphenalia of the boxing training camp was here: punch balls were rattling, heavy bags swinging to the hooks and jabs of sweating amateurs and professionals; boxers doing roadwork, boxers gambling at little card tables, or cuffing one another about in the ring under the expert eyes of masseurs, seconds, managers and trainers.

Ticker-tapes were going, field telephones ringing, type-writers clattering and wagers being laid in the eternal sunshine. Gaudy women, housewives, actresses and titled ladies came in a stream from Rouen, Le Havre, and as far as Paris.

Peasants and gipsies arrived from all points of the compass to the forest clearing, crowding in thick wedges around the small, square ring, lending the bright colours of their national dress, and a military band dominated all with blasts of martial music.

François Descamps, orator, hypnotist, acrobat and promoter, was in his element – entertaining the crowds with singing and dancing – haranguing political opponents, positioning film cameras to the best advantage.

And McAndrew, saying nothing but watching all, sat in a forked tree and sketched and drew with an industry that raised him at dawn and took him to bed at midnight.

The subjects were unending; the very physical application of the scenes below him caught him up – the village urchins, pickpockets, aged farmers, beautifully built athletes, titled ladies and blowsy Negro tarts who touted their wares on the edge of the crowd, unseen by the lurking gendarmerie.

With his bright, spade beard on his chest and his charcoal inscribing great arcs, nothing missed his hungry eye – the brown, muscled bodies of the boxers and their scarlet streams of blood; the sensuality of the girl troupe dancers who performed between bouts: even Carpentier's immaculate exhibition of box-fighting McAndrew exchanged for the drink-stunted faces of the ringside charlatans; the malevolent, hawk-like visage of those unsated by the spectacle of pain.

The young, eager faces of awaiting contestants, he saw and eagerly recorded; their smooth, unbled profiles contrasting with the cauliflowered, punch-drunk pugilists, the exploited refuse of Descamps' circus, of which Georges Carpentier was king.

Opponents of the Black Shadow came and went in vigorous progression, McAndrew vaguely noted.

Their route, resplendent in gold and silver dressing gowns, was an entry from the log-cabin, a bow to the cameras, a wave to the crowd to exuberant acclamation: square up in the middle of the ring at the gong; an attack by Rufus, arms flailing, the smacks of fists on flesh and bone, and *out*. Out to the world, apparently, in a collapse of crumpled limbs, then feet first to the exit.

Within fifteen minutes four sparring partners, white,

coloured, and of bulky proportions, fell before the black giant's searing attacks, and the film cameras whirred.

Meanwhile, McAndrew, still up his tree, recorded the proceedings with detached, artistic interest, until Descamps called, hands on hips, staring up:

"Come on, my artist friend! Get stripped for slaughter! You're next."

McAndrew vaguely wondered at the interruption, then lowered his sketching boards to the ground and came down to earth. The little man said:

"Five thousand francs on the Crédit Français at Evreux, but let me down and you don't get a sou, my friend. You dive at the end of the first round, remember?"

McAndrew stared at him.

François Descamps held his head.

"*Mon Dieu!*" he exclaimed, "He has forgotten!"

"You'll have to get that beard off," cried a handler.

"The beard stays on," said McAndrew.

Cheers of derision greeted McAndrew as he came from the log-cabin to the ring where Rufus Mambara was waiting.

The Scotsman had disdained both the ornate dressing-gown and the offer of official uniform; he came, instead, stripped to the waist, wearing only his tattered trousers and these reached only to his calves; his feet were bare.

The people ceased their derisory shouts and cat-calls when he climbed into the ring. The sun slanted down, turning his great head and spade beard into gold; his chest, bigger than the Negro's, jutted like a ship's bulwark, his biceps bulged: his journeyings in the East had hardened him; the heaving and hauling on dockside cargoes had slimmed him down and his brown body was cobbled with muscle.

On the other side of the ring, in scarlet trunks, Rufus Mambara's eyes shifted under his lowering brows, but McAndrew, apparently unperturbed by the coming event, smiled up at the sky.

The crowd went silent; then, sensing blood, it muttered, bassly, like bulls in an empty shippon.

McAndrew did not hear this. Somewhere up in the cobalt sky a lark was singing and he recognised its fretful cadence; knowing that somewhere below, perhaps among the feet of the careless crowds, there would be a nest . . .

Turning, he stared southward towards the road to Evreux; it shimmered like a purple ribbon through great forests of larch, and its freedom called him above the plaintive singing of the bird. A man's voice said:

"*Voila!* Good luck my British friend!"

Below the apron of the ring, Georges Carpentier was standing, his boyish face smiling up.

The gong sounded. McAndrew turned, facing the Negro, who attacked instantly, his great body brilliant with sweat and sun.

McAndrew, his gloves low, circled in defence.

The crowd was silent.

There was no sound now but the wind, and the singing of the lark.

The Negro's arms swung, but McAndrew was away, Mambara following ruthlessly, his movements ponderous, drunk with strength; his woolly black head thrust forward, as if inviting a blow. McAndrew retreated again, and Carpentier saw the fine muscles of his back ripple, and he danced clear as the black man rushed; McAndrew side-stepped. The Negro floundered into the ropes, striking air. A thick, white arm flashed out, a straight left, catching Mambara in the face.

It was a battle of Titans; the crowd stared agape; it knew its boxing. This white man, it now realised, was a boxer – no sacrificial goat.

François Descamps moved closer to the ring, cigar in mouth, glaring up, apprehensive.

Mambara attacked again, sliding flat-footed across the ring, his arms hooked in widening swings; McAndrew, frowning up from a crouch, ducked and weaved, taking the blows on his arms. Straightening, he sought a clinch, his great strength evident as he turned his adversary around like a giant doll.

Mambara said into his ear as they swayed on to the ropes: "Jesus, man, what you up to?"

McAndrew did not hear him.

He heard only the pulsing of his blood and the wild thumping of his heart.

It was conflict, and it suited him. He did not see the swaying black man before him, nor the white facial sea of the crowd. He saw only an opponent to be chopped and bludgeoned into submission.

Yet, withal, his brain was cool. And, as the Negro rushed again, his gloves madly swinging, McAndrew stepped inside and struck to the midriff. The black man gasped, doubling up. Standing back as the woolly head came forward, McAndrew, poised on his toes, hooked hard. Mambara took the blow clean on the chin with a crack like a pistol shot that cut through the ravings of the crowd. His head snapped back, his shoulders followed, his heels rose from the canvas and he fell with a crash. The gong sounded even as he fell, and men rushed out and dragged him to his corner.

McAndrew wandered back to his stool, turned and sat, to stare into the face of François Descamps, who was now in the ring, and his face jabbered soundlessly amid the savage roaring of the mob. People were leaping about, typewriters chattering, bets being laid amid the wild shrieking of women. And Mambara lolled in his corner, shaking his great head, fighting to gather intelligence.

Descamps shouted into McAndrew's face:

"I said make it look good, not kill him! You're supposed to dive. . . !"

McAndrew replied, in English, "I canna do it, mun."

The promoter opened his hands in a frenzied appeal. "Dive – dive! Ten thousand francs then, Monsieur. Just slip and fall." He grabbed McAndrew's arm. "We have a million invested! Four fights are booked in America . . . all you have to do . . ."

"Aw, shove off!"

Frantic, Descamps stared. "Who *are* you, for God's sake?"

The gong sounded like a toll of doom. The contestants rose from their stools, Rufus Mambara the slower. He ambled to the centre of the ring; there to stand, helplessly swaying, fighting for reflexes from his numbed brain, still stunned by the single, terrible blow that had felled him.

McAndrew, crouching low, came in.

In a shaft of sunlight he saw the Negro's face, contorted as he fought for balance; the rolling eyes white in the puffed, bruised cheeks, he saw: and measured the distance to the big man's jaw; drew back his right glove, and the bicep muscle bunched.

But the blow never came. Mambara sank to one knee, hung there perilously, before sagging at the waist. Then he fell, face down in the middle of the ring, his great black body shining in the sun, his shoulders heaving to the gasping intakes of his breath.

McAndrew turned on his heel, crossed to his corner, climbed through the ropes and jumped down from the ring.

Descamps yelled into his ear above the bawling of the crowd:

"Not a sou – you hear me? *Not a sou*, you two-timing son of a bitch!"

McAndrew, alone in the log-cabin, was gathering up his belongings when Carpentier entered: immaculately dressed, the boxer leaned against the frame, and said:

"My manager wants to know who you are."

"James Alexander McAndrew, Mister, and I'm on me way."

"Descamps also wishes to know how old you are?"

McAndrew lifted his rucksack and canvases and pushed past to the door. "If I tell him that he'll be as wise as me."

"You're forty, if you're a day, man. And the money?"

"Tell him to keep his money."

There was a pause. The Frenchman smiled. "Tell me, please – why did you do it?"

He received no reply.

"Because he was there, Monsieur – like a mountain?" He added. "I would understand that . . ."

No answer.

Carpentier said, "You have great talent, and I need such men about me. Soon, they say, I will be a light-heavy-weight . . . Will you not stay?"

"And fight you? Christ, mun, there's easier ways of dyin'."

Carpentier stood watching as McAndrew took the road to the south.

30

McAndrew left Evreux with a sense of jovial well-being.

It was a week since his encounter with the Black Shadow, and the future, financially at least, was brighter than for some time.

He had succeeded in selling his portrait of Gorgeous Georges to an art dealer in the town for three thousand eight hundred francs (three thousand six hundred for the signature and two hundred for the drawing) – but better, in Chartres, now also behind him, he had sold the remainder of his work (sixteen caricatures of the Carpentier training camp at Acquigny) for another four hundred.

Now, wealthy by McAndrew standards, he had stayed a night in the Hôtel de Paris in Chartres (where, with minimal success, he had tried to seduce one of the barmaids). Next morning he had bathed and changed into a new, grey morning suit with lapels of green velveteen: a lace-trimmed shirt, wing collar and new shoes he now wore: a black, wide-brimmed opera hat and a large silver-knobbed cane completed his attire.

With his bright, tight-curling hair lying on his shoulders, McAndrew now lay back in the deep-cushioned seat of the ten-thirty express out of Chartres. Puffing at a large cheroot, he watched the wine country of the Bordelais hurry past in the sunlit day.

A ruddy-faced schoolgirl, opposite him beside a broom in stays, regarded him, mouth open, with unfeigned awe from under her white poke bonnet: her large, blue eyes opening wide in astonishment when McAndrew sent her a secret, promiseful wink.

At dusk that day the Scot entrained by connection to Langon, where, according to Professor Spielman's biography, he stayed the night at La Grange, a little tavern on the outskirts.

Breakfasting early next morning, and leaving his suitcase and canvases in his room, McAndrew then ordered a trap to take him to the nearby village of Verdelais, there to pay homage at the grave of his friend and mentor, Henri de Toulouse-Lautrec.

The Countess Adèle, mother of Henri de Toulouse-Lautrec and wife of the Count Alphonse, put down the telephone in the Château de Malromé near Verdelais, and called for her husband's manservant. She said:

"That was the mayor. The verger reports that there is a man standing at Henri's grave . . ."

"Is that unusual, Comtesse?" asked the manservant. "Do not many visitors pay their tributes to your son?"

"This man is foreign. Yesterday he came, placed flowers, apparently, and stood for many hours; refreshing himself at the Bar Miami, he then returned to the cemetery and stood at the tomb until dusk. This morning he is there again."

The servant began, tentatively, "Madame, when the count comes . . ."

"But he will not arrive until next week. I had a letter this morning. Besides, you know that anything to do with Henri upsets him. I will go myself."

"Is that wise?"

"Probably not, but do not attend me, Dijon."

To McAndrew, his presence before the grave of his friend was the culmination of a pilgrimage: one that had begun as an ideal – to travel every yard on foot – but degenerated into a tourist's visit.

The homage, thought McAndrew now, was to seek an affinity with Henri that would reach beyond the tomb; one that would recount old conversations, revive old conquests and refashion the Butte through nostalgia.

293

Montmartre, he reflected, would never be again what it was in Henri's time – twenty years back in the 'eighties.

How, he thought now, could its charlatanism be re-captured, the phantasmagoria evoked?

For the reality of the Butte, McAndrew knew, was not the high-kicking Zidler girls of the Moulin Rouge, or the glamour of the brightly dressed Bohemians into whose water-jugs Lautrec had poured goldfish to make them cherish Spanish wine. Nor did the turbulent love affairs he and Henri had shared – the black net stockings, the frothy, lace underclothes, represent Montmartre in retrospect.

At the time, through the callow eyes of youth, yes, perhaps: but not so now. Too much time had passed. Too much had been taken out of context.

The Butte, as the Scot recalled it now, was Henri's tears at his mother's reproaches; disdain for his father's outrageous hypocrisy, his ironic laughter at his own monstrous afflictions. Even the irreligious, once lovely hags who now cluttered the hovels and attics of the Elysée-Montmartre had been honoured by time and biography's appalling fictions.

Did Henri's zestful, ignoble spirit still hover in the studio of Fernand Cormon? Did it still haunt the cut-throat alleys and dressing rooms of the infamous with their smells of grease-paint, powder and stale perfumes?

HENRI de TOULOUSE-LAUTREC MONFA
1864 – 1901

A decade ago. So much had happened. It was hard to believe, thought McAndrew, that the Little Treasure had ever lived.

He was walking down the cemetery path when the Countess Adèle came through the lychgate.

She appeared unreal, an apparition of white made golden by sun.

McAndrew paused, awaiting her.

The loveliness of youth may lie in the young, he thought,

but what could compare with the beauty of dignified age. . . ? As such, he determined, he would paint this woman on the mural . . .

The countess approached slowly, her presence enhanced by her fragility.

She was dressed in an embroidered tunic pulled in at the waist; the sleeves were of lace. And her skirt, full and heavily tiered, reached to her feet. She wore a wide-brimmed summer hat threaded with many coloured ribbons; around her throat was a band of black velvet.

Inclining her head in greeting, she lowered her parasol.

"Monsieur?"

Her calm, blue eyes moved over McAndrew.

He bowed, removing his hat.

"Your name?"

"My name is McAndrew, Countess Adèle."

"You have the advantage of me, Monsieur. You know mine?"

"I am your son's friend."

"Also an artist?"

"Also an artist. There will be more, of course, when he is hung in the Louvre."

She sighed, her eyes distant. "Not too many of those visit him these days. You knew him in Paris?"

"We shared lodgings in Rue de Steinkerque."

She smiled faintly. "From what I have heard of it, an address of distinctive character." She walked past McAndrew, opening her parasol to shield her face from the sun. "You are British?"

"Yes, Madame."

"So you have come far."

"Only from Rouen."

"And now?"

"Soon, I will return to Montmartre. But it was . . . necessary for me first to visit Henri."

"Of course. You . . . you will forgive us if we are jealous of his privacy? First the verger sees you and tells the landlord of

295

the Bar Miami, one of Henri's haunts. Monsieur Picard, he then visits the *maire*, and the mayor's wife, she telephones me." She clapped her gloved hands in a little delight. "Little can happen in Verdelais with such espionage. The news travels to the salons of Paris, popping into Château de Malromé on the way!" She smiled into McAndrew's face. "Where are you staying, Monsieur?"

"At Langon – La Grange."

"And when do you leave for Montmartre?"

"Tomorrow. Perhaps the day after."

"Then you will stay with me at Malromé – the count is away, you see."

"Madame. . . !"

"Monsieur, I insist upon it. Henri would not have it otherwise." She took his arm, but McAndrew did not move. He said:

"I have found him here . . . but is he at Malromé. . . ?"

The reply was instant. "Of course. I am at Malromé."

On their way to her trap, she added, "You know, Monsieur, you do not look the least like an artist . . ."

"Did Henri?"

She narrowed her eyes at the sun.

The Château de Malromé and its hundreds of acres was set in wine-growing country; situated on the road to Saint-André-du-Bois, it was two miles from Verdelais, and it was here that Lautrec often came for the summer.

Now, sitting in the trap beside the countess, listening to the clopping hooves of the pony, McAndrew saw its convex, slated towers grow out of the sun; a red-tiled roof stained the half obscuring trees like a splash of blood.

Along the gravelled drive now, and the driver stopped the pony. The countess said:

"Dijon will take you to your room, Monsieur; later he will fetch your luggage from Langon."

McAndrew did not hear her. He was looking over the sweeping country of the Bordelais.

*

Over afternoon tea, the countess said:

"I came here soon after the death of Richard, my second son. Henri was aged about four . . . I had parted with my husband, you see." She shrugged effectively. "Who could live with such eccentricity? Always it was the hunt – horses and harlots, Monsieur; no woman can compete. With one, perhaps, but never both . . ."

They were walking in the main hall of Malromé now. Spoils of the chase dominated the massive, austere walls; bridles and saddlery from Persia, stirrups from China. Yet this was the home that Henri loved, McAndrew recalled. To this he returned after the turmoil of Montmartre, its brassy music, female shrieks, the rattling of castanets. It was here that he had died; McAndrew sensed his nearness. The countess continued:

"My husband still visits, of course. Though age has treated him harshly, his eccentricity is undiminished. You are a Scotsman, so for you he may dress like a Highland chief; were you a Dervish, he would dance like a Dervish; for a Chinese, he would act a Cantonese opera."

McAndrew said, "He sounds to me like a man worth meeting."

"Once, perhaps, when younger. You have heard of his ancestors, the Counts of Toulouse?"

McAndrew said he had not.

"*Diex lo volt* (God wills it) – this is the family motto – hawks and hounds were the hobbies of Henri's father, grand-father, and those before them. Albi was their town château, Céleyran their great estate. And my husband, Count Alphonse, inherited every family trait of wildness and aristocracy. By comparison, Monsieur, I was *bourgeoisie* – even though a Tapié de Céleyran.

"Henri was born of ancient blood, but nothing could bridge the gulf between our families . . ."

"Nothing except the genius of your son?" suggested Mc-Andrew.

"Yes, perhaps, this sometimes happens." The countess sipped her tea. "Related to La Fayette and royal blood. The son of an aristocrat who would wash his shirt in a Paris manger and milk his mare for an evening drink, has little future." She sighed. "My ancestors, Monsieur, should have given thought to the perils of cognation. Even my husband and I were cousins. Henri, I fear, was the outcome."

31

Count Alphonse de Toulouse-Lautrec Monfa arrived at the Château de Malromé sooner than expected. In fact, he was outside in his chaise from Bordeaux soon after the countess and McAndrew, her guest, had retired for the night.

McAndrew, granted the room Henri had used when visiting Malromé, was in bed when he heard a hammering of hooves on the road to Saint-André-du-Bois. Going to the window of his room, he looked out on to a moonlit scene.

The count's chaise had stopped at the end of the drive, and an altercation began, which rose to quarrelling between a man and woman, interjected by loud protests from the driver of the carriage.

Now the couple descended to the road and the argument rose to a higher pitch – a man's commands, a woman's shrill denials.

The moon faded, bringing the road to darkness; gradually the wrangling ceased. McAndrew heard the carriage drive away in the direction of Verdelais.

Heavy footsteps began to crunch the gravel drive and the moon bloomed behind silver-edged clouds, momentarily exposing Count Alphonse.

Dressed in hunting breeches, a black cloak flying in the wind and a deer-stalker hat pulled down over his ears, he trudged, head down, with his hands clasped behind his back, towards the château entrance. Behind him, beautifully trained, two big deerhounds trotted, their noses to the ground.

Next came a furious hammering and the agitated chattering of servants. Light began to flood the lawns and courtyards as the house awoke. McAndrew opened his bedroom door to a sudden knocking.

The countess stood there in a silver gown, a candle held high; she said:

"Monsieur, my husband has returned. But pray do not be disturbed. I will present you in the morning – it is not necessary to come down."

Her agitation was apparent beneath her pervading calmness.

"Should you need me, I will come, Madame."

Nodding briefly, she held the candle higher, lifted the hem of her gown and swept across the landing.

From below stairs came the clatter of riding boots and the shrill blasting of a hunting horn. McAndrew closed the bedroom door. He heard the count's bawled commands to servants, the barking of his deerhounds. Later, from below stairs came singing, a drunken bawd of a song – a mess ditty of the 6th Lancers, by the sound of it – all this McAndrew heard, lying awake in the bed where Henri had died, until the house grew quiet and sleep claimed him.

He was awakened almost instantly by the skirling of bagpipes. Leaping out of the bed, McAndrew ran to the window, flinging it wide.

Below in the courtyard was Count Alphonse. Dressed in the uniform of a Highlander, bloated in the face and sweating wine, he was marching up and down the cobbles, pumping tunelessly on the pipes. Seeing McAndrew, he waved happily, and marched on, and the discord of those pipes, thought McAndrew, must have shifted the dead of Culloden. Up and down the count went, stopping at times to wave a claymore, yelling threats at the sky, then suddenly shouted up, with a moderately good Scots' accent:

"Do ye ken what's happening? It's in your honour, Highlander?" In French, he added, lustily. "Are we not kindred spirits – with you hanging royal clergy and we hanging monks? But have you one to compare, Scotsman, with our lustful Adelaide, the Toulouse-Lautrec no man could satisfy? *Mon Dieu*, all you've got is Bloody Mary."

"She'll serve," cried McAndrew, and slammed the window, turning as a low tapping came upon the door behind him. The countess entered when he opened it, and said:

"Do not bandy words with him, it only makes him worse; I do not wish you to be inconvenienced."

McAndrew grinned, rubbing his face. "Does every guest get this?"

"When he is home." She sat on a chair, a frail ghost in the blue light from the window. "As I said, it is a form of tribute. You are from the Sudan? – then he will be a Sudanese dancing girl and delight you with his agility. If you are from Spain – and we have entertained many Spanish diplomats – then he will be a matador. But he is best of all as a terrifying Saracen. I have even known him to be a Persian carpet. You are thinking he is mad?"

"It's a conclusion I've considered."

She smiled wearily, raising her voice above the wailing bagpipes. "Ah, but he is not. It is we who are not appreciative. Too much time, and inherited eccentricity . . . this is the trouble with this Toulouse-Lautrec. Too much money, also." She added reflectively. "At Le Bosc, when Henri was young, we kept a sea-chest filled with gold francs from which the family filled their pockets."

The sound of the bagpipes was suddenly replaced by the shrill cacophony of awakened hounds. McAndrew joined the countess at the window.

Into the yard below clattered a big, white stallion; the count was riding it bare-back, curvetting on the cobbles. Controlling it masterfully, he raised a hand of greeting to the window. And then he was away, firing a gun, galloping into the night with twenty hounds, in full tongue, streaming after him.

McAndrew said, "A gun also, Madame?"

"The guests, I fear," said she, "must take their chances."

By the morning of the following day the count had not returned from hunting.

"Is he always away as long as this?" asked McAndrew.

"Quite usually. There is a new inamorata abroad. She occasionally lives with him at the Hôtel Pérey, his Paris residence. When travelling to Malromé he keeps her at the hunting lodge near Saint-André-du-Bois. She is black, I understand – a dancer at the Café Noir."

"You make no protest?"

"*Mon ami*, my only protest is that he visits here at all."

"Just why does he continue to come?"

She smiled. "Our Toulouse-Lautrecs also owe a little to their avowed respectability. Convention must be served, you understand?"

"Yet he disapproved of his son's activities!"

"Of course. Do not hypocrisy and dishonesty make excellent bedmates? He actually refused permission for a statue to be raised to Henri, you know, and even burned some of his canvases . . ."

"No allowance being made for genius?"

"None. Official recognition has been a long time coming, so this hasn't helped, of course."

"A long time coming?" McAndrew ejaculated. "*Come!* A hundred works hung in the Indépendants and the Libre Esthétique but a year after his death? Nearly two hundred hangings in the Durand-Ruel . . . A *long* time? It is immediate! Even when we were together, his success was established . . ."

"In Montmartre?"

McAndrew nodded. "We shared rooms, as I said. But later he took his own studio in Avenue Frochot."

"You had a disagreement?"

"No, I had to return to Scotland."

"Your home?"

"In Scotland I am heir to a lairdship."

"Isn't that the Scottish aristocracy?"

"So the lairds claim. But we are the rogues and villains of the Highlands – sheep-stealers, cattle rustlers, arsonists, counterfeiters!"

"We have much in common, Monsieur!"

McAndrew ceased to smile. "I had much in common

302

with your son, Madame. He was my mentor; he taught me what little I know of animation, the configuration of sensuous line. It was a ritual purification, the abandonment of all the stupid conventions I had learned. He himself never acquired it, of course – it was genius presented to him in the beds of the Lautrecs. That was why he railed against the accepted teachings of men like Cormon and quarrelled with his fellow Impressionists. Character study by design, this was the essence; enquiry concentrated on the character and not the form.

"And degeneration?"

McAndrew smiled. "Oh come, Madame, you know your Smollett?"

"I confess I do not."

McAndrew said, "I quote him. 'Hark ye, Clinker, you are a most notorious offender. You stand convicted of sickness, hunger, wretchedness, and want.'"

"And brothels and harlots? You approve of these?"

McAndrew said, "Life cannot deny their existence. And traditional art betrays its own forgetfulness. Something had to be done. Henri drew Truth."

"But future generations will hold Henri's work to be indecent. The intellectuals . . ."

"Our true enemies are the intellectuals, fake and otherwise. Amorous in private, prim in public, they are running away from life so fast that they cannot stop; pausing only, as Degas said, 'To pick our pockets before shooting us.'"

"So much for Henri. What of you, now he is dead?"

"'*Je m'en vais chercher un grand peut-etre,*'" said McAndrew.

She laughed for the first time. "You, too, go in search of a great perhaps? I might have known you, too, lived on in Rabelais. I once asked Henri to draw me a cat – a kitten sitting by a fire – a cosy scene. Do you know what he replied? 'Dear Mama, I will immediately draw you a cat. It will be playing with a ball of wool, I shall even draw its purrs for you. But where will the little mouse go, *ma cherie* – in its belly, its mouth, or its claws?'"

"Typical of Henri. Meanwhile, would it be so wise of me to await the count's return?"

The countess rose. "Perhaps not. His moods are mercurial. Once Henri brought home a fellow artist – his name was John Lewis Brown. My husband first greeted him, and then pursued him from the château with man-servants, wolfhounds, and a gun."

"The gun continues to disturb me," said McAndrew. "Later, perhaps, I will die before a gun, but I have no plans for it at the moment!"

"Monsieur. . . ?" asked the countess, peering.

That afternoon the countess ordered a trap to take McAndrew to the station at Langon.

It was a day of bee-hum and the udder-smell of the cows lining the hedgerows. Their milk, said the countess, nostalgically, tasting of buttercups, reminded her of the dandelion days of childhood at Céleyran.

"Au revoir, Monsieur."

She stood at the entrance to the château, watching the trap swaying down the drive of Malromé.

As a splash of white against the poplars, so McAndrew remembered her; a purity audaciously stained by the Lautrecs and their mad excesses.

But McAndrew did not immediately go to Langon: first he directed the servant to take him to the Bar Miami in Verdelais; here, amid Henri's caricatures and cartoons, he drank steadily until late afternoon. Unaccountably (and later he put this down to the cognac) he entered the village church of Notre-Dame and there lit a candle to Henri, whose grave was nearby.

Entering the evening train from Langon with a first-class ticket to Paris (the cost defrayed by the Countess Adèle), McAndrew, waiting for the train to start, saw a coach and pair coming at speed. The driver, wearing the uniform of a Circassian knight – chain-mailed, with a visored helmet, armoured elbows and knee-plates, was furiously yelling;

tugging at the reins with one hand and brandishing a Turkish scimitar in the other.

With their chests and flanks foam-covered, the horses clattered over the cobbles, the coach precariously lurching as it skidded to a halt.

McAndrew sat upright in his seat.

The Circassian knight, his armour creaking, clambered down and opened the carriage door, his plumed helmet sweeping the gutter with a flourish.

McAndrew recognised him instantly – the Count Alphonse.

Stepping out of the coach with the dignity of a Negro queen, came Chocolat.

She was dressed in robes of black cashmere. Her face, her arms, covered with spiced oils of cinnamon, flashed in the sunset glare: her bangle earrings and bracelets shone gold.

She looked, thought McAndrew, rather like a black and gilt macaroon moving in a bowl of light. To get her on to canvas, he reflected, would need charcoal, more charcoal, and yet more charcoal . . . mixed with sun.

Straining in her hand was a gilt and silver chain, and on the end of the chain a Dobermann.

"Christ," said McAndrew.

The count escorted them to a first-class carriage; a whistle sounded, and the train was off.

"Bide yoursel' a minute, girl," said McAndrew, and rose.

The big dog growled deeply, its ears going up and its lips curled back;

Chocolat opened slanted, dark-lashed eyes as McAndrew slid back her compartment door. "*Pardonnez-moi. . .* ?" He bowed low.

The green eyes switched over him, like the eyes of a lynx, he thought; then they turned again to the window: she sighed, bored.

As McAndrew sat, cross-legged in a far corner the big dog raised its head and bared its teeth.

"Quiet, Cousin Dobie," said Chocolat, and smiled apologetically. McAndrew winked, and the Negress immediately turned back to the window.

"Button yourself up, son, you can't afford it."

"Ach, be reasonable, girl – you've got to pay for the best, ye know. Tell me where ye're sleepin' tonight and I'll send ye on a rocket to the stars."

It turned her. "*Jeez!* Do ye always propositin' ye women like that?"

"Aye, and I pray ye'll forgive the presumption, lady."

"Don't ye get your face smacked an awful lot o' times, Mister?"

"Yes, I do, but ye'd be amazed the number I sleep with."

"Ye'd be even more amazed, honey, if this Cousin Dobie removed the seat o' your pants, wouldn't ye?"

"The intention, lady, is not to remove me pants at this particular moment." McAndrew rose and sat beside her and the Doberman snarled ferociously, its white-balled eyes rolling, its teeth bared.

"Aw, shut ye gob, ye flat-faced tyke!"

Chocolat stared. "Who are you, Mister, for heaven's sake?"

"Me?" McAndrew thumbed his chest. "It's a good question. You're looking at the original Scottish loon, the laird of Ross and Cromarty, or so they claim – a remittance man escaped from the penetentiary of life – deranged, footloose and randy for ye, and you'd be advised not to let the opportunity pass, since ye'll never experience anythin' like it."

"Of all the pesky white-eyes Ah've met, son, you take the biscuit!"

"Nurture the thought," said McAndrew, "you'll find it a lasting experience. You're working at the Café Noir, Montmartre, did you say?"

Her eyes, like white saucers, threatened to jump from her face.

"How did you know that, for God's sake?"

"Me mither was a Russian fortune-teller and me father a

306

Circassian priest. So I can tell the future, as well as the past."

"Is that a fact?" Chocolat warmed to him.

"Aye, it runs in the family. And you're wasting your time with Count Alphonse, when you could be doing a humdinger with me in Paris."

"But how did you know. . . ?" she began.

"You stayed at the Toulouse-Lautrec hunting lodge near Saint-André-du-Bois, am I right?"

Her face showed incredulity.

"And like as not you're intending to join him at the hotel in Cité du Retiro?"

"I don't believe it!"

"Neither did I, at first. I couldn't accept that a beautiful creature could be so stupid – wasting her time on an aristocratic goat. The fella's worn out, or don't you care?"

"And you're intendin' to do somethin' about it, I suppose?"

"You're hove-to, Missus, and rollin' in a fine swell," said McAndrew. "Your rope ladder's down and I'm invitin' meself aboard."

"Bound for Montmartre, sailor? For that's where I'm going."

"A fine distinction, Missus – the Café Noir."

He gave her a happy grin. "Could ye get me in, do ye think?"

"What doing?"

He sat back, puffing at the cigar. "Cartooning, caricaturing – every café in Montmartre has its pet artist. Like Lautrec in the Moulin Rouge."

"He was Lautrec. And we've got a hundred artists at the Café Noir. What we want is someone to throw them out."

"Consider me engaged," said McAndrew.

"There's a bouncer already there. He's a six foot Turk and his name is Abdul. Shift him, and the job is yours. That's the rule for bouncers."

"Lead me to him," said McAndrew.

32

Abdul Mustapha Hamid (Mad Tiger), the Turkish bouncer of the Café Noir, bald, podgy, with a chest like a barrel and a stomach like a mountain (said Chocolat), rolled out his prayer mat, took out his compass and positioned it to point east to Mecca.

He was on his knees, head down, bottom up, and giving salutations to Allah when McAndrew entered the dressing-room of the dancers.

"Hey, what you bloody up to?" cried a shrill, cockney voice. "Abdul, what's this fella doin' in 'ere?"

Her name was Edie, she was half naked, and she came from Battersea.

A dancer from Paris called, her mouth pouted to the lipstick, "If he is good-looking he stays, yes? And this one is good looking, *n'est pas?*" She pulled her dressing-gown closer about her and winked at McAndrew. He, in the oblivion of a man possessed, was sketching swiftly, so did not hear either of them.

The dressing-room was between acts, a turbulent rush of half naked women and labouring dressers, and the very panic of it, mixed with the pervading smells of grease-paint, powder and flaunting, gaudy colours, snatched him into an agitation that touched hysteria.

Abdul came at a run. "Monsieur, you cannot stay here." He gripped McAndrew's sketch-board. "Please. . . ?"

"What harm is he doing?" asked a dancer over her shoulder. "You are a friend of Chocolat, are you not, Monsieur?"

McAndrew adjusted the board in her direction; her profile was smooth and pale against the flaring gas-jets, the shadows deep under her eyes.

"Come!" commanded Abdul the Turk. "Please leave quietly, Gentleman!"

The Turk's first requests were always polite, as befitted the rules of a respectable establishment. From this point on, it was said, he acted like a maniac.

"Not unless you completely insist on it," said McAndrew.

Abdul was coming out head first as Aristide Bruant, the baritone singer who owned the Café Noir, came in.

"It is a thousand pities," said he, "I was very fond of Abdul."

"You'll be much fonder of my friend McAndrew," said Chocolat, warmly. "He's a fine big lad, ain't you, honey?"

"It is the law of the bouncers, and I comply with it," said Aristide. "Soon, perhaps, somebody will come and, with luck, throw out McAndrew." He addressed himself to the Scotsman. "Abdul's wage was fifty francs a week – take it or leave it."

"Make it a hundred, for that's what Abdul got." McAndrew's stock arched proudly under his beard; he regarded Aristide with a belligerent stare.

"He will take it." Chocolat went on tiptoe and kissed McAndrew's cheek.

"You'll find that more dangerous than bouncing," said Aristide. "Fifty francs, big man – money in advance."

McAndrew took the money, went outside and gave it to Abdul the Turk.

The Café Noir was situated at Number Fourteen, Rue de Steinkerque, in the middle of Montmartre.

It was only recently opened – many said in competition with the famous Le Chat Noir, the cabaret café just around the corner from it, in the Boulevard de Rochechouart. Its sponsor, Rodolphe Salis, was complimenting his gains.

Cabarets in lower Montmartre were still proliferating, replacing the ancient elysium fields and coffee houses. On the mound of the Butte the church of Sacre Coeur dominated all, but below it the cobbled yards and courts with their rickety balconies were being slowly swept away in a revived, more vital Parisian gaiety: the Left Bank being slowly denuded by impresario visionaries with trumpet blasts of showmanship.

All Paris was enamoured of the Salis' tinsel establishments laden with their mock antiques, antlers, rusted arms purporting to come from the Revolution – blood-stained baskets into which the heads of aristocrats had fallen – all was grist to the prospector's mill.

Above most cafés lived the entertainers and artisans of the acts – seamstresses, lacemakers, set designers and clerks.

On the third floor of the Café Noir lived communally the *Dames de la Nuit*: following in the train of these came the wealthy élite of Paris, abandoning the old Café Cujas and the dance-halls of the Elysée-Montmartre, whose respectability was now tainted by cut-throats and Apaches who battened on errand girls, flower-sellers and waitresses, turning them into purveyors of perversion.

On the fourth floor of Number Fourteen Rue de Steinkerque lived Chocolat – now sharing it with McAndrew as a non-paying guest: above them, in the attic, lived a religious order of monks known as the Disciples of Pachomius, who, rarely seen but always heard, spent their time in incantation and abstinence. Therefore the entertainment of the Café Noir was often accompanied by unharmonious noises from above: Heaven, as Chocolat said, being resident in the attic.

From the gaudy Café Noir, raucous music blared out over its light-shot pavements. Here was danced the quadrille, the waltz, polka, schottische and decorous minuet. But, dominating all, the highlight of every evening, was the Can-can, led by Chocolat, the lead-dancer: she who specialised, like Aristide Bruant, in swashbuckling rudeness to the guests; who performed an individual act before the high-kick dancing of the Can-can troupe – the black-net stockings with their swathes of white, frothing petticoats.

McAndrew, in the middle of his second week as the official Café Noir bouncer, pushed his way through the gowned ladies and their frock-coated escorts, found a darkened alcove and from there watched the gas-lit stage.

Chocolat, scantily dressed in black with an open, hooped skirt and a crescent moon of luminous silver upon her head, was in form. She sang to the accompaniment of lusty orchestral brass:

"There ain't no beauty in the colour o' white,
There's no comparin' with a hide like mine.
For you whiteys got a skin the colour o' corn,
Too high in the womb 'afore you was born.
But the good God loves me like a race apart,
In the beat o' the pulse an' the thump o' the heart.
So He fried me proper in the oven o' the sun,
But you stinkers He denied and He did ye underdone . . ."

Cat-calls and jeers all through this, with Chocolat making rude gestures at the audience and throwing up her skirts, cavorting now, to show her bare bottom, and waving down protests with her fists. A man shouted, leaping up from a table:

"You moonshine woman! I could buy you for ten cents out of Harlem, same as I'd buy a pesky old bitch!"

Chocolat, striding up and down the stage now, yelling above the strident blasts of music:

"Is that so, you cotton-picking white man – we'd see to you good up in Harlem. White Trash – your head's been boiled too long in the sun!"

"Get down from there!" a drunk in evening dress now, fighting his way up from a table to the footlights.

311

"An' you, too, Trash!" yelled Chocolat. "Your time's over, and ma time's come!" She made a rude sign at him. A woman ,with an American accent shrieked from the crowded floor:

"I'm not putting up with this – pull her off, the cow!"

"You jist come up here and try," shouted Chocolat. "An' Ah'll land you one that'll heave you back to Philadelphia."

Bedlam now, with people shouting insults and Chocolat hurling them back, and Aristide, the Master of Ceremonies, called:

"Mesdames, messieurs . . . I beg you, take no notice. This particular artiste . . ."

Chocolat attacking him from behind now, tearing off the sleeve of his evening dress jacket, then doing neat cartwheels and handsprings around the stage (Chocolat the acrobat) as he pursued her in a riot of boos and whistles.

McAndrew watched, smiling, his fingers plucking his beard.

The act was original; its hostility made it different. Doubtless there were responding actors in the crowd, but it was good, he thought.

Now the orchestra struck up siren blasts of sound, drowning the growing altercation, and Chocolat sang shrilly, insulting the audience with gestures as she roamed the stage.

McAndrew heard a movement behind him, and turned.

Aristide Bruant, the owner, was standing behind him. He said in a rich, baritone voice, nodding across the room:

"You see who has come in, my friend?"

McAndrew straightened. Within a movement of waiters a man was standing alone.

"The Count Alphonse," said Aristide.

"Oh, aye?"

"A good customer of ours, McAndrew, and with money to burn. The father of Lautrec, the artist of the Moulin Rouge – remember?"

"Is that a fact?"

"And one who may not take kindly to sharing you with Chocolat, perhaps?"

"Ach, me heart bleeds for the fella."

"A frequenter of the Allée des Poteaux in the Bois de Boulogne, he often takes Chocolat riding there; at other times she visits him in the Hôtel Pérey in Cité du Retiro, his rooms in Town. Did you know this?"

"Mind you, I had the faint idea that purity wasn't her strong point, but I expect she knows her own business best."

"Do you know yours?"

"Give ye a tanner for it."

Bruant said:

"Such men don't share. Have you any experience with duelling pistols?"

"I'll give it serious thought," said McAndrew.

33

Chocolat's room over the Rue de Steinkerque was pretty; everybody agreed on this.

It was a large room, used originally as a seamstress' floor, where the daughters of local shopkeepers sat in rows before tables brightly polished by a century of muslin bales, silk, linen, and endless stitching for a few centimes a day.

Opposite the door was the bed. Flock-mattressed, brass-knobbed and railed and of fine proportions, it was, as Chocolat herself put it, 'ma professional necessity, though Ah also use it for sleepin', mind, an' it's got to be tromendos, see, in case ma Uncle Bojo arrives.'

In a far corner, in a wicker basket behind the door, slept Dobie Dawg, the Dobermann pinscher of untainted blood (according to Chocolat) but whose ancestry, because of his size, had clearly accommodated mastiff blood, and one or two bulldogs on the side, the bastard, said McAndrew. An opposite corner held a gas stove, upon which Chocolat, under protest, cooked McAndrew's eternal stews.

In the middle of the floor stood McAndrew's easel, his table and stool, a few rickety chairs. A big Le Clerc fire-place of Italian marble, totally out of place, completed the furnishings.

The floor was bare, Chocolat having removed the Persian carpet, as she called it, because of his paint.

In this room, during the summer of 1911 and the spring and summer of the following year, McAndrew painted, painted, painted.

The window, though small, possessed wrought ironwork trellis and a window-box, and from this hung lobelias, their blue petals contrasting with flowering red geraniums.

The exotic nature of Chocolat's window-boxes, people said, turned the bawdy Steinkerque into a little Sierra Leone.

From the window Chocolat kept abreast of what was happening in the Butte. With her arms folded on the sill she would watch the crowds thronging on the cobbled street below, and shriek her greetings:

"Bonjour, Madame! Give my love to Lauri Grenard!" (Grenard being a local councillor, of high breeding). This to an old crone selling fish, staggering half drunk along the cobbles.

"Monsieur Chevalier! Hallo, *hallo*!" She screamed with delight at the sight of a small, portly gentleman hurrying for a carriage.

Monsieur Chevalier paused, removed his top hat and bowed, smiling up. "Bonjour, Chocolat, *ma cheri*! Thank you very much. I am so grateful, my enchanting friend."

"Aw, think nothin' of it, honey – always ready to oblige."

"What's he so grateful for?" asked McAndrew, coming up behind her.

"I took some soup to his poor, old mother."

"He's too old to have a mother." McAndrew, the brush suspended, peered down to the street below.

"Man!" said Chocolat, "he ain't as old as he looks," and she threw back her head and shouted laughter. "Ah sure put life into his little parlour."

"Aye? Well, it stops now I'm aboard, ye understand?"

Chocolat spat, pushed him aside and went to the window, tossing a few centimes down to the cobbles below, yelling encouragement as urchins scrambled for them, calling up for more.

McAndrew saw her against a background of light; the dome of Sacre Coeur was caught in haloes of sun. Along the distant boulevards the flower-sellers were explosions of colour against the blue. Chocolat turned at the window.

315

"Time come you tell me what to do – you're out, Mister, understand?"

"Now, I'm here it stops, ye hear me?" He spoke automatically, now, lost in the canvas.

"*Jeez* – you big ape! Maybe you had folly-dolls before. You said jump and they went six feet high – but not this l'il chicken, no sir!"

"We'll see," said McAndrew, wiping his pallet knife.

"You're right. There's only one fella jumping in this one-eared, bum establishment, an' that ain't me, honey."

In the month he had been bouncing at the Café Noir, McAndrew was working with almost carnal frenzy.

Since moving in with Chocolat, everything, decent and indecent, fell under his brush. The tawdry baubles of Montmartre's night-life – the fetid air of the dressing-rooms with its half naked dancers, the faces of the market crowds, merry, sad, well fed or emaciated, came crowding into his consciousness. He drew the prostitutes of Steinkerque's third floor by the dozen.

In exchange for Chocolat's silence and passivity, he had, until now, given her free rein. If she was out – and he never enquired where – he worked from the moment the café closed until the early hours of the day; to fall asleep exhausted, spread-eagled across the bed.

"You goin' to carry on like this for ever, then?" Chocolat asked, and she knelt on the bed, took the whisky bottle out of his hand and heaved him over on to his face.

McAndrew's life, while with Chocolat, the dancer of the Café Noir, proceeded as inartistic, steepled events within the graph of a pictorial story, a sequence of vignettes.

By these, coming as they did between bouts of drunken, creative work, so he remembered her.

"Ma Cousin Dobie," said Chocolat, "is sure fond o' me," and she wetted her lips as the Mastiff-Dobermann padded across the floor towards her, one eye on McAndrew. Putting his paws upon her shoulders (on hind legs he was the taller) he panted into her face.

"Yessir, ma Dawg Dobie knows what's good for me, don't ye, sugar?" and she gave McAndrew a look to kill.

He, naked, was putting sweeping finishes to a caricature of Edward the VII. As prince, an earlier patron of the Café Noir, he was once a regular visitor to Rue de Steinkerque.

"What Ah'm getting at is this," added Chocolat. "This dawg is the only thing Ah trusts in a world o' two-legged tykes with beardy ole faces and lyin' old tongues."

"I'm fully aware of it," said McAndrew, not really listening.

The light was poor and with his brush between his teeth, he screwed up his eyes at the window.

"You know some'at more, Mister? This Dawg Dobie loves me from the tip o' his tail to the top of his nose, don't ye, son? – an' he don't ask for nothin'. He sits on his big backside and looks up into ma face and slobbers with love. He don't need the pushin' and shovin' the kissin' and the cuddlin' like you two-legged variety.

"Ah could go plain crazy and kick his ass and cuff him, but he'd just come back for more. There ain't nothin' in this world Ah do that ma Cousin Dobie don't see eye to eye." And she put her arms around Dobie's neck and kissed him.

"You're labourin' the point, Missus," said McAndrew.

Chocolat rose and walked back to the window. Her hands on the sill, she looked down on to the scurrying market crowds of cobbled Steinkerque below.

It was July. The day was warm with sun and air and the artists of Rue Norvins were setting up their easels among the pavement flower sellers, for caricatures of the thronging tourists . . . before the obscenity of an inevitable war.

The steps of Sacre Coeur, where the bells pealed and clanged, were crammed with the usual colourful humanity of the Butte.

"You going to Norvins to sell pictures today, Jimmy?" asked Chocolat.

"If I get no peace in here."

"Okay – that fits. Ah get a peaceful night, you get a peaceful day. Perhaps Ah'm only fit for a white man's bed, you think? That's all you're usin' me for, honey."

"Come away from the window, you're shadin' the light."

He saw Chocolat in profile against the blind windows of the houses opposite.

He had seen her before, of course, on the old African runs between the Clyde and Sierra Leone, when he was a cabin-boy on the big four-masters sailing to the Gold Coast with his father.

She was a Bahima, descendant of the Galla who once invaded Uganda.

Her face, like most Bahima, possessed no brows, and was short and straight, the skull coffin shaped. Once, long ago, he had sketched such a woman, washing on stones in the estuary of Bonthe.

They were a people originating in the Kenya highlands, their women being exported to the slave markets of Arabia, where they fetched big money from Arab princes.

Her limbs were delicately fashioned in ebony blackness; she was smaller than most Bantu, he thought, her hands and feet like a child's and her peppercorn hair, cropped short to her skull, made her into a boy.

"God, you're beautiful," said McAndrew.

"Reckon you're after some'at, you start talkin' like that." She drew herself up.

McAndrew watched her as she crossed the floor with her usual animal magnetism; a litheness that was almost stealth.

"Remember Ah mentioned ma uncle's comin' soon?"

He was drawing again, so ignored her.

"He's head man o' ma village back home in Moyamba territory. He's an important fella, I can tell you."

McAndrew was drawing with meticulous care, shading in the puffed cheeks, the narrow, bagged eyes and the swollen face, heavy with its beard.

318

"That's the king, ain't it?"

"Aye."

"Come into the café the other night, didn't he?"

McAndrew nodded.

"He used to jump the Chat Noir and Moulin when Lautrec was there, I heard tell." She added with professional reserve. "I knows a couple of ole girls down Rue d'Amboise used to sleep with him, three in the bed. This King of England was pretty good horizontal."

"You can say that again."

"It'll be three in a bed for us, too, when ma Uncle Bojo comes, mind."

"Can't he go on the floor?"

"Ma uncle ain't goin' on the floor for anyone, Mister. He's got a hut full of wives back home, and he ain't used to sleepin' by himself."

"Where the hell do I go, then?"

"Lest you turn out, of course, otherwise you're in the middle."

"Has she started praying yet, my friend?" asked Aristide Bruant.

"Not yet," replied McAndrew.

"She will."

McAndrew was beginning to sell pictures. He sold them from Chocolat's room where dealers came to buy: to the patrons of Montmartre who, every Sunday after Mass, made the journey from all corners of Paris to Rue Norvins near the church of Sacre Coeur; but more, representatives were arriving from respected art dealers, including representatives of the Musée des Arts Décoratifs and the Bliss and Albright of New York. It was to the latter that the caricature of King Edward was sold – two thousand three hundred francs, McAndrew's biggest sale to date. Chocolat said:

"You're doin' good with me, Jimmy. I turned your luck

right round. Right soon you'll be able to give up bouncing and do those queer ole drawings full time?"

"Perhaps."

There was a child McAndrew had seen in the Rue Fontaine.

She was scantily dressed and this did not perturb him overmuch, because it was summer. But her sad, luminous eyes of hunger stared out at him from a pale, old face, and her look, aged seven, was an affront to his sensibilities.

He had given her money in a small, grubby palm, and after a while forgot her.

The summer died, winter came. In front of a roaring fire he worked then, eating the brown stews Chocolat cooked, with relish. His face, now heavily bearded and unwashed, was gaunt with lack of sleep, and from a corner Dobie Dawg watched him with baleful, distrusting eyes.

Later, remembering the child, he had trudged the snow-clad streets to Rue Fontaine to look for her. People told him she had been taken to the Hôpital Lariboisière, there died, and had been buried in the Cimetière de Montmartre.

He had found her pauper's grave and put upon it Christmas roses.

There grew between this child and McAndrew an affinity that expressed itself in impassioned animation. And it was an emotion that actually made sound. Alone before the grave, on weekly visits, these sounds grew into chords of beauty that held colour and shape: all art, he was discovering, was responsive, one form to another . . . sound was colour, colour was joy; grief itself brought an almost unbearable recognition, through music.

This discovery began to possess McAndrew, and he saw the beggar child, not as poverty's wastage of the streets, but representative of rhapsodic tones. A great mural could be a symphony, the face of a hungry child a sad nocturne: spring was gay capriccio; summer a lovely merging of pastoral colours – serenity: autumn was adagio, winter a fugue of stereotyped whiteness.

This realisation brought in its wake a new creative force that astonished McAndrew by its complexity and inter-action. He wanted to shout aloud this revelation, and he fell to his knees by the frosted grave, calling the child's name.

According to Spielman (and his officially accepted McAndrew biography makes much of it) the artist's final confirmation of tonal-colour connection did much to dilute the profanity of his earlier subjects.

It was *vivace*, the art critics said. Its song of childhood shouted from the small face on the canvas.

Chantelle, the beggar child who died in Lariboisière, sold to the Beaux-Arts-Winton for two thousand francs, and was eventually hung in the Templa Musée of Brussels.

Fifty years later it sold to the Louvre for three hundred and eighty thousand.

34

McAndrew opened one eye, pulled down the bedsheet, and peered again.

Chocolat, as bare as an egg (he told Aristide later), was hand-standing on the bedrail: in the blue, eerie light of the room she was walking on her hands along the rail; reaching the big brass knob, she stopped, vertically motionless, as rigid as a stick of charcoal. Then she said, upside down:

"Now you tell me, Jimmy – you ever seen a woman stand like this on a bedrail in the middle of the night?"

McAndrew confessed that he had not.

"That's right," said Chocolat. "You got to come to black folks like me to see such wondrous perambulations. Ma Uncle Bojo, he says he's never seen such a perambulator as this l'il Chocolat." She then proceeded to do the 'splits' in mid-air, then turned her legs with increasing speed. The effect on McAndrew was paranoiac.

"Are ye comin' back in? Ah'm gettin' ideas about you, ma honey." He pushed back the bedclothes, mimicking her accent.

"Yessir, but first Ah got to say ma prayers. Ah was a pure white virgin child 'afore I got mixed up with the likes of you, so Ah got to sign my passport to Heaven."

And this, McAndrew told Aristide Bruant, the owner of the Café Noir, was the prayer she gave:

"O great god Wak," said she, "Ah come from a far country to this strange land, an' this wicked ole Paris has got me standin' on ma head . . ."

McAndrew watched her, listening.

*

From the floor above came the sound of plain-song, the chanting of the Disciples of Pachomius, and from the floor below the squabbling of the *Dames de la Nuit*, for there's some very strange people living in Fourteen Steinkerque, he told Aristide Bruant, and this is what he heard Chocolat say:

"O, great god Wak, Lord of the people of Galla and the terrible slumbers of the people in chains, lift up my face to the eagles of Heaven, pierce me with the spears of the sun if I forget my trust in Thee. O, fire high the silver arrows of the light, for the days swoon under the moon, and the halls of the wicked are bright . . ."

But McAndrew heard this in Bantu, and did not understand.

Chocolat prayed, again in Bantu (perhaps the most beautiful religious literature in the world). With a tiny effigy of the god Wak in her praying hands, she knelt, laying her forehead upon the floor, and said:

"I am sistered with love for you, O, great Wak: companion of my womb, I am sick with love for you. The stainless sun spills my loneliness at your feet. These are the roses of my thoughts; the fruits of my body I leave before you under the glass stars, in the orchard ways of my youth . . ."

McAndrew, still listening, heard Chocolat say in English now:

"When first I come here I was a pure honey child, and Ah'd never been did. But then this Jimmy fella arrives, and now Ah'm being did all the time, and Ah'm full o' the terrible waters. And that ain't fair, Wak; for all Ah'm asking is a bit more lovin', a bit more spoilin', and a lot less pixilatin', but this wide-assed bum, he treats me sore. So you hit this two-timer with the Evil Eye – push him under a horse, or somethin' – not that Ah'm wishing him badness, but he's that green jealous he don't let me out o' his sight. An' I ain't done nothin' to make him feel that way.

323

Ah's been as honest an' faithful as any no-fornicatin' Bahima gal could be. You talk to him, Wak?"

With this, she rose, stood on her hands again and began to walk around the room. When she reached the bed, McAndrew opened his arms to her.

"I'll mention it to him, too," he said.

McAndrew said, "The thing is this, Chocolat, if you love a fella, then you stay with him, understand?"

"Honey," said Chocolat, "Ah loves you unto my dyin' breath."

"Then you stay here and work and cook and mend, and I stay with you. Do I have other women in here?"

"Perhaps not, but you go down to the room below to sketch them – the *Dames de la Nuit* – what for?"

"For the posters and portraits – to earn us money."

"You don't go there for the pixilatin'?"

"Ach, ye darlin' thing, what do ye take me for? I'm in love, didn't I say? – I'm only pixilating with you."

"The other girls said . . ."

McAndrew clasped his hands in pleading sincerity. "Now, for God's sake! Would ye take the word of half a dozen tarts like that against me, ye honourable friend? I'll be bleeding to death for ye the moment you've gone. Where are you off to now, by the way?"

He had an unfinished sketch of the Disciples of Pachomius, hurriedly drawn while lying unseen on the roof, and he wanted to be rid of her. Also, the sales-girl of the *Dames de la Nuit* was coming up to sit for him.

"Ah'm off to Lariboisière to visit ma sick friend," replied Chocolat.

"You've got a sick friend in hospital?"

"Mamie Zinkoisen, the American girl just come."

"Sick? She was performin' yesterday – I saw her."

"Honey," replied Chocolat before the mirror, swinging her body this way and that, "she's so sick is that Mamie that mostus thinks she's a clay cold corpse."

"When will you be back?"

"When Ah arrive, more'n likely." She patted and fussed him, her eyes like saucers in her ebony-coloured face. "Meanwhile, don't hang around by the neck waitin'."

She was dressed in pink silk; round her cropped skull was a band of silver; her skirt was full, her arms were bare; she looked, he thought, like an apparition stepped out of jungle heat. Her chunky bangles rattled as she reached up her arms to kiss him. Dobie Dawg, from his corner, growled gutterally in his throat. Vaguely, McAndrew remembered that she had the profile of Count Alphonse Toulouse-Lautrec tattooed on her bottom.

"Give my love to Mamie," he said, now at the easel.

She smiled gaily, busying herself at the glass. He added, "You're sure you're going to the hospital, Choco?"

He heard his voice as an echo; even the mention of Hôpital Lariboisière brought to him the face of Chantelle, the child who had died. Distantly, he heard the reply:

"Ah, sure!" Turning from the mirror, she brazened up to him, hands on hips, slanting her eyes. "You think otherwise, son, you'm addling your head. Ah go by what ma Uncle Bojo says, and he's got no time for shananikins – if Ah strayed from you, the evil spirits would come right out an' collect ma virginity."

"Ach, that would be a terrible thing," said McAndrew and kissed her.

After Chocolat had gone McAndrew wandered the room; without her presence he felt strangely lost.

It was a phenomenon which he had never solved. He could have gone to the rooms below and charcoaled some of the women; his presence flattered them and he had the run of the place, in more ways than one.

They would sit in the parlour and pose for him on the brightly coloured couches in various states of undress, and these studies sold well in Rue Norvins of a Sunday.

Working in the brothel always brought him an affinity with Lautrec: as Henri did, he found in these women a warmth and companionship that he had discovered in nobody else; there was in them all something akin to piety when it came to personal honour. And he tried, in his representations, to capture the elements that Henri, in his opinion, had missed – their essential qualities of friendship and kindness that lay behind their rouged exteriors, and the tinsel decoration of their bodies.

Henri de Toulouse-Lautrec, McAndrew considered, for all his genius, yet lacked the spark of God men called humanity: Henri's very background had built in him disdain for poverty, and an aristocratic rejection of society's helpless.

It was this very necessity for compassion that McAndrew now exploited – compassion for the body as well as for the soul.

Lately, Aristide Bruant was employing him on stage-cartooning, and McAndrew relished the opportunity of lampooning wealth and privilege: an aged roué with a young girl at his table he would depict as riding her pick-aback in the Bois de Boulogne: a corpulent banker would be skeletal, picking up a centime out of the gutter, while his pockets bulged with money: blue blood aristocrats (and there were many visiting the infamous Café Noir for the new cult of being insulted) . . . ended on his canvases as flea-scratching peasants, pigs or mooing cows – brainless.

Aristide Bruant's practice of berating his customers, begun under Zidler at the Moulin Rouge in Toulouse-Lautrec's time, was proving even more successful at the newer Café Noir in Steinkerque.

Chocolat's particular act, an attack on colour-class, while having its effect of spontaneous gaiety, yet played a role. And Bruant, though of a compassionate nature off-stage (it was said that he fed all the starving dogs of Montmartre) exceeded decency when once in front of an audience, his bawdy songs blackguarding anyone who happened to take his eye, and in this McAndrew revelled. For Bruant, he knew – after years of deprivation and real poverty – secretly enjoyed castigating the rich and privileged, and encouraged his performers to do likewise.

326

Therefore, McAndrew was under no restrictions in his stage cartooning; his bitter, often cruel reproductions exposed the sicknesses of his clients and caricatured their weakness.

"Jesus, man," said Chocolat. "You can talk . . ."

But Bruant was delighted with his new protégé, and the Scotsman's fame was spreading over Paris with a speed greater than Lautrec's, in his time.

Newspapers like the *Paris Trumpet* and *Ce Soir* seriously speculated as to who would be next to fall under the bouncer-artist's vitriolic brush, and the Café Noir, since his appearances, was packed to the doors seven nights a week.

Diplomats and royalty (it was said that King Edward VII arrived with a party and was given the McAndrew treatment – unexpurged – and took it in excellent humour . . .) high-ranking civil servants, and especially politicians, were generally, it was claimed, giving the indecorous Café Noir a wide berth, said the columnists.

Probably it was his love of the lime-light that brought Le Compte Alphonse de Toulouse-Lautrec one evening to the Café Noir cabaret, when normally he might have attended, as routine, one of the higher-priced dance-halls of the Elysée-Montmartre. His very eccentricity would have accounted for his presence, yet Ratza Spielman, McAndrew's most important biographer, insists that he came as a result of the Scotsman's cartooning taunts.

Recently, it was known, McAndrew had confirmed the count's refusal to allow a statue to be raised to Henri, his son; further, that, despite the Countess Adèle's frantic attempts to preserve them, many of Henri's paintings had been burned by the family, and for this the Scot held the count responsible.

Certainly, Spielman's theory is supported by McAndrew's subsequent actions. His vitriolic hatred of Count Alphonse, it was said, was responsible for the man's presence, not the count's natural interest in the performances of Chocolat. But Spielman further contends that McAndrew's visit to France – probably brought about by contact with Jacques Collard at Atopia House – was for an express purpose – the death of Count Alphonse.

History cannot prove this, one way or the other.

The brown trees of autumn, the falling of brittle leaves, heralded the death of another Parisian summer: more beautiful, thought McAndrew, than any he had known.

It was his day off from the Café Noir; he was not on speaking terms with the work upon his easel, the *Dames de la Nuit* were not of particular interest to him, and Chocolat had gone (or so she said) to Lariboisière again to visit Mamie, the sick American dancer.

First McAndrew visited a perfumery in Rue de Rivoli, for a bottle to sprinkle upon the grave of Chantelle, also flowers with which to decorate the little stone he had now erected to her name; then he visited the retrospective exhibition of thirty-eight works by Henri at the Salon des Humoristes, the Georges Petit Gallery. The work of Van Dongen was also there, a painter he admired, though none of his famous purple period.

Like Lautrec, thought McAndrew, Van Dongen was vastly underrated, unwanted, even disliked. His purple period, then despised, the artist had used to roof his pig's cot; in later years, unknown to McAndrew, they were reverently dislodged, restored, and sold for fantastic prices.

Wandering the ornate rooms, McAndrew saw a face he recognised; an ageing Jane Avril, once the darling of the Moulin Rouge, stared at him with large, luminous eyes through her black veil.

"Madame. . . ?" McAndrew bowed to her.

"We have met before, Monsieur?"

"What man forgets . . . when once he has seen Jane Avril dance?"

She replied, "My husband died, you know. . . ?"

"I did not know."

The viewers wandered past them in the hushed whispering of art.

The woman sighed. "So sometimes I come to see Henri. Did we not all die with him, Monsieur?" She peered. "But I do not remember you."

"I was but small, you understand? Henri was the dwarf, but he was the large one – my friend and mentor; he taught me what I know."

"Now you are beautiful," said she. "Top hatted, wonderfully attired, you are quite beautiful. Why do I meet such men with my beauty gone? Surely you are not an artist also?"

Later, alone in the sun, McAndrew went into the Tuileries garden.

"No," thought he. "Compared with Henri, I am not an artist."

It was an era of flight; the new craze, ballooning, was taking away Parisian breath. Experiments in heavier than air machines, held usually at Issy-les-Moulineaux airfield near Paris, had transferred themselves, after initial success, to the Tuileries.

McAndrew joined the crowd, a hundred deep, around four great balloons whose crews were preparing for ascent. He recalled, watching from a distance, that this must be the Gordon Bennet balloon race, of which he had read in *Ce Soir*.

One by one the balloons rose into the air, their shapes black circles against the sombre tapestry of the sky. He strolled on around the edge of the crowd; leaves rose in dusty eddies about his patent leather shoes and spats. The race was under way now, the balloons soaring above him, one, two, three . . .

The sight of them stopped McAndrew in his tracks.

Motionless, he stared skyward.

For there was growing within him the old elemental song of freedom. The machines, in themselves, appeared a sudden gift – a franchise for liberty . . . an escape from the new-found safety of his existence . . . and the conventions that now jammed him between the Disciples of Pachomius' religious fanaticism and the depravity of the *Dames de la Nuit*. Even the continued impropriety of Chocolat appeared an immolation, the sardonic humour of his own cartooning revealed its crime of fratricide.

It was at this moment that he recognised Chocolat.

The fourth balloon of the race was going up; it hung, momentarily suspended in enormity fifty feet above the heads of the Tuileries' crowds.

McAndrew saw, smiling down from the basket, Chocolat's unmistakable black face: the same tulle dress she wore – the dress she had said that Mamie, her friend, preferred when she visited the hospital – the same bangle bracelets shone.

And behind her, with his arms around her waist while the crew worked, was Count Toulouse-Lautrec.

McAndrew watched, enveloped in the cheers of the surrounding people. The count put a heavy aviator's coat around Chocolat's shoulders; she waved vivaciously to the crowds below.

McAndrew waved also.

It was a seventy-two hour balloon race, he reflected, and grinned, tugging at his beard.

It would be an entertainment in itself, he thought, to hear Chocolat explain, in her halting, village patois, an absence of three days.

The lust for the open road, the necessity to energise himself again, to work again, naked and drunk, on the mural in Atopia House, beset him with obliterating force.

"Ah'll be seein' ye, honey-child," he said.

35

Chocolat said, when she returned:

"And when I got to Lariboisière to see ma friend, Mamie, they told me ma Uncle Bojo was arrivin' by the very next train . . ."

"Is that a fact?" asked McAndrew.

He thought: the child Chantelle . . . I need to finish her face. Her face must be transferred to the mural of Atopia; she was one of society's minor executions, achieved with solemn grandeur – perhaps even as a shade . . . yes, this is it . . . a shade staring out of the mural background: a crime of uncaring emptiness; perhaps painted in pointillism. . . ? the dot technique? Was Seurat alone privy to the form? McAndrew scratched his chin. But the effect must be captured, not authorised by professionalism, like Chantelle's murder . . .

Earlier – a week ago – before he sold the original of *Chantelle*, he began to copy it with the dot technique, and the effect was hypnotic. It absorbed his every waking moment. McAndrew performed his nightly stint, cartooning at the Café like a man in maddened haste. But his every waking moment was spent at the new *Chantelle*: the child's face stared luminously into his being.

There had even been benefit in Chocolat's absence with the count, because never for a moment had he been alone in Fourteen Steinkerque: there had always been Chantelle, the child he would one day transfer to the Atopia mural.

On the day Chocolat returned, he sold the original, but the one on the easel was not yet finished.

*

McAndrew had been drinking.

Sometimes, when thinking of Chantelle, he wept. Often, when he saw her face on the canvas, elated, he drank. So he worked on her portrait in secret, when a footstep on the stairs was enough to make him cry out, hurriedly hiding her away . . .

It seemed a mundane act of treachery even to share Chantelle with the canvas. Nor did he completely trust the brushes . . . who sometimes gossiped . . .

When Chantelle was finished, he told himself, he would transfer her to the Atopia mural, and let her die as all things die – slowly, in decay, with the crumbling of the plaster. This might expiate her murder in the streets, he thought.

Now he said to Chocolat while he worked:

"And then?"

"Then I went to the railway station, but Uncle Bojo weren't there, like I was told. You been cryin', Mister?"

"No! What did you do then?"

"Ah read this letter they give me about ma Uncle Bojo, and we took ourselves to Pontoise, ma cousin and me."

"To Pontoise? What for?"

"Because our Uncle Bojo got off at Pontoise, didn't he, Dobie Dawg?" She addressed herself to the Mastiff-Dobermann, affronted by McAndrew's disbelief.

"Why did he do that, for God's sake?"

"Get off at Pontoise?" She stared at him. "Because he thought he were in Paris. He's no ordinary fella is ma Uncle Bojo. He lives in a mud hut, man. He ain't used to gettin' around."

McAndrew thought: it would be best to kill her.

If, like Chantelle, she died, then she would be at peace and no more have to lie.

There was a sacrosanct silence about the little grave in the Cimetière Montmartre, a hallowed peace that could not be found in the bitter gold of whisky. Why the hell couldn't she have stayed in Uganda, where she belonged? Then she wouldn't have to die.

He held up his finger to the window and saw the flesh was

stripped from it; with detailed attention he examined this finger, seeing the shredded skin, the riven flesh, the splintered bone.

He drank again, the bottle high, eyes clenched. Gasping, he said:

"Go on, kid, Ah'm enjoyin' it."

"Go on what?"

"Tell me when ye found your Uncle Bojo."

"Ah did not."

"Why?"

"Because they'd put him on a 'bus for St. Rémy."

"*No!*"

"Ah'm tellin' you, Mister – he was sent south for Rémy-les-Chevreuse – on the road to Orléans."

"I don't believe it!"

Hollow-eyed, his face bulbous with whisky, hair awry, McAndrew stared at her with incredulity. "Orléans? Why the hell did they send him down there?"

"Search me!"

She whistled up Dobie Dawg, who came lumbering towards them. She said, "It's the honest to God truth, Mister – would Ah tell you a lie? So me and Dobie Dawg, we got on a 'bus for St. Rémy."

"And when you got there, Uncle Bojo was gone?"

"Christ, how did ye guess?" She stared up at him. "The whole damn trip took us more'n three days!"

"Ye . . . ye haven't been up in a balloon, by any chance, have ye, Choco? On the way, I mean."

Her eyes, white orbs, blazed. "Up in a balloon? What the hell would Ah be doin' up in a balloon, for Gawd's sakes? I had a dawg with me."

McAndrew said, "The truth, Choco, or by God. . . !"

"Up in a balloon, ye say? Did ye hear that, Dobie? He says you and me 'ave been up in a balloon. Jeez, what next? He's a most distrustful fella, ain't he?"

McAndrew was drinking hard.

Snakes were in his body.

333

Snakes twisting in growing sibilance; cobras, vipers and rattlesnakes curled and coiled in convoluted worls within the labyrinth of his chest; wound and entwined themselves sinuously within the confining muscles of his belly.

Upon his shaking hand, outspread on the floor, a rat squatted, preening itself in whiskered contentment. McAndrew peered at it through lowering brows, then shrieked.

"You're sure in a bad way, Mister," said Chocolat. "I reckon you ought to eat. You ain't eaten in three whole days."

"Ay, ay, for God's sake. . . !" muttered McAndrew. "Food . . . food!" He staggered to his feet and lurched to the table. Through a haze of sweat he saw the plate picked clean.

"Well, Ah never!" said Chocolat. "Ah never did in all ma life! Damn me – Ah gone and done it ag'in! I must 'ave given that stew Ah cooked to ma Dawg Dobie. And now there's nothin' – what we goin' to do, child?"

"O God! *Ellie*. . . !"

"An' Ah keeps tellin' you, Mister, ma name ain't Ellie."

McAndrew turned his face to the ceiling and bawled, tunelessly:

"Ellie! *Ellie!*"

"An' it's no good shoutin' for her," said Chocolat. "That Ellie lady never do come when she's called."

Chocolat said, "Ah've read my history, too, ye know. When I was a piccaninny, some biblical fella comes to our mud village and teaches us about Samson. Listen, Cousin Dobie, and Ah'll quote ye yards of it. This fella Samson, he burned the corn, ye see – he tied the tails of foxes together, set 'em on fire and burned the Philistines' corn, the bugger. Did ye hear that for education, Mister?"

But McAndrew, dead drunk, chin turned up, did not stir on the bed.

Chocolat said, "Then, natural', the Philistines comes up and says 'Who bloody done this, for Gawd's sake?' and

334

someone mentioned the name Samson, so they reckoned, right and fair, that they owed him one." She leaned above McAndrew's snoring face.

"You listenin', honey? Next time out this ole Samson he ups wi' the jaw-bone of a donkey and knocks off a couple o' thousand of 'em Philistines – no wonder they got it up their aprons."

McAndrew snored on, oblivious.

Going to the sink Chocolat returned with scissors, saying:

"Then he fancies a smooth l'il piece called Delilah, an' he told this Delilah piece a whole pack o' lies, like you told me, an' she reckoned somethin' up . . ."

She whistled. "Slip over here, Dobie Dawg and watch this, an' after I done it ye can 'ave a bit of his leg," and the dog came and watched while she cut off McAndrew's hair; first his hair she cut, then his beard, even his eyebrows she cut off, and the hairs of his chest.

"There now, Dobie Dawg," said Chocolat. "See what Ah done? There's more ways of skinning a rabbit than one, ye know. Mister James Alexander McAndrew, in ma opinion, ye now look like a baby's bum."

Next, from her hair she took a pin and held it above McAndrew's eyes, saying:

"Cousin Dobie, For all the sins this wicked fella taught me, I'll read ye Judges sixteen; twenty-one, which they made me learn by heart . . .

" 'But the Philistines took him, and put out his eyes, and brought him down to Gaza, and bound him wi' fetters o' brass; and he did grind in the prison house.' You hear that, Cousin Dobie. . . ?"

And, as she knelt upon the bed, the better to blind McAndrew, a knock came on the door and the Bahima woman opened it, and a man stood there, he who was a friar of the Disciples of Pachomius, and therefore one of high education, and this man said:

"Water, little sister? For our supply has ceased . . ."

After giving this man water, and knowing that the visitor

335

was sent from God, the woman of Bahima turned from the man on the bed and went away from him.

"Come on, Dobie Dawg," Chocolat said to the Dobermann, "You're comin' alonga me tonight."

Jean Pierre, the French Dwarf, was sitting at the bar of the Café Noir when McAndrew entered.

Beautifully attired in a coat of black velvet and trews, the lace at his wrists and throat was white: his yellow boater he wore at a cocky angle.

The little Frenchman raised his glass of absinthe; sipping it, he watched McAndrew in the ornate mirror over the bar, at first not recognising him.

McAndrew, looking smaller without his hair and beard, entered in the clothes of his stage act, as approved by Aristide Bruant: he wore a torn shirt, ragged trousers to his calves, and his feet were bare – a cynical representation of what the world expected of an artist of Montmartre.

With a half-empty bottle of gin in one hand, McAndrew pushed a swaying path through the floor customers to the alcove he used for watching Chocolat's act.

Aristide Bruant, ever kindly, saw McAndrew enter, and joined him in the wings.

He said, "But what has happened. Your hair, your fine beard? But where have they gone?"

"Give ye three guesses." answered McAndrew.

"Someone has cut them off? Ooh-la! But this is terrible! Some action must be taken. How can one go around cutting off people's beards?"

"Names have been taken, son. Consider yourself short, in the near future, of one dark bitch of a Bantu bloody Galla."

"My Chocolat? It is not possible! She would never do such a thing." Aristide pleaded up into McAndrew's face, his hands clasped together. "Look, for me, go home, *mon ami*. Your act I will postpone – I will say you are ill. No hair, no beard, and very drunk – how can your act be successful?"

"Look what's come in," said McAndrew, and nodded at the crowded floor.

The café was already full to the doors, every table occupied: the gilt and gold decorations flashed in the smoke-laden air; the gas-jets flared on the minor sea of faces, the evening gowns, the white shirt fronts of the escorts.

Waiters darted among the tables in a chinking of glass. Top-hatted society gentlemen, nervously aware of their descent into depravity, shot shifty glances at red-cheeked wheezing gentlemen, who, with bulging shirt-fronts, stuffed pigeons eggs and paté into their bloated faces and washed it down with iced champagne.

Vivacious Parisian gentry girls, experiencing the first-time thrills of Montmartre, chattered uproariously from rouged mouths (it would have to come off before they got home) – gesticulating furiously to newly arrived friends, come to take the plunge, and the floor shuddered to the Can-can.

Doe-eyed innocence was there also, the 'special-treat' maidens on the arms of prospecting uncles. Hardened dance-girls swept the floor with companionable dances going at ten centimes a time and promises upstairs for fifty francs. Marquises and comptesses, actors and actresses – even Jane Avril, once Henri Lautrec's lover, and la Goulue, his foul-mouthed mistress – they were in the company that evening, Aristide Bruant said, while Offenbach held court.

McAndrew, glass-eyed, pressed against the scenery to keep him upright and pointed at another – a table nearest to the stage where Lanky Doyint, the double-jointed, top-hatted entertainer danced, his slim feet floor-tapping around a franc laid on the boards. Martial music blasted out in strident brass within a thunderous noise.

"Count Toulouse-Lautrec – look!" said McAndrew.

Said Aristide. "This is his second visit, and we are very proud to receive him!"

"I've just *got* to go on – this is what he's come for."

"To be caricatured?" Aristide raised an eyebrow. "To be insulted, all right, we insult the customers – his eccentricity will account for that – but to be caricatured, my friend? And

337

you in this state? He is, you know, a very important man."

"Aye, you're right, son." McAndrew staggered. "We'll handle him with kid gloves and make him the talk of Paris."

"Be careful what you draw!"

"Isn't he used to going up in balloons? One thing's sure, Aristide, it'll increase ye profits."

Jean Pierre, glass half raised, was watching them in the mirror.

When down the Seine ports with a *Marie Prey* cargo, Jean Pierre invariably called into Montmartre.

Also, Paris was a convenient trysting-place; the train journey to Mignon Marat's village near Verdun was almost direct; this simplified their meeting.

For this purpose Jean Pierre rented a room in Rue Briquet, which, fortunately for McAndrew, was just behind Steinkerque. And while it was not possible, explained Jean Pierre to Mignon, to take a lady such as you into the cabarets of Montmartre . . . Would you deny me the pleasures of my youth? The gaudy lights, a drink. . . ?"

Mignon Marat was small, but a little taller than Jean Pierre; upon her face was a birth-mark, red; one cheek violently affected. But there was about her a demure prettiness, and her black hair reached to her waist.

"I love you, Jean," she said. "Could I deny you anything?"

He paused before her, smiling into her face.

"Not so for other women, *ma cheri* . . . Other women would want to know. I tell you – I seek a friend.

"Love is trust and trust is love. I cannot speak for other women."

She smiled.

"Please do not be long. . . ?"

He bowed to her.

36

Chocolat was on stage: in her silver peacock dress with its open skirt and great fan of feathers behind, she danced: with her giant head-dress of foil and feathers, glittering with sequins, she danced; with her naked breasts dusted gilt and gold, she glided up and down the stage and hoarsely shrieked her derision at the customers, and sang:

> "God gave to this woman a coal black face
> With a swing to ma walk that lent me pride.
> An' He set me down in a jungle place
> With a look in ma eye to defy white whips . . ."

The blare of music abruptly stopped. Coming front stage, Chocolat shrieked:

"An' Ah flourished – ye know that? You botherin' old Whiteys – despite you all, Ah flourished. . . !"

Hisses, hoots and gibes greeted this. People stamped their feet; people now on their feet, arms waving her down.

"Yes, sir – Ah did good! The great Jehovah, he sorted me out at your expense – and Ah don't give a ninny's bugger for the lot of you, an' Ah never did!"

And she sang, her voice shrill above the jeers:

> "For God He knew since the start o' Time
> That the action don't lie in the lips, ma son,
> But the way that Ah wiggle, and a-wriggle ma hips!"

And she lifted up her fan-tail of feathers, showing her bare bottom, including the tattooed profile of Count Toulouse-

339

Lautrec, and wriggled it up and down the stage to thundering acclamation and laughter. The laughter changed to delighted applause as Count Alphonse rose at his table and bowed to all about him.

"One day I'll have that tattoo off, and the skin wi' it," said McAndrew, and he tipped the bottle, drained it and wiped his mouth with the back of his hand. Staggering out of his hiding-place, thrusting people aside, he reached the bar. The barman said:

"Monsieur, if you please . . . no more. Monsieur Bruant, he said . . ."

"You fug off," said McAndrew. Leaping the bar counter, he helped himself to another bottle of gin.

But a sudden confrontation with Jean Pierre delayed him on his way out, and he stared into the dwarf's face. From the deep recesses of his numbed brain, he fought for recognition.

"*Voilà,*" said Jean Pierre. "We meet again, eh, Big Savage!" He calmly sipped his absinthe.

"You fug off, too," said McAndrew.

"At your service." Jean Pierre bowed.

Clapping began immediately McAndrew's easel and charcoal tins were carried on to the stage. Many people actually stood when the great wide sheets of Ingres paper were brought and the stage hands pinned them up.

McAndrew's fame as a cartoonist was spreading like a prairie fire; all Paris was now flocking into Montmartre for the privilege of being selected for his sardonic, often gross humour: talk had it (a fiction spread by the showman Bruant) that the Archbishop himself had filed a libel suit against the Café Noir, and McAndrew in particular, for his depiction of the cleric as a drunken, lecherous friar.

Jean Pierre, in his position of vantage, noticed that gendarmes were posted at the doors.

The applause rose to a tumult as McAndrew entered from the wings; this hushed a little when he was clearly seen to be intoxicated, and Bruant, now beside Chocolat, wrung his hands with nervous anticipation.

McAndrew, hands on hips but dangerously swaying, cried as the applause subsided:

"Ladies and gentlemen! The best that can be said of the Café Noir is that we tell the truth about ourselves. The food's indifferent, the hostesses dance like heifers, and Bruant's beer is worse than mare's milk . . ." and here he paused, grinning down at the count at a table a few feet away, adding:

"I mention mare's milk because one guest here is known to have given it a try . . ."

Bawled laughter followed this, and the count scowled.

Not a week ago a reporter had seen the count milking his mare along the Bois de Boulogne in full sight of other riders and the passing carriage of the President of France.

"Indeed," added McAndrew, now apparently sober. "Talk has it that the President stopped, and he had some as well."

The count's face became bucolic and he scowled up at the stage; his guests, delighted at his discomfiture, held their heads together, nodding assent.

"And since," continued McAndrew, "it is my disposition to select for my attentions the noblest person in the room, who else must I choose for my subject tonight but one who has chosen to grace us with his presence – Le Compte Alphonse de Toulouse-Lautrec Monfa – better known, without a doubt, as the father of our revered and much lamented Henri, the darling of the Moulin Rouge!"

Out of the corner of his eye McAndrew saw the count, already apoplectic, lift a commanding hand: moments later Aristide Bruant, summoned to his table, was engaged in agitated discussion. The Scot shouted, getting into his stride:

"Therefore, I have the honour to present our guest in a role best suited to him . . ." He grinned around the assembled faces.

"As an upright and foremost member of the French aristocracy . . . like so . . ." and he wielded the charcoal, inscribing two long, vertical lines. "Descended from the Count de Chambord of the Bourbons, the legitimate pretender to the French throne – who might challenge his claim to royal blood? What aristocracy can compare with such ancestry? – the Counts of Toulouse and the Viscounts of Lautrec!"

He approached the stage gas-lamps, crying, "Take a bow, sir, take a bow!"

The count, his brow cleared now, nodded about him; applause rose, and McAndrew, arms raised, brought it to a higher note. Turning, he drew swiftly, and a dignified figure, tall, narrow and erect, took shape.

"What splendid, audacious spirit was his, my friends! *Diex lo volt* – that is the family motto! Did not God Almighty will it that our subject, Count Alphonse, should be head and shoulders above all others?

"The Holy Land crusades! Ten times excommunicated by the Pope – is that not a record of which to be proud. . . ?" He turned to the easel and, with lightning strokes of the charcoal, made a narrow head and shoulders, then shouted to the floor:

"True, this family enjoyed a debauch – don't we all? For this aristocracy, recall, were history makers of unbridled energy – 'Let us not confuse love with matters of copulation,' said one Lautrec to an enquiring duchess. And of whom was he speaking? To Adélaide de Toulouse, of whose lusts, as history relates, no serf, king or animal could satisfy . . . What nobility. . . ?" He opened his arms to the count. "What grace. . . !"

Mutterings began among the audience as McAndrew turned again to the easel, cartooning in a *cuirassier*, in his decorative uniform, gold braid and epaulettes . . . yet all curiously vertical, a slim line version of the original – elongated. The figure's height out of all proportion to its width.

Turning to the audience, the Scot shouted:

"Though a hawker, falconer, hunter and shooter – our subject was also a devoted soldier, remember, a product of the academy at Saint-Cyr. Indeed, he was the darling of the 6th Lancers, ever ready for battle, but – through no fault of his own – was never to hear a shot fired in anger!"

The count rose at his table, his fist raised, and McAndrew

342

shouted, "But this was not our guest's fault, my friends. An officer and gentleman must obey his own demands of patriotism if his country calls. And we here owe to our nobleman the honour and dignity accorded to all who perceive their public duty. Was it not from the loins of this illustrious soldier that our beloved Henri, the artist, sprang. . . ? – among countless others, of course . . . The Little Treasure? The *enfant terrible* of the Moulin Rouge?"

The people's protests suddenly diminished into an ominous quiet. And, in the ringing silence, McAndrew swung back to the canvas, drawing with colour now, hazing in, below the feet of the elongated figure, a blaze of red.

A configuration of earth (upon which the figure stood) made shape. People craned their heads sideways, the better to recognise the form.

The cartoon finished, McAndrew faced the audience for the last time.

"See," he cried. "Our noble count is now standing on a field of blood – but not the blood of the battlefield, my friends – oh no! – the blood of the hunting field . . . for at this occupation – the killing of things – he is particularly adept."

Silence.

"And so, ladies and gentlemen . . ." and here McAndrew swayed dangerously, the gin bottle back in his hand, "we see him at his best – the professional between the sheets – the adulterer, seducer, libertine, rake, fornicator – he who accused his son of all such things, and burned his paintings in the face of posterity!"

Saying this, McAndrew turned the cartoon on to its side.

The earth, red-stained, now became the body profile of the count in English hunting-pink . . . and from the figure's belly projected the *cuirassier* in uniform, a phallic symbol.

McAndrew cried in the shocked silence:

"The twenty-eight variations, as many of you know, can be obtained from Burton's Kama Sutra, but not the twenty-ninth. This, as accepted in Paris, is known personally only to Le Compte Alphonse de Toulouse-Lautrec Monfa. *Diex lo volt!*"

*

343

In the ensuing pandemonium, the count rose to his feet.

Approaching the stage he drew from his breast pocket a visiting card and calmly tossed it at McAndrew's feet, saying quietly:

"Tomorrow, dawn? The Cimetière Parisien de Pantin Bobigny?"

"Mister," said McAndrew in English, "in the name of ye dead son, I'll give ye me undivided attention."

37

Wandering aimlessly down Rue Briquet, McAndrew was singing, though Aristide Bruant's suggestion that he should leave the Café Noir at once, had cut him to the quick. Waving his bottle of gin, he was doing a two-step, and bawling, to the tune of Dolly Gray:

> "Goodbye, Choco, I must leave you
> Count Alphonse says I must go.
> The old bastard says he'll kill me,
> 'Cause he knows you love me so . . ."

McAndrew was still singing and dancing when night-capped heads came out of balcony windows, and irate voices shrieked, in French:

"Go to bed, you mad-brained English!"

"I'll have ye know I'm a highland Scot, Tosh," yelled McAndrew, glaring up.

"Then get back to Glasgow, ye noisy sod." This from a northern English voice.

"Then you come and bloody shift me," cried McAndrew. He stared down the street where windows were coming open and heads coming out, and yelled:

"And put your frog faces back, ye pesky lot – it looks like a cattle truck."

Fists were shaken and night-pots being emptied down as McAndrew began to march up and down, bellowing as he went:

"Company will march past in review order. *By the left* . . . look to ye front, man, look to ye front. . . !"

Military strains now rose into the Montmartre night as he marched, shouting commands, arms swinging to the regulation pace. A chorus of protests rose; doors were slammed, pots clattering as weapons were being collected.

"Right, Englese, now we come!"

"Aye, and do ye'selves better'n at the Battle of Waterloo – come on, then!"

"Now we arrivé!"

"And Agincourt!" Staggering, the bottle tipped high, he guzzled and profaned, killing détente. Then he paused, listening to a clattering of boots on stairs, and cried:

"Violence now, is it?"

On his way to Steinkerque he was bawling the kit inspection ditty:

> "Comb, spoon, knife, fork, lather-brush,
> toothbrush, razor, laces . . . and oh, where's
> the housewife?"

But when he neared the light-shot pavements of the Café Noir, and home, his pace slowed to a creep; with a finger against his mouth, he went on tip-toe, now . . . being afraid of Chocolat.

Distant clocks were striking one a.m. The attic of the Disciples of Pachomius was silent, but the third floor, abode of the *Dames de la Nuit*, was beginning to wake: strident music came from its darkened windows, the soprano shrieks of women, the gutteral muttering of men.

Earlier, McAndrew had seen Chocolat drive off with Count Alphonse in his new scarlet Panhard-Levassor motor-vehicle, with Cousin Dobie (showing his teeth) sitting on the back seat like a postillion guard, and there came to McAndrew a small flush of pity; Cousin Dobie granted no distinction when it came to a set of trews, he reflected, velveteen, whip-cord, or otherwise.

The room in Steinkerque conveyed a sense of emptiness as he entered with his key: McAndrew saw, through a haze of gin, the easel with its small, sad face staring out . . . the face of the child, Chantelle; the moon entered through the open door, bowing first, exposing the drab furnishings within. And then a soft growling from a darkened corner told him that Cousin Dobie was, in fact, already home, even if his mistress wasn't.

The doubtful greeting appraised McAndrew with a small, eerie comfort, for if Dobie was in, then Chocolat was never far away.

Then he noticed a small, black head on the bed's pillows, and smiled: her silence clearly betokened feigned sleep – reasonable behaviour upon Chocolat's part, he thought, after the trauma of the night's experiences.

Aristide Bruant, McAndrew dismally considered, would be difficult to assuage in the morning. That was . . . and this he pondered at some length . . . if he was still alive in the morning, after his encounter with the brave Alphonse.

The tombstones of Bobigny cemetery became etched upon his mind, a macabre pictoria seen through the fumes of gin.

Stripping off his clothes, McAndrew got into the bed, to lie there in dizzy dreams of slanting ceilings; finally to turn over and put an affectionate arm around the still, black form beside him.

"Och, ye darlin' creature. I don't know how ye put up wi' me."

The effect was almost immediate.

His mouth touching skin and bone, McAndrew opened one eye, peering through a bushy brow. And the visage that arose in that eerie light was not the face of Chocolat, but one riven with ancient tribal scars: the mouth he had kissed was not the mouth of Chocolat, but the leer of a skeletal hag: the breast he had touched possessed no softness, but was an empty rib cage strung with sinew. And the hand McAndrew slid beneath the sheet caressed something so unusual that he gripped the object, and pulled. And an apparition of ebony blackness arose in the bed beside him, opened its mouth and bawled from its cavernous void:

"*Jeez!*"

347

"Bloody hell!" ejaculated McAndrew, and was out of the bed at a leap, just as Chocolat came through the door, crying shrilly:

"You dirty ole beggar, McAndrew! What the hell you doin' in that bed to ma Uncle Bojo?" and she raced around the room after him, swinging her handbag.

There ain't never been such a commotion down Rue Steinkerque, said Chocolat later, since the Union come and put the Codes o' Practice on the *Dames de la Nuit*.

Round and round the room went McAndrew with Chocolat after him, Cousin Dobie Dawg howling and ma Uncle Bojo rotatin' his honkers, said Chocolat. "An' Ah'm tellin' you, Mister," she explained to Bruant, "Ah ain't never heard such a palaver in all ma life, no sir. What with that Dobie whoofin' and ma Uncle Bojo squealin' and the dames from downstairs shriekin' – well, ye can imagine. For them professionals don't take kindly to a queerin' of the pitch, an' that's understandable."

"I myself disapprove," announced Aristide, archly.

Meanwhile, McAndrew, half way up to the attic met the Disciples of Pachomius coming down, so fled before them with Dobie Dawg in pursuit.

"And what happened then?" asked Aristide, lighting a cigar.

"You'll never guess," said Chocolat. "Up Steinkerque that queer fella goes with the *Dames de la Nuit* after him with cobbles, Cousin Dobie on his ass and the Disciples headin' him off, since they don't go for this he'in and he'in stuff, neither, apparently. And right and proper, too, Ah say, for ma Uncle Bojo's a respectable married fella wi' eight fat wives at home in Bojoland, and he don't reckon to get pixilated in Paris without his prior permission, no sir." Chocolat was breathing heavily.

"I absolutely agree," said Aristide Bruant.

Going very fast was McAndrew, with half the gendarmerie in Montmartre after him, waving truncheons and blowing whistles. Along Rochechouart he went with his drawings under his arm and his trousers around his knees, being

348

rushed by every Madame in Steinkerque, said Chocolat, "for this fancyin' behaviour's very bad for trade, ye know, and ma Uncle Bojo reckons that his privates are particular, and Ah says it's a cryin' shame that he's got to come to Paris to get holed up, for this never happened to him more'n a couple o' times before, not even in Sierra Leone."

"Quite so," said Aristide. "And then?"

"Then that ole Scotsman, he jist plain disappeared," said Chocolat, in awe. "Jist like Beelzebub – one big puff o' smoke, an' he vanished. And this 'as put the wind up ma Uncle Bojo no end, believe me, for like he says, it's a hell of a thing to be did by the Devil Incarnate, yes sir . . ."

"And Mr. McAndrew?"

Chocolat emptied her hands at Aristide. "We ain't seen hide nor hair o' him since."

"Thank God for that," said Aristide.

Jean Pierre, waiting in the shadows, caught McAndrew's wrist as it went flailing past the top of Rue Briquet, and levering, twisted him into the shelter of an alley. "This way, Big Savage. Quick!"

"*Jesus!*" said McAndrew.

Jean Pierre, with his small legs folded under him, sat on a kitchen chair in Rue Briquet, unspeaking . . . while Mignon served McAndrew with bread and wine.

He, sagging bleary-eyed over the table, tore off huge chunks of the hot, crusted bread and guzzled it down with red wine from a bottle.

"The cheese, Monsieur . . ." Mignon whispered. "You do not like Rochefort cheese. . . ?"

"Eat it," commanded Jean Pierre. "She bought it especially."

With the canvas of Chantelle hugged against him, McAndrew ate, watching the dwarf. Jean Pierre lit one of his eternal cheroots and stared back at him through its smoke. Mignon said, smiling with piquant charm:

"You will sleep now, Monsieur Savage? There is but one bed, but it would please us if . . ." she faltered.

The room held a strangely perfidious quiet.

McAndrew said, "What time is it?"

Jean Pierre consulted his fob watch. "Two o'clock."

"Call me at five, I have work to do."

"So soon?" Mignon appealed to the dwarf. "Jean Pierre, your friend is exhausted . . ."

"It is necessary, Mignon. Owing to his stupidity, it is necessary."

"But why?" She looked from one to the other. "Surely . . ."

"Don't ask questions, woman. It is necessary." Jean Pierre added, to McAndrew. "At five o'clock I will have a cab waiting. But I will not be there, you understand? You are a fool, so you will handle fool's business alone. This man will kill you."

"And you, meanwhile, go to hell," said McAndrew.

After the Scot was asleep, sprawled across her bed, Mignon said, "It is strange, Jean Pierre, the way you speak to each other. . . ?"

"It is the language of men."

"Of English men?"

"Not necessarily."

On tiptoe, he kissed her; first upon her lips, then upon the red birth-mark of her face: in McAndrew's snores, he kissed her.

38

McAndrew, sitting in the back of his cab as it clip-clopped through the still dark streets, raised to his lips the flask of absinthe he had stolen from Jean Pierre and drank, gasping. With red-rimmed eyes he stared through the cab window at an awakening Paris.

All down the Boulevard de la Chapelle blind windows were opening their eyes to the dawn: he heard the shrill protests of harassed mothers and the squalling of potted babies, the deeper commands of waking men.

Smells of bacon and garlic drifted deliciously to his nostrils, and he gratefully savoured them: these faded into lush cow-pat and buttermilk smells as the big country of Bobigny came rolling up out of the mist. A jay was singing – he heard its song above the jangling harness.

Tombstones and heraldic angels assailed him then, stark black against a reddening sky, as the cab driver stopped it outside the cemetery gates.

"You require me to wait, Monsieur?"

The man raised a lined face, staring through the ground mist to a distant field: here, outlined against the clouds stood a coach and two white horses. The cabman sighed: clearly, thought McAndrew, he had made such journeys before . . . and gone back empty-handed . . .

"Och, no, Mister. It's me last couple o' francs, ye see." This he said in patois, and warmly.

"I'd be prepared to wait, and free."

McAndrew bowed.

There was about the cabman a quiet gentility, McAndrew

thought; the man's eyes drifted over the Scot's ragged clothes, the bare feet blue with the cold. So momentarily, McAndrew stared up and the cabman stared down, his cadaverous face sunk with shadows: God Almighty, McAndrew thought – it's the bloody undertaker, and he gave him a happy grin; tipping high Jean Pierre's silver flask, he drained it, then tossed it to the cabman . . . who neatly caught it, and handed it back. His voice was deep:

"Do not give away your luck, Monsieur. When a man leaves this world without his permission, best he departs with at least one reasonable possession, which will exclude, of course, his wife . . ." and McAndrew grinned wide.

"Och – that serves ye . . . did ye hear that, Ellie?" he said aloud.

Three men, all top-hatted and frock-coated against the morning cold, were standing beneath overhanging branches in a misted field.

One, the coachman, of gigantic proportions (the count's bodyguard) held the horses: the second, no higher than his shoulder, was a surgeon; he was clutching a small, black bag of instruments.

Count Alphonse straightened when he heard McAndrew coming.

"He comes. I am surprised!"

"And whistling, the fool!"

They stood listening, for the night mist still obliterated the road to Pantin.

"Let us pray he has breath enough to whistle upon his return." The surgeon mopped his small, sweating face. "You are shooting to kill, Alphonse?"

"This one – certainly."

"You realise the dangers, of course?"

"There is no danger. He will not be missed."

"He will certainly be missed. Is he not in regular employment? And you publicly challenged him, remember?"

The count turned away. "None heard it."

"But he has your card, has he not?"

"Yes, and it will be in his possession."

"Then I shall retrieve it . . ." answered the surgeon, "before I certify his death in Larisboisière. Duelling is an offence, my friend – even a Toulouse-Lautrec is not above the law."

"Which is a pity," replied the count. "Time was we could defrock a priest, outrage and hang him in public; things are certainly not what they were." He nodded towards McAndrew's footsteps coming out of the mist. "Make sure that this one lands in the right department, that is what I pay you for."

McAndrew, whistling his head off, came barging out of the mist, staggering.

"He do look as if he's taken a drop or so, mind – beggin' ye pardon, gentlemen," observed the coachman, jovially.

"Do not be impertinent, man – keep your place," admonished the surgeon.

"'Morning, gents!"

McAndrew looked, thought Count Alphonse, like some monstrous frog spewed up from the bogs of Bobigny; he was shivering, his hair tufted and glistening water, and his ball eyes radiated cold. Approaching, McAndrew cried happily:

"Pistols at dawn is it? Hell, mun – do you really consider yourself affronted? All I did was do a drawing – and isn't it a fact that ye eat your dinner wi' it?" In patois French, again, he spoke.

Stiffly, the count led him to the open door of the coach: arranged on its back seat was a variety of weapons.

"Rapiers? Cutlasses – pistols; kindly make your choice."

"Jesus, ye bloody mean it, don't you – you're going to put an end to us?"

"That is my intention."

McAndrew grinned wide. "*Diex lo volt*, eh? God wills it. But the motto of my clan's a hot one, too – *Nemo Me Impune Lacessit* – so dunna say, son, that ye haven't been warned!" He smiled happily about him.

The Latin raised the surgeon's face first, then the count's.

353

"None challenges me with impunity. . . ?"

"'None *threatens* me . . .' It's the translation you're both misfirin' on, if ye do not think me bold . . .'"

The count said, loftily, "My wife informed me that you are from some vague lairdship, and I am prepared to believe it."

"Och no, laddie – that's not the point," replied McAndrew. "But it's only fair for ye to know who you're cudgelling with, don't ye see? For we've been blood-letting up in the glens while you bloody frogs were stitching the Bayeux Tapestry, an' I'll take ye on with claymores or Catch-as-catch-can, as you like."

"The man is a gabbling fool," asserted the surgeon.

"But also an aristocrat," added Count Alphonse.

Picking up a pistol he sighted it distantly, saying, "There's much more satisfaction in killing a gentleman . . ." He moved away.

"If ye insist on it," said McAndrew.

The surgeon said, as he handed McAndrew his pistol:

"Monsieur James Alexander McAndrew, laird of Ross and Cromarty – so you tell us – because of your noble birth the count has declared that he is prepared to be lenient. Are you listening?"

"Ah'm hangin' on every word, Your Worship."

"You insulted him publicly," continued the surgeon. "You did so both with intent and premeditation – indeed, you did it again, just now. The newspapers have referred to it, with the result that he has been widely pilloried – unfairly, and without giving you the smallest provocation. Do you understand my French?"

"Perfectly – pray continue."

"Therefore, says Count Alphonse, if you are prepared again to perform in this iniquitous Café Noir, this time making a full apology, and recant your baseless attacks upon his noble character, my client would consider sparing your life."

Silently, McAndrew pondered this, saying, as he brushed

his eyes, "Aw Jesus – now there's a real gentleman. Ach, that's entirely good of him. He'll not be killin' me?"

"Do what he asks, and you can go free."

"And causin' me no injury, neither – no beatings, or anythin'?"

"I've already told you – retract, and you go free."

McAndrew raised his face.

"Go tell him that I'm killin' him for what he did to his son."

The surgeon was affronted. "His son. You mean. . . ?"

"His son, Henri, the artist of the Moulin Rouge, whom he renounced, ostracised, and whose works his family burned . . . Henri, my friend, who lies in Verdelais. Tell him, Monsieur Docteur, that when I heard of Henri's death, I decided to kill his father in the name of posterity – that I came to France – to Montmartre, for this purpose . . . to insult him and finish it here, in this field and on this day. Do you, now, understand what I am saying?"

The surgeon replied, "Monsieur, you are ill, do you realise this? Worse, you are drunk. You are an artist, they tell me; the count is a military duellist, an expert in killing. You will die, sir, make no mistake, and probably most painfully. Listen to me – whatever the errors of the past, whatever the revenge . . . I beg you to retract the injustice you have done. There can be one, and only one possible outcome to this fight."

"Go and tell the bastard," said McAndrew.

39

Jean Pierre left his cab at the Bobigny cemetery entrance, and hurried through the tombstones to the duelling field.

Earlier, after awaking McAndrew from sleep, he had followed him across Rue Briquet to Rochechouart Boulevard, hailed a cab and followed McAndrew's chaise at a safe distance.

Fortunately, he reached the rendezvous in time: McAndrew and Count Alphonse were actually standing back to back, the surgeon with his handkerchief upraised, when Jean Pierre entered the adjoining wood and watched from the shadows of trees.

The surgeon's commands rang out:

"Gentlemen! You will advance for ten paces, then turn, and fire in your own time, but within six seconds from the time you turn. Is that understood?"

Count Alphonse lifted a finger. McAndrew said, "For Christ's sake get on wi' it, mun."

"Are you signifying that you understand my instructions?"

"He understands full well," replied Count Alphonse, in French.

There was about this man an inborn elegance, thought Jean Pierre, and this was not possessed by the Scotsman. The count was bareheaded, his shirt of white, ruffled lace; his breeches, tightly fitted to his straight, slim legs, were of scarlet, his riding-boots of chamois leather, reached to his knees. And he held himself well, thought the dwarf – one could not deny it; an arrogance that came from the beds of La Fayette and his contemporaries.

McAndrew, by contrast, was a hulk; a towering figure of tufted beard and mouse-cropped hair, in rags, splay-footed on the autumn floor.

And there arose, even as Jean Pierre watched the scene, a sun of almost regal splendour; it brushed spun gold upon the forest refuse; it painted up the lichened trees with a new and vital greenness, which was like the beginning of the world. The sunlight shafted the morning, the day was born.

"Gentlemen, stand by!"

The count was thinking that soon this parody would be over, and his confidence held no boast. Other men, confirmed duellists, had faltered before the pistol's blaze, and fallen; he always aimed to kill. His only worry was Hôpital Lariboisière . . . and a trustful surgeon would negotiate that. Footpads or Apaches could always be blamed for wounds, or death, in the area of Montmartre . . .

McAndrew was assailed by no particular emotion as he waited for the handkerchief to fall; strangely, however, thoughts of Ellie Kendall began to enter the untenanted areas of his mind.

He saw her, in that infinite delay between firm finger and handkerchief, not as womanhood's representative . . . the female tiger . . . but as one of sudden gentleness: not upon the fields of warring dominance, but of affection, and kindly tolerance.

But, he wondered, did any woman alive possess such sweeting attributes? The poet's search for one was both notorious, and vain . . . based on maternal teachings, no doubt, and never mistress fact.

By contrast, McAndrew had discovered, the love of one man for another was infinitely more precious, and enduring. It existed unspokenly, except, perhaps, through a curse; unattached to pillow turmoil and gasped, soon forgotten pledges.

357

Yes, men, he had found, did not require the fragile proofs of love: though the weaker sex, they were unattached to cheap, romantic situations; no physical contact bolstered love's perfection.

What woman (and this was the thought that possessed him now) would seek to fire a gun at another to settle a point of honour. . . ? They who possessed no honour when it came to their sisters, and few moral truths when it came to their men.

McAndrew grinned to himself; Christ, he thought, he could talk . . .

The handkerchief fell. He began, automatically, to walk.

Within him, strong and alive, was a warmth for the Count Alphonse . . . not for Ellie.

Jean Pierre emerged from behind his tree the moment Mc-Andrew turned, and fired.

Light flared from the pistol, smoke rolled out. The count staggered slightly, then drew himself upright.

A small, scarlet stain of blood began to widen on the bicep of his shirt.

The clattering of McAndrew's weapon reverberated through the forest, the birds ceased to sing.

Seconds passed. Both men stood motionless. The count raised his pistol, sighting McAndrew. Taking deliberate aim, he called:

"Stand sideways gentleman! You are a barn door. God, these stupid British!"

McAndrew stood square, tearing open the shirt at his chest, and cried, "Shoot, ye swine, and be damned to ye!"

"Two seconds," called the surgeon . . . as the count's pistol shot flame and smoke.

McAndrew shuddered to the impact of the ball. His earth heaved. His sky flared. Suddenly, he spun with the impact, then fell, face down, and lay still.

The count wearily turned away, gesturing over his shoulder. "Get rid of it," he said, and the coachman moved.

"*Wait*," said Jean Pierre, and entered the clearing.

First he knelt by McAndrew, his fingers against the Scot's temple, then he rose.

"He lives," he said.

"And who are you?" asked the count.

"I am his friend."

"A friend who brings bad luck, perhaps?" The count nodded to his coachman. "We do not need one such as he at Lariboisière, it is dangerous. Beat him, and send him away," and he pulled on his morning jacket.

The big man lumbered over towards Jean Pierre.

The dwarf suddenly somersaulted, and kicked the coachman in the face: as he fell the little man was upon him; his hand chopped down. The coachman sighed, and lay still. Jean Pierre said:

"Treat men like sheep, Monsieur, and you turn them into tigers. My friend is large, so I shall need your help to lift him – also your coach, to carry him to my house. Nobody is taking him to Lariboisière."

Count Alphonse moved swiftly, leaping for the coach and its weapons; Jean Pierre moved faster, kicking shut the door with his foot. Hands on hips, he faced them both; the surgeon, he noticed, was trembling.

"Lift my friend and put him in your coach, gentlemen; and do it gently, or I will kill you both."

With the surgeon driving the coach belonging to Count Alphonse, and with an unconscious McAndrew lolling on its back seat, the dwarf directed it across Pantin and along the Boulevard de la Chapelle, to the room in Rue Briquet, where Mignon was waiting with hot water and bandages.

"This, Big Savage," said Jean Pierre, staunching the blood from McAndrew's head, "is at least one absinthe you owe me. And Mignon, I pray, will see that I get it." Then he took from McAndrew's pocket the silver absinthe flask, saying, "Meanwhile, it is most honourable of you to return this to me, my friend."

Book Five

40

1913

The firm of Cambourne Freighters, now renamed Ross-Cambourne Ltd., had expanded considerably in the years since McAndrew had left Ellie.

Under Ross Bolton's guidance the number of freighters had increased to thirty-two, and were now employed on sea routes all over the world.

Ellie, whose maxim had always been to put away enough corn in seven fat years to last through seven lean ones, had played unwittingly into Bolton's hands.

He, for his part, used the Kendall capital wisely in speculation, proving himself more adept at economics than at the helm of a ship.

Let the city be glutted with gold, thought he, before its capture.

The close communities of South Wales at this time were not without their social standards, but these varied according to supply and demand.

The businessman who covered the legs of his settle (because of the bare effect they might have upon the children) could enjoy income from a Portsmouth brothel. Not sixty years before, slaves were being flogged in Bristol by gentlemen on their knees in Church.

Nevertheless, it was necessary that the adulterous but profitable House of Cambourne should be seen to be acceptable.

Ellie and Ross Bolton, if ostracised by the gentry (who

were also at it, said McAndrew) yet enjoyed a happy social
life with their fellow captains of industry: adultery, like
prostitution, being made respectable by quality.

As Ellie breakfasted from a silver tray, she began to think
about McAndrew.

It was over twelve years, she reflected, since he had left
Cambourne. Tom was only three then, now he was nearly
sixteen.

She dully munched her toast, staring ahead.

In those twelve years her shipping fleet had flourished. But
it was to McAndrew, her husband, not to Ross Bolton, she
realised, that the initial success was due – those were the
hard years: Ross had merely linked the firm with the
meteoric rise of Barry, now the biggest coal port in the world.

Nor could she herself claim credit for the firm's extra-
ordinary expansion.

During her long illness, a condition of the blood from
which she was not yet recovered, she had handed over her
assets in the company to Tom, her son, through Jake as
trustee. It had given Ross virtual control; now, in retrospect,
Ellie began to wonder if this had been a mistake, and she
longed for the time when Tom, still at school, could take over
the reins from Jake, and eventually, take control from Ross.

This, she concluded, was the natural scheme of things: as
one went out another came in.

Lately, however, she was given cause for a deeper worry:
Jake was proving an unreliable trustee.

Her father, once the respected head of the Barry Bible
Class (which used regularly to meet under his theological
guidance) was now to be seen more with the tipplers of the
local publics than with his students of Divinity.

Unaccountably, Jake had taken to drink.

Hebrews ten: thirty-one, once his constant quote, he now
replaced by the bawdy doggerels of the Chain Locker and
Three Bells.

The situation Ellie found disturbing, to say the least.

*

Even more disturbing, the graph of exports was flattening.

Oil, not coal, was now the cause of jubilation, and Barry was beginning to feel the pinch. People were getting out of coal; oil-burners were taking over. Rumblings of war had begun on the Continent.

If war came, the old Navy coal-burners would be sacrificed to oil. Barry's jugular vein, the black wealth of the Rhondda, would irrevocably be cut. And Ross-Cambourne, geared to coal, would be practically out of business.

Ellie had no illusions about it. She rose from the bed and went to the window, looking out on to the Big Wheatfield.

The sun betokened a glorious July morning, but when she saw the tinker caravans, high up on a ridge, she frowned. Was it some strange trick of the sun, or did they appear closer? Had they even entered her fields, something she had forbidden them to do? Then worry about the firm nagged at her mind again.

Vaguely, she wondered what Uncle Jason would do . . . was Ross correct – that they should sell up, go north to Whitby and into trawler fishing? The proposition was attractive, and beautiful Whitby, so close to her Newcastle home, invaded her mind. Sitting down, Ellie stared at her face in a mirror.

Age, she saw, was now touching her face with his ancient fingers, etching the lines of illness around her mouth.

At forty-two her youth had gone, but men had made her face what it was, she thought.

Vaguely, she wondered then what would happen if McAndrew returned; he had come back once, of course, with disastrous results, but her sense of impending disaster snatched at the possibility of his help. With her father drinking, the need for his strength was apparent. But how would she treat him were McAndrew suddenly to arrive? Ellie pondered this, her comb suspended. Probably as badly as before, she thought: genius, at best, is a neurotic child, and her practicality would revolt.

And what would McAndrew suggest under these new economic circumstances? Ellie didn't know. But of one thing she was sure – she'd do precisely what he advised. With McAndrew a woman had a certain knowledge – what he did would be for her good – having no lust of personal gain.

Ellie smiled wryly: the same could scarcely be said of Ross . . .

A tap came on her door.

"Yes?"

"That girl's here, Ma'am," said Megsie.

Pinta and Tam Shenks were standing in the hall. A young girl was standing between them.

"'Mornin', Missus," Pinta pulled his hair; Tam Shenks, wide-shouldered, darkly handsome, pushed the girl before him.

"So this is Rachel?" said Ellie.

"Come down from the tinker caravans, mind," said Megsie warningly.

"Yes, I know."

"She's a good girl, Missus," said Pinta, "ain't she, Tam? She's a good family girl, if ye get me – good wi' kids, an' that."

"Are you her grandfather?"

"Uncle, Missus. I watched her growed," said Pinta.

Ellie smiled encouragingly at Tam Shenks. He, drunk with strength, moved flat-footed, his hob-nailed boots scraping the floor.

"You'd like to work for me?" she asked Rachel.

The years had done more for Ellie than age her; they had warmed her into a new and kindly tolerance.

Rachel drew herself up.

Her dress enhanced her tinker aura – a typical wanderer. Her legs and feet were bare, her bodice red and gathered at the waist with a scarlet girdle; her skirt, above her knees, was of black homespun, and her hair which reached down to her waist, was auburn in lustrous waves; its colour, thought Ellie, was astonishing.

But it was her eyes . . . slanted in her high-boned face,

366

they gave no doubt as to her antecedents: the effect was completed by large bangle earrings.

Ellie once knew a girl like this in town; a gay promiscuous brat, with a talent for evil. She was settled now with a husband and family, and her name was Tuesday. In her time she had been called to Cambourne for the favours of the master, in the bad old days when Teddy Grey-Cambourne ruled the roost, and all the hens as well.

Now here was another potential courtesan; of equal beauty, and with the same trim, virginal figure . . . possessed, it appeared, of the same adolescent sensuality.

Was it wise, Ellie wondered, to bring such temptation into the house, when Ross was known for a roving eye? She said, kindly:

"You'll have to work, ye know."

"She'll work, or she'll get the back of my hand," said Tam Shenks.

"I take it you're her father?"

"So I heard say, Missus." He guffawed, suddenly at ease.

Ellie said, "Would you be happy here, child?"

"Aye, Mum," replied Rachel.

To Ellie's surprise the girl's voice was beautiful.

"Can you begin tomorrow?"

"She can begin right now," enjoined Pinta, and twisted at his ragged cap. "We . . . we was wondering, Missus, really speaking, us being a bit short . . ."

"No," said Ellie. "And she works here on one condition only – that you clear your caravans off my field. You have permission to be on the road, I understand, but not on my land."

Ross, in riding habit, came through the door as the two men went out. His smile was gay and he was beautifully turned out. Her life, thought Ellie, was adorned by handsome men of imperfect quality.

"Good God, who are those two?" He looked over his shoulder.

"The father and uncle of Rachel, our new maid – or so they say."

"The one taking Megsie's place?"

Ellie nodded, going into the drawing-room. "And Megsie's starting in the kitchen where Cook left off, bless her."

"A tinker as a maid? You surprise me?"

"Why not? Everybody's telling me we're a classless society."

"She'll steal your silver."

"Nobody steals from me, Ross. Try it and you'll see.".

He smiled at her. "Subtlety, my love, is the art of being a woman. You've always excelled at it. By the way – it's the end of summer term, isn't it? When is Tom arriving?"

Ellie was going up the stairs. She looked down at Ross standing in the middle of the hall. She thought – life was only a dream. A dream from which one awakened to find oneself alone.

"Tom?" The name brought her to actuality. "On Wednesday – the six-thirty from Cardiff."

"Are you meeting him?"

"I don't feel up to it. Saul's going to fetch him in the trap."

Ellie was watching Ross. There was about his aesthetic face a sudden cold austerity, something she had noticed before when they discussed her son.

"This," he said with mock gaiety, "is a time when the blood is singing," and he strode across the hall.

"Oh God, don't start that again! And don't blame Tom because you don't get on – the boy tries hard enough. Heaven knows what he's done to warrant your dislike." Lifting the hem of her skirt, she went up the purple-carpeted staircase.

Ross delayed to call after her, "You expect too much, my charmer. Loving you is a sort of consecration, but there's no particular reason why I should adore your son."

He watched her as she painfully climbed the staircase.

She possessed, he thought, the virtuosity of plain wife-hood, a good commodity in a cook; in bed she was a bore. Yet there was fluency in the way she held herself, unusual in the working class.

Others, he thought, inherited the cloak of nobility; Ellie, like her accent when occasion demanded, merely put it on. From the start, he thought, she had proved herself to be a walking falsehood.

"By the way, I shan't be in tonight;" he called after her.

"Excellent," said Ellie.

Rachel, momentarily free of Megsie, listened in the shadows of the hall.

Rachel served at table on the night Tom came home.

He had come, Ellie recalled pleasurably, at his usual blustering pace, the image of McAndrew in miniature; the same bright head and rumbustious nature.

With one hand on Saul's shoulder, he had vaulted out of the trap, tumbled his suitcases on to the drive and run up the entrance steps to greet her: here he swung Ellie in a circle until she begged to be released. In tears and laughter she kissed him, smoothing his hands, flicking off his coat the golden dross of the road, meanwhile chattering, and cherishing him.

Saul Plentyman, the groom, monumental and massive, arrived with the cases. His bald head gleamed, his nose was flat, his ears were little bobbles of brain battered out of his skull; he moved past them, cat-like, with slow, lethargic grace.

"The usual room, Ma'am?"

Ellie, still in Tom's arms, nodded over her shoulder and they were momentarily alone save for a parlour and scullery maid racing hand in hand for the protective custody of the kitchen.

The pony stamped impatiently on the drive, dying to be gone.

"Did . . . did you have a good journey?" Ellie's pallor had gone; her face was flushed; Tom thought she looked beautiful.

"Marvellous."

"And the train was on time?"

Tom didn't immediately reply. He was looking past his mother to the main entrance.

Rachel was standing there in her new maid's uniform; demure, self-possessed. She dropped a hint of a curtsy, as Ellie turned.

"Cook's made a cup of tea, Ma'am."

"We'll be there directly," Ellie called, and Tom said, his face askance:

"Good God, what's that?"

"Our new housemaid."

"What? Crimes! Things are looking up at Cambourne!" He stood watching as Rachel disappeared into the hall. "What does Ross think of her?"

"So far he hasn't voiced an opinion."

"Where is he, by the way?"

"It's a standard question. I haven't the faintest idea." Ellie wandered through the hall. "But he knows you're due home today, so he'll probably be in tonight."

"You still having trouble?" It was the way he asked it.

Ellie paused, putting out her arms to him. "Nothing for you to bother about, and certainly nothing I can't handle."

"You look better," said Tom, "I'm pleased – you look much better."

Loneliness, thought Ellie, is a major ingredient of absolute love, and much of this was dissipated by Tom's arrival. The very vitality of his presence brought to her a stimulus that encouraged the future.

Over the years there had grown between them a clear and honest understanding beyond that normally enjoyed by mother and son. So it was difficult to realise, she thought, that behind the mask of such manhood, there was really only a boy. Often she wondered if she demanded too much . . .

Tom said suddenly, and out of context:

"You're coming to terms with it – Ross, I mean."

Ellie sighed. "Tom, when I was twenty I thought I knew it all. At thirty I began to doubt it. Now, at forty, I realise how

370

much I have to learn. They call it the art of life. Ross and I are all right – we understand each other. Stay concerned with your own importance, I can take care of mine."

He smiled at her, and in that smile she saw McAndrew; plainly, even at sixteen, he considered life to be a wry comedy. He replied, "God, you lot do take life seriously. It's a mistake, you know."

"Our generation is like that – Victoriana – clutches of martyrs in search of stakes. We make and enjoy our own particular Hells. Meanwhile what the devil am I talking about? Tea?"

She thought determinedly, for God's sake keep your mouth shut, he hasn't even got his foot through the door. One wrong word and all the skeletons will come dancing out of the Cambourne closets.

"Rachel," said Ellie, sitting down, "this is Tom, my son."

The girl lifted her face, smiling faintly. Tom said, "How do you do?"

"I . . . I recognised him from the photograph, Ma'am," said Rachel softly, then resolved again into a sentry's professional silence.

They stood in a small, silent communion; even Ellie appeared uncertain.

Tom was staring as if Rachel, at close quarters, allowed him a luxurious suspension of belief. She looked, he thought, like a cuckoo-clock doll dressed in black and decorated with white lace.

It was a brief but efficient scrutiny, and clearly Rachel enjoyed it.

"You may go now," said Ellie.

"Thank you, Ma'am."

Ellie poured the tea. "Do all young men gape at girls in that manner, or is it confined to Westminster Public School?"

"When we're upended. Gosh, she's gorgeous! We've got nothing like it in our neck of the woods."

"Confine it to distant admiration. She's a housemaid, remember, and a tinker at that."

371

"You remind me of our latest joke," said Tom, waving her down.

Ellie sipped her tea. "I hope it's suitable for my maternal ears."

He grinned at her over the brim of his cup. "The princess said to the prince, 'Do the poor make love the same way as us? If they do, we ought to put a stop to it, it's far too good for them.'"

"Really, Tom. What next!"

"If you're doubtful about the facts of life, don't be afraid to ask."

"You young people! I don't know what the world's coming to – talking like that to your mother."

"Meanwhile I'm suffering from abdominable fortitude – got any toast?"

"Of course, darling. I'm so sorry. You must be starved. I'll ring for some."

"I'll go and make it, if you like."

"On the contrary, you'll stay here!"

"Keats was only twenty-six when he died," said Tom. "I'm following my baser instincts. Have a great time while you can – toast included."

"It's a puerile sentiment," said Ellie. "And somewhere I seem to have heard the theory before . . ."

"Put it down to my impious nature." Getting up, Tom kissed her face and went down to the kitchen.

McAndrew, thought Ellie, smiling faintly, would never be very far away from Cambourne . . . all the time his son was about.

41

Biographers of McAndrew state, with one exception, that Ellie was merely guilty of an error of judgment in engaging Rachel to work at Cambourne. But Professor Ratza Spielman, the Viennese authority, (normally more concerned with allegations of McAndrew's murder of Constanze) cites an Agreement between Ellie and Ross to which, through Seddon and Partners, Ellie's solicitors, he was privy.

This Agreement, entered into during 1903, granted Ross a third share in the company, and, simultaneously, two-thirds to Tom, with Jake as his trustee.

But the clause additionally stated that, should the new partner engage in 'moral turpitude' (presumably Ellie's attempt to protect herself against amorous adventures) Ross's interest could be terminated on her application to a ruling court.

She was badly advised, said Spielman, for the clause was probably *ultra vires* as a result of Ellie's own defection – as a common law wife.

Spielman advances the theory that Ellie, regretting her initial generosity, brought Rachel into Cambourne as a bait for Ross.

Accepting her business acumen, this is not without foundation, but one fact is certain.

Ellie, when she brought Rachel into Cambourne, was unaware that she was McAndrew's daughter.

Nor did Rachel know that Tom was McAndrew's son; this became clear through her subsequent behaviour.

*

It was mid-summer.

In the country of Cambourne all was solitary, and the early harvest was swaying golden in the wind from the Channel.

Here the old Bristol sailing barges with their brown, bat-wing sails were beating across the sky. Larks were singing above the elms of Sully, badgers burrowed in earth. The liquid amber of a fox moved in the sultry stillness, its bright eyes watching anglers on the bank of the river.

Between Penarth and Sully, about two miles from Cambourne, Tom sat easily in the saddle of Ross Bolton's big mare, gently plodding along St. Mary's Well beach.

Here the sand, rippled by the morning tide, secreted rock-pools, the home of cuttle-fish and sea-spiders, shrimps and star-fish, which he used to collect when a child.

Often, with Ellie watching, he would come with spade and bucket – after his father left her, but before Ross came permanently to live with her, and there was for Tom a cleanness about this place that nothing could dispel.

Now, on this visit for the summer term, he had started to come here by night, partly because he found peace by the sea; mostly to get away from Ross, recently arrived.

Tom had no illusions about their relationship; clearly Ross disliked him – and probably, thought Tom, this was because of his innate hatred of McAndrew. He, in his turn, actively disliked Ross Bolton; a dislike fuelled by the disdain with which Ross treated his mother.

Adults, to Tom, were an enigma. If they were out of love why did people stay together? He pondered this as the big mare plodded on. At a time when Cambourne should have been alive with sun and warmth, the rooms within were as cold as a dead heart; nothing seemed more important to these two than the war between them.

Marriage, Tom was beginning to think, was a fight for survival; one in which silence was misconstrued as strength and generosity as weakness.

Lately, therefore, rather than face the tension of the after-dinner silence, Tom had taken the mare and galloped her down to the sands of Mary's Well. Here, in the flat unvarnished sea he would bathe, swimming out into the bay with strong, confident strokes; there to tread water under the stars while the ships of the Channel thudded past unseen.

Now it was afternoon. High above him was a golden topaz. Over the vast, unbroken sea, the clouds of a perfect summer trundled like pot-bellied monks. The sands flashed golden to each new rush of the sun.

Rachel also watched the sea, and saw a distant horse and rider.

As Tom approached, she drew back into sheltering rocks.

Above her a lark was singing. Tom heard it too, and turned up his face, his eyes screwed up to the sun.

Naked to the waist he rode. With his bright hair and body burned brown by the sun, Rachel thought he looked like a primitive young god.

Only once a week, during her half day off, could Rachel come down to Mary's Well beach, and this she had done since working in Cambourne. And, while Pinta and Tam Shenks had insisted that Ross Bolton, the master, was more important than a schoolboy in terms of conquest . . . Rachel had set eyes on Ross only on one occasion.

Since then, apparently (according to Megsie who knew the Upstairs business in detail) the master had been working up in London.

Therefore, Rachel had turned her attentions to Tom: his adolescence called her, his vitality invaded her dreams in her attic bed above the stable yard.

When Saul Plentyman, the groom, was brushing down the mare in the mornings, this was a sign that Tom, that afternoon, would ride. But the Missus had to be watched, of course; Rachel realised this. At meal-times, in the silence of switching eyes and fluttering winks from Tom, Rachel maintained a discreet aloofness.

Ellie guarded her offspring with the ferocity of a meat-fed cheetah.

Only on the shores of Mary's Well, away from the strictures of adults, lay freedom, thought Rachel. And here she would sit in the shelter of rocks and await Tom's coming, as now.

She had known other boys, of course; the giggles of the coppice were a part of tinker living. 'Till my tackles come pledged, so to speak,' thought Rachel in her tinker-tongue, 'then things be different.' But never in my life, said she to herself, if Tam Shenks and that bloody Pinta got their way, would I make love to a pretty young gent – and give him his due, Tom McAndrew were that.

Rachel longed for him with a healthy if unrefined desire.

Later, Rachel noticed, when the nights grew hot, Saul Plentyman groomed the mare in the afternoons, so she took to roaming the shore at night, in hope.

Ross Bolton, a few days earlier, had returned to Cambourne, and Rachel sensed the baser aspirations of an older man. Tom's approach to her was gay; a wink that meant a roll in a haystack. But Ross Bolton's eyes, lifting under his dark brows as she stood waiting at the sideboard, were the advances of a licentious adult: a splendid affront to Missus, provided you didn't get caught.

So whatever Pinta and Tam Shenks was up to, it were working. Give the master time, they said; let 'im take it slow.

Christ, he's nearly forty, thought Rachel – it's time he was blutty dead.

Meanwhile, first things first, as Gran used to say.

Tom McAndrew was of her age, her youth, her time. And it was two whole months, said Megsie, before he was due to leave Cambourne.

Saul Plentyman had groomed the mare that afternoon . . . The day had been hot. Night came, brilliant with stars. A crescent moon was sitting on his bottom on top of the stable when Rachel, pulling on her black stockings, buttoned her shoes and went down to bathe.

From her attic window she watched Tom go clattering out of the stable yard.

Sitting on her bed in the dark, she listened to the big mare galloping down Bendricks.

*

376

Rachel did not go into the sea immediately.

The dead-eyed cottages above the shore sat like bull-frogs awaiting a spring, the sea shone its blue, oiled glass, the sky was streaked with mare's tails in the fatal glow of the moon: phosphorescence was flashing along the brows of the little waves in jagged traceries of light.

Far away to the east, sheet lightning momentarily lit the Channel and peering, Rachel saw Tom coming; a distant speck in the west. Now she could hear the beating hooves on sand; louder, louder.

Swiftly, waving her arms out of her shift, Rachel knelt in the shadows, peeling off her shoes and black stockings. Then raced, nymph-like for the tide-swim; splashing her way through the shallows and diving full length.

She swam tinker-style, the dog-paddle she had learned in childhood.

Tom, reining in, stared seaward at the tumbling phosphorescence.

The mare slowed to a trot, then halted – unknown to him, near the rock that sheltered Rachel's clothes. And he remembered, as he saw the person swimming, of other times when he had bathed like this; days that were golden and bright with flowers, when Cambourne had the gift of laughter.

Somewhere in the tree-fringe of the shore a night-bird was singing. Suddenly aware that he was spying, Tom gently spurred the mare.

"Wait!"

He heard the cry from the sea, thinking, at first, that it was a gull. And so he did not go, but tethered the horse to a pinnacle of rock and ran closer to the tide-swim, lest the one who called might be in trouble.

And so Tom waited, and Rachel, seeing him there, waded slowly out of the sea.

Above her, a white gull hung in the wind, crying hoarsely. Tom heard the gull crying, yet did not, because Rachel was making shape before him. The mare snorted, stamped the

377

sand impatiently. There was nothing in his world then save the moonlit wave-lap . . . and the woman coming closer.

Rachel stood before Tom and the wavelets played around her ankles, and there was between them only her nakedness.

The night-bird had ceased to sing, the gull his crying.

The lightning flashed again. Thunder muttered and barked, clattering on the rim of the sea like distant ravening dogs.

"I come, Tom McAndrew."

Tom knew a sensation beyond time and place; a strange savagery called him.

"Are . . . are you all right?" He spoke but did not hear his voice: there was thudding in his ears an unknown wish: never before had he seen a woman naked.

Rachel came nearer.

The cold wetness of her body touched the wind and he felt this coldness, and the dull, numb core of his being reached out for her, yet he did not move.

"Aren't ye comin' in?" asked Rachel.

She smiled and he saw her teeth shining in her sun-black face and the whiteness of her body, which was sea-cold when he touched her, and in his throat there was a strange convulsive restriction and in his mouth a dryness, because he had touched her, and made her real.

Rachel said, pulling at his hand:

"Come on, son. Why stare? Ain't ye seen bare nakedness before? Aw, come on! Take off ye clothes and come on in."

Tom grinned and wiped his mouth with the back of his hand.

"Damn me!" he said.

"Off wi' them!" Rachel dragged at his hand now, pulling him into the shallows. "I'll give ye sixpence if ye beat me dog-paddling to Bristol!"

"Hell!" said Tom, and ran back up the beach, tearing at his clothes and flinging them down on to the sand. And Rachel saw this and shouted laughter, and her laughter rang around the rocks and down the chimneys of the moon-washed cottages, and the old people heard and tuned their ears, thinking it was a gull.

"Glory bloody hallelujah!" shouted Tom, and frantically waved his arms out of his shirt.

"Wait there! I'm coming!"

Now he was hopping around on the sand, tearing at his riding-boots, and Rachel shrieked with a new joy as she watched his growing nakedness. Socks and pants went sailing up, riding breeches and vest followed and he turned, as bare as birth.

"God, they'll strip the pair of us for this," he cried, and raced down the sand towards her, and Rachel came up to meet him and snatched his hand, and together, like primaeval sprites, they plunged into the shallows.

Ankle deep, calf deep, thigh deep – now wading, turning their bodies to the swill of the tide. And the moon shone and the phosphorescence played on their nakedness, and there was nothing for them but sea and sky as they dived together, and not a single watcher, save one . . .

The mare, uneasy, turned up her muzzle to the wind. Her eyes rolled white as she snorted her fear. But none save Mrs. Tinker Bob heard her as she came down from the Bendricks, through the sentinel rocks and over the sand.

Mrs. Tinker Bob, McAndrew's friend, stood beside the mare, and at her feet was a white bone half buried in sand, and this bone was part of a mare's skull bleached by sea and wind.

When Mrs. Tinker Bob's foot touched the skull again the mare whinnied, knowing in her primitive brain that all that had happened before would happen again, and fear of death moved in her like a chill disease, but the woman did not know of this.

She knew only that Rachel, the daughter of McAndrew, and Tom, the son of McAndrew, were together and naked: that this was an idiocy, for them, and for their children.

Therefore, the fear of the mare and the fear of the woman was for different reasons.

When the mare whinnied again, Mrs. Tinker Bob put out her hand in comfort.

And, shivering with apprehension, she watched Tom and Rachel playing in the sea.

42

Smoke curled upwards from the fire Tom was building.

He built it Scout style, firing it with bleached driftwood gathered from the beach; the little kettle Rachel had brought sang and steamed: there was nothing about them but sea and sky, the drifting smoke and their glances, one to the other.

They knelt on either side of the fire, watching the kettle, and Rachel laid out a tea-cloth, and on this she put raisin cakes she had stolen from under Megsie's nose, also scones she had taken hot from her oven.

The sun burned down with amber heat, a majestic fire that threatened to consume them. Away to the east huge cumulus clouds were gathering; above the estuary the sky was sulphur-coloured.

Earlier, they had laid together hand in hand, eyes clenched to the blood-red sun, and in their silence Tom had known a fine rhythm, the senses of manhood, and could have shouted aloud with exultation at the discovery.

Soon, he knew, he would make love to Rachel, a knowledge born in desire and dreamy expectation. It was not enough to bathe and run on the sands; soon they would make love.

Soon, thought Rachel, Tom will make love to me, and I will not resist him, but she remembered the words of Mrs. Tinker Bob, the woman of the caravans:

'The mole don't burrow in the nest of the thrush, nor the fish swim in the earth o' the badger . . .'

True, the old girl had warned her that to court with a gentry chap were dangerous, but she did not understand the moral: old hag-women like Mrs. Tinker Bob talked too much, anyway, Rachel thought now. And who was she to threaten to tell Tam Shenks? Spyin' on them! Spyin' . . . when it was a drink-sin of delight to lie like this, hand in hand with Tom McAndrew . . .

Did she love him? Of course not! thought Rachel. How could a grown traveller woman love a boy? Yet it was a titillating lift to the senses to have him close, and old Tam Shenks could take a jump.

"What are you thinking of?" asked Tom.

"Don't matter any," said Rachel.

"You thinking of me?"

"Ain't thinkin' of anyone, really speaking. Just that I reckon I could lie all me years like this, instead of sloggin' it out in bleedin' old kitchens."

"I'll arrange it with God for you."

"Reckon I could just go poppin' round the whole wide world with you, Tom McAndrew, and never think of marryin' a bloody old tinker, with babby after babby in the old red vans."

Tom rose up on an elbow, smiling into her face. "You marry me, Missus, and I'll take you round the Universe."

"I ain't never been round that, so far," said Rachel. "The kettle's boilin' – you see her?"

Rising, Tom went to the other side of the fire and knelt there, and Rachel knelt, too, so that they looked one to the other, and she knew a fierceness in her, a calling to his body, and this grew into an ache and she raised her hands and put them upon her breasts because of the aching. And yet he seemed unaware of her predicament. In the longings of her attic bedroom, when she had put on black stockings and laid there sleepless, so the aching returned.

"Tonight we swim?" she asked.

The wind moved in the rocks where they were concealed, tousling her red hair, blowing it across her face.

"After tea, if you like."

"Too many people knocking around, Tom McAndrew. Get me hung, you will; if Tam Shenks hears of me naked bathin' again, he'll tan me black an' blue."

"Let him try."

"And your mam'll send me down the road."

"I doubt it."

"Aye well, there's somethin' in that, really speakin' – you got a good old mam, you 'ave. Megsie do tell me of her – she were a real old rooster when young, apparently, but now she's soft like Wilberry cheese, says Megsie. I likes working for 'er, mind."

"Where's your mother, Rachel." He asked it only to hear her voice, which was like dark velvet, and as beautiful.

The girl shrugged. "Don't really knows the goin' of her, for she died, and nobody spoke of her much, save my poor old Uncle Brookie, an' he's passed on now." Rachel smiled into the sun. "Seems as though some big wanderin' chap arrives and pegs her out under old Tam Shenk's nose, so to speak – he anna me dad, ye know – just talks of it.

"Aye, this soldier chap comes up, see, and pegs out my mam, Rosa, and she died . . . bringing forth me. And no one's seen hide nor hair of 'im since, though old Mrs. Tinker Bob knows more'n is good for her, I reckon, the way she chatters . . ." Rachel smiled. "Tinkers are prattlin' magpies, ye know – always savourin' other folks business, like you lovin' me, for instance."

"I love you," said Tom.

She pushed him gently away when he reached for her, saying, "Hey up! Folks might be peekin', mister. . .! *Ease off!*"

"Tinkers worry too much, if you ask me." Tom jerked his head at the sea. "Come on in and I'll teach you more than dog-paddling!"

"Ah so, me lovely! But I reckon we'd best swim in the dark places, lest black devils like old Pinta and Tam Shenks do haunt us, eh? You ever seen your dad, Tom McAndrew?"

He said, taking off her accent, "A couple of times . . . seems as though he was some big wanderin' soldier chap who arrived and pegged out my old mam – under Ross Bolton's nose, so to speak . . ."

She giggled at this, her head back, and Tom caught her

long hair in his fingers and held it to his face, then hooked his arm hard around her waist and drew her against him.

He saw her eyes large and startled in the moment before he bent to her mouth: they fought in a passion of gasps and kisses.

"*Wheeah!* Save us! Bread and cheese now, is it? Loose me!"

For answer his hands moved to her breast.

"Hop off! Ach, I'd never have believed it. Sixteen is it? You're grown up. Loose me lest I come to a mama!" She wriggled away in the sand. "Cool yersel' a morsel, mun. Later we'll be loverin', when the moon come up, and then I'll come warm and sweet for ye, with nobody watchin . . ."

Tom said, his eyes moving over her face. "You are strange, strange and beautiful . . ."

"All the chaps say that. I'm the best o' the tinker mutton chops, they do say in the village, and as sweet as a nut . . ." and then, as if to herself, she murmured, ". . . but the mole don't swim to the thrush, nor the fish fly to the badger, that they say, too, mind."

"What was that?" Tom gripped her hand, his eyes shining, and she was instantly gay.

"Ach, siddle ye down by here!" and she patted the sand. "Don't bother none, Tom lad."

"But what did you say? Come on, now!"

Rachel shrugged. "Oh, jist some bloody old traveller sayin' from old Mrs. Tinker Bob; she's alus prattlin', like I told ye."

He tried to kiss her again, but she held him away, "No, no! Later, when the moon's got her skirts up. Then I'll do ye so fine that ye'll never forget this tinker, wi' nakedness or black stocking lovering, just as ye please. How do that suit ye?"

Tom said, "You've done this before, haven't you. . . ?"

"Aye, plenty. Blessed are the fornicators, for the others don't know what they're missin', I heard say. But sparkin' with you, I'll ne'er forget, Tom McAndrew."

She put her head on one side, smiling prettily, and pushed her auburn hair back from her face.

"Tea?"

*

383

They drank the tea and ate the scones and raisin cakes, looking at each other across the little fire, and each knew that what they had planned would come to pass, in due time, when the moon was lying on his ear.

"Tonight?" said Rachel. "You promise?" she asked.

"Can't be tonight," said Tom. "Ross Bolton's coming home. I'll have to stay in."

She was petulant. "Where's he been all this time, for God's sake? Tho' he's a fine lookin' chap, for all that!"

"Up north, so my mother says. We're selling the shipping fleet."

"Is that a fact. And then?"

Her interest didn't appear unusual to him: tinkers were unusually curious.

Tom shrugged. "Don't know much about it. Coal's dying, says Ross, and we're buying up trawlers – for sea-fishing up Whitby way, so my mother told me."

"That cause you'll be leavin' Barry?"

"More than likely."

Rachel pressed his hand against her lips. "You leave me now, Tom McAndrew, I'm goin' to be a lonesome old gal. If they take you northern, will ye take Rachel, if only for wickedness?"

Later, Tom looked at his watch. "We'd better go."

"Me too, lest that blutty old Megsie do have me. She's got an eye for Saul Plentyman, did ye know?"

Tom gave her a grin.

"She reckons I'm after him, I think. Give 'im one glance and she gets it up her apron, but he's a lot too plenty for me, the bald-headed old coot."

"You're my girl, remember that. Remember that always." Tom drew her to her feet and kissed her mouth. "I love you, Rachel."

"We gotta go, Tom McAndrew, or there's trouble comin' round these parts – we gotta go."

Rachel went racing through the sand dunes; Tom galloped the mare along the beach, back to Cambourne.

And Pinta, from the shelter of his rock, watched them both.

Jake did not come for dinner that night, though Ellie had asked him to come for sure, because Ross had returned to Cambourne.

In the drawing-room, while Rachel served the coffee, Ross settled himself in an armchair. Ellie, on the other side of the fireplace, was doing her eternal embroidery.

"Coffee, sir?" asked Rachel.

Tom took a seat on a skew by the window, looking out on to the falling dusk. From here he could see the Big Wheatfield and the glow of the tinkers' bonfire: unless he was mistaken, he thought, the five caravans were now on the edge of the wood. As if reading his thoughts, his mother said, stitching:

"The travellers are in the field again. Yet, if I've told them once, I've done so a dozen times."

Ross, brandy glass in one hand and a cigar in the other, frowned at the fire.

"Your people, Rachel. What do you say for yourself?" He smiled up at her as she passed with the coffee-tray.

"Don't rightly know, Master. Old Pinta do reckon he's got permission, mind."

"Not from me," said Ellie. She lowered her embroidery.

Ross interjected, "I told them they could come down closer to the wood, for shelter."

"You might have mentioned it."

"Darling, I simply didn't give it a thought." Ross sipped his brandy, staring into the fire.

"Anyway, it's midsummer." Ellie lifted her face. "Rachel, tell Pinta, or whatever he's called, that I want to see him tomorrow."

"Yes, Ma'am."

"And Rachel . . ."

The girl paused again.

"Prepare my room. I'm having an early night."

Ross said, "We've got a lot to talk about, you know. Don't you want to hear what happened in London?"

Tom rose to leave.

"No, stay," said Ross. "This also affects you. Isn't Jake coming?"

"God, don't ask me!" Ellie sighed.

"In the Chain Locker when I last heard." Smiling, Ross examined his cigar, his teeth appearing in his dark-handsome face.

He was, thought Tom, a particularly soiled specimen of life and often wondered how his mother tolerated him.

Strangely – and Tom had noticed this before – Ross appeared to view Jake's drinking with malicious satisfaction. Banality lay in the man's unspoken words. Having the power to hurt Ellie, he used it ruthlessly, while she, for her part, treated him with an air of careless amiability.

In his mother's face Tom discerned a sort of penance for past sins; and clearly, through the years, she had lost her talent for sincerity. As for Ross, he appeared to Tom to switch it on and off like an electric light.

Between them was a frightening artificial gaiety.

Often Tom wondered about his father; vaguely, he recalled a place by the river and a fish cooked in moonlight. The only concrete event he connected with McAndrew was the night he had crashed through the french doors, a blood-stained scarecrow of a man, and clearly Ross feared his return: personally checking all the doors and windows every night, and ensuring that Saul Plentyman, the giant groom, was on the prowl.

Ross also kept a revolver in his room; Tom had seen it.

His mother, to Tom, was a constant source of worry. As the years passed, even her cares seemed to decay. But, while her eyes held a sad docility, she nevertheless exhibited a fine, peremptory air when confronting Ross over some new escapade, amorous or financial. He was, as Rachel put it, a boy for the gals.

Ellie was dressed that night in a brown taffeta dress with a bustle, and lace at her wrists.

She appeared, thought Tom, like some patient queen

386

landed with an undesirable libertine as consort: she admonished; protected and maintained her dignity. And though her love-life had proved a litany of disaster, Ellie had yet, in his opinion, managed to maintain both her good looks and demeanour. It was illness, not Bolton, that was spelling her demise. But that same illness was granting her, as tonight, a nun-like flawlessness of complexion: her comportment, like her make-up, was perfect.

Bolton said, getting up and standing before the fire, "You'll recall that we had an original offer of four hundred thousand for the fleet unladen? Well, I went north and Barrow Yards Limited – now the Barrow Consortium – raised this to twenty-eight thousand pounds more. I think we should accept."

"How does that compare with the bids from the Reardon-Smiths and the Corys?" Ellie did not look up.

"The Corys pulled out at three hundred and fifty thousand and Reardons haven't confirmed their tender." Ross sipped his brandy. "The local people are on the same tack as us – if war comes Barry will hit the slide."

"Aren't the expectations premature?"

"Perhaps. This was my argument. The possibility of war with Germany is sheer conjecture. Oil is the bugbear; conversions are already on the go and the freighters know it. Ten years from now every coaler will be in the breakers' yards."

"As Barry will be ten years from now, according to Uncle Jason."

"But Uncle Jason isn't around these days. Face facts," said Bolton. "The problem is ours. But I wonder what would Teddy Grey-Cambourne have done?" He paced the room, pulling at his cigar.

For reply, Ellie held her embroidery up to the light. Bolton said:

"You don't appear concerned about all this, or are you?"

Outside in the woods a bird clamoured peevishly. Ellie said, with the embroidery in her lap:

"I saw a golden aureol today. It allowed me to come quite

close. It had an eye like a black rain-drop. I was entranced."

"Marvellous!" whispered Tom.

Ross said, "Ellie, Ellie . . . for God's sake show some interest. Do we sell, woman, or not?"

Ellie raised her face. "Ross, I'm just too tired to care. Four hundred thousand – twenty-eight thousand more, what does it matter? Sell to Barrow and let's have an end to it." She stared at the clock above the fireplace. "I wonder where Father's got to?"

"Don't give him a thought. He won't have an opinion even if we explain it – he never does." He tossed back his brandy at a gulp. "Surely you want to know what bid I made for Whitby Trawlers?"

"How much?" asked Tom, and Bolton slowly turned an astonished face:

"Good God! The babies are out of their long clothes! Would you understand if I told you?"

"Quite probably."

"Two hundred and ten thousand for the trawler fleet, but it's our business, not yours."

"On the contrary," interjected Ellie, "it's very much Tom's business."

Tom said, smiling, "This appears to leave a pretty handsome surplus. What's happening to the couple of hundred thousand?" and Ross replied warily, turning to Ellie:

"Do I really have to explain – to a schoolboy?"

"Why not?" Ellie peered at her sewing. "I want to know as well. Besides, in a year or so from now Tom'll be in the firm, or have you forgotten?"

"Presumably we're investing?" asked Tom.

Bolton sighed. "Yes, but I hadn't considered where." Getting up again he poured himself more brandy.

Tom said, "We'll only get two or three per cent at the bank and the Barry Company's paying ten . . ."

"God Almighty! Aren't these the very people we're trying to get away from? Invest with them? We might as well stay in shipping."

"I didn't suggest it. But there's brokers in Leadenhall

offering twelve on Krugerrands. Anyway, isn't insurance the big thing now?"

"And where did you learn all this?"

Bolton was white-faced. Standing with his back to the fire he was exuding a frightening hatred. "At this rate you'll cut a swathe through the aristocrats of inherited wealth, young man. Is your economics teacher one of the new cult – a modern South Sea Bubbler? For, if war comes – and Germany's already sabre-rattling – economies will collapse overnight. Investment abroad is dangerous."

Ellie said, getting up and putting away her sewing, "I've had enough. There's more clatt 'na dinner, as they say in my town. In any case, I want Father in on this." She gathered up her sampler saying, 'God is love'.

Tom said, as she closed the door, ". . . I think I'll go up, too."

"Oh no, you don't – I want a word with you," said Ross.

"Saul tells me you're using the mare a lot."

The older man's face was now flushed with the brandy.

"Yes. You gave me permission."

"I gave ye permission to ride the mare, not the bloody locals – and a servant in the house, at that."

Tom closed his eyes, then said evenly, "There's a new age of enlightenment around."

"Don't you bandy words with me, you young upstart! You're mother's ill, or perhaps you haven't noticed. God help us – do ye have to pick a bloody tinker?" He stared at Tom with a mixture of contempt and anger; the boy smiled back calmly, saying:

"But the tinkers are the aristocrats these days, or don't you know? It's a new concept, Ross; we're the mongrels."

"Intellectual clap-trap! Tell that to your mother!"

"Strangely enough, I think she'd understand . . ."

"Then try her! She'd have Rachel out on her ear in seconds." Ross glared with anger, swilling the brandy around his glass with nervous agitation. "You were turned out by the same factory as your father, this is your trouble –

the sweepings of a Scottish gutter, but you're starting the rut earlier than I expected. Keep away from Rachel, ye hear me? Keep away, or you'll have me to contend with."

"Meanwhile, keep my father out of this!" Tom drew closer, "and my mother, too." He was white-faced now and trembling.

"Christ, I'd be glad to!" Bolton gulped at his glass. "Where do ye think Cambourne would have been today if it hadn't been for me? I've built it up to what it is, despite the perambulations of your mother and that drunken sot of a grandfather." Ross levelled a shaking finger. "Listen to me – tread wary, McAndrew, or I'll have ye, as God's me judge. I've had my bellyful of Cambourne and I'm not putting up either with your disobedience or your high-handed bloody insolence, so take your pick. You will not see that girl again, d'you hear me?"

Tom said. "They can hear you over in Barry."

Ellie, undressing in her room above, heard the raised voices and sat on the edge of her bed, her hands over her face.

Rachel heard them, too, and moved down the shadows of the hall before Tom came out of the drawing-room, slamming the door behind him.

43

Jean Pierre sat on his high stool at the Chain Locker bar and watched the big navvy at the other end of the room. The dwarf reflected, as he sipped his absinthe, that this was the biggest navvy he had yet seen in Wales; handled properly, he could provide excellent sport.

The man stood apart from his companions, mainly dockers, who were flooding in after the evening shift; boisterous and drunk, most of them. It was the ending of the six weeks pay, and their pockets were filled with sovereigns.

The fair-haired, blousy barmaid, frantically pouring the foaming quarts, followed the little man's eyes with growing apprehension; touching the landlord as he passed, she jerked her head.

"Yes, I know," said he.

Jean Pierre raised his absinthe. The saliva trickled from his swollen lips. The landlord said, his fat face gleaming sweat:

"You ashore for long, Jean Pierre?"

The Frenchman nodded. "Long enough . . ."

"We want no trouble, understand?" The reply was trembling with nervous courage.

"From me?" The dwarf thumbed his chest. "Trouble from me, Monsieur? Stupid! Me, Jean Pierre? Do I ever cause trouble?"

The big navvy drank, his heavily-browed, reddened eyes sweeping the room.

A cock-fight was going on in a corner, a flurrying of feathers, shining spurs and shrieks. The big man knuckled his face, drained his quart and pushed his pewter-pot across the counter.

"Same again."

His gaze steadied on to Jean Pierre, whose bald eyes were shining with a strange, metallic light. Filling the navvy's pot, the landlord said, his face averted:

"Now, leave him alone, Frenchie. Any trouble, and I'll call the police."

Jean Pierre was remembering a child who begged at an attic window, and below, on the street, people passed without an upward glance, not wishing to be involved. The child smashed the glass with his fists and screamed, until he was dragged away into darkness: then there was nothing but big hands tearing at his clothes, and pain. Jean Pierre said now:

"It is possible that the police may come too late, Monsieur. He is what you call – a very good specimen?"

The cock-fight grew to an obliterating shrillness; blood spattered the saw-dust in a clashing of spurs. Money chinked. The dockers roared, and the dwarf, his eyes on the big man in the corner, sipped his absinthe.

Jake Kendall, Ellie's father, came in. His face was written with gloom.

Unlike the others, he showed the dwarf scant respect, but barged up to the bar, elbowing his way for room. Jean Pierre's glass spilled as he raised it. The absinthe splashed his white silk shirt and stained his velvet coat. Always when the *Marie Prey* docked, the Frenchman dressed with fastidious elegance.

Anxiety in the landlord's face changed to pleasurable greeting and relief as Jake arrived.

"'Evening, Jake."

"Be careful, little man," said Jean Pierre, and brushed away the stains with a white, silk handkerchief. He closed his heavily-lidded eyes as Jake gripped his shoulder.

"Thou seest before thee," said Jake, "A man on his bloody uppers. Father to Ellie Kendall, friend of Lord Grey-

Cambourne, brother to the respected Uncle Jason – and not a guinea to his name. They have consigned me to the princes of hell!"

"You'll get no credit in here," added the landlord, polishing glasses. "Beside, debtors ain't religious, are they!"

Jake wiped his mouth with the twitching anticipation of the alcoholically infirm. "I forgive you, sir, your pious little mind."

"Anyway, you're already drunk," said the landlord.

Jean Pierre did not hear this.

He was still watching the man.

"Ye fat bastard, I'm as sober as a collier's canary," said Jake.

"You're drunk, I say, and you'll get no credit, Jake Kendall – away with ye. Argue, and you anna welcome."

"Am I heck as like," said Jake. "Pity me, for God's sake, Amen. The Psalms, my friend. Psalm one hundred and two, verse nine. '. . . I have eaten ashes like bread and mingled my drink with weeping . . . my days are like a shadow that declineth and I am withered like grass . . .'"

"Bugger off," said the landlord. "Sadie girl – nothin' for Mr. Kendall until he settles up, understand?" Turning, he thumped the bar before Jake's tearful face. "Ye got the five-barred gate credit like the others, mun – ye had a pound for every rung – then ye got the diagonal, which means you're out – six sovereigns in all. Ye don't play fair, sod off."

Jake said, his hands as if in prayer, "'. . . If thine enemy hunger, feed him; if he thirst, give him drink . . .' A pint, Welshman, in the name of Jesus?"

"I said sod off; there's no more credit here. If ye walk round the garden long enough you're bound to find a crab-apple, aren't ye!"

Jake shouted, his face aflame, "By the living God! If me son-in-law, James McAndrew were here, you'd change ye tune, ye insulting swine!"

The gaze of Jean Pierre moved from the big navvy to Jake with slow, sullen interest. His globulous eyes stared out of his hairy face.

"McAndrew? The Big Savage? What of him?"

"Ach aye! And if he were here he'd savage the lot of ye!" cried Jake. "A pint? You'd think I was asking for the crown o' St. Peter!"

The dwarf suddenly grinned wide, took a shilling from his yellow waistcoat pocket, spun it up and the landlord caught it.

"Give him what he wants," said he. "Big Savage was my friend."

"Ach, wee man, you're a gent! Frog legs or not, you're a bloody toff!" cried Jake.

He took the quart pewter the landlord gave him, blew off the top, and sank his mouth deep. The ale-froth stained his whiskers, and he gasped, "God speed and quiet seas to ye, sailor. Another, Frenchie?"

"Buy him another and you won the Battle of Waterloo," said a tiny docker, pushing to the bar. He was a small, sinewy Northumberland man; later he joined the Old Contemptibles, and was killed on the Marne; Jean Pierre didn't give him a glance.

"My son-in-law a friend of yours?" asked Jake. "After the outing ye handed him?"

"That is why he is my friend, Monsieur."

"Mind you," explained Jake with a new independence, "don't get the idea that I'm in penury." His voice rose above the screeching of the cock-fight and the bantering roars of men. "This is life, marrer – one day up, next day down, like a pretty woman's drawers. This time tomorrow I'll be in the money . . ." he glared at the landlord. "And I'll be taking me custom elsewhere, too, let me bloody tell you."

"Another?" he asked, expectantly, of the dwarf.

"If you wish it, Monsieur."

"Vive la belle France!" said Jake, and opened his throat and poured down the third with scarcely a swallow. With a tiny fist he beat his pigeon chest. "I'm one o' life's tragedies, ye know. They use me bad, and I anna appreciated."

"Is that so?" asked Jean Pierre, abstractedly.

Over the rim of his glass he watched the big man in the corner again.

394

It would be pleasurable, he was thinking, to hear such a giant beg, before being kicked through a window. The *Marie Prey* was due out on the night tide. What was a good shore leave without a good fight?

Jake said at the white froth of his ale, "We're selling the fleet, ye know . . ."

His voice was drowned in the cock-crows of a victor. The men were suddenly silent, like cows nosing a stall. Three times the bloodstained cockerel crowed. Money was changing hands in greed and muted tempers. The landlord asked:

"What was that, Jake Kendall? I didn't get it."

"We're selling Ross-Cambournes."

"The freighters? In God's name, why?"

A coterie of men gathered around them, peevishly intent, their eyes darting in their work-grimed faces.

"Christ, that'll kill us – they're selling Cambournes?" said one.

"What for?"

Jake swelled with bull-frog importance. "Because this damn-hole place is on the slide, that's why. We're going into fishing. Up Whitby way – buying up trawlers."

"Jesus, that'll sink the piece-rates!"

Their voices rose in harsh protest. A man said, "It's the beginning of the end, lads. Oil's comin', see? And these rotten financiers know what they're about."

The landlord said to Jake, his hand up for silence. "And where do you come into this?"

Jean Pierre was no longer listening; he sat as a man removed.

Surrounded by the dockers, his eyes, bird-like, were now fixed on the navvy in the corner. With one big hand gripping his pewter, and the other knuckling his mouth, the man stood silently, his eyes closed.

Jake said pompously, "As trustee in the firm, my presence is desired up in London, ain't it!" He staggered, holding on to the bar. "In other words, gents, brass to brass – do I make 'em jump." He levelled a finger in the landlord's face. "So very soon, marrer, I'll 'ave money to burn, and ye can keep this excuse for a pub. What's more, you can bed your barmaid."

A man said, and his voice was cultured, "You're trustee for the son, aren't you? I heard talk of that. You're signing on the lad's behalf?"

"Ye hit it on the head," said Jake.

"Then be careful what you're signing."

"Especially with that bloody twister Ross Bolton in the saddle," said another.

They jabbered and drank: outraged, appalled.

"So Cambournes're getting out! God Almighty!"

"It's the start of the rot!"

"Bloody gentry pansies – they pick us up and toss us over!"

"The beginning of the end of Barry."

"That's life, anna it?"

"It'll be the Corys next."

"Then the Reardon-Smiths!"

"Oil's come in, coal's on the slide, see? You can't expect . . ."

"What about the Rhondda? It'll hit them a lot harder'n us . . ."

"Poor sods!"

"Bugger the Rhondda. I've got five kids."

"Then ye shouldn't 'ave been such a randy old dad."

"When's all this happening, for Christ's sake?"

"Tomorrow – I just told ye, didn't I?" Jake drained his pot and pushed it away. "Another, landlord, and make it a whisky. By this time next week I'll buy your bloody pub. Drinks all round – what about that? Drinks on Cambourne Freighters – in advance!"

"Excuse me, please, Monsieur . . ." said Jean Pierre, and slipped down off his stool.

The big navvy was still in the corner, hunched like a man in a dream.

As the dwarf wandered towards him, a drunken sailor

396

came through the door of the Chain Locker, confronting him. Jean Pierre paused, hands on hips, staring up.

The sailor swayed dangerously, his cap on one side.

"Where's the piss-hole, Matlow?"

Jean Pierre caught his arm, steadying him, saying, "The directions are simple. Listen, my friend. Go through that door . . ." and he pointed, "proceed across the yard until you come to a door marked 'Gentlemen'. Ignore it. Go straight through the door marked 'Exit'."

"Thanks, mate," said the sailor.

Jean Pierre reached the navvy. The carnality of his aggression touched his face.

The man was a giant, ponderous, heavy-footed. He turned to the Frenchman, blinking with red eyes from the stained rivulets of a bearded face. And the barmaid, light-footed, ducked under the counter and ran across the floor with disconcerting speed.

Interposing herself between them, she said:

"You're on the wrong horse this time. Leave him alone, Jean Pierre, he's just lost his missus."

The dwarf faltered, licking his thick lips. Then a smile broke upon his face. Raising his straw hat, he bowed low, saying:

"Monsieur, I apologise to you for interrupting, but I was wondering if you would do me the honour of drinking with me?"

The big man lifted a swollen face.

"I . . . I'll get 'em," said the barmaid.

Ross Bolton arrived at closing time.

In evening dress, top hat and cloak, he strode up to the door of the Chain Locker and flung it open.

"Jake!"

Jake was still there, but within him was the kinship of the drunk. Turning from the bar he examined Bolton with sad, bleary eyes.

All faces turned as Bolton slowly entered.

Strangled into silence by a fever of curiosity, the room

397

seemed to die. Their mugs lowering, the customers stared from one to the other, hostile yet respectful, and Bolton said in a loud, declamatory voice:

"I thought I'd find you here, Jake. *Out!*" He pushed the door wider.

Jake lowered his face. Jean Pierre said gently:

"If you do not wish to go, Monsieur, it can be arranged for you to stay, perhaps?"

The old man saw Bolton as if at the bottom of a locked dream. Bolton he saw; he saw also the Frenchman, and there hammered within his brain a warning confusion of over-turned tables, smashing glass, fists, boots and blasphemy.

Treason, also, beat like a pulse in his drink-laden head, like a hammer . . .

"I'm waiting," said Bolton.

The bar stood in silence; not a man moved. Jake shambled over the saw-dust and out into the night.

Slamming shut the door, Bolton gripped him by the collar, whispering into his face:

"Where did you get the money? You drunken sot! Do that again and you won't get a penny, understand? You'll sign, by God, but you won't get a single penny! What did you say in there?"

Jake closed his eyes. "Nothing . . ."

"I hope not. One word . . . one word, you understand, and by God, I'll put an end to you!" He pushed Jake away. "Now get your head under a pump. I want you on the eight-ten to London in the morning. And until you sign, you don't get another penny."

Not two miles away, Tom was already in the sea, waiting for Rachel.

The night was mercurial, its blackness brilliant with stars, and the moon hung over the sea. Black-breasted gulls, silent for once, hovered over the shore of St. Mary's Well like ghosts of migratory owls: the night was barefooted, breathless with warmth.

Tom moved lazily, the overarm litheness of the trained

swimmer; now floating on his back, looking at the sky. And felt against his naked body, the pulsating thumping of distant propellers – steamers ploughing through the Channel.

Westward he could see the glow of Barry docks, and heard on the wind the activity of the loading, for the port was running full spate.

Shaking foam from his hair he momentarily trod water, looking shorewards to the thin, yellow strip of St. Mary's sand, but Rachel did not come.

He was wading out of the sea half an hour later when Rachel arrived.

She came breathless, her arms wide in greeting, and flung herself against his wet body, and they stood clasped together in the warm sea-wind; a man and woman joined as one, and Tom pressed kisses upon her mouth.

"Dear God!" gasped Rachel. "It were that damn old Megsie. I reckon she don't know if it's slated or thatched . . . And old Saul Plentyman's hanging around, an' all. You know, Tom, I do reckon he were spyin'."

"On you?" Tom wiped the water from his face.

"On us, boy! There anna a damn old thing I do these days, but old Saul Plentyman's sniffin' it. 'Where ye off to now then, little Missus?' he says to me. 'Got some fella chained up down Barry, 'ave we?' 'I should be that lucky,' I says to 'im. 'When I get out me tackles, Saul Plentyman, they don't need chainin' – they needs locking up!'"

She laughed gaily, her head back, and the mare, tethered nearby, heard this and whinnied, because of the mare's skull near her feet.

Tom said, "I love you, Rachel, I love you!"

"Ay ay, but bide a bit, fella! Button up ye bits and pieces, for we got all the time in the world." She seized his hands, smiling into his face.

Her hair she pulled down to her waist, and drew him closer into the shadows of the rocks: he saw her hands moving swiftly, like white flowers in darkness; her growing nakedness as she flung off her clothes.

399

"Reckon you're the luckiest old fella in Barry, then some! I don't do this strippin' for every lad, ye know," and Tom heard her, knowing that all they had planned would come to pass, and none was left in the world save them.

"Shall I leave me stockings on, to drive ye barmy?"

There was no shame in her. And, when Tom opened his arms she leaped to him, and he knew the warmth and the softness of her, the thudding of his blood, a strange and primaeval cry, a growth of flowering strength.

Rachel knew of this, too, so that they whispered and gasped unintelligibly within the kisses, her body responding to the sudden gale of his strength: enwrapped now, they sank down slowly in sand, at the feet of the mare, and the mare knew of them, but was inattentive, because of a sister skull half buried beside them.

"*Now*, Rachel?"

"God save us, mun – I 'aven't had me swim."

"Please, now?" His hands sought her, he was kissing her face, her hair.

"Get me damn hung, you will. You come rough I'll go up the family way."

"It doesn't matter. Rachel, *Rachel*. . . !"

"*Crumbs!*" said she, and fought herself free. "You'm a real hot fella for sixteen, Tom McAndrew. I jist anna known a fella like ye, so loose me quick," and she scrambled to her feet. Bending, she gripped his hands and drew him up beside her. "Down to the sea, for Gawd's sake, mun, and cool you off. You're grown up – more like Ross Bolton's lovering . . ." and she hesitated . . .

"Ross Bolton. . . ?" said Tom.

"Aye aye, if it happened. . . ! But he wouldn'a be half the man as you, Tom McAndrew."

She shouted laughter, her head back. "That were nearly a large mistake! *Whee-up!*"

"Hush, for God's sake" whispered Tom. "And don't mention Ross Bolton again!"

"Och, cool down! An' cool that fella with ye!"

*

Rachel ran, Tom followed, and saw the whiteness of her against the dark sea, a woman without legs, because of her black stockings. And sand-pats rose from her feet as she ran, and little grains pattered on his face.

Through the shallows now, running side by side, for Tom had caught her up, and they dived full length into the little threat-breakers coming in from the east, for a storm was brewing, and the sea was unquiet.

Now they swam in deep water together – Tom with his long, easy strokes, Rachel beside him with her ungainly dog-paddle, and from the beach a man was watching, and this was Pinta. Behind the shelter of a rock a second man watched, and this was Tam Shenks, and in their hands these men held sticks.

But Tom and Rachel swam on, her long, red hair floating out like a wreath behind her; Tom caught it, cherishing it against him, and brine was salt on their lips as he kissed her.

Sometimes, in the fringe of the breakers their whiteness was discernible; at other times, in the deep, green troughs, they were lost to view. But Tam Shenks and Pinta waited by the mare, and in their hands they held willow sticks cut from the trees of the Big Wheatfield, deep into which they had taken their caravans.

And so they waited, Pinta in darkness, Tam Shenks holding the mare, and near his boot was the skull jutting up from the sand, but none saw this save the mare.

Presently, hand in hand, unsuspecting, Tom and Rachel waded out of the sea.

"Soon you will belong to me," he said, and paused in the shallows, turning her into his arms, and kissed her. "And after that you go to no other. You promise?"

"I promise."

"Promise it real – real and good? For ever – you'll belong to me?"

"On the grave of my mam, Tom McAndrew. I promise."

So they walked up the beach to where the mare was standing. And she, seeing them coming whinnied and shied, her forelegs beating the air, because Tam, in moving, had unearthed the skull.

And the skull jutted up, its socketed eyes staring black in the moonlight: seeing it, the mare shrieked and shied again, and Tom seized Rachel's wrist and twisted her behind him in the moment before Tam Shenks's stick came down. The stick missed Tom's head, but caught his shoulder, but he did not feel the pain.

In a moment he was McAndrew's son. He saw, in a gleam of the moon, a man's head and shoulders make shape within the shrieking of the mare, and a jaw: this he hooked hard with his fist, and felt the smash of knuckle on bone. Tam Shenks fell. Then Pinta came, flaying with his stick, and Rachel turned and fled.

Tom went in, crouching, the image of his father, ducked the hooves of the mare, and hit up short. The mare went one way, Pinta went another, and dropped.

But Tam Shenks was on his feet again, bawling with rage; blood streaming down his chest.

"Run, Rachel! *Run!*" yelled Tom.

Man and boy faced each other on the sand and the skull of the mare, grinning sightlessly, was between them as they circled. Tam Shenks said:

"By God, young 'un, I'll bloody do you for this," and swung his fist. Tom ducked it, but the next blow took him full, spinning him sideways. Instantly, the man dived full length, but the boy rolled away, sprang up, and caught him with a hook to the face and a left to the throat.

Gasping, fists clenched, Tom waited; Shenks rose, (seeing Pinta moving feebly . . .) and ran, head down. The butt took Tom in the midriff, pumping out his breath. He slipped to his knees, gasping, and Pinta struck him from behind.

Tom fell forward, face down in the sand, motionless.

Pinta and Tam Shenks picked up the sticks, and beat him.

Later, when the beating was over, they carried Tom down to the sea and bathed the blood from his back.

Then, when they were sure that he was fully conscious, they put him into the mare's saddle, and slapped her rump, so that she would take him home.

Pinta said, "Tell your mam we're in the Big Wheatfield now, by Mr. Ross's permission, and nobody's movin' us out. And you – make yourself scarce – back to school with ye, and think yourself lucky you're alive.

"So much as look at our girl again, ye lustful young bugger, and we won't be responsible."

With Pinta carrying Rachel's clothes and Tam Shenks carrying the sticks, they then went in search of Rachel. Finding her hiding in the stables of Cambourne, they took her out and beat her, also.

44

McAndrew, with his hat on the back of his head (and sport-
ing sprigs of thistle), was bawling a barrack-room song to the
tune of 'Johnny Comes Marching Home', as he tramped
along.

"Somebody signed the Private's pass. Horoo! Horoo!
Somebody signed the Corporal's pass. Horoo! Horoo!
Then somebody trod on the Sergeant's arse
As he was lyin' for dead in the grass
Oh, Sergeant dear, ye looked so queer
When the Colonel's wife, she thanked ye.

So wi' drums and guns and guns and drums. Horoo! Horoo!
Wi' guns and drums and drums and guns. Horoo! Horoo!
Where are the legs with which ye run?
Sarge, your bollicking days are done!
Me darlin' dear, ye look so queer
Sergeant, I hardly knew ye!"

Since early morning he had marched, after the *Marie Prey*
had docked at Cardiff; coming alongside in Tiger Bay with
pit-props for the Rhondda from the forests of Brittany.
McAndrew had paused to sit on the quay and paint exotic
flowers of red and green and gold – blooms that sprouted in
profusion from the crevices of the old stone flags: vagrant
seeds fallen from crates shipped in from the West Indies.
And Jean Pierre, the French dwarf, standing on the
fo'castle head, had watched.

McAndrew had come aboard at Le Havre after tramping in
from Nice: he and the dwarf had not exchanged a single word

on the sea trip, but it was clear to the Frenchman that the painter had been awaiting the *Marie Prey* for the homeward run, and he was flattered.

Now, squatting on the hot deck of his ship, the little man rolled one of his eternal cigarettes and squinted up at the sun. Perhaps, he thought, he and the Scot would meet again. In Spring Garden Lane, Hong Kong? In Spain, as two years back . . . in Barry Port, or Rouen? He did not know.

"*Voilà!*" he said, "this is life!"

Perhaps never again would they meet, he thought, except to fight, feet, fists or duels.

The dwarf spat from the corner of his mouth and his slitted eyes followed McAndrew as he strode away through a forest of masts and spars.

With his hands deep in the pockets of his ragged trews the big man went, his tattered shirt fluttering in a hot wind, and on his back he carried his pallets and canvases.

Picking up a melodeon, Jean Pierre played a merry little French tune, his back against a deck buoy, and the music came to McAndrew as he strode through Roath Dock.

"*Au Revoir*, Big Savage! Join me in a toast to madness! Lucky you have a wooden head, yes?" called Jean Pierre, but McAndrew did not return his wave.

Jean Pierre sighed deep. Are we not all mad? he thought. For it was strange, how certain he was that the destiny of McAndrew was somehow linked with his . . .

A voice called from below decks, "Jean Pierre!"

"Yes, *mon capitaine!*" The little man groaned, put down his melodeon and walked stiffly to the companionway.

"This donkey engine. The safety valve is stuck again!"

"Then treat it as you would a donkey, my friend," called the dwarf. "It goes better under a stick."

"Oh yes? One day this donkey will kick you in the face, Jean Pierre – you come and beat it."

The days were hot for autumn. But at night, with the rise of the big September moons, out came the matron of cold with her red nose and wringing hands, chattering about winter.

405

The trees of the Blorenge mountain, still being decimated for the Top Town furnaces, began their painting of russet-green and brown. The old River Usk sparkled and sang in a tinkling descant of ice; frost rimed the hedgerows in the early mornings, cows were coughing tubercular: the foxes of Abergavenny, ears pricked for the baying of hounds, sneezed with cold in their mist-wreathed lairs.

But this particular morning was warmer than most, with all the perfumes of the dying summer in its nostrils. And, as McAndrew set off from Tiger Bay (named after a river in Peru) with thoughts of France, Montmartre in particular, and Chocolat, far behind him, there was a richness in his blood, and the countryside echoed to the pounding of his boots.

Shouting good mornings to magpies for luck, waving to badgers and rabbits squatting in the fields, he went with a flourish that matched the morning.

At dusk that day McAndrew set three snares for rabbits; slept in a thicket by a brook and awoke ravenous, to find them empty. Furious, he roared at the morning, and rooks and crows rose from the tops of elms like burned paper in the western sky. These he cursed also, fists up, maddened by hunger.

Later, he lay full length and, face submerged, sucked up icy water. Rising, belly full, he wiped coldness from his beard and chest, and yelled at the sky.

"Sod ye, then! I'll do without ye," and he pulled the snares out of the earth and flung them away. "I'll eat off your blood-sucking gentry, and be damned to ye!"

Strapping his belongings upon his back, he set off for Abergavenny.

The sun was nearly overhead as he came down the Monmouth Road and he smelled the housewives' ovens and the scorching of their ironing boards, and imagined white, starched aprons hot from the fire. Into Cross Street now and the whole glorious country from Brecon to Ponty was alight with the sun.

*

It was market day and hopes of a generous housewife faded when McAndrew realised they would be out selling their produce. And he found them in the Market Hall, the mountain women of the Top towns streaming in with their goods. Pigs were squealing, cattle bellowing, plump matrons crying their wares, flourishing their hands in shrill soprano cries amid the bass shouting of their mountain men.

Tinkers and tailors were here, arrogant mountain fighters, packmen from the valleys, chickeners with a hundred scraggy necks swinging: ducksie farmers, goosers – all were here, with urchin children crawling under the stalls in theft and drunks from the King's Head next door tippling hot-poker Guinness.

Lobscouse was bubbling in cauldrons, loins of pork being sliced, chittlings and gravy on the boil, faggots and peas sizzling, and the perfumes wafting up were enough, thought McAndrew, to glutton the soul of St. Peter.

But it was no place for plunder with the police on the prowl for pickpockets, so he decided to dine at Morgan's, the best hotel in the town, and this required a formula of confidence and good manners.

With a fine arrogance McAndrew strolled into the spacious hotel foyer and smiled around, his broken boots splayed on the thick-piled carpet.

"Will you kindly sit here?" A waiter indicated a table in a corner.

"On the contrary," interjected a cultured voice. "Would you care to join me, sir? And as my guest. . . ?"

McAndrew looked the speaker over.

She was small, dressed in black lace, and old; and she raised a courteous, tired smile from under her black veiled hat.

"Now, that's entirely good of ye, Ma'am! I'm from Stirlingshire, ye see, and we've custom up there never to dine alone."

McAndrew sat down opposite the lady at her table. She

was eating delicately, a tiny, wizened piece of English gentility in a Welsh town.

"The name," he said expansively, "is James Alexander McAndrew! I'm a sea-farer, d'you see? On the march to see me sick old mother." Looking around for the waiter, he snapped his fingers.

The other guests whispered behind their menus; big hats were inclined in McAndrew's direction. The waiter said, discreetly:

"Is . . . is everything all right, Lady Heston? I can recommend the Hors d'oeuvre à la Français. Followed by the Coquilles de Saint-Jacques, à la mode Saint-Malo . . ."

"Dear God, I canna accept!" McAndrew brushed his eyes.

"Oh but you must, sir. François," Lady Heston said to the waiter, "the full menu, if you please, beginning with the Hors d'oeuvre and a good outsize steak . . ."

"Sirloin, preferably," said McAndrew. "Half a pound, and garnished with fried onions . . ."

"And a bottle of Lafite, if you have it, François?"

McAndrew glanced up to see her smiling brilliantly, and he followed her gaze.

"Aha!" Lady Heston exclaimed, "here comes my darling Felicity . . ."

McAndrew rose as another woman approached.

The newcomer was dressed in a white tussore suit, and wore a big picture hat with a red rose on the brim. McAndrew guessed her age at forty. Her green eyes moved over him with the appraisal of a tiger at a kill. She was beautiful, and knew it; looking, he thought, like a matronly bride who had been lifted off her knees in church.

"You'll just never believe it, Felicity," cried Lady Heston while McAndrew adjusted the younger woman's chair. "I was about to go hunting for goods in the market, when this fine hunk of a man comes sitting under my nose. Mr. McAndrew, this is Lady Felicity Barre – Felicity, this is James

Alexander McAndrew – tramping his way to Stirlingshire to visit his dying mother . . ."

"Well, we all have mothers, Mr. McAndrew," said Lady Felicity, "and dying ones are guaranteed to melt the heart. Ah, here comes your food! Eat heartily!" She smiled prettily, "Then afterwards – to Linda Vista, where we'll fit you out with decent clothes . . ."

"Ach, no! That's too much!"

"Yes, we insist! A good meal, a bath, a night's rest and you'll feel a different man. We pass this way but once, you know."

McAndrew scarcely heard her for he was eating voraciously, gasping with hunger, shovelling the food into his capacious mouth, wiping his whiskers with the back of his hand.

The eyes of the two women met. Lady Felicity fluttered a wink over the rim of her glass.

45

Bathed, powdered, resplendent in yellow silk pyjamas, McAndrew lay in the duck-down featherbed in the main bedroom of Linda Vista and contemplated his good fortune.

Earlier, he had seen the moon sliding over the top of the Blorenge mountain and watched the pulsating glow of the Blaenafon furnaces where unseen pygmies laboured in the red-bung flashing of the iron.

Earlier still he had seen Crawshay Bailey's engine fussing over the Llanfoist iron bridge and heard the otters barking from the Usk where the stars, tumbling in its spate, were sumptuous jewels.

Later, on the edge of sleep, the door of the adjoining bedroom opened and Lady Felicity entered.

McAndrew saw her in the silent torpor of a dream, and slowly sat up in his great, canopied bed.

She came slowly, translated into shape by the flung moonbeams of the latticed windows. With her black hair piled high upon her head, she looked, thought McAndrew, like someone stepped from the Imperial Bath; a woman of splendid breasts and the carriage of an empress. Naked but for a purple skirt that reached to the floor, she came with quiet enquiry, bending over the bed and peering into his face.

"Are you asleep, Mr. McAndrew?"

On the edge of his dream she had entered his world of unreality, and for once he was unprepared. Lady Felicity said:

"Please, I beg you, do not think me cheap."

He answered, chuckling deeply:

"It seems to me I've run into a black widow – they eat their husbands, I've heard say." He pulled aside the blankets. "Come on in, girl."

"No, wait. Please wait. . . ! I . . . I really must listen for Lady Heston. Naturally, she'd be most distressed . . ."

"If she found you in bed wi' a sailor? Ach, go on with ye! She's been a flipperty-jinx in her time, has that one! Come on!"

"Just another moment . . . *please?*"

The moon faded again as she crossed the floor. Blackness gathered her now, and McAndrew could see nothing; the room appeared suspended in an empty, monastic silence.

Getting out of the bed he tiptoed to the door and tried the handle. It was locked.

She appeared to have gone right through it: a wraith which neither iron nor timber impeded.

The brandy he had drunk at dinner acted like a swig to the senses. Reluctantly, McAndrew assumed that it had all been a fantastic and glorious dream.

It was one of the casualties of bachelorhood, he concluded, that when ever he dreamed of fair women, they were approaching the maternal phase of a disappointed nymphomania.

Next time (and he grinned to himself in the darkness) he would dream of a woman of double chins, a vacuous humour, and the prospect of twins.

"Mr. McAndrew!"

McAndrew opened his eyes.

Lady Felicity was dressed as before, but this time her movements were quick and feverishly alert, her eyes wild, her hair dishevelled.

"Quick, for God's sake!" She gripped his shoulders, shaking him into wakefulness. "Burglars! Quick, Mr. McAndrew – *burglars!*"

411

"Jesus," he breathed, "there'd be no strife in this world if it weren't for bloody people. Where, for God's sake?"

"Down in the hall!"

There was about her nakedness this time a voluptuous indelicacy.

"You're sure now – burglars?"

"I tell you I saw them – they were taking the silver."

"You'd not be puttin' one up me jumper now, would ye?"

For reply, she suddenly smoothed his hair: the performance of this small office gave new promise to their relationship. McAndrew said, releasing her:

"Wait, then, and I'll go and do the sods."

Putting her hands behind her back, she smiled coquettishly, saying:

"That, Mr. McAndrew, is where the vulgar classes diminish themselves. Adjectives dilute the content of speech, or didn't you know? And when you do come back, something a little more refined than rape – if you please – assuming, of course, that you perceive the grammar?"

When McAndrew returned to his bedroom after a fruitless search of the house, Lady Felicity was no longer there.

When the town hall clock struck twice, Lady Felicity came again.

McAndrew awoke from a shuddering drowse, wondered where he was, then stared at the naked vision framed in the adjoining door. Lady Felicity said:

"It's the classical strategy of opportunity, Mr. McAndrew. Why do you not avail yourself. . . ? It knocks but once, you know . . ."

He replied from the bed, "There's a witch's stench about the room. Get yoursel' a broom and go round chimneys, woman."

"Do you want me, Mr. McAndrew? You have only to ask."

Flinging back the clothes, he twisted and flung himself towards her, hitting the floor full length.

"I'll bloody kill ye," he said. "As God's me judge, I'll kill ye!"

He was kneeling now, watching as she retreated through the thick-panelled door. He heard her turn the key.

When the town hall clock struck four, Lady Felicity came again. The heavy door of the adjoining room swung slowly open.

"Mr. McAndrew. . . !" Her voice cajoled him.

There came from the bed an inarticulate shout of fury.

At five o'clock Lady Felicity stood at the end of the bed. McAndrew opened bleary eyes, and closed them.

"Forgive me," said she, "for being uncharitable. But how can you possibly sleep like that, snoring, while I lie awake?

"You, my friend, are chained by your own vulgarity, you are ponderous, inelegant. You live by the rules of crude strength and betrayal, one without honour or veracity. When educated, you disgust with your conceit and foppery; when uneducated, like you, your perversions are an appalling affront to the dignity of womanhood. You are miscreated, McAndrew, insensitive, as are all your set: you are but a moving vehicle of phallic instrument – venal, egocentric and depraved. Have you the audacity to think that I would let you enter me? – the sweepings of a gutter?"

When McAndrew opened his eyes again, the room was empty.

Morning came bright with sun. The Usk River meadows were golden with foxgloves, water mint, self-heal and milfoil, and the gardens of Linda Vista, cultivated by unknown but loving hands, were alive with waving ferns and flowers of every colour.

McAndrew, standing by the window, could hear the curlews shouting from the river: a heron was standing on one leg in the shallows, the distant castle was caught in ropes of sunlight.

A knock came on the bedroom door and Lady Heston

413

entered as McAndrew opened it. In her arms she carried a pile of clothes.

"Did you sleep well, Mr. McAndrew?" She laid the clothes out on the bed.

"Like a top, Missus!"

"So did I. So that is excellent." She patted and fussed, adding, "Now, pray do not be offended, but here are some clothes from the wardrobe of my dear husband. Like you, Mr. McAndrew, he was a giant of a man." Her smile faded. "Twenty years ago he left me, but I was luckier than poor Felicity – I did have some years of marriage. And we were so very happy . . ."

"And then?" prompted McAndrew.

She shrugged, empty. "And then I met Felicity. She was alone, too, you see. But it was harder for her, of course, being younger. I hope you were kind to her last night, my friend?" Her bagged eyes searched his face.

"Milady, I were the soul of male generosity. The sweet creature was sleepin' when I left her."

"Dear me, how poetic! The moment I set eyes on you I knew you two were a match. Her husband left her, too, you know. . . ?"

"Is that a fact?"

"Walked out at the altar. There's a room full of wedding presents upstairs, covered with cobwebs. And he appeared to be such a gentleman. I . . ." Lady Heston hesitated. "I have to choose her . . . her consorts very carefully, you understand. She won't take anyone. After all, she is a lady, isn't she?"

"Right down to her toenails."

Lady Heston made a small, wry face. "I suppose, if one wanted to be very unkind, I could be called a procuress, but, well . . . I do so love to see young people happy." She clasped her small hands together. "Besides, times are changing – women are the predators now, aren't they?"

"You can say that again."

"And it's all so romantic! The French would approve, I'm absolutely sure."

"Ach, indeed! A Frenchman would go up a tree for Lady Felicity – and I'll carry the memory of the darlin' creature to me grave. But there's one thing botherin' me now . . ."

"What's that?"

"I left her this morning without a goodbye."

"Well . . ." Lady Heston contemplated this.

McAndrew added swiftly, "I'd not make it difficult, ye know – no dyin' farewells. I'd just like to express me gratitude to the darlin' lady – her givin' affection to a big, awkward fella like me."

"I . . . I don't know," said Lady Heston, indecisively. "You see, it . . . it isn't in the rules, so to speak . . . Usually, the gentlemen just dash off without a word in the morning, you know? After they've had the money, of course."

"The . . . the money?"

"Of course! Ten pounds and the suit of clothes . . ." She regarded McAndrew warmly.

"I'd even go on me knees to her, the sweet child," said McAndrew.

"Really? You would? Oh yes, I'm sure she'd like that! Look, if I give you the key, do you promise me faithfully you'll be out in five minutes – so she can go back to sleep?"

"What I have in mind, lady, will take me one minute flat," said McAndrew.

"You see before you the moving vehicle of the phallic instrument," said McAndrew, locking Lady Felicity's door behind him. "Shift over."

46

Princess Maria Joseldon was about McAndrew's age, but hadn't worn so well. The thrust of wealth under the will of Lord Grey-Cambourne, consequent over-eating and an ancestry of Bavarian beer-drinkers, had laden Maria with premature obesity.

The lithe and winsome princess who had charmed Teddy Cambourne's senility sixteen years before, was no more. Bedecked with vulgar jewellery, in a flamboyant dress of scarlet frills and sequins, Maria held court in Number Fourteen Duke Street, London, W., and fed her rouged mouth with chocolates from Harrods; cooling herself betimes with a Japanese fan of intricate delicacy. The September morning was hot and she perspired gently under the piled up black mantle of her hair.

McAndrew, strolling along Duke Street in the sun, took his time, this being appropriate to his present elegance.

In his morning suit, lately the property of Lady Heston's husband, new shoes bought for ten shillings, a walking-stick in his hand and a half-a-crown bowler hat on his head, he knocked at the door of Number Fourteen, and Nell, maid to Princess Joseldon, stared up. Turning abruptly, she fled, presenting herself before the princess in stammering breathlessness.

"Oh, Ma'am, there's the most gorgeous man standing on the doorstep!"

"His name?" asked Maria.

"Didn't ask him, Ma'am."

"Gorgeous, you say?"

"Absolutely gorgeous!"

"Show him in," said Princess Maria.

Dusk was falling on the London parks; a red sunset sank over the city, painting the tops of the autumn trees: sunlight shafted the oppulent drawing-room in which McAndrew and Maria sat in luxurious ease, amid nostalgic memories of Lord Grey-Cambourne.

"He didn't entirely approve of you, you know," said Maria.

"I am grieved to hear that," said McAndrew.

"It was merely, I think, his recognition of a kindred spirit – he said you were a rogue."

"Then he said it more than once, Ma'am."

Maria sipped smoke from a long-handled, Egyptian cigarette. "But he was in a quandary, because also, he didn't completely trust Miss Ellie, your wife."

"He made that clear, too."

"And he secretly hoped, I am sure, that you and I would . . . how you say in English, get together. . . ?"

"Better late than never, Princess."

"But too late, nevertheless? Look at me." Maria regarded her expansive figure. "You should have arrived earlier, my friend – not always was I so unattractive." She clapped her plump hands together in a small, charming gesture, and her accent, thought McAndrew, was music.

"I was once, shall I say, like Guy de Maupassant's charming little countess – she who window-tapped and was subsequently under-paid – remember?"

"Lord Teddy surely paid you well . . ."

"But not because of my beauty – because I was with child."

"I didn't know that," said McAndrew.

"My daughter," said Maria, as if making a vow of chastity, "my darling Josie, was but four years old when Teddy died. She is seventeen now . . ."

417

"And living here?"

"At the moment she is in Cambridge – Girton – but in three days from now, she will be home." Maria's eyes grew large with joyous anticipation. "And then, my friend, the house will come alive! She is charming, she is exquisite – more, she is talented. The most beautiful pianist, Mr. McAndrew! More wine?"

McAndrew nodded; rising, he helped himself from a decanter.

"Yet Teddy did not marry you?"

"He could not, because he was already married – few knew this. So Josie, not I, became his love." She smiled at McAndrew over the rim of her glass and her eyes were smudged with the tears of mascara. "I, in turn, achieved the status of a vehicle – I had produced for him the greatest achievement of his life. You find that trite in this modern world?"

"Not at all."

Maria rose, wandering around the ornate room of red velvet curtaining and heavy chandeliers. "He would enter this house after a tiring journey from Barry, brush past me with scarcely a word, take the child from the arms of the nurse, and disappear with her.

"When he was at home he would bathe her, feed her, change her, dress her. It was idolatry, Mr. McAndrew, yet love in its purest form. As for me – I was a nonentity, part of the furniture. He made love to me, of course, but only as a release of his emotions. I played no other part in his life. Only for Josie he planned – marriage to a handsome man of wealth and good breeding. He spent his evenings thumbing through Debrett to find him."

McAndrew said, "A fixation?"

"Of course. But how could I tell a man of Teddy's enormous intellect that he's being a fool over his daughter?" Maria sat down again. "I . . . I was young. I did not know how to combat it . . . combat?"

"That is correct."

"It was a form of madness; and it expressed itself in his

terror of losing her. Something from his childhood, perhaps?

"I . . . I recall an occasion when we were at a concert. He was reluctant to go, I remember, but I begged him to attend. It was in Stuttgart – Josie was about three years old – it was a year before her father died. An item in the programme was *Pavane for a dead infanta*, by Ravel. I saw it too late in the programme notes. During the performance Teddy began to weep. It was clear that knowledge of the piece had returned to him. It was embarrassing. Before the end, he was so overcome that attendants had to assist him from the hall."

"You had little chance, Ma'am, with that kind of intensity."

"Of course, so I did not resist. And after Teddy died, I carried on where he had left off. Look at me!" She opened her hands in acceptance of defeat.

They sat in silence, contemplating each other, and Maria said:

"And what of you? – the *enfant terrible* of the Cambourne estate?"

McAndrew pulled at his cigar, grinning at her from his chair.

"You left your wife, they tell me."

"She left me, in fact," he replied.

"For Ross Bolton."

McAndrew nodded through the smoke.

"They thrive, I am told. They call it Ross-Cambourne, now, did you know?"

"I did not know."

"And your son?"

"Tom?" He examined the end of the cigar. "Ah, poor Tom!"

"On the contrary, he will soon be very rich. Sixteen, is he not, a year younger than my Josie. Soon he will be going into the firm?"

"I . . . I am a little out of date," said McAndrew.

"You should not be. Your wife betrays you, all right, but . . ."

"Do you mind if we do not discuss her?"

419

"If you wish, sir. But your son – this is different – unless all ogres live in Britain and all victims in Bavaria, where I come from. You owe him a duty, do you not?"

"No doubt." McAndrew fixedly smoked on.

"And you – what of you?" she asked.

"Me? There is very little to tell."

"There is very much to tell, my friend." Maria narrowed her dark-lashed eyes. "You are an artist, they say – one of peculiar talent. A Neo-Impressionist of bright colours and contours! And you have just returned from Montmartre?"

"You are well informed, Ma'am."

"Of course. All bored people are well informed, they deal in the lives of others. And now?"

"And now?" repeated McAndrew, disinterested.

"What do you plan to do with yourself?"

McAndrew gulped at his wine. "The intention was to travel mesel' to Scotland – to Cromarty, to be precise . . ."

"You have a home there?"

"I've more, lady. I've thirteen thousand acres and a baronial hall stolen from the crofters; property's still theft, though it's a Marxist theory. At the moment me brother runs it."

"Thirteen thousand acres! Are you a laird?"

"Well, I thought I was, for me marvellous brother Angus was on his deathbed, you see. And he sent a telegram to Paris tellin' me to return and claim the estate – by Scottish law, ye'll understand, all property devolves upon the next surviving eldest son, which is me." He drank again, draining the glass.

"And so you'll be leaving. . . ?" She pouted sadly.

McAndrew shook his head. "With your permission, I will not. For I telephoned the old beggar yesterday and he told me he'd decided to recover, which is typical of bloody Angus, beggin' ye pardon. He's been on his death-bed half a dozen times to my certain knowledge, and I should ne'er have left Montmartre."

Princess Maria filled his glass. "So, you'll be staying in London. . . ?"

"If you'd not think it presumptuous. The lairdship's my responsibility – the tenants have a right to consideration – but . . ."

She interjected, "It appears to me, sir, that you have no real desire to become a laird."

"Me, Ma'am? – I only want to paint." McAndrew frowned up at the chandelier light.

"And so, you would like to stay here, with me?"

He warmed to her. "Ach, I would. Teddy Cambourne told me I'd get a welcome – but I have to advise ye, Princess, though being in need of shelter and sustenance, I'm in a state of penury. I'm a remittance man, ye understand – normally paid to keep away. But the administration has gone for a Burton; like Billy Bunter, me postal order hasn'a come through yet . . ."

"It is of the smallest importance," said Princess Maria, and rang a bell.

Nell, the maid appeared silently on the Persian carpet of the room.

She had been kneeling in prayer – that McAndrew would soon leave. There was a boy from Camden Town whose father was a Pearly King; the boy was coming in on an early tram, and it was Nell's evening off. Her flat chest and spindly legs belied the passionate beating of Nell's heart. There would be hot, red saveloys and pease-pudding steaming on the Cheapside stalls, and afterwards a walk in the park, and so far he had not kissed her . . . She thought, 'O God, it's my evening off. Please make him go . . .'

Her gawkish locomotion and flat chest had so far denied to Nell even the promise of kisses.

Maria said, "My dear, I want you to forego your evening off. Mr. McAndrew will be staying indefinitely. Get Agnes to help you prepare his room – the one next to Josie's – she's going to adore having an artist in the house. You will do that?"

"Yes, Ma'am." Nell turned to go.

"And darling . . ."

"Yes, Ma'am?"

"Do try to achieve it with a little more grace. . . ?"

Nell thought: you fat old bastard. May you fry on the grids of Hell. There is no God: there cannot be a God.

Princess Maria smiled with an inner, growing exultation. Her eyes opened wide in her powdered face.

"Welcome to our house, Mr. McAndrew. You will work, of course, while you are here? There is a conservatory with a north light . . ."

"That sounds reasonably suitable."

Rising, Maria refilled their glasses; McAndrew rose as she held it out to him in a toast. They stood as people momentarily obsessed with countenance; McAndrew, a foot the taller, smiling down.

The chandelier light made gold of his hair: his spade beard shone lustrously: never had she seen eyes of such astonishing blueness; they seemed to reflect the man's inner soul. His very maleness dominated the room; it was uncouth and vulgar. Men had looked at her like that before. Their glasses touched. The faint clink shattered the silence. They drank, their eyes unmoving.

"That . . . that scar on your hand, Mr. McAndrew . . . how did you come by it?"

It appeared necessary to break the impasse.

He flexed the big, brown hand before her. "A mere flesh wound, Ma'am. A friend of mine and I attacked a Boer machine-gun during the Relief of Ladysmith. His name was Caesar – a rare animal, actually – an ex-patriate Boer. I got a bayonet through the hand – close-quarter fighting."

"God you must be brave!"

"I was a soldier, Ma'am." It was a remark that said nothing in particular; McAndrew stared about him, drinking slowly.

"And Caesar, your friend?"

"He lost a leg, and subsequently died."

"I am very sorry . . ."

McAndrew smiled, showing big, white teeth. "When did you say your little Josie might be home. . . ?"

47

Josie came home from Girton College in late September, when McAndrew, stripped to the waist in the roof-top conservatory Maria had set aside for him, was painting with the devouring energy of a man at his final canvas.

The northern façade of the conservatory faced the street below, and McAndrew, his pallet knife suspended, watched the open carriage in which the princess was bringing her daughter from the station.

Nearing the window, McAndrew saw it threading a path through a Duke Street crammed with midday shoppers and horse-trams; a broad snake of pavement life that reminded him of Paris with its brilliant colours and activity. The sun burned down from a sky of sapphire intensity: this astonishing September was celebrating the youth and gaiety of an autumnal spring.

McAndrew unashamedly followed the route of the carriage with the intentness of a man who is watching his final copulation before the abyss of impotency.

This animal mood had been upon him since striking the shores of Tiger Bay, and he had yearned for Chocolat with an unrequited lust. Nor had his connection with the Lady Felicity brought relief; in fact it had sharpened his need, for he had not enjoyed her. Therefore, with Maria Joseldon in mind, he had hoped to discover the libertine Teddy Cambourne had promised: instead, he now found himself bound to so dull a prospect for food and watering.

Already he had existed for a week without a woman. The experience was scarcely to be borne.

And so, McAndrew followed the carriage and the movements of the young girl within it with the intensity of a man who has never seen a female before.

And Josie, straw-hatted, golden-haired, acted with the spontaneity of a child home from school, and McAndrew thought she was charming: her laughter drifted up to the window where he watched.

With his shirt stained rainbow colours by brush and pallet wipes, he reached out, gripped the half-empty bottle and drank, but his eyes did not move from the scene below. Josie, unaware of a watcher, fought to keep her boater on in the wind, and leaped about with child-like excitement; pulling her mother to her feet in shrieks; now assisting a wobbling, overdressed Maria of frills and fancies down the carriage steps to the pavement.

McAndrew didn't even see Maria: he was watching Josie.

She was dressed in a navy blue uniform and wore a skirt that reached to her calves: her stockings were of black worsted, her shoes black brogues; a drabness that enhanced her beauty, thought McAndrew. It was impossible for him to believe that this perfect human being could have been sired by the dwarfish Teddy Cambourne . . . from the lop-sided grossness of one like the Princess Maria.

"God Almighty," whispered McAndrew, and wiped his bearded chin with the back of his hand.

They came in a clattering commotion up the narrow, spiral stairway to the roof conservatory; a gasping, excited Josie, a wheezing and sweating Maria; and stood side by side in the open doorway in smiles and stares. He saw the incredulous eyes of the girl upon him.

Josie came nearer, to stand before him smiling up. Maria, gasping with the climb, patted her chest and said breathlessly:

"Darling, meet our guest – an old friend of your father – James Alexander McAndrew."

Bottle in hand, McAndrew regarded Josie.

Life, he thought – now that he could see her more clearly – had not yet cast her features into that of a woman; there was in her face no malice, no bitterness in her eyes, and his thoughts became suddenly cyclonic . . . he would snatch at this innocence before it was betrayed by a day, a week, a month: he would catch it in the brush and chain it to a canvas.

As Soutine had captured the garish beauty of Rembrandt's *Flayed Ox* by pouring fresh blood over his putrefying side of beef, so he would abduct this pristine innocence before it was wooed by caprice.

Josie said, with wonderment in her voice, "How do you do, Mr. McAndrew?"

McAndrew did not reply. His eyes were moving over the smooth, oval contours of Josie's face.

Maria, her hands clasped over her stomach, was regarding the pair of them with a warm, maternal pleasure. She said, huskily:

"Really, I suppose you could look upon him as a sort of pretending father, could you not, my darling?"

Nobody replied.

Josie had been home a week when McAndrew took her and Maria to the park to see the swallows fly away.

Earlier, he had seen them in thick, regimented lines on the sagging telegraph wires outside his window, and they betokened, for him, the essence of escape by flight, a phenomenon never to be caught by brush stroke.

And now, with Maria walking one side of him and Josie on the other, they strolled in Regent's Park in the bright afternoon sun amid the suppressed elation of Londoners at last sated with warmth, for the summer had been glorious. Josie said:

"Where do they go?"

Vagrant children were running among the crowd with hoops; uniformed nannies walked by preceded by prams and contained within their personal superiority: a defence against young guardsmen from Knightsbridge barracks, who, puttied and white-belted, marched past with ceremonial precision, their boots clanking on the tarmac.

425

"The swallows?" said McAndrew, "South Africa, mainly – about ten thousand miles return, resting on the way, of course. Think of it!"

"You know about birds?"

"Ay, ay, on and off."

"Do many fly away in the winter?"

"Yes, but tits and warblers, woodpeckers, nut-hatches, and robins, and many others stay. But, come late autumn, off go the swifts, thrushes and fly-catchers and a hundred other species, making for the sun."

"I would like to leave like that," said Josie, reflectively.

"Fly to the sun?"

"I hate the winter when everything dies . . ."

Maria said, comfortingly, "But the seasons must die so that life can be lived again. Is that not right, Mr. Mc-Andrew?"

He saw beyond the podgy profile of Maria the smooth out-line of Josie's face; against a green tracery of trees and a clear, blue sky McAndrew saw her, and thought of a place of warmth and the white porticos of a sun-struck building against Medi-terranean blue; the Mediterranean, as Toulouse-Lautrec had said, which was too beautiful to be painted.

And it was abhorrent to him to think that he was too old for this child, when her life was just beginning.

He would have liked to shed the complaining years and taken her hand, to find in her the youth he had lost before it had begun. And then, strangely, without warning or com-passion, the face of Ellie was framed in Josie's face, and Josie's voice, when she spoke, had the lilting north country intonation of Ellie. The wind moved, bringing to his nostrils a faint perfume, and this was the perfume Ellie used.

"Oh Christ," said McAndrew, making no sound. "*Ellie!*"

The swallows were wheeling across the sky in swelling abundance; the day was filled with their chattering and the sweeping of their wings.

Radiant, Josie pointed up, following their flight until they swooped low over the trees of the Serpentine, and dis-appeared.

"More!" cried McAndrew. "Look, more are comin'!"

Maria said, out of context, "Do not leave us, Mr. Mc-Andrew. Please do not go . . ."

He heard, but ignored her.

For already the call of the open road was pulsing in his blood. He heard the thumping of boots, felt the buffeting wind, and smelled again the smouldering wood-ash of the roadside fires; the damp, sweet earth-smell of wayside hedge-rows.

They took tea at the Ritz. It was a weekly treat, apparently, accorded to Josie when she was home from college.

Amid the grotesque decoration of egg-and-tongue, cyma recta and reversa and the gilded metopis of the French Renaissance, they sat beneath the delicate carvings of plaster acanthus and honeysuckle, crystal chandeliers, stylized tulips and pomegranate leaves: the vulgar tarnishings fraught with memories of under-paid nannies, Oscar Wilde and the Relief of Ladysmith.

Flowers were abundant in the tearoom; roses from English gardens, pink, white and yellow; begonias and anemones; larkspur and montbretia of astonishing beauty, and the tinkling of spoons and bone china vied with the funereal scent of lavender and potted ferns.

And all about them, contented with their English existence, diocesan and military gentlemen, society ladies, youthful suffragettes and blue-jowled, barking businessmen buttered and jammed hot toast and drank luke-warm tea with a chattering resolve to get as much down them before leaving for Henley.

"Oh, the larkspur!" whispered Josie.

"Lightness and levity," said McAndrew. "That's what she stands for."

"Really?" Josie's young face shone with pleasure.

"Begonia? What does she say?" asked Maria, not to be outdone.

"Dark, *dark* thoughts, my lady!" He made a sombre face.

Josie was delighted with him. "Anemones?"

427

"Forsaken, I fear, my little one."

"And roses. . . ?" Josie's face was unsmiling now, intent upon his.

"Ach, there I can do ye better – t'is the language of the flowers, ye see? For a rose, deep red, like this one," and he touched it, "I offer ye bashful shame; for a dog rose, pleasure and pain. For a rose from la belle France, you'll be meeting a man by moonlight, and for a musk rose, you give me your fine, capricious beauty . . ."

"You made all that up!"

"Och, I didn't I tell you! It's the language of the flowers. And for a nephitos rose you'll weary with infatuation. Didn't you know all this, for God's sake, it's schoolgirl stuff!"

"James Alexander McAndrew," said Maria, "you are a mine of information, but I don't trust you!"

"I'm more than that," said he. "I'm a terrible fella for the women, given half a chance!"

"I think you're quite beautiful," said Josie, unsmiling.

"Oh dear," said Maria, patting herself, "this is certainly no place for us."

"Have you been here before, Mr. McAndrew?" asked Josie.

"Aye, many times – and call me James, will ye?"

"Where were you educated?" She was staring at him with a hidden apprehension apparent not only to her mother.

"Edinburgh and Oxford." McAndrew stretched himself with athletic grace. "Me feyther didn't approve o' the Scottish system, ye see, and he reckoned to Anglicise his sons. But they sent me down from Oxford, I'm ashamed in me heart to say." He sipped his tea, winking at her over the cup.

"What for?" Josie was bird-like, instantly intent, her face flushed and beautiful.

"Ach, I had an affair wi' a Battersea waitress, and they didn't think a lot of it. You're talking to the inventor of original sin."

"Did you put her in the family way?"

"*Josie!*" admonished Maria.

"I did me best. She were a plump, west country piece wi'

428

black hair and peaches and cream, and she were five years older'n me . . ."

"Without a doubt you were led astray," said Maria, defensively.

"Ach no! It was me who did the misleading. Her old man comes up to Oxford wi' a stick and generally playing hell around the corridors, so I slipped out o' the back to save me skin."

"What was her name?"

"Er. . . ? *Rosa.*" He had clearly given this thought.

The waiter came to pour more tea. The room was now crowded with elegance. The talk within the white and pink-clad walls was moderated and discreet. McAndrew thought he had been nowhere before which exhibited such discretion.

"Rosa? What a beautiful name!" said Josie. "What happened to her?"

"Search me. I was at sea."

"You mean you abandoned her?"

Maria interjected, "Darling, I suspect that James was very well off without her. Girls of that kind are out to catch a man, you know."

"But she was going to have a baby!"

"Aye," said McAndrew, with sadness, "the poor, wee soul."

"And you walked out on her?"

"I hadn'a the money to do otherwise."

"But what about poor Rosa?"

"May the good God bless her for the sad, rejected creature that she was. And may I be stricken dead if I ever commit the likes again."

"You actually left her to fend for herself? Really, I think you're disgusting!"

"Josie, please calm yourself!" whispered Maria, smiling around as the big, summer hats tilted towards them in mute enquiry.

"I do, I think you're disgusting! And I'll never speak to you again! That's a dreadful thing to do!"

Rising, Josie flounced away without a backward look.

"Let her go, let her go," said Maria, confidentially. "She's got one of her moods again. Outraged innocence! Believe me, she can be the most impossible child."

"Dear God, I've upset her," said McAndrew, staring after her, and Maria patted his hand in gentle commiseration.

"Never mind, James," she said, "you have still got me."

48

A week later, haunted by the presence of Josie in the house, available but unpossessed, McAndrew was working in his studio with the primitive energy of a man who has but one canvas left before senility.

He worked naked, striding around the conservatory with fierce exclamations and animal grunts, not stopping to eat or attend Maria's frantic knocking on the locked door above the spiral staircase.

The canvas was large, of Rabelaisian content and demoniac possession.

Of garish content and unnatural, grotesque shapes, colour was everywhere – the luminous translations of vivid emotional response, and always the influence of Lautrec's Post-Impressionism challenged the traditional.

Tumbling down the steps of the Sacre Coeur, sprawling over the gravestones of the Cimetière Montmartre, were the scapegrace hordes that infested the Butte. Writhing under a glaring moon were the debauched dregs of Rue Muller and Faubourg-Saint-Honoré – the dancers, posturers, tumblers, acrobats.

Here were the *filles de joie* turning out of the cabarets, the drunkards out of the bars; there the pimps and ponces of the Moulin Rouge, in whose exposed brains dead rats were dancing a saraband. Now the prissy perverts with obscene tattoos on their chests and buttocks; the arabesque dancing of La Macarona, black lace and diamanté underclothes flashing back the sulphur-coloured dawn.

All were here in a gastronomic feast of sensuality: the wan

faces of drowsy lesbians, the green-eyed chorus of the Chat Noir with their top-hatted, sophisticated escorts; also the strange, icy beauty of Madame Fernod of the old Elysée-Montmartre, beating time to music amid her purple-coloured draperies, the songs of Salis.

The precocious and voluptuous La Goulue who ended in the gutter, high-kicking her black-clad, exquisite legs in the Can-can; a little seamstress dancing a quadrille before her corruption by the licentious Café Noir.

Waitresses from the Tuileries leaped from clouds – the endless sacrament of the poor to the rich – all drawn with pristine clarity, their youth enhanced in beauty, but their limbs crippled and their dresses fantastically mispropor-tioned. It was near-genius in search of Toulouse-Lautrec.

Old crones were tippling or defecating; smooth-faced nuns passed in detachment, oblivious to the defiling antics of half-naked guttersnipes, bare-footed and depraved. It was satanic, a diabolical intervention that spewed from Mc-Andrew's mind with obsessive force . . . the dirt-pickers of Paris scratching for vermin amid brothel senility, the lunacy that had died in shrieks in Lariboisière; the naked con-tortions of the prostitutes of the Rue d'Amboise – all were here; fat-stomached friars, surrounded by galleries of wine and flowers, jovially pulling babies to pieces and frying them on grills.

And above all, peering from corners, the black face of Chocolat laughed down in total benediction at the comic and profane; an unchanging Chocolat, thought McAndrew, the first apostle of realism.

But one portion of the canvas McAndrew left undrawn: the void was central and dominant – a vacant and capricious nonentity waiting to be filled.

When he was exhausted McAndrew gulped down what was left of the whisky, then slipped to the boards at the foot of the easel, to lie outstretched in shuddering, sweating dreams, while Maria knocked unavailingly on the door.

*

Maria was working at her obesity with dedication born of desperation.

She had been labouring thus from the day McAndrew had arrived in Duke Street.

She bathed three times a day, wallowing in sweating nakedness in a steam-filled bathroom and emerging from the bath like a boiled lobster: progressed, stage by stage, through the pages of a *Get Slim* book, conducting vigorous exercises on the floor of her bedroom, her fat limbs waving in contortive agony.

She wrote away to Godalming for a booklet on a weight-watcher's diet and a pamphlet on *How to lose Ten Pounds in a Week*, for which she paid five guineas, two in advance. She attended the Turkish Baths in the Strand every other after-noon, began a diet of lettuce and bananas, restricted her liquid intake to water and raw lemons, took four inches off her waist and six off her bust in a fortnight, and managed to return to their original position every whale-bone in her stays.

The third week found her attended in the morning by two Amazons as black as Nubian slaves: these, professional masseuses, laid her out and rubbed, chopped, slapped and kneaded her until howls of anguish arose from the curtained bedroom. But pain brought in its wake astonishing success; by the end of a month Maria was beginning to return to womanly shape.

The process was assisted by worry, because not only had Josie begun to walk around the house like one narcotised, but the artist who had hypnotised her had now locked himself in his conservatory studio, and refused to emerge.

The advent of night invariably found McAndrew on the prowl, Maria discovered.

The route was inevitable – down to the kitchen to eat his fill – (he once consumed a raw chicken and left its entrails on the floor) and then down to the cellar to replenish his horde of whisky.

Maria, by now, was considering the possibility of wooing McAndrew by the subtle gifts of womanhood.

The man's sudden appearance, his arrogant, male domination had rekindled within her desires she had long considered expired. Indeed, the wish to own him had recently become a biological necessity.

McAndrew's presence, however uncouth, eccentric, Bohemian as it was, had awakened in Maria's ample breast a suffocating and primitive passion.

Therefore, given the ability to get into her stays again; granted Josie's return to Cambridge, a considerable bribe of money (exceeding by far anything she had parted with to McAndrew yet . . .) the princess now considered it within the bounds of possibility of having James Alexander McAndrew either before the altar or in her bed within the next six months.

McAndrew, aware that much was now expected of him both in expiation and good manners, treated Maria and Josie with the kindness due to their station, and to the behaviour expected of a guest.

He suddenly stopped drinking, attended table propitiously, and maintained a gentlemanly attitude worthy of one about to take his place in high society. Now beautifully attended by the tailors of Savile Row at Maria's expense, he was the Scottish laird again, the aristocrat with lace and decorum.

It was the night before Josie returned to Girton College that McAndrew selected for the *coup de grâce*.

The painting, finished but for its final adornment of the figure within the void, rested on the easel.

Sober, McAndrew worked until the city clocks struck two, then opened the door of the conservatory and stole down the spiral staircase and along the red-carpeted corridor to the room where Josie slept. It was his sobriety and care that allowed Maria to sleep peacefully.

The door of Josie's room opened to a touch, exposing the narrow, schoolgirl's bed within. Her suitcase, already packed, stood by the little dressing-table; her high-laced boots, the toes turned in, waited side by side on the floor; her petticoats and lace-frilled drawers were draped over an arm-chair by the casement window.

McAndrew stood at the bottom of the bed and watched: Josie breathed with the untroubled rhythm of innocence; an in-nocence, he thought, that was the mantle of her childhood. And his conscience, long thwarted and suppressed, nagged faintly in the depth of him.

McAndrew had actually turned to leave when Josie stirred and opened her eyes.

"You've come for me?" she asked, and sat up in the bed.

For reply he approached, and held out to her a rose.

"For a rose from la belle France you'll meet a man by moonlight, remember?" he asked.

"I remember," said Josie, taking it.

McAndrew offered her another. "A musk rose, also, for your fine, capricious beauty . . ."

"I remember that, too," said Josie. "I've been lying awake, you see, because I knew you'd come. There'll be the most dreadful row at college, of course. Old Clappers will play Hamlet. Are you going to put me in the family way, like you did poor Rosa?"

"That's not the intention at the moment," answered McAndrew, helping her out of the bed – she was now hold-ing a rose in each hand. "First things first, girl. The inten-tion, at the moment, is to put you on to canvas."

Josie, with her head held high and her long, fair hair down her back, followed him like a wraith of white silence, along the red-carpeted corridors of the landing, past her mother's door and up the spiral staircase to the roof-top studio.

Maria, in a hopeless dream of youth, went snoring up the path to Heaven while Josie, hand in hand with McAndrew, went with him to the gates of Hell.

"If things like this happen when you're seventeen, I'm not going to bother to grow up," said Josie. "Do I keep me nightie on?"

"Nightie off," said McAndrew.

*

435

She stood, McAndrew thought, like some minute Diana, and possessed a pure relationship with the subject; a perfect female in shape, so that her body became almost of the brush; an admixture of flesh and mystic colour that laid itself on the canvas with clarity and ease.

So well she stood; surely as Venus before Correggio or Susanna before Rubens? McAndrew thought. And Chocolat, she of the mocking, awkward stance, was no match in dignity.

Josie stood upright, her head tilted slightly in an unmistakable arrogance that matched the theme – that of purity besmirched. Therefore McAndrew painted her, though such innocence had as much right on that canvas of devils, he concluded, as a nun in a whore house.

It was nearly dawn before he had finished, and in all that time Josie had not moved, so he captured her with pristine clarity: she holding the position to the end with charm and repose.

McAndrew looked upon the canvas, knowing that with virtue's incomparable addition, he had painted a work of great valedictory purpose: a worthy enrichment of the unfinished mural at Atopia.

The winter of 1913 and the spring of the next, fateful year, is lost to posterity, in respect of McAndrew.

Westminster police records confirm the abduction of Josie, the daughter of the Princess Maria, as being on the eighteenth of October, but Maria claimed her daughter's absence as two days earlier than that.

Nor is it known, by statement evidence, where McAndrew took Josie in the abduction.

Perhaps only Maria knew how slight the crime, for Josie, apparently, had proved a willing victim. There was no evidence of a struggle in the house in Duke Street; she had taken nothing with her save the clothes she stood up in, being careful to leave behind her anything that savoured of the schoolgirl.

Presumably, she was now a woman.

They had left, said a tearful Maria to the police inspector, at four o'clock in the morning, and nothing appeared to be missing save the artist's canvases, the contents of the larder, and two bottles of whisky.

Police reaction was immediate.

The Stirlingshire police were alerted but without success; no laird being unearthed in the county who laid claim to the name of McAndrew. The motto he enjoyed – 'No man threatens me with impunity' – in itself caused an affront, this being the motto of the Stewarts – nothing to do with the McAndrews. The clans bristled. McAndrew was, in fact, in more danger from outraged Highlanders than the police of Westminster and King's Cross, where a couple of the description of McAndrew and Josie were seen to entrain soon after dawn . . .

Speculation rose in the newspapers. Most concluded that, McAndrew having been a seaman, had spirited Josie abroad. His progress from Montmartre to Le Havre was tracked; enquiries made aboard all ships from Brittany, including the *Marie Prey*, where Jean Pierre, now hawking in the streets of Tiger Bay, mumbled incoherently in French patois behind the leather mask that covered his disfigured face. For the winch donkey-engine, exploding in a sheet of flame on the foredeck, had seared his features with shafts of super-heated steam, and the dwarf was blinded.

Now he stood outside the Golden Cross at the top of Bute Street, Cardiff, or sometimes, after a white-stick tramp to Barry, outside the Chain Locker, selling matches and boot-laces.

Questions, also, were asked of the landlord of the Morgan Angel Hotel Abergavenny, where McAndrew had once been seen at lunch . . . therefore, of the ladies Heston and Felicity Barre, who naturally insisted that the artist had never been under the roof of Linda Vista.

Police were alerted in Barry and Cardiff; Ross Bolton

437

himself was questioned, as was a now bed-ridden Ellie . . .
Even Tom was interviewed at Westminster School.

After six weeks of intense but fruitless inquiries, the name
of Josie, aged seventeen, daughter of the Princess Maria
Joseldon, was listed under 'Missing Persons'.

That was the last that was heard of either she or
McAndrew during the winter of 1913, and the spring of the
following year.

Nobody, apparently, had thought of even glancing in the
direction of Atopia House, where Mama Meg, ageing and
less talkative, still held court . . . and where a mural, com-
missioned by one named Uncle Dumb (long since dead . . .)
was still unfinished . . .

49

The mural finished, McAndrew left Atopia House hand in hand with Josie in springtime and the air was soft and warm, blowing south over the Yorkshire dales.

The Staindale brook was shouting with sun, misting her rainbow colours above the little waterfalls to the broader Thornton Beck, and the trees of Dalby Forest were blowing live and green in the wind. Badgers crawled from their earths and blinked at the sun, the dormouse stirred from her winter sleep. Reed buntings and kingfishers began their swooping flights above the reedy margins of the dykes, the 'ticky-tic-tic' and melodious 'teu-teu' of their sister, the lapland bunting, was exchanged for the high-pitched chirruping of the yellow wagtail, and McAndrew cocked an ear to listen as he and Josie went swinging over the dales: the whole, greening country of hills and valleys was alive with the rustle and tumble of April.

Early May found them down south; a giant scarecrow of a man walking with what appeared to be a ragamuffin boy, for Josie had her bright hair plaited under her cap.

The middle of May, when the celandines had faded and the sea pinks were in bloom, saw them deep in Wales, after following the Avon down Evesham Vale and treading on the gold-dross pathways of the Forest of Dean.

Four days later they were in the tap-room of the Golden Cross at the top of Cardiff's Tiger Bay.

"Got a room, landlord?" asked McAndrew, towering over the bar.

The man, as skinny as a workhouse broom and with an

eagle eye on him, was an undersized gnome from the bogs of Connemara.

"Father and son, did ye say?" the landlord asked, and peered at Josie, while she, with her ragged cap on one side, fixed him with her eyes of cornflower blue.

"Aye, me missus walked out on me, ye see," explained McAndrew, "so we're on the road," and he slapped down money. "Whisky for me, small beer for the lad."

"No wonder she departed," said the landlord. "For that's the fullest set of breeks this side o' the Greek Orthodox, no offence intended, son. Christ, ye'll have me bum in the county gaol for runnin' a disorderly house, so ye will."

"Would ye have me dear son expose his chest for proof, for God's sake?" asked McAndrew. "Is that what you're asking?"

"Heaven, no," said the landlord, "the shock'd kill the customers. Will three bob a week shoot ye dead, unless it's an unbearable hardship for ye to share a double bed?"

"We'll take it on a temporary basis," said McAndrew, "for this is a dump if ever I saw one." He sank his whisky and picked up his canvases. "And if your customers snore I'm makin' an official complaint. Where to?"

"Up to the attic and first left over the roof," said the landlord, "and in the name of God don't mention the name of Barney Corrigan if the Sally Army investigates."

The customers roared at this, lifting their mugs; a few younger men wolf-whistled Josie as she followed McAndrew up the stairs.

"Is it always like this?" she asked, in the attic.

"Ach no, child." McAndrew took her into his arms. "But you're dealin' with real people now, see – not the Burlington poofs and the Regent Street rogers, and I'm kicking that landlord from here to Rat Island if the fleas talk Irish."

"Are they your people, then?" asked Josie, examining the bed.

"Aye, every one, and I count 'em friends. She makes a fine Welsh stew, does Cardiff town, and the people she cooks are the salt of God."

"We'll be staying here long, Jim?"

She was standing by the window now, looking over a sea of crazy roofs and tumbling chimney-pots and they stretched down to distant Tiger Bay.

McAndrew looked into Josie's eyes.

Ellie's eyes, too, were of cornflower blue, he remembered. Josie said:

"Tiger Bay, you said they call it?"

"Aye, little love, we're home," said McAndrew.

Tiger Bay!

This was the Welsh port owned by the Marquis of Bute, one vying with Barry for title of the biggest coaling port in the world. A melting-pot of every nationality born since the start of Time, it shared no heritage with its sister Cardiff, but was of itself – a big sprawling enclave of docks and waterways, dividing within itself two civilisations, white and black.

The white population were the 'haves' – the coal magnates, shipowners, craftsmen and coal-trimmers – the upper crust of the wealthy and artisan classes. But, twenty-five nationalities populated the other side of Hayes Bridge: here the crews of the stinking fo'castles and galleys, half-starved for shareholders' profit, crowded into the squalid courts – the gin drinkers, the laudanum addicts of David Street, Union, Mary Ann and Millicent. And the Sailors' Home near Pier Head was crammed with the dross of human society.

Prostitutes sauntered among the taverns and bars in search of customers, many of whom, impoverished and ill, sought refuge in the Royal Navy mission ship at West Docks, or died unheeded, five thousand miles from home, in unfrequented hovels, doorways, doss houses and culverts.

Chapels like Bethania and Bethel, Wesleyan and Bethany Baptist, flourished side by side with brothels, grog shops, Chinese laundries and opium dens.

Wing Sang's 'Celestials', the Chinese pig-tailed Tongs of stranglers and cut-throats, haunted the gambling dens, where a sailor could lose his pay packet and be floating in the dock next morning. All was less than a sea-mile from Cardiff city's respectable St. Mary's Street, where Rawlins White lit a Protestant candle of martyrdom that illumined the high finances of Cardiff's city elders; they who later hanged an innocent Dic Penderyn for riot protest against their obscene profits.

Here the graves of the respected and loved lay in the shadows of alleys as disreputable as Silvertown, Soho, Harlem and the Bronx.

In the Cornish Mount, later that evening, there's more goin' on, says McAndrew, than Muldoon's bloody picnic, and he's right.

Half the night ladies of Peel Street are here, some still wearing their trade white aprons, and Tittyupover, head Mamasan of the tribe, leads the dance.

Scot McNally's accordion is blasting the time, Irish fiddles are screechin', Slanty Alf, the Chinese steward from the *Kobe Maru*, is puffing on his ophicleide, Spanish Joe from Malaga farts deep on his big bass horn, and Tittyupover is in form, tossing up her skirts to show her petticoats, and round and round she goes in the reel, while Bandy Jock does a Jolly Tar hornpipe and Big Bess Fergie clicks the castanets.

Major Gillis, cashiered from the Gurkhas and now lodging with Mrs. Posh in Christina Street, bawls the Eton Boating Song on champagne brandy (he's a fireman aboard the *Nellie van Ville*). Three West Indians from the Peel Street Easy Houses shoot dice, quarrelling falsetto, and six pig-tailed Chinese 'dry swim' mar-jongg in a corner to lend to the racket, and you've never heard such a blutty commotion, says Miss Alicia Smith, the Japanese barmaid, since the Splott Glee Club got into *Judas Maccabaeus* in the Cory Hall last winter.

McAndrew, with Josie following (still dressed as a boy) pushes open the street door, shoulder-charges the customers, and hammers the bar for ale. And Josie, momentarily alone amid the confusion of bodies, white, black and yellow, stares about her in growing consternation.

442

With a mug in one hand and a port and lemon in the other, McAndrew steers her into a corner, and he's just killing the quart when the street door goes back and Solly Fisherman rushes in.

"I left me pension wallet and a bottle o' stout for me missus on the bar," says he in a panic.

"You're wallet's still here," says the barmaid, "but the bottle's gone, tell ye missus, and I'll thank you, Solly, to decline your insinuations."

"Ach, thank God," says Solly, patting his wallet.

From the Cape Horn beerhouse next door to the Anglesea, White Swan, Golden Cross and King's Arms, the trumpets are playing and the mouth-organs going, for the port is crammed with luggers, steamers, coalers, paddlers, brigantines and sloops; cargo bummers from the West Indies, passenger liners from Europe, smuggling ketches from Africa and tramps from China.

Even the Kendall Freighters are here, now called Ross-Cambourne: the Cory ships and the Reardon Smith's, and you can walk from one side of Roath Docks to the other on their decks, they say.

The froth and dregs of the world is here; mulattos with their tribal scars, Portuguese and Indian, Lascars and Singapore Chinese, even a Tibetan performing a Demon Dance in the Glastonbury, wearing the mask of the 'Door Messenger of Yama', the God of the Dead.

Old crones are shrieking in the 'Snake Pit' of the waterfront Windsor Arms as the apparition approaches, kicking up their skinny legs all in a row, and not a tooth among them, says Madame, clattering the spittoons.

From the corners of the earth the sailors are flooding into Tiger Bay; the matlows of France with their hooped vests, looking for wine and women – and Peel Street can handle them, don't you bother, says Mrs. Claire of the waterfront taverns and grog shops where the German sailors roam, far from their beautiful Rhine and Danzig.

The Swedes are in the Norwegian lodging houses and the

Norwegians are in the workhouse Spike, grubbing a day's pickings on fourpence a night. Gamblers, beautifully turned out in tight breeks and resplendent waistcoats, farm the seamy dens; drunkards and wine-throaters reel down North Church Street, Sophia Street and Maria, flinging their money at the windows of the prostitutes.

The Spanish cafés and Maltese bars are thronged to the doors, with every colour God could create, says McAndrew – Chinese opium smugglers and hashish grooms moving like footpads in dark corners; women washing sailors' underclothes for two shillings a twelve-hour day, and West Indians singing calypsos and playing their steel bands.

Devon and Somerset policemen keep their boots up in Hodges Row when the Bay is filling, I can tell ye, says he – and if anyone shows disrespect to a Sally Army girl when she's collectin', I'll bloody kill 'em, says Bessie Bunter, the landlady of the Crown.

And it's the same wi' any bairn, too, remember – with the Bay at its worst a wee one can play her Hoopla or One, Two, Three Oolaary up against a wall, or hopscotch on the street. For the first hobo that touches a child down in the Tiger goes into the dock, d'ye hear me? asks Bridget O'Leary, the washerwoman – aye aye, the bugger goes into the dock, sure to God, and we leave the bugger to drown.

All right, says she, we've got our pros, we've got our randies, and there's gambling and opium and other goings on, but no more'n any other seaport, and at least we're honest. So give me Tiger Bay men any time over the so-called gents of Cardiff. You want a going over?

No, Missus.

Then mind what you say about the folks who live 'ere.

And so the music rises and the horn blasts blare and up goes Tittyupover again, doing her somersault act, while the customers yell their applause, including Mrs. Bernadette O'Hara, who has come home to die, aged eighty, and she lifts her fifth Guinness.

"Aye, me lads," says she, "this is a respectable establishment, and I'm applying to the Pope for a permit to die in

444

peace, God bless him," and she crosses herself. "Up ye go again, Titty me love, and show your respectables, for we'll all be as cold as clay corpses tomorrow."

"Don't look so shocked, me lovely," whispers McAndrew into Josie's ear. "You're lookin' at the people of the earth . . ."

The shouting and music died to a whisper.

"Dear me," says Bridget O'Leary, "here comes little Chu Chu."

Chu Chu is a marmoset monkey no more than eight inches high; dressed in a black frock coat and tiny trews, he has upon his head a little top hat and in his hand he holds a foot-long walking cane, silver-topped. He comes arrogantly, tapping men's toe-caps to pay him due respect.

The bar is silent, the boards slowly cleared by the customers to make a ring; Chu Chu stands motionless, his top hat lowered, his silver-knobbed cane under his arm.

"Have ye come to dance for us, Chu Chu?" asks Miss Alicia, the barmaid, and she nudges McAndrew. "He comes every Friday to the Cornish Mount – don't ye, my charmer? – never seen anything like it, Mister. Takes care of himself – his master, Old Soria, died, you see? So he just keeps working round the publics . . ."

Of a sudden the marmoset begins to dance.

"Bless his little heart," says Tittyupover. "He's better'n George Elliot any day o' the week."

Chu Chu began to dance.

And McAndrew swiftly drew out a board, and with charcoal began to draw.

There was at first no sound but the pattering of tiny feet on the boards and the coloured chalks and charcoal squeaks of McAndrew at work.

Levering himself up on to the bar counter for a better view, the Scot stared down at the scene below him, and drew, breath pent, with swift, professional strokes.

445

He saw the blunted features of the outcasts, those bereft of hope; the bulbous faces of the depraved, he saw; ale-soaked cheeks, thickened and nosed – the sickly, undernourished who preferred ale to food, but also the angular, skinny faces of deep-sea sailors, high-boned and ill; the crews of the big cargo-bummers, whose owners counted their profits in millions in Cymric House, while they ate weevil biscuits and putrid salt-beef on the Bay of Biscay runs.

The rouged and powdered faces of the prostitutes he saw, and slashed them on to the board; the genial smile of Mrs. Posh (now sick of weeping for Dai who lies fifty fathoms deep). McAndrew caricatured the yellow-faced Chinese with their key-board grins and flared nostrils, they of the drowsy, opium-heavy eyes slanted in their bony cheeks.

The wide, bright blue eyes of Bridget O'Leary, he captured perfectly (milking for two I am, mind, and another six at home – ten 'fore I'm finished – Christ, mun, I do love kids) – and her virtue he achieved at a stroke. He drew, watching all, while all watched Chu Chu, and beside McAndrew, unnoticing as he half-turned, Miss Alicia, the barmaid, cupped her chin in her hands and put her dimpling elbows on the bar, and her teeth were white in her flat, Oriental face.

McAndrew drew with incredible speed, his face alive with apprehension lest a single element be lost.

And Chu Chu danced in the pin-drop silence, twirling his cane, waving his top hat, crossing his tiny feet in minute and enchanting patterns, and Josie saw it, and was entranced.

Slanty Alf, the Cantonese steward watched, as did Big Bess Fergie, the dock-loader, she who worked with men and fought them bare-knuckle on equal terms. Spanish Joe, with his bass horn lowered, had one arm round the thick shoulders of Bandy Jock, hushing him into silence.

Major Gillis watched with the bleary eyes of the lost alcoholic, in dreams of distant India and the Raj: the West Indians, pulled from their dicing, shared their space with a big Nigerian, his face as black as watered coal. And the Chinese Chang Tai-lo watched (though his comrades didn't bother . . .) he who was a dreaded 'Celestial' Tong, and last night had killed a Turk for opium: Soot McNally who cleaned the boilers of the coal-burners, stared with coal-grimed eyes from his wasted, tubercular face.

Most of these were kneeling, but behind them, standing – crammed solid in the press – were the ladies of Peel Street with their clients on their arms: sipping gin, they stared from rouged and mascaraed faces, compassion on their mouths – the best human beings in the Bay, said some.

And, as Chu Chu danced, in came Bridget O'Leary, who was washing for fifteen and just dropped in for a stout, she cried, until she was flapped and threatened into silence.

For Chu Chu, alone in the world now, was dancing, and this was a Tiger Bay event. So Bridget put her chin on the scarlet shoulder of Tittyupover, and beamed down into the ring.

Chu Chu danced on, twirling his cane as his master, Old Soria, the dead Puerto Rican had taught him: now crossing his little feet on the boards, pirouetting, swaggering with the cane held bowed above him; waving his top hat as Soot McNally now accompanied him on his accordion.

So the marmoset danced and the accordion played and the people began to clap, and, as they clapped the time, so Chu Chu quickened the pace, bowing, prancing, leaping.

The tempo quickened. Soot McNally's big boots hammered the rhythm, and the people called for ale; glasses and mugs were passed around. The accordion pumped and blasted and still Chu Chu danced; the music rising to a higher, blatant song, them coming abruptly to a stop in a hammering of boots.

Then there was nothing but the chanting of the people and the tinkling of the dancing money, which Chu Chu collected in his hat.

When he had finished he bowed. The cheering and clapping rose to a tumult.

The marmoset then deliberately crossed the floor and

447

knelt before Josie. On one knee he knelt, an act of submission.

Laying down his hat and cane he opened his arms to her.

McAndrew auctioned the drawing, which was bought for two pounds by Major Gillis.

"Good payment!" said McAndrew.

"Gawd, that's nothin' in the Bay!" cried Miss Alicia. "Old Solly Fisherman, the jeweller, had a diamond ring in his window last week – a hundred and fifty pounds, and he sold it. Right, you lot – make way, if ye please," she called.

A Salvation Army girl came in selling *The Warcry*. The men dug deep into their pockets for coppers.

The girl was young, slim, bright-haired like Josie. Momentarily, their eyes met across the room.

After she had gone, the barmaid cried:

"Don't make sense, do it? The police are in Hodges Row, too bloody scared to come out, and she comes in here and lifts our money!"

"You come again, my ducks!" cried Big Bess Fergie, as the girl went out.

With his canvases under one arm and the other around Josie, McAndrew went into the night, and the moon was blazing over the Bay, making bright needles of its forest of masts and spars.

Seeing this, McAndrew remembered Barry Port and the old *Sarn Helen*, and Ellie . . . Then he heard a baby cry from a curtained, terrace window, and he remembered Tom, his son . . .

"What are you thinking of, Jim?" asked Josie.

McAndrew did not reply.

The night was suddenly cold. Chu Chu made a small complaining sound, and shivered.

Josie held him closer against her throat.

50

Tom came home from Westminster School in the late spring of that year – a dispensation granted him because of the illness of his mother. But Ellie was not at Cambourne, her doctors having decided that she needed treatment in a Kent nursing home, a care unavailable to her in Barry. Neither was Saul Plentyman (acting under orders from Ross Bolton) there to meet Tom at the station in the family trap, a duty he always performed.

And so, on his arrival at the station, Tom hired a gig to take him home.

The old familiar sights and sounds embraced him as the pony's hooves beat a metallic rhythm through Barry's crowded streets. And the sun beat down in swords of fire upon an industry heightened into panic proportions.

Railway engines were shunting, the sirens of *Nancy* and *Betsy*, the little saddle-tanks, were shrieking, their wagons clanging and clattering through the turnouts. Mule whips were cracking, great shires and drays straining to the carts, a thundering accompaniment to steam cargo-bummers lying out in the Channel – one by one they bellowed for lighters.

As if screwed by rag-bolts to the bed of the ocean, barges and ketches dipped and nosed in line astern, with cotton wool on their snouts; craft from Zanzibar, Spain and the ports of Brittany, their maws wide in exchange for the wealth of the Rhondda.

Fussy little tugs hooted and whooped, dragging out to sea the big coal-burners. Skin-boats, the big banana traders, glided in like ladies.

449

And over the sun-drenched scene the bawled commands of overmen, foremen, crane-deckers, rose like an obscene chorus as clattering snakes of wagons poured down their bright cascades of coal from the Welsh valleys.

But more – with the threat of war in the political air, a new freight was abroad – the secret canvas-covered flats of howitzers and ammunition wagons from the factories of the Midlands. And these added to the cacophony of confusion and noise . . . cannon that would later sheet the faces of nations with destruction, and the poppy lands of Flanders with blood.

"God!" whispered Tom. "I've never seen anything like it!"

"Changed a bit, has it, since you was here last?" asked the driver.

The sing-song articulation of the man, broad-faced and humorous, brought to Tom the old nostalgia for Wales.

"Young Tom McAndrew, ain't it?"

"That's right."

The Welsh weren't nosey, thought Tom, only curious.

"Your poor mam's not at Cambourne, ye know, sir. . . ?"

"Yes, I know."

"Gone into hospital in England, but comin' on tidy, so they tell me. Reckon you'll find a deal o' change at the big house now, though, beggin' your pardon."

"Likely so," said Tom, putting an end to it.

They were taking the dock road now, at Tom's request, going to Sully via Bendricks, and the road was jammed with artisans and labourers – men going off shift confronting others coming on.

The driver said, "The lodging houses are fair crammed, ye know. Six to a room – the beds are never cold. First we 'ad the navvies, now we got the dockers; the place is bulging at the seams – the old town ain't what it were, and I was born and bred in Barry. One moment peace, next moment bedlam.

"They call it progress," Tom observed;

"I calls it Sodom and Gomorrah. But mind you, this old

town'll keep its soul! *Diawch*, what's happenin' here?" The driver reined the pony to a halt.

On the corner of Dock and Bendricks a crowd was gathered.

Here a man was haranguing the workers, standing on a hillock, his fists upraised, and Tom recognised him instantly.

Old Jake, his grandfather, unaware of Tom's presence, bawled, his wizened face raised to the sky:

"Do not drink wine nor strong drink, thou, nor thy sons with thee, when ye go into the tabernacle of the congregation! That ye may put difference between clean and unclean. . . !"

"Ach, go home, old man!" shouted a man. "A pint never did anybody any harm!"

And Jake cried, "Leviticus ten, verse nine! The God of Israel has spoken! And you see before you one who is himself defiled!" He shook his blue-veined hands upward. "Once I was clean, but I abused myself with strong drink – as a stag defiles itself in its pit! Listen, brothers, listen. . . !"

"Ye drunken old sod!" yelled another. "You're a fine one to lecture us on abstinence – with your back teeth awash in the Chain Locker every night?"

"Yes, yes! But that was before I saw the light!" wailed Jake, near to tears. "'Give ear, O ye heavens, and I will speak . . .' I beg you to listen. Cursed are the publicans! 'Their wine is the poison of dragons.' But now I repent, for I have transgressed and betrayed my loved ones through drink. 'I have erred in my vision like the fallen prophets'."

"*Diawl!* Hook him out of it, for God's sake!"

"Ye daft old faggot, you're plaiting ye legs now!"

"Give him a whiff o' the barmaid's apron!"

"Send him back to his Bible class."

Tom was already pushing his way through the men. Reaching Jake, he gripped him and hauled him down.

"*Tom!*"

Jake stared askance into the boy's face.

"Aye, it's Tom, Grandad! Home now?"

"But who shall speak to the ungodly?" Jake fought himself free.

451

The driver of the gig joined them.

"Give me a hand with him, man," said Tom. "Make way, lads, make way," and he shouldered a path through the crowd, pulling Jake after him.

The old man sank to his knees, and wept.

"Pull yourself together, Grandad! Come on – home to Cambourne . . ."

Jake raised a tearstained face. "To that place of fornication and iniquity? Not I! Nor you, my son – I beg you!" He clung to Tom, swaying on his legs. "A nest of vipers, the hole of the asp!" He wiped his face, the action of the thirsty drunk. "O God forgive me!"

Tom sighed. "Where are you living now, then?"

"Church Terrace – Number Four . . ."

"That's Cadoxton – opposite St. Cadoc's," explained the driver of the gig.

"We'll take him there first," said Tom.

Neither he nor Jake saw the French dwarf standing nearby in the gutter. Laces and buttons and pins and matches he was selling from a tray suspended before him; Jean Pierre, though hearing all, saw nothing from behind the leather mask that covered his mutilated face.

After they had taken Jake to his cottage, the gig took Tom on to Cambourne, and the first person he saw in the stable yard was Saul Plentyman, the giant groom.

"Where's Mr. Ross, Saul?"

The groom replied:

"Down town, I heard say, but back soon, sir, accordin' to Megsie. And Miss Ellie's coming home Friday, anna that good news?"

"So the doctors told me. By the way, have you seen Rachel? She still works here, doesn't she?"

The big man hesitated, then said, "Now, that I don't rightly know, young master."

"You don't know?"

The gig drove away, the driver waving goodbye with his

whip. Saul stared senselessly in its direction, his flat face grooved with apprehension.

"Well, not workin' here exactly, if ye get me . . . Though she's around mind . . ."

Tom stared at his growing discomfiture.

He asked, "And Megsie, where's she?"

Relief mingled with exuberance in Saul's semi-idiocy. He bellowed unintelligibly and Megsie appeared from the kitchen, wiping her hands on her apron.

"Well, if it anna Master Tom!" she exclaimed, brightfaced.

"Didn't you know I was coming?"

"Not a word, dear soul!" She kissed him, hugging him.

"But I wrote to Mr. Ross."

Megsie, plump and portly now, patted and fussed him with inarticulate warmth. "Well, I expect he didn't think to mention it. But your mother's comin' home day after to-morrow, you heard?"

"Yes, I know. And Rachel – where's she?"

Megsie adopted an air of one not to be tampered with, her chin uptilted. "Now you think better of that question, Master Tom. Ye know full right I don't approve of upstartin' and goings-on . . ."

"Is she *here*? That's all I want to know."

"She's here all right, don't you fret!" Now it was a mood of disassociation.

"What does that mean?"

"Likely you'll find out, 'afore you're much older."

"You're talking in riddles, Megsie – come clean."

The woman walked away, saying over her shoulder, "You go and 'ave a look in the Big Wheatfield, Master Tom – an' then ye'll see how that Rachel's a'flourishin' – grown too big for her boots, you'll find."

"The Wheatfield?"

"Like I say – you go and look. Rachel and her tribe 'ave taken over, God help us."

Tom went to the rear of the house.

Beyond the duck-pond, under a line of elms that divided the fields from Cambourne's sloping lawns, five red caravans stood in a tinker semi-circle, not thirty yards from the lounge windows of the house.

When Tom returned he said to Megsie in the kitchen. "They've moved in, have they?"

"Ay ay. And once them tinker dollies get their claws into somethin', there's no shiftin' them. And they got their hooks into Cambourne, take my word. Your Grandad Jake moved out . . ."

"I know."

"And likely he's the start o' the rest of us – a fine kettle o' fish it is for Miss Ellie to come back to, and her so ill, bless her heart." Megsie fanned herself, one of her flushes.

"And Mr. Ross – what does he think about it?"

The woman turned, pale with anger. "Don't you talk to me about Mr. Ross, young Tom – never no more. I jist ain't used to the goin's on around here, in Cambourne." She shook herself in dull, surly anger, adding, "An I'm tellin' you something else, Little Tom – if it weren't for your mam, ye wouldn't see this Megsie for dust – and you don't help any, neither, come to that . . ."

"Me? What have I done?"

"You know dang well what you done, for God's sake – foolin' around with that little tinker brat, an' now she's high-handing it around as if she's Queen o' the May." Sweat sprang to Megsie's face.

"That . . . that's all over now."

"An' I should think so, too – it anna done your poor old mam any good, I can tell ye . . ." She paused, fighting her tears, adding, "Aw, come . . ." and she reached for him, clasping her against her. "Siddle ye here with old Megsie, and promise me . . . no more moonlightin' wi' that tinker bitch, now you've come home. . . ?"

Megsie had changed, he thought: before Bolton's arrival, she was one of antic and wit, but Cambourne had aged her, bewildering her comfortable sense of respectability.

Now Tom saw beyond her the unmistakable figure of Rachel walking swiftly along the drive to the front of the house. Megsie followed his gaze.

"Aye," she said, "that's what I mean – riding habit. She's been out gallopin' the mare, I expect. You left a tinker maid, son – since you've been away she's behavin' like the mistress of the house."

Saul Plentyman, still of a brooding silence, carried Tom's cases up to his room.

It was his own room. Hands clasped, Tom wandered around it in pent loneliness, his sense of emptiness enhanced by his mother's absence from her room next door.

From here he could see the Big Wheatfield.

Standing clear of the curtained window, he watched the tinkers coming and going between the five caravans on the edge of the lawn:

Pinta, he saw, also Tam Shenks, stripped to the waist, washing in a bucket: Mrs Tinker Bob, he saw, a woman he didn't recognise, and Evan Kinto, bent with age, a man he didn't know.

Other tinkers were there – women like Mrs. Florence, Rosa's mother, now as bent and scraggy as a witch, and a bearded giant of a man whom the others called Timoshenko, and this man was playing on a melodeon and bawling a tuneless song.

There was also a tinker in rags, of quiet gentility, whom the others called Lover, and another who was blind, tapping with a stick. Many young ones were there, too – young bucks of wide shoulders and brown arms – and pretty tinker girls in coloured costumes, and children – the children were everywhere; babies, toddlers, teenagers riding bare-back on the ponies.

These people, as Megsie had said, were taking over Cambourne, and it was astonishing to Tom that Ross Bolton was allowing it. For years his mother had been ordering them out of the Big Wheatfield: now they were practically in the house.

God knows what would happen, Tom thought, when his mother came home.

Later, he dressed for dinner, but kept to the room until he heard Megsie sound the gong in the hall: the discordant clanging was like the tolling of doom.

Ross Bolton, standing in the hall, was dressed with a fastidious grace that bordered, thought Tom, on the effeminate.

"Good evening, Tom. Welcome home, though I must say I expected us to meet a little earlier. We've a great deal to talk about."

"No doubt."

Bolton sat at the head of the table, his usual place. Tom sat on his right: his mother's chair at the other end of the table was empty, yet her place was laid with such care that it seemed as if Ross Bolton expected Ellie to walk in at any moment and sit without comment.

The new maid, a village girl of pale countenance and awkward gait, hovered before the serving-hatch with the nervousness of the untrained.

Bolton said, while the maid served the soup:

"You had a good journey down?"

"I did."

"But disappointed to find your mother hadn't returned?"

"I didn't expect it. Friday she's due home, isn't she?"

Bolton nodded, sipping his wine. "She's ill, you know . . ."

"I'm aware of it."

Tom was staring at the dresser.

It was here that Rachel used to wait, he thought: it seemed a century ago that Rachel used to stand there demurely, hands clasped, eyes downcast. Bolton's voice invaded his thoughts:

"You may be aware of it but you don't seem to appreciate it. Your mother may not live long . . ."

"I know that, too."

"Her blood complaint was initially delayed, but the progress hasn't been sustained."

"She should never have gone away."

Bolton emptied his hands over the table. "Had she stayed here you'd have accused me of inaction. London specialists aren't available in Barry. She needed special care." Bolton added with calm resignation, "It comes to us all." He waved

456

the maid away as she took his plate. "And this brings me to a business point. I'm due to London in the morning, so I've got to raise it now . . ."

"Couldn't it wait until she's dead?"

"Don't be dramatic!"

The maid was serving Ross again and he sat back in his seat. "Death is one of the basics, and I've got a business to run. You know, I take it, that your grandfather has passed over your interests to me?"

"I do now." Tom stared vacantly around the room.

"You're not interested?"

"Not particularly."

"Perhaps not, but you'll listen to what I have to say."

Tom said, "I know it already – you've sold out to the Barrow Consortium for four hundred and twenty-eight thousand."

The other nodded. "Your mother agreed to it, remember?"

"And you've bought a Whitby fishing fleet for two hundred and ten thousand, which leaves a couple of hundred thousand in your personal account, am I right?" Tom added bitterly, "We've been through all this. The only difference now is that you've pushed the McAndrews out of it."

"It's in your best interests, Tom. A directorship, when you come of age. . . ?"

"*God!* You know what you can do with your directorship!"

"It would be in your mother's interests, especially if she wants to stay on here in Cambourne."

"What does that mean?"

Bolton put down his knife and fork. "That I'm off up north. If I'm running a fishing fleet in Whitby, I can't do it from Barry."

"So, you're also walking out on her?"

"Don't you think she'd prefer it. We've long since ceased to be congenial company, haven't we?" Bolton raised his glass. "Indeed, I thought you'd be glad to be shot of me. After all, you've still got Cambourne."

Tom pushed away his plate. "What else have you left us?"

457

"A settlement of two thousand a year – even without the directorship, the pair of you could live very nicely."

"This will kill my mother. The fleet was all she lived for . . ."

Bolton got to his feet. "Perhaps, but she's likely to live that much longer without me around to pester her." He raised his face to the door of the room.

Rachel had entered.

Tom rose from the table, staring over his shoulder. Rachel entered slowly and with grace.

She was dressed in a white, silk gown that reached to her feet: her hair, turbanned upon her head in a chignon style, increased the effect of womanly dignity; her diamond ear-rings flashed, pearls were at her throat. Without a word she sat in Ellie's place at the other end of the table, facing Bolton; her face was cast down, her eyes lowered.

Tom whispered, "*Rachel. . . !*"

Bolton said, "The McAndrews have come to the end of the road, Tom; you might as well accept it. And I won't be going to Whitby alone, as you can see, even if you don't approve."

Tom said, "God Almighty!"

"There's not a lot you can do about it, you know. In the view of Jake, your trustee, your interests were best handled by me personally, and I assure you that they are. You still have Cambourne – true the fleet is mine – be fair, I built it up, you know . . . and a settlement of a couple of thousand a year . . ."

"A couple of thousand!"

Bolton shrugged. "You'd get a lot less if you had to work, my son. And in the circumstances, I doubt if you'd get an appeal through the courts. Besides, you're still rich – there's your father's money, remember. It's still in his name, I take it – unless, of course, it has vanished in debauch. . . !"

"If he were here, he'd kill you!"

"No doubt, but he isn't here, is he? And, what's more, he belongs to the same roguish company as I – with rogues, you know, there's a mutual admiration society on the go – at his rate of delinquency he'd be the first to admit it!"

458

"You're a bastard, Bolton!"

"Yes, of course – hasn't that always been patently obvious? But do try to be a little less Victorian."

51

It was a contemplation, thought Tom, of the absurd and the sublime; the usual elation that filled him when returning to Cambourne was sullied by the absence of his mother, the presence of Ross Bolton, and his apparent loss of Rachel.

He was undressing in the moonlight when a light appeared under his bedroom door; he heard the rustle of a skirt and saw a note pushed through on to the carpet of his room. Picking it up, he read:

> Darling Tom,
> Please, *please* meet me tonight. At the Spinney. Eleven o'clock. Don't let them see you.
>
> Rachel

Tom did not move. With the note clutched in his hand, he knelt there, listening to the sounds of the house: of Megsie clattering about in the kitchen below, and Ross pacing his room, which was above. Faintly from the Big Wheatfield he heard the sounds of music.

Rising, he went to the window and looked out into the night. A bonfire was blazing within the semi-circle of the tinker caravans. And near the bonfire was a woman Tom now remembered. Her name was Mrs. Tinker Bob, and she had once called at the stables for water: tall, erect, she was staring towards the house.

The moon hung low, speared by the poplars of Cambourne; the night seemed breathless with expectancy.

Tom glanced at his watch. The hands said ten-thirty. Hurriedly, he dressed again. A few minutes later he was out of the house and walking swiftly down the road to St. Mary's Well.

Rachel arrived riding side-saddle on the mare; she came at a gallop along the sands to the Spinney, and Tom, from the shadows, saw her coming in the moonlight. She was still wearing the long, white dress she had worn earlier at dinner, the hem of which she had tucked up under her knees, and her legs and feet were bare.

The mare snorted as she was reined to a canter, and her nostrils dilated, her white-balled eyes betraying her fear, for this, to her, was a Golgotha.

Rachel tethered her in the shadows of overhanging branches, and then walked slowly along the beach.

"*Tom!*"

Tom watched her. She looked like the wraith of a lost soul; indelibly part of the night, but unreal. Her hair was loose upon her shoulders, and the sea-wind took it, blowing it momentarily about her face. She called again, but her voice was drowned in the faint thumping of the breakers.

"You there, Tom. . . ?"

He came slowly out of the shadows; the mare saw him and whinnied.

Rachel quickened her pace, then ran into his arms.

"Aw, God!" she said.

He held her, uneasily, spitted on indecision, and she turned in his arms and stared up into his face.

"Aw, God help me," she said. "I prayed, ye see – I been prayin' all week as how you'd come back to me."

"And Bolton?"

She was instantly alert. "What about him?"

"Come off it, Rachel – It's obvious what's going on!"

Furious, she pulled herself away, her anger enhancing her rich, dark beauty.

"Hell is it? *Dai Dafto*! Is all the badgers alike 'cause they've got four legs? You got a damned cheek . . .!

461

"God, what do you take me for? You're living with him. What's more, you're doing it in my mother's house!"

"You believe that?"

"Of course I believe it! Everybody in the place knows what's happening."

"Pinta and Tam Shenks . . ."

"To hell with Pinta and Tam Shenks!"

"Aye, and to hell with you, too, if ye take me for a girlie! I done nothin' wrong, I tell ye – not yet, anyways. Perhaps I go up north with Bolton, perhaps I don't. But I don't sleep with nobody no more, Tom McAndrew, not since I found you." Her eyes pleaded. "They beat us both, remember?"

Tom stared about him, seeking mental escape, but she gripped his arms and swung him to face her, saying, breathlessly, "Aye, but you only 'ad it once. I've had it six times and more, before they got me into Bolton's bed – and then I were out, mind – faster than a monkey up a stick. And Bolton reported, so they beat me again, and Tam Shenks, he comes and stands on the lawn and Pinta and the young bucks come wi' sticks, but I got out o' the window. Aw Christ, I 'ad it sore . . ."

He stared down at her. There was a patent ability in tinkers, a poetic beauty that decorated the lies by tinker-tongue, and he hesitated, his feet shifting in the sand. Rachel said:

"Only once he had me, honest to God. And that was 'afore I met you, Tom McAndrew – cross me heart and spit on the Cross."

The wind moved between them; the sea, flat calm and hazed with light, was star-garlanded. Riding lights were bobbing in the distance, the skin-boats making east for Bristol, and their diesel knockings thundered on the sand. Rachel stared about her in a sudden, renewed fear:

"They'll 'ave us ag'in, mind, if we stay by here."

Tom emptied his hands. "Where to, then?" He added, distraught. "What are we doing together, anyway?"

"Because I loves you, Tom McAndrew. Take us to Sully, is it?"

"The Island?"

"Somewhere we can talk? You don't want me, all right – I didn'a come for loverin', Tom – just to be wi' ye, is it? Take us over to the Island – even Tam Shenks don't look for us there . . ."

Tom sighed, glancing at the moon. "The tide's right. It'll give us three hours, at least . . ."

Rachel jerked her thumb at the wide expanse of sand seaward. "If we take the mare I reckon we've got longer before the tide comes back in. Nobody is peekin' at folks over on Sully . . ."

"You've been there before, haven't you? God, I must be mad!"

"O *ah*!" She was suddenly joyful, her eyes screwed up and shining and her face was pale in the soft, warm light. "That's right – I been sky-larkin' over on Sully since I took to me bodice, but never no more. Not now, Mister, since I come sparkin' for Tom McAndrew."

Turning out of his arms she whistled for the mare and the animal broke the tethering branch and came to her, its head low, and nuzzled Tom for comfort.

They mounted her, Tom with the reins and Rachel with her dress tucked up and astride behind him, and the mare took the shrimp-pools slowly, knowing the journey by heart; picking her way with her double load among the rock outcrops, passing the broken ribs of the wrecked ketch where sailors drowned, and plodded, head down, over the quarter-mile stretch of sand that divided the Spinney from Sully Island.

And so they went together, Tom with the reins loose in his hands, Rachel behind him, her arms about his waist, and soon the Island came up out of the moonlight, in emblazoned silver, and its high escarpment rose from the east. Rachel cried at the sky as she leaped down on to the sand:

"And that's us – old Tam Shenks, Pinta and Evan Kinto can take a runnin' jump. Just you and me, Tom McAndrew, and to hell wi' old Bolton, too – just me and you, eh?" And she gripped his hands and drew him close to her as the mare went in search of grass.

463

Tom held her and they shivered involuntarily, for the wind was suddenly cold, like blowing over dead sailors' graves, for this do come a spooky old place at times, said Rachel.

"Come!" she cried then, and ran.

Tom hesitated, still untrusting. Then she shouted, "Oh, snakes alive! I be joyful ag'in now you've come, fella! Ach, look at your poor old monkey face – why so doleful? Catch me, kiss me, Tom McAndrew! Last one up the top of the hill is brainless."

She was off, her soaked dress held up, her brown legs twinkling.

Tom ran his fingers through his hair, grinning, then went after her, his feet slipping in the sand in plodding pursuit.

Josie Joseldon said, lying on the bed in the attic of the Golden Cross in Bute Street:

"It is strange that I should be in love with you, Jim McAndrew. I am seventeen years old and you are twice my age. You are all the things that I am not, I am all the things you were. And truly, the first time I saw you, I knew that I would love you and get nothing in return.

"Is it true, for instance, that you have a son called Tom, about the same age as me? Who did you love for him, Jim McAndrew, before you heard of Josie?"

Lying there, staring at the ceiling, she listened to the sounds of the street below; the knife-grinder with his mule and cart, the lamp man with his donkey and hooded wagon and a dozen oil lamps swinging, smelling of oil and kerosine.

Josie heard the clattering coal-wagons making for the docks, the big shires hauling their eternal beer-flats of the brewers; the high pitched quarrelling of Welsh wives, and their sing-song kindness, the bawling of babies, the steel hoops clanging down the Bute Street pavements, and she said, in her mind:

"It is clear to me now that you are not in love with me, Jim. So, is it possible, I wonder, to have a one-sided love affair

464

with oneself – one partner giving, the other taking all? So that one speaks words of the heart and hears replies from the heart of a rival?

"Why is it, I wonder, that kindness, if given too often, dilutes into an impoverished gift? That affection, given too readily, is misconstrued as weakness, that gentleness becomes only a fool's dance and love, if pledged, becomes disdained? Because, that is how it has become between you and me, Jim: my love affair is now with myself.

"Sometimes, you know, when you are making love to me and I hold you within myself, I hear the voice of another talking inside you, and the words this woman says are the words I am speaking myself, but it is not my words you hear, my darling, but hers. How can it possibly be that I give to you so much of myself and receive so little affection back? My woman's intuition tells me that female cunning holds back one small thing to call her own – something that no man shares. But I love you so well, you see, that this is not possible for me to do.

"Really, I sound like a stupid schoolgirl, talking this way, but . . . has this been my mistake, I wonder, in giving you my all?"

The cockle man was coming down Bute Street. Josie heard him cry, almost inarticulately, "Cockles, mussels, cockles, mussels. . . !"

The child in Josie warmed to him.

One must take a basin (it could never happen in Girton, of course, and certainly not in Duke Street . . .) yes, one took a white china basin, and into this basin the cockle man would pour them and you took them to the sink and washed them, and even after washing them there would still be grains of sea-sand at the bottom of the bowl.

Then you would boil them and eat them hot, with bread and margarine and vinegar, and no caviare of Duke Street (which she had eaten many times) could compare with a two penn'orth of cockles and mussels bought in Bute Street from the man who lived on Rat Island.

"Oh God, Jim, what am I going to do?" said Josie, and

465

turned her face to the window where the evening sun was slanting on to the boards.

"Sometimes in your sleep you call her name . . . 'Ellie, *Ellie. . .* !' you call. Is she your wife? If so, why do you not speak of her, except in sleep?

"Once you painted me. It was on that first canvas you did in Duke Street – the one you took to Atopia House and transferred it to the great mural there – *The Feast of Madness*.

"And it was true madness, Jim, because the face of every woman on that canvas was the same – different bodies, different shapes, different ages, different clothes . . . but all their faces were the same . . . Do you realise that the face of one woman only is painted on your mind. Is this the woman you call to, the Ellie you keep for your dreams?

"How is it possible to combat this? Perhaps, were I older, I would know how to do it. But, because I do not know, I conduct my love affair alone, with outward affection returned, without inner response. So I am not of myself – I, Josie Joseldon, the daughter of the Princess Maria – my name is *Ellie*. And the role I play in your life, Jim McAndrew, is to give myself to you as another.

"Don't you think it sad that I should lie here crying, while you are downstairs in the bar? Indeed, I would go back to Duke Street if I did not love you so well, and . . . if you did not need me so much, even though you forget my name is Josie."

Jean Pierre, the French dwarf, tapping with his white stick, came into the bar of the Golden Cross, climbed awkwardly on to a high stool and sat there with his leather mask covering his face and his straw hat perched upon his head.

A few loungers glanced up, but only McAndrew, who was hunched over a quart in a corner of the room, really saw him.

The dwarf sat unmoving, alone in his blindness; his tray of wares he had left on a seat near the door.

McAndrew lit his pipe, his hands cupped to the blaze of the match. Jean Pierre, for his part, took from an elegant cigar case a small cheroot; this he put between his thick lips, the only part of his face visible, but did not light it.

McAndrew rose ponderously and went to the bar counter, beckoning soundlessly to the Irish landlord.

"Absinthe," he whispered, waving towards the dwarf, and slapped down money. The landlord nodded and put the absinthe on the bar in front of Jean Pierre.

"Paid for," he said, in passing.

McAndrew waited, his thick, muscular arms on the bar. Jean Pierre's hand went out, found the glass and raised it to his lips.

"*À votre santé*, Big Savage," he said.

McAndrew did not reply but lit the cheroot between the Frenchman's lips, then went up the stairs to the attic, and Josie.

McAndrew believed Josie to be asleep on the bed, therefore he washed with care in the tin bath in the corner of the room, fearful of awaking her. And she, with her eyes half closed, watched him with a joy of possession she had never known before.

Stripped to the waist, he rubbed the soap over his big, brown body and the suds laid a mantle of bubbles upon his great, leonine head and golden beard.

It would have been bearable, Josie thought, had he been one to pass in a crowd – one of the hundreds who filled the publics to which they played night after night. Chu Chu, the marmoset, stirred against her on the bed, and she held him deeper into her warmth, fearful lest he should awake and betray her.

Yes, night after night now they played the publics in Tiger Bay, she and Chu Chu dancing, McAndrew doing his caricatures, selling them these days for five guineas a time.

Yes indeed, she reflected again, with any other man but Jim McAndrew it would be possible to return to her mother: now that the trouble was upon her, she longed for the comfort of a woman's advice . . .

Often she had wondered if she should tell McAndrew of her condition.

She was in her second month now and the early sickness had begun. But she was fearful that he might leave her if he knew about the baby . . . McAndrew's moods were unstable; they vacillated between yawning chasms of despair and scintillating joy, and he was painting with a fever that contained them both – studying late into the night the theories of the Japanese aesthetic, the basis of Gaugin's Synthetism.

And, while in every way he showed Josie affection and care, there existed in his every action the independence of a roving spirit; he longed, she knew, for the literary and artistic circles he had found in France, both at the Château Malromé and the old Café Noir.

More, he was discovering new worlds within Cardiff itself: well-known patrons of the arts were now venturing into the Bay to see him at work; the nouveau riche dilettante with its unbred gentlemen and faintly vulgar wives, who saw in Welsh Tiger Bay a smudged replica of French Montmartre.

This worried Josie further. It was bringing to him (and this she sensed) a new identity of fame, and he was working in the attic studio like a man possessed, often calling her from sleep to stand for him, weary or only half awake after an evening of dancing.

From the Salutation to the Ocean Wave and the Cape Horn publics she danced – to the White Swan and the Antelope – six and seven houses in a night.

It could not continue.

Soon, Josie knew, she would have to tell him about the baby . . .

As if by some intuition McAndrew was suddenly aware of her eyes upon him, and his hands paused on the towelling. Approaching her in half nakedness, he bent above the bed.

"Me sweet, wee Josie," he said bassly, and kissed her. "Me dear thing, I'd die for ye, do ye know that?"

Josie wondered if he would. Or if, in her later travail, he might even paint her black, as he had boasted, when in his cups, of painting Chocolat white . . .

The coming of the baby could mean the kiss of death. She was living now within a cubic world of Rabelaisian colours, of luminous, emotional responses to light and shade; a monumental primitism one moment, traditionalism the next.

"Will you stand for me, darlin'?" He shook her shoulder now.

"Oh, Jim, I'm tired. . . !"

"Aw, come on, woman! Nobody's askin' ye to bleed to death – for God's sake – ye can sleep any time . . .

"And hold your stomach in! D'ye know something, Josie? For a young 'un you're gettin' a fine middle-aged pot on ye, so ye are!"

She held her stomach in.

The great thing was to keep your self-esteem, thought Josie, even if you had to take your clothes off.

52

It was two o'clock in the morning when Tom and Rachel left Sully Island. The sea appeared shrouded in snow, a transfiguration by moonlight, and the low thumping of the breakers had subsided into a dull, threatening swell.

The lovers came slowly, their arms around one another, to a place of sand in the lee of the wind, where the white mare was standing. She raised her head and whinnied a welcome to them, but they did not reply.

"What now?" asked Tom.

"I anna goin' back, Tom McAndrew. I ain't never goin' back, you hear me?"

"It's going to be tricky."

"No it ain't. It's no more tricky than tinker-duckin'. . ."

"Tinker-ducking?"

"Takin' the broad road instead of the narrow – movin' out on the caravans away from the babbies. Lots of tinker girls do it, and never come back."

"Running away, you mean?"

"Ay ay. I'm for Tom McAndrew 'cause he's my fella. Not for no bugger am I goin' dry, not that Ross Bolton especially. He's got to move sharp, I tell ye, to take me bodice."

Tom looked at the sky. Rain-drops, steady at first, began a soft pattering on their upturned faces. Rachel said, quickening her pace, "Meanwhile, we best get shiftin' lest the rain do come with the change of the tide."

"The change of the tide with the rain, you mean," added Tom, and gripping the rein of the mare, he ran, with Rachel following. On the edge of the sands they looked to the distant Spinney over the wide, intervening causeway.

"We've left it a bit late, I think," said Tom. He glanced at his watch.

"Ach, dunna fear, lad! Take us on the old mare, and we'll gallop."

Tom shook his head. "Too dangerous, among the rocks."

"Dear me, yes, the old moon's dyin'," and Rachel stared up at the sky as the moon disappeared behind storm-swept clouds. She squared up then, a fighting stance and showed her fists. "What say ye, then – do we stay all night?"

"Can you imagine what will happen in the morning!"

"Or run for it, then – you first with me after ye, and God help ye if I catch ye!"

The rain began a downpour. Tom cried, above the suddenly rising wind, "Let's try it, then, we can always come back." He stared at the distant mainland.

The tide was coming in fast now, building itself up in flat, swimming layers.

Rachel cried, "Try the old mare, I say. She knows this place like the back of her hoof – come on, mun – we can always loose her and run for it."

But the mare shied when Tom tried to mount her, and even when he clambered over her back, she shied again, whinnying, as Rachel, hooking her arm around Tom's, tried to get on behind him: precious time was lost.

The rain was cascading, the moon vanished behind purple, scudding clouds. But now, with Rachel gripping his waist, Tom dug his heels into the mare's side and she took the Island lee sand first at a dangerous gallop, her flying hooves sending up spray.

Tom reined her in when they reached the narrow causeway, a pattern of rocks worn by generations of journeyings from the Spinney to the Island. Here were the treacherous rock-pools and outcrops that forbade speed and the horse picked her way expertly among them. Now forelock deep in the incoming tide, she slowed to her own pace, and Tom let her have her way.

471

Rachel shouted above the wind, "*Dammo di*, it do come in fast don't it! Heel her, for God's sake," for the tide was layering up in little foaming patches, and, reaching the point of no return, they heard its thunder: a building up before unseen forces, the towering tides of the distant Channel, now lost in rain and spray.

The mare struggled on, up to her girths in water, her hooves scrabbling for a hold over the pinnacles of the rocky causeway; now sinking precariously into hidden seaweed pools. And this bucking staggering flight nearly unseated them both.

The wind was howling now, whipping up the breakers, and these flooded in, splashing against the mare's flank, threatening to overturn her. Tom shouted above the growing thunder:

"We'd best jump and run, girl. If she slips we're off!"

"I'm already off!" shrieked Rachel, and fell sideways into the flood. And the bore took her, sweeping her legs from under her, so that she had to grip the mare's saddle to stay upright. The tide became fiercer every moment now.

The mare was whinnying pitifully, wallowing in aimless circles as the sea began to claim her. And the added weight of Tom and Rachel, grimly hanging on to reins and saddle, bore her down against the sea's strengthening thrusts.

In her small brain there moved a primaeval thought of long dead ancestors: this memory took her into thunderous caverns beyond the tides, where the little fishes go . . . the little fishes that swam in the eyeless skulls of a hundred mares and stallions from the ship that foundered off Avonmouth, piling up their carcases a century ago.

Knowing this by instinct, and the bubbling, distended agony of death by water, the mare leaped high, shaking herself free of the restricting humans. She wallowed and plunged, and the sea took her joyfully, overturning her, so that she went high at first, breasting the sea that bore her down . . . before slowly sinking, to rise again, head streaming foam, in a somersaulting of flying hooves.

Flung clear, Tom and Rachel were initially separated,

sucked down by the flood. Tom rose first. Flinging water from his hair, he grabbed at Rachel as her white dress billowed past on the racing tide. He gripped the dress and hauled himself upon her; was sucked under water again, but rose at once, kicking for air – and gasped at it, one great lung-full, before the weight of Rachel again pulled him down.

The incoming tide between island and mainland was six feet deep now, the race rising to its bore. And as Tom gripped Rachel's hair and pulled up her face, the mare, pawing water, floundered past them in the foam-topped waves.

"Tom! *Tom!*"

Rachel screamed, but the scream died as the sea washed over her.

Clasped together now, with Rachel's long hair and white dress trailing behind them, they were drawn under by unseen hands, down, down into green coldness: like mating fishes they went, enwrapped together in stillness, and the undertow took them and hurried them along, down, down.

And then, by some unknown force they were lifted up; lifted and projected up to the surface – momentarily to float there among the eddying swim, and Tom shouted once, unintelligibly, before a whirlpool took them again, spinning them round, sucking them down again into a world of silence.

With his lungs slowly filling Tom stared into Rachel's ashen face, knowing it in but a second snatched from time. He saw her eyes, wide and startled; her open mouth he saw in a ringing silence – the redness of her tongue and lips, and her hair was flowing out like red seaweed behind her.

There was coming to them an eerie, bubbling peace as, clasped together, over and over they rolled. And the current took them in that last embrace, making them eternal lovers.

They were gripped together within a world of icy silence; beyond the call of sound, free of pain, removed from the instinct to stay alive. It was enough, it seemed, to lie in the arms of the sea; to sink lower, lower . . . to be thrust up yet again and sink again . . . into the comfort of oblivion.

They did not struggle now; their mouths no longer gaped

473

for air, their eyes were closed. The last tribulation of death by water drowned the need to survive.

Over and over, still together they went, like dolls in death, the playthings of the sea. Their faces were pressed together, their limbs quiet.

In this manner they sank to the bottom of the Channel and glided along in each other's arms, bumping gently over stones twenty fathoms down. And came to rest beneath an overhanging crag among the sand dunes of the sea.

There they rested, with the incoming tide but faintly disturbing them: only Rachel's hair moved now, floating out; binding them together, like a shroud.

Above them the tide was full, the wind quiet, the rain had ceased.

53

It was Saturday night in the Golden Cross and the bar was full, and not only with dockers, navvies and seamen: city gents were there with willowy ladies on their arms. Fat, bejewelled ladies were there, commercial gentlemen from the Tiger Bay and Cardiff halls of business, men in evening dress on their way to the Royal, the Queen's or the Angel hotels.

They had come to see McAndrew draw and Josie tap-dance.

And she, dressed in a man's black evening dress and tails, with a top hat on her fair head, her face corked black and a silver-knobbed cane in her hand, tap-danced in a circle around Chu Chu, the tiny marmoset, similarly attired.

McAndrew, perched high on the bar counter, drew caricatures of the customers with a speed and artistry that left them gasping. They, thronging in from the street, stood on chairs and tables to gain advantage, the rich rubbing shoulders with the poor.

In a corner of the room, away from eyes that might be outraged by his deformity, Jean Pierre, the French dwarf, played on the melodeon George Elliot's music-hall song. And every customer in the place was singing, the Welsh among them in full harmony:

> By the light (*Tap-tap-tap. Tap-tap-tap . . .*)
> Of the silvery moon (Silvery moon, silvery moon)
> I love to spoon (*Tap-tap-tap. Tap-tap-tap . . .*)
> To my honey, I'll croon (I'll croon, I'll croon)
> Honey moon (Honey moon, honey moon)

475

Keep on smiling in June (In June, in June)
Your silver beam will guide love's dream
We'll be cuddling in June . . .(*Tap-tap-tap. Tap-tap-tap* . . .)
'Neath the silvery moon. (*Tap-tap-tap. Tap-tap-tap* . . .)

And, as the verse was repeated from a hundred throats, so
Josie and Chu Chu danced together in the ring of people, he
raising his top hat, Josie twirling her cane; crossing their feet
in the tap-tapping, bowing to one another.

And the clients, their faces entranced, sang, hypnotised by
the saw-dust ring before them.

Beefy faces with blue jowls or bottled noses watched;
knife-cut chins, lanterned jaws and double chins of good
eating and layered fatness – sideboard whiskers set on
throaty collars, wing-tipped and starched; the fuzzy-wuzzies
of Big Business, the baldies of commerce, all were here, and
the Adam's apple leaping of the skinnies, too, were watching,
and every one was singing. And the faces were merry of
countenance – merry even though wan with illness, bloated
with ale; and many bright with goodness.

"By the light, by the light, by the light, of the silvery
moon . . ."

Sweating cheeks, flabby cheeks, the hollowed bones of
hunger; faces beaded with gin or powdered; the dignified
make-up of genteel ladies, the rouged cheeks and carmine
lips of the libertines, all were there in the Golden Cross that
night, with Irish Joe Lillie, the landlord up on the bar
counter doing a leprechaun gig with his arms akimbo, his
little boots cocking up, and his one-armed missus beating the
time with the copper stick she used for easing out the customers.

McAndrew drew and drew on his boards with charcoal,
frowning up under his heavy brows at potential clients, with
the quality women making the best of themselves in poses
and the common women unaware, stamping their clogs or
clapping to the time . . . "I love to spoon . . . love to spoon,
love to spoon . . . to my honey, I'll croon . . ."

Josie and Chu Chu danced, the landlord did his gig, Jean

476

Pierre pumped on his melodeon, and the people sang, swaying, swaying, swaying . . . and even the tom cats stopped their caterwauling to listen on the cut glass, said Josie afterwards, when the Golden Cross got going on George Elliot that night.

And in they came from the street, joining in the palaver, cried Irish Joe.

Bobbie Jones and Copper Nobs the Tiger Bay policemen came, and 'Have a pint with me, love,' said Sophie, the Italian barmaid, and they had just drowned their teeth when the chorus began again, and they were in there beating time with their pewters, and the dancing and singing nearly raised the dead in the C of E over in Llandaff, said Tittyupover, who was going religious these days, folks said, having seen the light.

Even the Sally Army girl was singing, said McAndrew afterwards – "And do you know I sold six canvases that night, and two to the Chamber o' Trade – for hanging in the Mayor's parlour, would ye bloody believe it? Twenty-five smackers, Josie – there's some bottles o' whusky. . . !"

Round and round goes Josie, dancing to Chu Chu who stands in the middle, twirling his silver cane, throwing up his little coat-tails, and the saw-dust is on his tiny patent leather shoes.

All the clients are beating the time now, with the dancing rising to a climax of tapping and colour.

When the song ended the dancers were stilled, and there came from the room a bellowing shout, and everybody was around Josie, patting and kissing her and trying to get at Chu Chu, who was up on Jean Pierre's shoulder (having now adopted him) and McAndrew was handing out the drawings and collecting money, with Josie wrapping the caricatures and old Constable Nobs trying to kiss her.

Constable Jones has a bag of fish and chips under his helmet, with a cod's backbone hanging down by his ear, shouts Bridget O'Leary, who has just come in for the washing to keep her eight kids, and more expected.

The last customer had just been assisted out with the

477

landlady's copper stick when old Jake Kendall, Ellie's father, appeared in the doorway.

"Ease off, old man, it's time," said Irish Joe, the landlord, and pushed him off the threshold.

"Hold ye horses a bit" said McAndrew, staring into the dark. "This man I know . . ."

Josie, with Chu Chu in her arms, stood aside as Jake entered. His face was wasted and wet with tears and he swayed to the fumes of gin. He said up into McAndrew's face:

"Thank God I found ye, Jim! Ellie's needin' ye, by God!"

McAndrew said levelly, pushing Josie behind him, "Is that a fact? Has she ever needed me before, then? In a dozen bloody years? Away, ye skinny wee scoot!"

"Ye son's dead, Scotsman . . ." Jake wrung his small, red hands. Tears welled up in his eyes and splashed down his tattered coat.

"Ye what?" McAndrew bent, staring down.

Silence.

Beyond the public door, pale-faced children of the night were standing in the rain; their faces puddles of wetness.

McAndrew reached out, gripped Jake and shook to rattle him.

"Ye old swine! Ye're lying to bring me back. . . !" But his grip suddenly relaxed and he bent to Jake, his eyes growing wide with horror, and the little man swayed in his hands.

"My Tom . . . did ye say. . . ?"

"Your Tom's dead, Jim. Drowned. They got his body off Bendrick's sands. The dwarf told me you was in Cardiff, but I've been three days findin' ye in Tiger Bay . . ." He went on tiptoe, peering up. "You've got to come . . . I tell ye, you've got to come, Jim – our Ellie's goin' mad."

McAndrew raised his hands and put them over his face.

Josie took McAndrew, leading him away; Jake followed uncertainly.

Jean Pierre, still in his corner and with Chu Chu still on his

478

shoulder, stared sightlessly into the lamps from behind his leather mask. Josie heard the landlord say,

"Watch him, Missus, for God's sake . . . I know his sort, he'll smash the place up, so he will . . ."

"Come with me," said Josie, and took McAndrew's arm.

"Hush you, hush . . ."

"*Hush*, I say. . . !"

They gathered about her, whispering advice.

"Just leave him to me," then said Josie. She turned to Jake. "Where is his wife. . . ?"

"She's in Barry, woman! Don't ye even know?"

Josie said, "Get a trap . . ."

"A trap. . . ?"

"A trap, man. And wait outside." Over her shoulder as she led McAndrew away, she said, "He'll be down soon. Wait, I tell you."

"Wait, did ye say?" Jake's voice rose. "His son's dead, and ye tell me to wait? Ye cheeky young whelp, who the hell are you. . . ?"

"*Wait*," said Josie, "or he may not come at all!"

Jean Pierre took Chu Chu off his shoulder, and held him against his face.

After McAndrew had gone with Jake to Cambourne, Josie took off her male evening dress and lay on the bed in near nakedness, not even bothering to wash the cork and white paint from her face.

The attic was hot, the atmosphere pervaded by an acrid smell of paint and charcoal; the easel, standing near the window, had upon it a half-drawn portrait; fingers of moonlight felt the shadows.

Josie stiffened on the bed when she heard stumbling footsteps on the stairs; rose and covered herself with a gown when she heard the unmistakable tapping of Jean Pierre's stick.

Never before had the dwarf come to the room.

Sitting on the bed, tense, she watched the handle of the door.

There came a faint knock.

"*Josie* . . . It is I, Jean Pierre."

"What do you want?"

"Little, but it is necessary that I talk with you, Mademoiselle." His accent was lilting; his voice, deep and pure, was untroubled by the mask.

"Can it not wait?"

"It cannot."

Josie hesitated, then crossed the room and opened the door.

The dwarf said, sitting facing the bed, "You will be leaving here now that Big Savage has departed?"

"Big Savage will come back to Josie, Jean Pierre."

The little man nodded. "But if he does not return, will you still stay and dance?"

Josie looked at the window. "Perhaps not."

"*Sacrebleu!*" He clasped his hands in pleading and bent towards her. "Of course you cannot stay – it would not be possible." He hesitated, "If you do not stay and dance, would it be possible for me, Small One, to keep the marmoset?"

"Of course, Jean Pierre." Josie rose from the bed.

The Frenchman opened his hands to her. "For you Chu Chu is a friend, but for me a living – also a companion, you understand. He could be my eyes, *n'est pas?*"

"I would want you to have him, Jean Pierre."

Perched on the chair, with his legs crossed beneath him, he looked, thought Josie, like some small, primitive monster spewed up from the night. The window moonlight was upon his face and the mask shone dully above his thick, shapeless mouth: his small hands were gripped together as if in supplication; his flat, straw hat perched ludicrously upon his crown and at a merry, rakish angle.

The child in her banished the fears of the woman; he was like a small, outrageous doll, with which a child could play. Yet she sensed his dangers. His voice, bass and beautiful, belied the exuded sense of evil. Men feared this one;

strangely, despite his afflictions, women did not. Josie said, moving closer:

"Is there something more important?"

"Of course. Do you think I have come here to talk to you about a monkey? – even I, Jean Pierre, who is an expert when it comes to monkeys? You will listen?"

"Of course."

"Big Savage will not return to you. Do you hear that?"

"I hear it, but I do not believe it."

"In your head you do, so believe your head, Small One, and not your heart . . ." He reached out, touching moonlight. "Come, sit at my feet . . . more, Small One, let me touch your face, so that I can see to whom I am speaking? Come, do not be afraid. Is it not excellent luck to be touched by a dwarf. . . . ? Come . . ." He cajoled her, waiting. "Please. . . ? It is so small a gift . . . just a touch. . . ?"

Josie closed her eyes, then slowly moved, kneeling before him.

The dwarf reached out a small, hairy hand: with infinite gentleness his fingers touched her forehead, then slowly traced the lines of her face, her hair. "The colour of this?"

"My hair is fair."

"Ah, such a pity! When in my mind I had painted it black – the colour of Mignon's hair." He turned his face upwards as if in contemplation. "So beautiful was Mignon's hair – she could sit upon it you know – indeed, many said it was the most beautiful head of hair in Brest. But I did not know – I saw no others . . ."

"Mignon. . . ?"

He ignored it, saying, "Tonight, down in the bar, the gendarmes came, did they not?"

"Old Constable Jones and Nobs? They are not gendarmes! They are friends!"

"Who knows? Sometimes they are friends, yes, but sometimes they are also policemen, and tonight they come to watch. Who is this school-girl? they ask – the child who dances in the taverns, yet speaks with an educated tongue? Who is this who acts the wife to a mad artist – he whom men

481

call the Big Savage? *Eh Eh?* It is a good question, is it not? So they come to drink, these gendarmes, but also to watch. And tonight, perhaps, they telephone the gendarmerie in London? The professors at the Cambridge school, perhaps – or a mother in Duke Street? Who do they telephone, Small One?"

Josie said faintly, her hand to her throat. "You know, don't you!"

"I am no fool. I make enquiries. Blind I may be, but I talk and others reply; I hear, and am heard. I taste, and the taste is bad to me; I smell, and it is not good. Listen to Jean Pierre, for my life is finished and yours is just begun, eh?

"*Listen*, Small One. Big Savage has gone, and he will not come back to you. Two people he loves in his life – himself first, and mostly, and then his wife, the one called Ellie. She is ill. Perhaps she will die, I understand. But even if she dies, he will not come back . . . because he has never really been here."

He opened his hands to her in pleading. "Be sensible. It is necessary in life to accept the truth. He is gone. You are alone. Soon the police will come and take you . . . and this I will not allow. While I live, no man will take you where you do not wish to go. You are with child, are you not. . . ?"

Josie rose to her feet, staring down at him. The little man said:

"I think you are with child because when passing your window I hear your sickness. Big Savage does not hear you, but I hear it, and am sad. For this happened to my lovely Mignon Marat, when she was in the same condition. Come, come, *mon amie*! How is it possible to dance with a baby in your belly?" His arms opened expansively. "*Voilà!* Be sensible – go back to your mother, the Princess Maria, in London. If she loves you even as much as I, she is in tears like me. Go home, my small Mignon . . . go home and forget this mad McAndrew. He is my friend, that is why I talk for him. Pack your belongings, and before the gendarmerie come, I will take you."

"Why are you doing this?"

Jean Pierre smiled behind the mask.

"Because you are not called Josie, the woman who served Big Savage, in the bed and in the bar; no, you are not!" He clapped his small hands together. "Your name is Mignon . . . Mignon Marat, I call you, when I hear you dancing; and you do not come from London with a fine education, but from *Carmaret-sur-Mer.*

"You are a peasant with red lips and black hair, one who serves in the Café Village, and who waits for me at the end of the lane near my parents' house, but to whom I cannot go . . . because of this." And he touched the mask. "Only this woman held me; to her I once made love, but to no other. You understand, Small One? There are certain things it is not possible to do. And so, when I hear you speak and dance, I call you Mignon and change the colour of your hair."

483

54

Megsie was standing in the entrance of Cambourne when the trap arrived; McAndrew leaped down from the trap, and, followed by Jake, ran past her into the hall. Taking the stairs three at a time he ran upstairs and burst into Ellie's bedroom.

The sight of Ellie lying motionless struck him into immobility.

Slowly, without sound or expression, he approached the bed.

Megsie, panting, watched him from the doorway.

McAndrew stood there, staring down; Megsie said:

"I . . . I came in this evenin', Mister. Nigh six o'clock, it were, and she were gone."

"Ach, Jesus!" said McAndrew.

Jake joined them, moving around to the other side of the bed, his hands screwing together, but he did not speak. Megsie said:

"It were Tom, ye see. The . . . the tinkers was in the house after Mr. Bolton left, you understand? When . . . when she come home four days back he was gone, but she didn'a say nothin' about that. The tinkers was here – down in the ground-floor rooms, but she didn't say nothin' about that, neither.

"But then, the day she heard Tom died, she had a stroke . . ." She looked up at McAndrew with tear-filled eyes. "She . . . she were that ill when she come home, mind. I . . . I did all I could, really speakin'. . ."

Jake said, bitterly, turning away. "It was the tinkers. Like I told ye, Scotsman, they come in and took over when Bolton went, and . . ."

McAndrew said, staring at Ellie's upturned face:
"Where's Bolton?"

Jake shrugged emptily. "Up Whitby way by now, more'n likely."

"Whitby. . . ?"

"He sold us up and bought high in fishing. He took her fleet and it killed her."

"How was that possible, man?" McAndrew turned to Jake. "The fleet was Ellie's."

Jake mumbled, "It . . . it was Ellie's until she gave Bolton one third . . ."

"All right, she had a controlling share."

"She didn't. She passed that over to Tom."

"How? He wasn't of age."

Jake said, his face low. "She . . . made me trustee . . ."

"And you passed it over to Bolton?"

Jake made a small weeping sound and knuckled his face.

"God Almighty!" said McAndrew.

The three of them stood together now, staring down at the bed. McAndrew said, gently, "Leave me now . . ."

"Mister . . ." began Megsie, "there's something more that's happened – something even Jake here dunna know . . . I . . ."

"Go now," said McAndrew.

"But . . ."

McAndrew made a short, gutteral cry: it was out of context with his mood or the situation; it possessed no matrix of recognisable sound.

"*Get out! Leave me!*" It was a bellow.

Together Jake and Megsie hurried from the room, with backward, fearful looks over their shoulders.

It was near dawn when McAndrew left Ellie's bedside. A dim light was burning on the landing. He descended the stairs upright, one hand gripping the banister, and crossed the hall. Turning the handle of the drawing-room door, he swung the door back upon its hinges.

The room was in a shambles of disorder.

485

Chairs and tables were overturned, ornaments smashed. Broken glass littered the floor: empty bottles from the rifled cellar were everywhere, on the mantelpiece in clusters, in the fire-grate, lying half emptied across the Persian carpet. Half-finished food, opened tins and bread, half-eaten chickens, rabbits, rounds of cheese were left where they had been dropped by guests who had departed in haste. The large, jagged wine stain was like a dried wound on the Kashmir table-cloth. The shutters had been smashed, the great chandelier that once hung in splendour, the pride of Ellie's Cambourne, lay in a tangled heap in the middle of the room, its gold-plated fitting ripped off for loot; even wallpaper had been stripped away in panels, faintly waving like coloured sails on the walls.

There moved in the deep recesses of McAndrew's numbed mind a mixture of compassion and fury.

The empty hearth, sloped with cold ashes from the fire-place to fender, epitomised more than all he had seen, the sudden demise of Cambourne as he had known it.

Then the acrid tang of smoke stung his nostrils, and McAndrew moved towards it, filled with a sudden, pervading weakness.

The night was star-lit, breathless, as if strangled by a fevered ague.

A sudden redness blazed from the lawns beyond the smashed windows, and he remembered a summer day, a child and a fish, and a bright happiness that even obscured the sun. A dog fox called in the distance and its mate replied, and the sounds stilled him. Now the tinker bonfire fanned its dying embers, and he smelled, also, the reek of wild garlic that hung in the woods beyond, and there grew within him a small jubilation as the open road called again.

Mrs. Tinker Bob was standing beside the dying fire on the lawn outside the french windows.

"'Evenin', Jim McAndrew," she said.

He nodded, wandering towards the fire, facing her across it.

"Ye've done us well, woman," he said. "Congratulations. I couldn't have handled it better. But once ye took the place, in God's name why did ye leave?"

"Because of death."

"Ach, balls! What's death? Ye lived in the house, didn't you? Ye scurrilous tinker bitch! Ye should have burned your vans and made the best of it. With the lad drowned and his mither gone, ye could have made Cambourne yours, or wouldn't Bolton allow it?"

"It was Bolton who gave us Cambourne." The tinker drew herself up and pulled her red dress closer about her. "But when Rachel was found drowned this mornin', the young bucks were afeared o' the country, and were off."

"Rachel?"

"Ye haven't heard?" Mrs. Bob moved closer to the fire.

"Me son's dead and so's me wife," said McAndrew. "What more do ye want from me? Get goin', before I shift ye," and the tinker answered:

"Listen, McAndrew. Another body was found this mornin', and this was Rachel's, the lover of your lad Tom.

"She were Tam Shenks's tinker girl out of Rosa Florence – do ye recall the name, McAndrew, or do I remind ye? – but Tam was never the father, as you know well. The father was you – do you remember I told you, years back? Aye, aye – Rachel and Tom, both sired by you – brother and sister, though they never knew it, mind.

"And they drowned together, God rest 'em, between Sully Island and the Spinney: days back they found your Tom; only this mornin' they fetched out your Rachel . . ."

She crossed herself in a sudden, jumbled prayer, adding, "Ye can 'ave Tom, but we're havin' Rachel, for the tinkers claim their own. It's the law."

Mrs. Tinker Bob added, "She were McAndrew sired, and therefore entitled to her worldly share, we reckoned. So Pinta brings her 'ere for her pickings, see? – wi' Ross Bolton in mind, understand – in case he fancies her, an' he did . . . but she fell for your Tom instead, an' there's no accountin' for that . . ."

McAndrew lowered his face, and the tinker said, "And now she's a dead 'un. But, though sired by you, she had Rosa's tinker makings, so the young bucks 'ave got her in the van. She's our'n, McAndrew – see to your lad – dunna come pesterin'," and she strode off into darkness.

Megsie said, "Mister, anna it time you got the funeral man?" Her eyes flourished tears. "I mean, you got the death certificate, an' all that, but . . ."

"Aye, woman," answered McAndrew, "I've sent for him."

"Then shall I ask old Saul to hurry him?" Megsie gazed about her in pent grief. "I mean, it don't seem right an' fair, do it, to have the dear lady lyin' upstairs, and no priest, or anything. Mind you, I laid her out decent, and . . ."

"God bless ye, Megsie," said McAndrew, and, away from ears, said to Jake: "She went easy, man. Be at peace. tears won't bring her back."

"Aye, yes, but I killed her, didn't I?" Jake wept aloud, his face veined and purple with grief. "I can't stand it, can I? But you never loved her, as God's your judge."

"Jake. . . !" McAndrew held him. "Pull yourself together. How long would it take to get the old *Sarn* in steam?"

"The *Sarn Helen*? What for, for God's sake?"

"Think, man, think . . ." McAndrew gripped him. "You know what for. Don't ye remember what Ellie said – she wanted to be buried at sea. . . ?"

"At sea?"

"Do you recall Albert Horton's lad – the grease monkey – Ellie took him on, remember – the boy who died of burns in Gibraltar, and Ross Bolton buried him at sea. . . ?"

"What are ye talking about?"

"Off Cape Ortegal he was buried, remember? From the old *Elida*. And Ellie, when she heard it, said she'd like to go that way an' all – she told you herself, too – now think . . ."

"O, aye," whispered Jake, rubbing his face.

"Then I ask ye again – how long will it take you to get a head of steam on the *Sarn*? Have we got her still?"

"O, aye, in Two Dock. She were the first o' the Kendall fleet."

"*How long?*" persisted McAndrew. "How long to get her steamed for sea?"

"To fill her, fire her, get her a head? Hell, mun, what are ye asking?"

"I'm asking ye to give your Ellie her dying wish," said McAndrew. He added, "Is there any decent thing you've ever done for her, save sire her? Have ye ever been anything but a trial and burden to her, like me? It's what she wanted and what she asked for, and if you don't grant it her, I will."

"But the undertakers . . . Megsie said . . ."

"We're the undertakers. And now I'm asking you again, Jake – how long?"

"An hour to feed and fire her – six hours from then."

"Get going," commanded McAndrew.

"Without a decent, Christian burial? Man, be reasonable!"

"Confusion to ye enemies, Jake. You're a better father than I gave ye credit for. Be back here after dark."

"But a coffin, man – a *coffin!*"

"She'll have one, and one she loved," said McAndrew. "The old *Sarn Helen.*"

"God forgive me," said Jake. "It'll be the eternal fire for me, for what you're asking!"

"If you don't go through with it, you'll get worse from me."

After Jake had gone to fire the *Sarn Helen*, McAndrew went to Ellie's room, and dressed her in her wedding gown, the one she had worn (and had hung in moth balls) in Seion Chapel, Bangor, nearly eighteen years before.

Upon her hair he pinned the mantle of white lace, and lace was at her wrists and throat; her shoes of white satin were upon her feet.

After he had done this he stood, smiling down at her. He thought she looked beautiful lying there in her wedding dress. Then he locked the bedroom door and sat beside the bed, not troubling to reply to Megsie's repeated knocking.

"Lie easy, I'm with ye, darlin' girl," he said to Ellie.

He did not have to go to the east wing for his own clothes. As if through nostalgia, Ellie had kept them with her own.

The tartan trews and jacket, if tight, still fitted; he stood before the mirror in the bedroom and positioned his cap with care, brushing up the eagle's feather to a jaunty angle, spitting on the silver brooch of the Stewart clan to polish up the motto, if not his own, and the lace jabot arched proudly at his throat.

"Aye, you'll fit," said he. "We make a fine pair, so we do, eh, Miss Ellie?"

When darkness came Megsie ceased to knock, and McAndrew heard Jake coming with the trap above the night singing of birds.

Unlocking the door, he looked down into the darkened hall, then picked Ellie up into his arms and ran swiftly downstairs and over the lawns to the road.

"Ach, holy Jesus, how beautiful she looks!" said Jake, peering.

The pony's hooves clattered on the road, and faintly above them they heard Megsie's voice, calling, calling.

"Get goin'," said McAndrew, and gathered Ellie against him.

"You'll never guess," said Jake, "who I saw this afternoon on my way through the docks. She was making her way to the Barry Dock Hotel after shopping, and looking as pretty as a picture . . ."

"Who?" asked McAndrew.

"Mrs. Bolton, Ross's common law wife."

"Did she speak?"

"Aye, she did. She asked what was happening now Tom had died, so I told her about our Ellie, too."

"That was wise."

"And that Bolton had taken the spoils and was headin' it for Whitby."

"Did ye now," said McAndrew. "What happened then?"

"She asked me the time o' the next train out of Barry."

"You're becoming intelligent, Jake," said McAndrew. "I'd not like to be in Bolton's boots. She'll give him Whitby trawlers and Ellie in particular."

55

Aboard the *Sarn Helen* McAndrew unlocked the door of the little aft cabin and laid Ellie down . . . on the same bunk where she had borne Tom; he straightened her dress and put a pillow under her head.

"I'll be back, girl," he said; and locked the door behind him.

In the boiler room he found Jake firing the box and he looked at the steam gauge.

"What's she up to?"

"A hundred and eight. I can't gamble her higher."

"If ye do her plates might go. Leave her at that," said McAndrew. Framed in the doorway he looked up at the dawn lightening sky. "Can you take a run at it?"

"Likely so, but there's a wee bit of a sea coming up, ye know, and the traffic's thick."

"She'll handle it. We only want her once. Steam her and I'll cast off." He smiled down at Jake. "Good man. Thanks. Once we get her in the Channel I'll see to the lifeboat."

"She's rusted. Her chocks are heavy."

"I'll see to those, too."

In the Harbourmaster's Office on Number One Dock, the officer on duty said:

"There's lights port and starboard on the old *Sarn*."

"You're dreaming."

"I tell you there is, and a riding-light."

The second man rose from his desk, staring through the gloom at the forest of masts. He reached for binoculars.

"Must be hooligans. Best telephone the police."

"She's moving out . . ."

"Don't be daft! She's up for scrap."

"She's been up for scrap these past ten years and more – but she's moving, I tell you – look, slow astern."

"Can't be. Her boiler wouldn't stand it!"

The binoculars came up. "Look for yourself."

"Hey up . . .!" whispered the second man. Going to the telephone he rung the handle. "Give me the Dock Police," he said, and then, as an afterthought, "Also Mr. Bolton over at Cambourne House."

The telephone rang in Cambourne. Megsie did not answer it. She was trying to get into the locked door of Ellie's bedroom.

The sea was brisk and perky, and the swell was coming down the Channel, heralding a storm.

Clear of the port entrance, McAndrew took the wheel and steered a course. Jake joined him on the *Sarn Helen*'s bridge, saying:

"Where are we bound?"

"Not so far lest she blows a valve. You take her, Jake – to a mile nor'-nor'-east of Flatholm – keep her about a mile out. The chart says deep water there – deep enough, anyway, to gi' a woman a decent burial."

"Ah, she'd like that," said Jake.

"Snug within the Channel she loved, even within sight of Barry."

"And hear the traders comin' and going above her? God, what more would she ask?"

The dawn was coming up in blood and the tide began the run, the big swims that came in from St. George's and the Atlantic and built up the sea that drowned Tom and Rachel.

And on that tide the bummers came, the skin-boats and tramps, the coal barges and liners, making east for the Welsh ports, or west for the New World, riding shoulder to shoulder, green to green, red to red. Up and down the Bristol

493

sea-towns on the old Slave Trade routes upon which this wealth was gained.

With Jake at the wheel, McAndrew firing the boiler and Ellie locked in the aft cabin, the old *Sarn Helen* went, threading a course like a needle for Flatholm, and the sun began its bubbling on the rim of the sea, to come up red and flaring into a dawn of fleecy clouds, and warmth.

Reaching their destination, Jake swung her to port, turning in a slow circle, leaving behind them a wake of foam. The old Clyde puffer leaped at the wheel then, rattling her chains like an animal tethered, rolling on the pea-green sea.

McAndrew, below, opened the bilge cocks and the sea gushed in; then went hand over hand up the ladder to the foredeck where Jake was waiting.

"Are we ready?"

McAndrew gasped, "Aye, mun, ready."

"You've opened the cocks?"

"Wide – for'ard, aft, amidships. Give her half an hour and she'll fill on pressure."

Jake narrowed his eyes at the mainland where the lights of Barry and Cardiff were fading with the dawn.

"She'd best hurry. The coastguards saw us out, don't worry. Any time now they'll be after us."

"Would ye like to see your girl?" asked McAndrew.

"I would that . . ."

They stared at each other.

"After that, give me a bit o' time with her?"

Jake nodded. "Of course."

McAndrew said, "I've loosened the chocks and the lifeboat's dangling: all you've got to do is slacken her down, and lower. Then ship oars and hang around for me, eh?"

"Don't be too long," said Jake.

McAndrew went with him down to the aft cabin and opened the door.

Ellie lay on the bunk like a woman sleeping.

"Gi' ye two minutes, man." McAndrew looked for'ard. The *Sarn Helen* was already settling by the head. Even as he stood there he heard the for'ard bulkhead go down.

*

494

When Jake had left Ellie and was aboard the lifeboat, rowing clear, McAndrew called down to him: "Right, mun, give me five minutes – just paddle around . . ." and Jake, ten feet below in the lifeboat, nodded and wiped spray from his face, though McAndrew knew it was tears. The old man cried in a broken voice:

"Pilot boat coming up two points west!" and he pointed.

McAndrew ran round to the *Sarn Helen*'s stern, staring seaward.

The unmistakable silhouette of a coastguard cutter, sails heeling her, was dipping in the sea with foam on her nose, three miles west.

"You make a quick goodbye, and jump," called Jake.

"Great God in the mornin'!" yelled McAndrew. "D'you think I'd be daft enough to hang round for the suction?"

He then went across the quarter-deck to the engine-room, and stood there for a moment, staring at the distant pilot cutter which was ploughing in a freshening breeze.

McAndrew looked at his watch, calculating that he had less than twelve minutes before the coastguards came.

First, he swung back the boiler fire-box and gave the fire-grate draught, and the bright coals glowed and flared as the small stuff sprayed it: he stoked carefully, selecting his coal, slammed the fire-box shut with his foot, and watched the steam-pressure needle climb. A hundred and six pounds per square inch, a hundred and ten . . . a hundred and twenty-five . . .

Next he shut down the steam-pressure valves, the cylinder release and the mechanical gain, then he turned off the water feed to the boiler. The fire-box belched its relief, shooting out a yard of flame as he stood aside.

McAndrew stoked her higher, selecting his fuel from the smalls and dry slack, and slammed shut the door before the fire shafted out. Standing back, he watched again as the steam-pressure needle rose . . . a hundred and thirty pounds . . . a hundred and forty-five, then it swept upwards, passed the danger red of a hundred and fifty.

McAndrew shouted then: "Blow yersel' to Kingdom

Come, me darlin'. Blow, *blow*. . .! They'll not get ye, Ellie, soon ye'll be sleeping deep and cool – over me dead body will they get you!" and he shut down the safety-valve with a spanner, clamping it tight.

The *Sarn Helen* was rattling her hull as the steam pressure grew.

Thick smoke was bubbling from her funnel in long black wreaths that stained the morning, laying a mantle of oil on the foam-topped sea, and coastguards from Barry to Cardiff and south of Bridgewater Bay raised their telescopes and binoculars. And, while Jake waited, paddling around for McAndrew, the men in the approaching pilot's cutter went about in a shower of foam, and yelled from their wet faces, pointing as a mushroom of blackness was forming above the slowly circling steamer.

McAndrew left the engine-room and went to the fore-cabin, the cabin he had occupied a century ago, it seemed, when he was young.

With a blow of his fist he splintered his locker above the single bunk, dragged out oilskins, jerseys and thigh boots, and flung them aside.

A bottle came next and he knocked off the top, set his mouth around the splintered glass and swallowed the whisky in gulps. It struck his palate with blood and liquid fire, and he momentarily gasped, then tipped up the bottle again, drinking it to the bottom before flinging it aside.

"Well, I'm buggered," he said, his eyes alighting on his bagpipes.

Beneath his feet the old *Sarn Helen* bucked and heeled to the tide; rudderless, she was swinging aimlessly in the Flatholm undertow, drifting into the lee of the island.

"Well!" said McAndrew, and pulled out the bagpipes and turned his eyes to the ceiling.

He said, "So ye left me these – thanks for nothin'! Ye've taken me all, do you realise that? My woman and my son. Ye had to kill your own son, could you not have left me mine?"

He raised a shaking finger, his face incensed with growing

rage. "Can you tell me one single thing I've been granted to thank you for? Just one? Just enough love to cast aside – just enough talent to beg for more – do ye make a hobby o' this, for God's sake?" He waved a big hand in disgust. "Och, fella, it's no good talkin' to you, for you've been beat two thousand years – the Devil's in charge of the world, so Old Nick, me great, satanic majesty, I'm appealin' to you!"

Staggering on to the deck he left the cabin door swinging behind him, and shouted at the black funnel smoke pouring out above him:

"Hey, Lucifer, Beelzebub, or whatever they bloody call ye – hearken unto this! Grant this poor bastard and his missus peace . . ."

He rolled around the sloping deck, blaspheming, shouting insults. "And blow me, her, the Barry bloody Railway Company – Cambourne Freighters and all their connivings to bloody eternity. D'you hear me? Especially me, James Alexander McAndrew, for all me sins, celestial and supernal. Let Pandemonium reign. . . ! if only I could get my hands on that bastard, Bolton!"

And then he stopped; swaying, he stood on the fore-hatch, staring shoreward to where the pilot-cutter, on her last tack, was coming at full speed with a wide wake behind her. McAndrew said:

"Oh Christ! *Tom! Ellie. . . !*"

He staggered to the edge of the hatch, tripped and fell, rolling headlong as the ship lurched. And he heard, beyond the dull roaring of the sea, the groans and strains of the bulging boiler plates as the steam head rose. And the siren cock burst then, ringing out over the Channel a full and discordant blast; higher gushed the steam, and the siren rose to a shrill, tenor note.

Jake stood up in the lifeboat and shouted through cupped hands;

"McAndrew, McAndrew!"

Above the siren McAndrew heard the thin wail of his voice.

"Sod off!" he said, and, hand out, reached the aft cabin

door as the *Sarn Helen*, taken by the rising wind, heeled once, and leaped, wallowing in deep, green troughs.

McAndrew paused, then shoulder-charged the door, falling to his knees within.

The room's darkness was instantly banished by flooding sunlight, for the dawn was full now, red and raging over the sea; all within was tinged faintly red, including Ellie's gown.

McAndrew was still upon his knees.

"Ach, ye darlin' wee thing," he said and put his arms about her.

The *Sarn Helen's* boiler exploded. The engine-room erupted in a plume of flame, shooting skywards into the sun, and its detonation, thunderous at first, slowly died to clattering reports that echoed to the horizon. And Jake saw, as the debris rained down, that the old tramp had settled amidships; now dividing herself as if cut through the middle with a knife . . . slowly to sink, bows and stern cocked up.

The sea took her, so that she hung for a moment in its arms, before sliding down into the depths. The suction came then, as the pilot boat hove-to alongside Jake's lifeboat – drawing both craft instantly towards the debris of the plunge.

They turned slowly in the whirlpool, side by side, like dancing dolls on the breast of the sea.

In the pilot cutter, returning to Barry with the lifeboat in tow, a coastguard asked:

"What were the pair of you doing out there, anyway?"

"Our business," said Jake.

"He knew what he was about, that one. If it weren't for the boiler we'd have had him, Clyde Puffer an' all."

"O, aye?" Jake raised a tearstained face.

"Four of us, mun!" They were broad-chested and fighting Welsh. "Talk sense."

"Fourteen of ye," said Jake.

They sat, watching him, then one shouted above the hiss of the sea, "Did you hear that other noise. . . ?"

498

"The siren? Aye, the cock-valves blowed off," answered another.

"No – that other noise – above the siren. It sounded for all the world like blutty bagpipes."

"It were," said Jake. "It was *MacCrimmon's Lament.*"

"MacCrimmon's what?"

"If ye haven't heard of that," said Jake, "your education's been sadly neglected."

Book Six

56

1945

John, the son of Josie and McAndrew, walked swiftly in bright spring sunlight; ran up the steps of the National Gallery and then up the stairs to the Hall.

In the uniform of a Royal Air Force squadron-leader, with his gas-mask on his shoulder, he joined the throng of people standing before a great mural.

The mural, seven feet high and signed by one named Salieri, had been recently removed from the banqueting hall of Atopia House; it spread over half the length of the gallery.

With a centre piece of an ancient patriarch sitting in a chair, Uncle Dumb, the oil painting overflowed with colour and activity.

Three hundred and sixty-five people were thronging around a solid phalanx – the family of Atopia House.

Mama Meg, Miss Pan and Toppy, crowded together on the canvas. Banker was there, Rosa Florence and Evan Kinto, Pinta, her step-father – Mrs. Tinker Bob dancing in her red dress, Vladimir Timoshenko with his melodeon and Blind Jack tapping with his stick, but seeing all.

Tittyupover was there, and Chu Chu, the marmoset in top hat and tails, and he was dancing. Mrs. Posh was there, with her arm around Major Gillis – Spanish Joe and Bandy Jock, Lover Alf stealing from a housewife; Constanze, stood alone.

Gunner Jenkinsop and soldiers were formed on a barrack square, the ceremony of the drumming-out: Lord Windsor and Jake were in morning dress, with Megsie opening the portico door of Cambourne to them, and dropping a curtsey:

the Princess Maria Joseldon, in gargantuan obesity, was undergoing massage beneath the ornate chandeliers of Duke Street; near her, in rags, drooped Mrs. Bernadette O'Hara of Bute Street, come home to die.

Marie Antoinette with her ladies-in-waiting dominated the foreground with aristocratic airs: Miss Pan, deceased soon after the death of Constanze, dined demurely at her card table outside her tent with a candelabra and bottle of Chianti, attended by an astonished Saul Plentyman. Ross Bolton stood with his hand on Tom's shoulder beside a soldier spreadeagled on a gun limber, being flogged. Lady Felicity Barre walked arrogantly across the bedroom floor of Linda Vista, bejewelled in her purple skirt; a tiny Lady Heston crouched apprehensively in a corner, holding a key.

And Ferdinand de Silva (who died in bed) keeping guard, marched along the battlements of Atopia in the blue uniform of *Uspallata*: Conrad sat on a nearby gravestone drinking red wine, or blood.

Mr. Toppam (now in Broadmoor for the murder of Constanze – unfit to plead . . .) was busily hanging his dolls; Brunel was hunched before a graph of higher calculus, while from his brain deluged water from a broken viaduct. Effington-Smythe (still at it, said his shareholders) shoplifted from his store with unfeigned delight; Vicar Groper, long dead, whispered into the ear of an affronted waiter.

Banker sent surreptitious notes to Miss Pan via Brookie, whose sister, Rosa, waved gaily from a haystack. Mama Meg counted buttons, Jean Pierre sipped absinthe, Tuesday waited behind the french doors of Cambourne, Lord Grey-Cambourne tussled a handkerchief under the nose of a Siberian bear.

And over all, dominating all, the nude figure of Josie rose as if from the turrets of Atopia into the sky, an Aphrodite of unifying fertility concept, her arms outspread, embracing all, while around her legs and feet gay Parisians danced – spilling through the doors of the Folies-Bergère, the Moulin Rouge and the Café Noir. This, the canvas McAndrew had painted in Duke Street, was superimposed against a backcloth of Sacre Coeur with its great dome and statues, ramparts of marble and flights of ascending steps.

Down these steps tumbled the libertine hordes that haunted Montmartre, a part only of the three hundred and sixty-five humans on the great canvas; the failed artists and sculptors; touts, layabouts, anarchists, toughs, Apaches and pickpockets.

Here, with sudden gaiety and abandon, under brightly striped café awnings, the people wined and feasted in brilliant sunlight; floss-headed seamstresses hurried down Rue d'Amboise and Rue de Steinkerque, Lautrec's brothel haunts of a decade before: crippled soldiers begged for alms around the fountain of the Place Pigalle, and Concorde.

Ellie stood alone on the foredeck of the *Sarn Helen*, in profile against the Strait of Menai, her hair flying in the wind.

Nearby, before the grave of her son, the Countess Adèle stood against a sunlit Château de Malromé and its rolling vineyards along the lane to Verdelais, and the bishops of the city, depraved by wine, offered her bits of half eaten dogs.

John McAndrew looked around the faces of the people about him. A man asked softly, of his friend:

"What is it called, you say?"

"The Feast of Madness."

The squadron leader glanced at his watch. It was midday and he was due to meet Hilary, his wife, in the Savoy Hotel at one o'clock.

He was wondering where his mother, Josie, had got to.

She was the moving force in this public exhibition of his father's mural, and she was due at Paddington on the eleven o'clock train from Barry.

Now clear of the immediate crowd, he sat down on a bench; behind him, but within his immediate hearing, two elderly women were discussing the relative merits of the mural. One said:

"According to the introductory notes prepared by Professor Ratza Spielman, McAndrew's biographer, it was restored by the Princess Josie Joseldon, the mistress of the artist, listen to this," and she read from the Notes:

"'James Alexander McAndrew, the Post-Impressionist painter, is known to have visited Atopia House (known locally as The House of Eccentrics) between the years 1894 and 1913, during which period he worked on the mural at the request of a recluse and his housekeeper.

Upon the death of the housekeeper in 1940 (who left Atopia House and its appurtenances to McAndrew's surviving son) the Princess Josie Joseldon, his mother, had the mural removed from the wall of the banqueting hall of Atopia and restored.

The difficulty of this becomes apparent when it is remembered that the work is on lime and haired plaster; clearly it was the artist's intention that his work would eventually crumble into decay, beyond hope of regeneration . . .'"

John McAndrew picked up his own introductory Notes and read on:

The mural scenes depicted are difficult to correlate as representing every aspect of McAndrew's life, though Princess Joseldon believes this to have been his intention.

Throughout, the influence of Toulouse-Lautrec is apparent; the French scenes being reminiscent of Lautrec's depictions of the Montmartre of a decade earlier . . . the dancing of Jane Avril and La Goulue being recreated in the entertainment of Chocolat and her Can-can troupe of the infamous Café Noir, where McAndrew is known to have worked.

The depiction of his earlier life (he was dismissed from the Army for frequent desertions) is seen as a protest against military discipline; the period 1896 to 1900, though sparsely represented on the canvas, portrays his entry into a world of commerce, where his rise was both meteoric and tragic, for he deserted his wife Ellie, (late of

Cambourne Freighters, the South Wales shipping firm) yet died at his own hand during her burial at sea in the summer of 1914.

The harshness, the caricatural vision of James Alexander McAndrew's work owes much to Japanese prints, the source of inspiration to so many of his fellow Post-Impressionists: the rich, garish colours and bellicose dynamism of brushwork are intended to enhance the character of the subjects rather than express a natural visual experience. The themes are both bitter with irony yet compassionate in symbolic content.

The 'furia' of painting (Lautrec's own expression) applies more to James Alexander McAndrew than to Lautrec himself, his chosen mentor: the *Paris Review*, commenting on the French Faculty of Art's Premier Award for *The Feast of Madness*, states . . .

The woman was speaking again. John McAndrew closed his mind to the bustling pressure of the people.

"I wonder," asked the woman's friend, "why he signed it 'Salieri'?"

"Search me," came the answer. "There's nothing in the Notes about it."

"After all, they think he was mad, don't they. . . ?"

"You can say that again. D'you realise that every woman there has exactly the same face? It doesn't matter who they are – young or old, their faces are the same. He must have been mad to paint a thing like that. I reckon it's obscene."

John McAndrew looked at his watch.

Vaguely, he wondered if Hilary had yet reached the Savoy.

He was tired; tired of the war, of activity, even of peace.

It would be simpler, he thought, to play the role of the laird up on the family estate in Ross and Cromarty. Anywhere away from noise and people, and the constant crucifixions by James Alexander McAndrew.

There would be more reporters awaiting him at the Savoy,

of course, unless he was unusually adept at side-stepping them.

Wherever he went these days there were reporters.

It was worse than bombing raids.

57

John saw Hilary before she saw him: she was standing in the foyer in her light blue uniform of the W.A.A.F., looking expectantly around. He was sitting on a high stool, bright-headed, bigger than any man there, when she came into the Savoy bar. He said:

"Good girl, you made it. But my mother's late. I wonder where she's got to?" He raised a hand to the barman.

Hilary nodded. "You know Josie. She has no idea herself where she is from minute to minute. She'll not settle up in Scotland, you know. She'll never rest until she's turned Cambourne into the McAndrew Gallery. By the way, they've discovered a new painting down there under the old wall-paper in the east wing, apparently. 'The Whore at Toilet.'"

"So I've heard, and I've had no peace since they found it."

"How's the exhibition going?"

"Had a job to get near it. But I obtained what is generally known as a spectatorial review – one old girl actually thought it was obscene."

"That's not the consensus of opinion. The art world is raving." Hilary touched his hand. "Don't you think we'd be better up north with Uncle Angus's lairdship, than slumming it down here in Duke Street? You're not going to get any peace, you know. As I came in I heard more reporters asking for you . . ."

"Bastardy being of paramount interest in a press release. Who cares about the art of James Alexander McAndrew?"

"Don't be bitter, John – Josie isn't."

He drank, savouring the whisky. "Perhaps not, but then I didn't even know the guy, did I? At least she had that doubtful pleasure."

"There's another view," said Hilary, playing with her glass. "You've got the money, so you accept the liability. Everything costs something in this world, you know." She smiled faintly. "Do you remember poor old Seddon standing here five years back?"

"God, he tried his best, didn't he? What a war!"

"The war's over, John. A lot of people have gone under in history – trying to keep the McAndrews alive . . ." She smiled brilliantly and took from her pocket the Gallery's Introductory Notes, adding, "I picked up one of these as I came over. Have you read it?"

"Yes."

"But it still won't do you any harm to read it again – the comments of the art section of the *Paris Review* . . . And God, they're hard to please! Listen, John – savour every word – who cares about legitimacy. . . ?" and she read:

" 'The same generality of madness evoked in this work is akin to that suffered by Van Gogh, and, to a lesser degree, by Gaugin. Derangement is apparent in every line of this mural, especially in the artist's depiction of the women – nun, harlot, barmaid, beggar, titled lady and housemaid – all, to McAndrew, possess the same face . . . their features on the canvas are identical.

According to photographs, it is the face of Ellie, his late wife, but at time of press there is no proof of this.

Yet it is this very derangement, combined with opulent colourings, scope, and meticulous execution that raises James Alexander McAndrew, through intellectual vigour, to a higher status than that yet subscribed to conventional Post-Impressionism. He has added a further dimension, that of sound; a musical lyricism sharply defined within the sensuous lines and often garish colours.

Of Rembrandt and Soutine, Goya, Nicolas de Staël, Utrillo and Toulouse-Lautrec, the Company of Outcasts

510

among whom McAndrew walks . . . of all these only three have achieved the Divine.

Toulouse-Lautrec himself, never enslaved by Post-Impressionism is, in the opinion of the writer, the pupil of McAndrew, not his master. And the world would have accepted this before now, had this artist's name been Salieri.' "

Hilary looked up then and her face became suddenly alive. "Oh, look!" she cried. "Here comes Josie!"